What readers are saying about Conor and the Crossworlds

"Hello from The only radio station in the world owned and operated by kids, WKID 96.7 FM, located in Clearwater, Florida. For years we were looking for an exciting book to read live on air to our listeners. All the books that we thought would be interesting to read on air turned out to be very confusing to our listening audience, but three years ago we received our first book from Kevin Gerard titled Conor and the Crossworlds. After receiving the book we thought it was just going to be another boring book, BUT NO! JUST THE OPPOSITE! This book was awesome!! Not only did we love it and were able to relate to Conor because he was our age, but our listeners really loved to hear us reading the story on air every night. They begged us not to stop reading it due to the great suspense of the story. Every night when we would stop reading for the night the phone would start ringing with listeners very upset and wanting to know what happens next, of course our response was "you will have to tune in tomorrow night." If we ever had a night that we were unable to broadcast we would receive hundreds of e-mails and phone calls. We just wanted to say thanks again for writing such a great, exciting story and we look forward for the next book."

– Adam and Eric – WKID 96.7, Clearwater, Florida

"The Conor and the Crossworlds series is one of the best series I have ever read. It is full of action and friendship and a bunch of stuff it is awesome!!!"

– Alicia – Desert Hot Springs, California

"Conor and the Crossworlds is the perfect blend of fantasy and adventure. Action around every corner.....Conor is my favorite character for his courage and bravery! People can relate to him."

– Andrew – Portland, Oregon

"I'm from the high school in Burlington, Vermont that you visited. I didn't really get a chance to properly thank you, so I'd like to do that now. Not only is your series, Conor and the Crossworlds, one of the most imaginative, brilliant and overall best fantasy reads ever, you've also inspired me to write more than I can ever express. Keep speaking at schools; you're very motivating, and I'm so grateful for your stories and kind words. Thank you!"

– Burlington, Vermont

"Gerard does it again! This book is even better than the first. So imaginative and a fast read."   *– Erica – San Diego, California*

"I think that Conor and The Crossworlds is a genius series! They made me want to read again; they are definitely my all time favorite books. I think Conor's stories will be a huge success. I can't wait for the next one!"   *– Max – Desert Hot Springs, California*

"Thank you again for the gift you gave to my son. He has never been so excited about reading and wanting to read. That is the best gift of all."   *– Penny – La Mesa, California*

"In the book series of Conor and the Crossworlds, I loved the stories at the very beginning when I started reading them. I personally admire Conor because of his bravery and courage to put other people before himself, and I loved the fact that there are creatures that have powers that no person can ever imagine. When I started this series I was hooked from the first page and couldn't wait for the next book to come out. Now after three, I can't stop thinking about the next book to come out and try to imagine what could happen in the next book..."   *– Jacob – Norco, California*

"I am so very impressed. I remember the darkness from the third book more than anything, although the second book had such cool fight scenes and new characters. For some reason this story is pure pleasure for me, I think because it was quite visual and exciting, but also very tender. The ending was absolutely amazing, it evoked all the feelings you would expect from an extremely well-written fantasy."   *– Karen – Tierrasanta, California*

"The Conor and The Crossworlds books are great! Full of drama and adventure, it has everything a book worm needs to be satisfied with the book she/he devours! It's a suspenseful adventure, waiting to pull you into the journey and complete it."   *– Shannon – Oceanside, California*

"Hi, it's Ryan.

Big fan!!!!!!!!!

Love the books, but, I'm thinking you should make a movie. I want to see what colors the places are, I want to see how big they are. I can see the pictures; I just see them in black and white. And I'm almost done with the second book. I met you at the Clairemont branch Library 50th Celebration. That's where we bought the first book. Who won the key thing, or is it still going on? Please reply..."

– Ryan – San Diego, California

"I have been reading the series since Kevin came by my school. It was and will be full of emotion, exciting characters, and meaning. All the books have great plots, and I can barely wait for the next couple of books. Conor is a perfect mixture Harry Potter, Bobby Pendragon, and Percy Jackson."

– Wesley – Indio, California

"Now that the Harry Potter series is over, it's time to find a great new book series, and Kevin Gerard has the answer. His new book series, Conor and the Crossworlds, is possibly the next great teen book series."

– Titan Toll Chronicle – Glendale, California

"I like your books. They're very suspenseful. I think your books will be worth more in the future. What I think I'd like to see in your next book would be more characters. I like the design on the front cover of Book Three .

– IMS student – Riverside County, California

I am in the sixth grade. I like all of the characters you put in the Conor and the Crossworlds books. I even liked the words you put in the books and the action in the story and how you describe it.

– IMS student – Riverside County, California

The characters that you put in the book are amazing. I can actually imagine in a dream a giant cat taking me for a ride in the sky. You have made some really amazing books."

– IMS student – Riverside County, California

"I just love the Conor and the Crossworlds books! When I pick them up I can't put them down! I feel like I'm in another world!"

— *Jocelyn – Manchester, New Hampshire*

"I love the Conor and the Crossworlds books because they have a really good plot. I like how in an instant Conor's life goes from ordinary to getting to experience being in an alternate world beyond imagination. When Conor starts gaining abilities from serving as a warrior for the Crossworlds creators, it makes me wish I could escape to an alternate world of my own and meet majestic cougars like Purugama. The third book "Surviving an Altered World" is my favorite because of the quest for the five keys. The plot for the third book was awesome and the scavenger hunt that the author did for the five keys that went across the United States was a lot of fun! That's why I love the Conor and Crossworlds books. Not only that but I've always liked writing, thanks to this series I am inspired to write so much more!"

— *Jade – Lumberton, Mississippi*

"Kevin Gerard's Conor and the Crossworlds series is an essential "must have" for any library or fantasy fan. Conor's story stands out in the ever-growing fantasy genre as a fun, safe adventure for all ages. Mr. Gerard's work does not stay on our shelf very long and patrons are eagerly awaiting the next installment."

— *Michael – Hattiesburg, Mississippi*

"Reading Conor and The Crossworlds is like watching a movie in your head, and not spending time on the T.V. so my parents don't get mad."

— *Shannon – Oceanside, California*

"When you came to my middle school you said you would give me a copy of your book free if I got mine published. I am proud to say that my book is 452 pages long and is on its way to 3 different publishers! I hope you are ready to hand over that book!"

— *Lucy – Desert Hot Springs, California*

"Crossworlds
Conor and the Crossworlds
Replenished my soul with every page
Only something with
Significant power
Sinks within my gaze.
What it must be like to live
On champions glade
Right beside the champions
Like Eha, Therion, Ajur, and Maya
Don't forget Surmitang and best of all Purugama
I will seek refuge in the Crossworlds."

– Wesley – Indio, California

"I love these books because they are very adventurous. Every sentence traps me inside the book as if I am in it. I never want to stop reading these books, I just love them so much."

– Joseph, La Jolla, California

Conor
and
The
Crossworlds

Book Four: Charge of the Champions

KEVIN GERARD

Crying Cougar Press

San Diego, California

Published by Crying Cougar Press
San Diego, California

© 2005 Kevin Gerard. All rights reserved.
First published in 2009.

Edited by Katie Chatfield
Cover art by Justin Gerbracht
Cover design by Molly Nicholson
Interior illustrations by Jennifer Fong
Typesetting by Julie Melton The Right Type

ALSO BY KEVIN GERARD:

Conor and the Crossworlds:
Breaking the Barrier

Conor and the Crossworlds:
Peril in the Corridors

Conor and the Crossworlds:
Surviving an Altered World

Conor and the Crossworlds:
The Author of all Worlds

Visit the author's website at:
www.conorandthecrossworlds.com

FOR MY MOTHER
AND HER INFINITE CAPACITY TO FORGIVE...

BATTLE RANKS
COUNCIL OF SEVEN

CREATOR
ABILITIES:
Corridor Construction
Power Allocation
Animation of Life
MAGIC – *Untouchable*
IQ – *Advanced*
BATTLE SKILLS – *Exceptional*

CHAMPION
ABILITIES:
Corridor Travel
Power Transference
Structural Manipulation
MAGIC – *Extraordinary*
IQ – *Superior*
BATTLE SKILLS – *Excellent*

SEEKER
ABILITIES:
Corridor Travel
Unlimited Vision
Superb Trackers
MAGIC – *Limited*
IQ – *Good*
BATTLE SKILLS – *Formidable*

GUARDIAN
ABILITIES:
Corridor Travel
Translation
Superb Healers
Magic – None
IQ – *Excellent*
BATTLE SKILLS – *Limited*

BATTLE RANKS
CIRCLE OF EVIL

DESTROYER
ABILITIES:
Identity Transfer
Power Allocation
Animation of Environment
MAGIC – *Impenetrable*
IQ – *Advanced*
BATTLE SKILLS – *Tactical Brilliance*

SHADOW WARRIOR
ABILITIES:
Corridor Travel
Invisibility
Weapons Construction
MAGIC – *Exceptional*
IQ – *Superior*
BATTLE SKILLS – *Excellent*

SLAYER
ABILITIES:
Corridor Travel
Limitless Energy
Blinding Speed
MAGIC – *Good*
IQ – *Poor*
BATTLE SKILLS – *Superior*

KEEPER
ABILITIES:
Corridor Travel
Cell Construction
Imprisonment Specialists
MAGIC – *Limited*
IQ – *Good*
BATTLE SKILLS – *Limited*

Conor
and
The
Crossworlds

Book Four: Charge of the Champions

ESCAPE AND RECOVERY

CHAPTER ONE

A peculiar quiet hovered over the realm of the creators. Not the kind of silence that soothed the spirit during a visit to the beautiful planet. This seemed altogether different, as if the creators and those who served them had simply melted into the scenery. Not a soul enjoyed the natural beauty of the realm. No one roamed the spacious grounds. The crystal waters trickled throughout the area as they always had, but no one enjoyed their therapeutic qualities. The lush forest awaited its guests with open arms. The branches and leaves standing guard over the entrance drooped languidly, however, from the lack of visitors on this day. For the first time in centuries, the Council of Seven had been summoned. Anyone not called to witness the proceedings waited patiently for the decision of the supreme gathering. No one wished to disturb the creators while in session, so the expansive grounds retained a mystical silence the entire day.

The gathering place for the Council of Seven sat in the middle of the most pristine setting in all the Crossworlds. Everything, down to the last blade of grass, was prepared and placed with all the sensory organs in mind. To see the realm of the creators was to look upon a cherished place from every cultural description dating back thousands of centuries. No one invited to walk these beautiful grounds came away unchanged. If you enjoyed no other senses, the sight of the realm alone would cause you to fall to your knees in admiration.

The first thing anyone saw upon arriving was the large variety of flora blanketing the grounds of the realm. An array of lush trees joined together at precise points throughout the grounds. A multitude of natural colors burst forth from the gatherings in a breathtaking display of physical well-being. In between the giant guardians marking the pathways throughout the realm, endless collections of supporting greenery connected the trees in a natural harmony unrivaled anywhere in the galaxies. Luxurious lawns invited visitors to remove their sandals and let their toes feel the soothing embrace of the soft grass. Huge walls of jasmine and honeysuckle sprang from the floor of the pathways, spiraling up tree trunks or falling lazily from heavier branches. Not a stray leaf appeared anywhere; no discoloration existed on any tree, bush or blade of grass. A first-time visitor would wish only to stay forever to gaze upon the enticing gardens.

The intermittent appearance of water complemented the flora perfectly. Coming around a corner of a pathway, one might observe an immense waterfall crashing down a distant cliff face. Falling gracefully from an opening in the rocks, the free-flowing water seemed frozen in place by its precise descent. One might stare at the natural wonder for the length of their visit if not for all the other subtle placements of liquid relaxation all about them. In more than a few locations a series of meditation pools enticed visitors to enjoy their soothing tranquility. In some areas only a few connected pools existed. In others, however, huge collections of attached pools meandered away from the walking path. Almost every series of ponds contained a soothing, continuing waterfall that distributed the flowing liquid from pool to pool. The sight claimed many visitors when walking the paths of the realm for the first time. Asked repeatedly if they wished to see the remainder of the grounds, the visitors simply waived their hands as they walked among the breathtaking, interlocked pools. In still other areas, natural water walls framed the resting places for the creators and their visitors. One had only to sit for a moment to gather in the serene effect. As the clear liquid fell gently down the face of the wall, small leaves and tiny flowers of every color flickered lightly with each drop that passed over them. The water flowing down the wall followed a direct course. Not one drop fell along an imprecise path. Each aspect of the water wall seemed purposeful. Visitors resting within their confines would find themselves slumbering peacefully within minutes.

The creatures roaming the realm of the creators seemed perfectly attuned to their surroundings. Unafraid of any visitors, all animal, fish, or bird life curiously examined everyone walking about the grounds. Exquisitely colored fish swam lazily among the connected pools. Visitors choosing to place their hand into the waters would find the fish gladly swimming over to inspect their peculiar appendages. Climbing into the water and sitting amongst the different varieties of fish brought the visitor a truly amazing experience. Slowly at first, and then with greater urgency, fish would accumulate around the visitor's body. Each would jealously garner a moment of attention from their guest and then break away so another of their kind might also enjoy a brief interlude. Every fish, down to the tiniest occupant of the pools, remained in excellent health always, a gift from the creators for the companionship they provided.

Any visitor walking the grounds of the realm soon found their path accompanied by an amazing collection of fascinating exotic birds. Not an overpowering number of chattering pests, no, these small groupings merely kept the visitors company along their way. One could see them preening their feathers while resting within the confines of the flourishing foliage. At times the multicolored companions flew down to their guests, landing lightly upon their shoulders. If the visitors sat amongst the connected pools, the birds found solace resting on the visitor's knees. At no time did the birds bother or haggle with the guests for offerings of food. They simply shared the environment with them, craning their beaks to look up into their eyes, or chirping softly. It seemed that they existed to make a visitor's stay that much more enjoyable.

Often while strolling along the grounds, a guest came upon one of the many majestic beasts that roamed the forests of the realm. Visitors would often recognize animals from their home world, but they would see strange creatures in the realm as well. It would not be uncommon to encounter bears, deer, cats of every sort, and even a gentle breed of dog here and there. Other indescribable creatures from other planets crossed their paths as well. Dagells from Stemwich, similar to a deer but more muscular, macheens from Hordugan, a furry lizard the size of small dog, and Ezuvex from distant Wilzerd, an extremely intelligent bear-like creature that spoke every language in the Crossworlds. All these creatures walked without fear throughout the realm. Once they took up residence among the creators, they enjoyed a peaceful existence with no natural enemies. Visitors were encouraged to interact with the animals they encountered. The guests became transfixed while doing so. No one from any planet within the Crossworlds community could ever have imagined such an enjoyable experience.

The final pleasing sight for all visitors to the realm of the creators came from the crystal sunlight that bathed the entire area during daylight hours. The clusters of trees eclipsed the proper amount of light, allowing a gentle blend of filtered and direct brilliance to reach the grounds. No visitor ever received more light than his or her eyes could tolerate. Whether looking up into the trees, toward a glistening waterfall, or across a small valley at a group of animals, the light always remained perfect.

The temperature in the realm could not have felt more agreeable as well. With the sunlight flawlessly filtered through the trees, and a gentle breeze always flowing throughout the grounds, visitors seemed to smile every minute they walked peacefully about the grounds. Anyone choosing to speak of the weather remarked that it represented the best day they could ever remember in their home world.

Many other sensory experiences complemented a visitor's visual enjoyment as well. Guests could close their eyes at any stop along a path and listen to the natural ambiance of their surroundings. One might hear a waterfall crashing upon a distant cliff, or the sounds of animals calling out to their fellows. By quieting the mind, one could note the gentle conversations of small packs of birds close by. The soft dribbling waters of the connected pools faded in and out of a visitor's audible range. A guest could even hear the water walls, as silent as one's own heartbeat, after a period of meditative concentration. Finally, the soft winds, always present within the realm, touched the ear ever so lightly now and again.

Anyone walking the grounds felt compelled to stop from time to time and close their eyes, inhaling deeply. The natural fragrances drifting through the realm demanded nothing less. The air alone smelled so fresh and clean that at first visitors had trouble breathing. So used to their own polluted atmospheres, visitors found it astonishing when their lungs took in a larger volume of air as they first became exposed to the environment. After a half hour or so, they marveled at their newfound physical strength. The pure oxygen of the realm transformed their bodies within minutes of their first exposure. Now breathing deeply for the first time in their lives, visitors happily roamed from place to place, ingesting the exquisite scents. The soft winds carried the fragrant smells of nature past the visitors as they walked the groomed pathways. Immense beds of jasmine and honeysuckle, flowers of every kind, and the clear scent of pools of crystalline water danced around a visitor's glands as they walked along the paths.

Upon seeing, hearing and smelling such perfection, guests could not help but touch every aspect of their surroundings. The creators encouraged this, because the organic elements in the realm responded favorably to a guest's contact. Although produced and nurtured by magical means, nothing caused the flora and fauna to exhibit robust health like frequent interaction with visitors. Upon arriving, one immediately touched the pathway as they walked, feeling the velvety softness of the soil beneath their feet. A guest often approached the large trees along the trail, grasping the soft, auburn bark and squeezing it gently. They grabbed at the stringy branches shooting off from the bushes along the walkway. Gliding their hands along its length, they felt the nubs of new life running down the spine of the branches. Touching the clear water in any of the pools, water walls, or waterfalls caused visitors to close their eyes and remain motionless. The water felt so exquisitely clean they hesitated to remove their hands.

With all the grandeur of the lower realm, the grounds faded

into obscurity next to the chamber of the Council of Seven. As befitting as its station, the chamber was nestled atop the highest hill in the realm. To anyone walking below, the crest would appear to be nothing more than another natural aspect of his or her surroundings. Had they the opportunity to climb the hill and visit the chamber, they would come to a different opinion entirely. The pathway up the rise mirrored other trails around the realm, with its soft, velvety soil, groomed to perfection. After cresting the hill, however, all similarities to the lower realm ceased.

The chamber rested in the exact center of the rise, directly on its crown. Numerous trees from uncharted worlds circled the hall surrounding the chamber. The thick branches and lush leaves swirled around the enclosure, creating a natural barrier with few entrances. Giant crystals of every color and size emerged from tree trunks, dripping water, wine, honey and teas of every description. One had only to produce a cup and hold it under one of the crystals to receive refreshment. The trees and crystals eclipsed every line of sight into the chamber with the exception of one direction. Direct sunlight beamed from above, bathing it in a healthy, warm glow. The refracted light from the wide variety of crystals created a soft, multicolored hue inside the chamber.

Not a single doorway led into the central meeting room. A circle of corridors, each bearing the shade of one of the seven councilors surrounded the hall. No one could enter the chamber of the Council of Seven except by moving through one of these corridors. The council members alone prepared their portals for another's journey. This ensured the safety and security of the supreme councilor and the other six members of the ruling body.

The chamber itself exhibited no opulence at all. Few accessories dotted the room. A clear table, held aloft by a magical spell, provided a hub for the assembly. An oval cut into the table's center, roughly eight feet in diameter, served as a well for anyone presenting a case before the council. In this way, the presenter could always face whoever currently challenged or supported their position. No chairs circled the outer rim of the table. The council members brought their own seats, stood, or floated softly on a cushion of air. Refreshment stations stood in the four corners of the meeting room. Servants from the lower realm remained on hand to assist the members in case they required anything at all.

The council chamber displayed the only signs of life in the realm this day. High on the crown of a hill in the most beautiful of all locations in the Crossworlds, a select group from the ranks of the creators listened to an argument placed before them. Very few had been invited to the chamber to sit in on the discussions. The decision would be left to those who had walked these pathways for eons. The Council of Seven, their servants, and one other high-ranking creator had passed through the ring of corridors. The councilors had received their briefings and refreshments. They floated around the clear table, listening to the petitioner present her case.

Those standing quietly at the bottom of the hill would never hear any of the exchanges in the session. However, if they stayed long enough and stared toward the top of the hill, they would behold an intriguing sight indeed. Every so often, a silvery light flared brightly from within the chamber. To an onlooker who lived in the realm, that vision could mean only one thing.

CHAPTER TWO

"We must find him!" demanded the Lady of the Light. She delivered her impassioned pleas in a firm but deferential manner. Connecting with each member of the council as they entered and exited her line of vision, the Lady locked her eyes to theirs without blinking. She had been given the most privileged of audiences and she knew this conference could end without explanation. She presented herself and her case with equal precision. The creators, assembled comfortably in the council chamber, sat quietly, listening to her pleas. "He gave up everything for us! He sacrificed his own life and that of his companion's to fight as our Champion! He recovered the five keys of the creators *by himself* while we hid from the wrath of the evil ones! Without this accomplishment, we might not be here today conferring with each other. He did everything we asked of him. Will we turn our backs on him now?"

With a stiff upper lip and a stern look in her eye, the Lady paced purposefully in front of the Council of Seven, the supreme gathering of the creators emeritus. She argued her case aggressively while looking directly at each of her superiors. She paid particular attention to those she knew she could influence. She pushed the council to use all their available resources to search throughout the Crossworlds. Conor must be found, she submitted vehemently. To do anything less would be a disgrace to the integrity of the council.

"What of the thousands of worlds under our protection?" boomed the voice of the first councilor, his golden aura flaring about his shoulders. "Many worlds exist in a state of chaos. Thanks to the Circle of Evil, more planets under our protection fall into disarray with each passing day."

"Without our Champions to do battle for us," he said, "we must summon our own magic to hold off the might of Seefra's armies. Will we deny these other worlds the security they deserve, all for the sake of one young man from a planet at the very edge of our dominion?"

"And what of the five keys of the creators?" continued the first councilor, now standing to keep still so he could face the Lady of the Light. "We have no secure knowledge of their whereabouts. Conor Jameson's companion cannot be found by any of our most accomplished seekers. We must assume she still possesses the keys. We must also assume she remains a prisoner of Seefra's shadow warriors. How much longer will it be until he overcomes the spell you placed on the metallurgy of the keys? What will become of Conor's companion the instant they decipher the components of your magic? Would you have us lift our protection over her and send those resources in search of your young earthling?"

The first councilor leaned forward, placing his large hands on the transparent table in front of him. "You conveniently forget, my Lady, that we currently operate without the Champions of the Crossworlds at our disposal. We fear that their location will forever be a mystery to us. Indeed, they might never honor us with their service again. Do you comprehend the meaning of this? For ten thousand centuries, first with the protection forces and then with Maya and his brother Champions, our cause has reigned supreme. With very little intermission, we have held the Crossworlds in a state of peace for all that time."

The first councilor's golden aura flared again as he raised his voice to the Lady of the Light. The force of his speech seemed to surge from the entire chamber. "I remind you that it was *Conor Jameson* who summoned the chaos we now endure by revealing the nature of his association with us. After receiving explicit warnings from both Purugama and Maya never to speak of his amazing adventures to anyone, he chose to ignore the cautions. With everything he had learned, he chose to put not only his own life in jeopardy, but untold millions of others as well. And you find the nerve to stand here and make demands of us? You ask too much of this gathering, my Lady."

"I ask too much?" replied the Lady of the Light with a raised voice as she approached the inner curve of the council table. The silver coating around her body sparkled brightly as she felt the hold on her emotions slipping away. "This warrior helped defeat Drazian at the tender age of *ten years*. He overcame Gandron and Fumemos at twelve. He very nearly destroyed Seefra *in his own fortress* at the same age. Now, after vanquishing Loken at fourteen you will abandon him to the cell of shadows for the remainder of his life? I ask only for what he has earned – our undying love and limitless support in this supreme quest. How can you possibly grant him anything less?"

The Lady paced about the interior circle of the council table. She looked at each member in turn before returning to face the first councilor. "My Lord," she began, not with anger, but with love in her heart. "I cannot deny the truth of what you say. Conor erred grievously. Believe me when I tell you that no one knows this more than he. He sits somewhere now, alone and despondent. I assure you his thoughts are only for others, not for himself. This young man has proven himself beyond anyone's expectations. He has not only displayed an array of incredible physical abilities, but also the emotional and spiritual capabilities of one not encountered by us in many centuries. I admit that I have grown extremely fond of Conor during my association with him. But I stand before you to-day requesting assistance for a young man who may even be more than we can presently comprehend. After all, did we not discover a great deal about Maya after we brought him to live among us?"

The Lady of the Light composed herself, clamping down on her emotions in preparation for her final statements. "Consider this, my Lord, and esteemed members of the Council of Seven. Conor may be our only hope. He may in fact be able to find and recover the Champions from whatever forbidden corridor they presently occupy. He may even locate and rescue his companion and return to us the five keys of the creators. Even without these assurances, I would strongly recommend that we use every force at our disposal to locate him. I beg you, for our sake and for the sake of the Crossworlds, find Conor and bring him to me."

The Council of Seven conferred silently for many moments, whispering to one another with heads bowed. They thought deeply about Conor Jameson, the newest and youngest Champion of the Crossworlds. He had indeed served the creators bravely while barely into his adolescence. He had accompanied Maya on perilous journeys to repair the corridors, facing dangerous opponents every step of the way. At any time during those challenges, he could easily have walked away, frustrated by their expectations of him. He had persevered, however, in the name of his mentor. Mighty Purugama had taught him extremely well, passing on everything he received from Maya to his young protégé. Besides, ridding the Crossworlds of the likes of Gandron and Fumemos certainly didn't hurt Conor's cause either.

Retrieving the five keys of the creators with little outside assistance also shed a warm light on Conor's case. The journey to repair the corridors held its own terrifying turns, but at least Maya had traveled alongside him. This young Champion captured the five keys virtually on his own, although his companion provided more than a small measure of assistance. The beginning of that quest had not been without challenges. The Champions had been taken captive and could not assist him. The creators had been openly attacked for the first time since the Crossworlds had come into existence. If not for the sincere affection the Lady of the Light held for Conor, perhaps no one would have fought to warn him, or given him license to use their powers so openly. Surely the young man deserved their deepest consideration.

With their silent deliberation complete, they began to argue loudly amongst themselves. Some members of the council reiterated every point the first councilor had brought forth in the gathering.

"Without his brash behavior, we might not be sitting here conferring at all. Does that not count for anything?"

"It certainly counts for far less than the bravery of his exploits. I say his freedom is of paramount concern. Can anyone on this council assure me that he will not play an important role in the future of the Crossworlds?"

"Yes, but what part will he play? Will he save us or destroy us?"

"If we cannot determine that, then we must go to him immediately. We cannot expose ourselves to the consequences of an incorrect choice."

"I say leave him to his fate. If he is such a grand warrior, then why has he not freed himself? Let him prove his worth by coming back to us by his own initiative."

"We are the Council of Seven! Have we not called for assistance from time to time? You make a valid point, my Lord, but there is no precedent for your argument. If we do not vote to locate this Champion at once, then I shall immediately resign my commission to this council."

"Your threats will not influence this gathering."

"Enough!" commanded the supreme councilor. All discussion ceased as the members awaited the final words of the meeting. "I will not allow this council to act in a manner that demeans its importance. This is a serious matter, one that deserves our most fervent attention. Let us choose our path and convey our decision to the one who fights for the young man's freedom."

Bowing their heads and closing their eyes, the creators transferred their thoughts to the supreme councilor, with the vote arriving at five to two. Judging his worth against all other considerations, the members had come to a swift conclusion. The supreme councilor motioned for the members to be seated before addressing the Lady of the Light.

"We admire your passion, my Lady," assured the Lord of all Life. "Always remember, however, that what we do is for the good of the Crossworlds. Your young Champion may be all that you say he is, but to us he is just another instrument. As with the Champions of the Crossworlds and the protection forces, Conor Jameson exists only to serve us."

The Lord of all Life showed the slightest hint of a smile before continuing. "Fear not, my Lady. One of our most capable seekers has been watching over your young Champion for years. We dispatched him many months ago with orders to locate and liberate him. Although we've had sparse communication for some time, we have every faith that he will accomplish his mission. When he finds him, he will deliver him here for a period of rest and recuperation. You, my Lady, will serve as executor of his rehabilitation. Does this satisfy your pleadings, creator?"

The Lady of the Light bowed in deference to her superior. The silver sparkles disappeared and her aura cooled upon hearing their decision. "All that I ask has been granted, great one. I will prepare to receive our Champion without delay."

THE CELL OF SHADOWS

CHAPTER THREE

Conor lifted his eyelids again. He couldn't remember how many times he had opened his eyes in the gloomy cell. He lost count somewhere past the fifteen thousandth time. That occurred so long ago he couldn't even remember the days. He kept opening his eyes, hoping to see a source of light from somewhere inside his cell. He had lived in complete darkness for so long he wondered if his eyes would ever be able to stand the light of day again.

He kept opening them whenever he found himself awake. He would lie in the black, soulless cell, opening and closing his eyes. He played a game with himself, trying to convince his mind that the next time he opened his eyes he would see something other than darkness. It worked for some time, but now Conor opened his eyes merely to keep from going out of his mind.

He had lived in the bizarre cell for well over a year as far as he could tell. He knew the dimensions of the box precisely, sixteen feet long, twelve feet wide, and ten feet high. Having marked it off just to keep busy, he felt certain of his calculations.

The walls of the cell were a complete mystery to Conor. He could press his arm almost all the way through any of them. There was no solidity at all. If he tried to walk through one of them, however, the darkness collapsed all around him, forming an impenetrable barrier. It looked almost as if an army of shadows gathered around him any time he attempted to escape. After trying this a few times, Conor watched the other walls react as he tried to walk through one of them. The shadows from the other walls zoomed toward the battered area of the cell, fortifying the place where Conor hoped to push through. It was either an incredibly sophisticated piece of equipment or a living being. Knowing the Crossworlds as Conor did, he guessed the latter. If organic, then it served its masters well. It never tired, never needed to replenish itself, and it understood its function perfectly.

After many attempts at the walls of his cell, Conor once tried to dig his way out. The floor of his cell, after all, remained as it had been all along, a loose collection of dirt and rock from the mesa. Clawing his hands bloody, Conor managed to dig the beginnings of a crude but serviceable tunnel under one of the corners of his cell. As he leaned back to rest, he could see the reinforcements sliding along the walls in his peripheral vision. The shadows raced over to the corner from every direction, forming a tightly packed wedge directly underneath his tunnel. He didn't even attempt to dig around it. He just stood up, nodded his head in admiration, and walked to the other side of the cell.

A few times he attempted to trick the shadows into making a mistake. Using a rock he found while digging one day, he carved out a tunnel in one corner of the cell. As he expected, the shadows flowed over to his position, concentrating their energies and blocking his path. At the instant he saw the shadows blending together, Conor jumped up and ran toward the opposite wall. He figured that the shadows had depleted themselves in order to cover the tunnel, and he might be able to get through one of the thinner walls. He felt he actually might have made it a couple of times. The wall had definitely thinned and as he pushed his way out he sensed a tiny membrane of light. The shadows quickly recovered, however. He felt them collecting around his body, reinforcing the wall, slowly pulling him back into the cell. He marveled at the organic quality of the cell structure. He actually felt the shadows gripping his arms and legs while they gathered together to reclaim him. The cell performed its functions perfectly, even as a prisoner Conor had to admire it.

Not only did the cell of shadows keep Conor captive, it also kept him alive for months on end. In all the time he had resided within the shadowy walls, Conor had never seen a bite of food or a sip of water inside his cell. Yet, aside from the normal growth of a teenage boy, he hadn't lost or gained a pound during his long stay. By some form of powerful magic, the Circle of Evil had designed the cell with recuperative powers. Since he felt nothing while awake, Conor deduced that the cell fueled his body while he rested. Something in the structure of the cell walls must have infused his body with every nutrient needed for human survival.

Another surprising facet of his bodily functions lay in the fact that there didn't seem to be any. Conor had not relieved himself, nor had he felt the need to do so ever since he awoke in this bizarre cage. Apparently the designers had taken complete control of his biological functions. Having studied humans for eons, they must have determined exactly how to keep a young man prisoner indefinitely. He couldn't even remember producing a drop of sweat, even while exercising or attempting to escape. Astounding as it appeared, Conor always asked himself the same question. *Why would they keep me alive?* He had fought with the creators and Crossworlds Champions and destroyed many of their most potent warriors. He had pledged his life against their forces and worked diligently toward their ultimate ruin. Even so, they had successfully imprisoned him without injury or torture. If they had kept him locked within these walls for all this time, then certainly they planned to keep him indefinitely. But why keep him alive? Why continue to nourish him? Why not destroy him and finish the creators? They must have the five keys since they had captured Janine.

Conor balled his fists in frustration again. His girlfriend could be anywhere. She could be undergoing the most painful torture imaginable. She could be gone already, disposed of after their quest for the secret to the keys had concluded. How could he have let her go so easily? How did he allow both of them to be fooled so completely?

Janine had no part in this except as an unwitting accomplice. She had been selected as the keeper of the keys and for that she paid the ultimate price. She fought bravely by Conor's side during their journeys together. She never complained once even though she had plenty of reason to do so. Even while witnessing sights no person should ever see, she continually walked forward to their next objective. He wondered if he could have collected the five keys without her assistance.

He would gladly remain here in the cell of shadows forever if it meant that she had safely found her way back home. Thinking of her safety had helped him come back from the brink in the early days of his imprisonment. He cried himself hoarse for a week worrying about her. For another month he admonished himself time and again. He couldn't rid himself of the terrible guilt he felt. Every time he closed his eyes the image of Janine's face morphing into

Seefra's disgusting countenance resurfaced in his mind. When he recalled the image of her standing alone in the final corridor he would snap awake, screaming for his girlfriend while swinging his arms in an attempt to bring her back to him.

After months of imprisonment, he realized that the magic of the five keys was the main reason they kept him and Janine alive. They must not have found the source of the Lady of the Light's spell on the keys. *When they did finally resolve the riddle, however...* Conor closed his eyes, cringing at the thought. They would make him suffer by forcing her to an excruciating demise.

And, Conor wondered, *what of the Champions of the Crossworlds*? Had his blunder sealed the locks on the cage of fire forever? They had almost escaped as he and Janine collected the five keys. How frustrating it must have been to smell freedom and then have it snatched away at the last second. He remembered the sorrowful despair he saw on Eha's face as he lay within the bars of the cage. To a cat, they had all looked defeated. Purugama, with his mighty wingspan, suffered the entrapment more acutely than the others. Forced to keep his wings folded around his body, he endured the worst of the cage's energy when he could no longer hold them to his sides. Standing at the extreme edge of the cage, he would unfold one wing, gingerly stretching it out to the limits of the bars. Invariably, the tip or one of the ribs would brush against the barrier, sending a surge of fiery energy toward the offender. Even worse, the cage of fire sent bolts of punishment at different intervals, so at times the great cougar received a mildly painful sting. On other occasions, however, the pulse of energy blasted through his body so forcefully it nearly knocked him unconscious.

They had been imprisoned in the cage of fire for roughly the same amount of time Conor had lived in the cell of shadows. He wondered if the cage kept the Champions alive in the same way this cell nurtured Conor. Or if not, maybe the creators had found a way to care for them. He thought of Maya, the wise Lord of the Champions. *What must he be thinking while locked in a cage with his brothers for so long?* Knowing him as he did, Conor supposed he spent his time trying to communicate with the Lady of the Light, hoping to find a way to defeat the cage. *Still, cats are passionate and curious creatures, and at times Maya must have felt tremendous frustration.*

Surely Ajur and Surmitang had roared their aggravation for weeks. He couldn't imagine Surmitang, the proud Sumatran tiger, held inside a cage with no hope of escape. The shame of his situation must have bled away his strength by the day. And Ajur, Conor could see him now, crouching in a corner of the cage, pecking away at different components, testing it for weaknesses. Ajur, the strong, bull-headed plodder, would try to find a way to escape the cage of fire long after the Crossworlds had slipped into oblivion. At times he would feel overwhelmed and defeated, but he would shake those feelings off and continue his work faithfully.

The only Champion left was Therion, and Conor hadn't a notion of where the giant lion might be. The creators had given him life, but a life of solitude for all time. Even though the majestic beast had tried to destroy him, Conor whispered a short appeal to the Lady for his health and happiness.

The young man paced at the far end of his cell, watching the shadows follow him every step of the way. He had built a mound of dirt at this end of his cubicle, sort of a crude cot for sleeping and resting. He had even built a small riser at the head of his bed, which served as a rigid but serviceable pillow. He lay back on the mattress of soil, interlocking his fingers and placing the backs of his hands against his eyes. He let the eyelids fall while trying to visualize the day he would walk out of his prison. He focused on the image of light, any source of light that helped diminish the darkness he existed in every day. He thought of the Lady, how the pure light of her aura burned so intensely at times. He thought of the sun, a star he hadn't seen in so long it almost couldn't appear in his mind. He thought of the lights in his room, of flashlights, of headlights on cars, and of candles. He thought of every source of light he could imagine, trying desperately to ignore the stone darkness that existed beyond his closed eyes. In this way, he played his game again, the game that always ended the same way, with him opening his eyes to the black of night. He lay there with his eyes closed for the longest time, in no hurry to open them again.

On the wall farthest from where Conor lay, a pinprick of light silently pierced the infinite darkness of the cell of shadows. It receded, leaving no trace of its penetration behind. A few feet from the first incision, another miniscule beam of light bored through the cell wall. It, too, backed out of its path, blinking out as it exited the cell. One inch above the sandy floor, another penetration appeared, this time in the form of a flat beam of light roughly four inches across. As quickly as it appeared it dissolved into the cell wall.

Conor sensed the impression of light somewhere in his mind. He didn't open his eyes immediately, because he had imagined this very thing so many times before. He lay there on his sandy bed, his hands covering his eyes, swearing to himself that a source of light had entered the cell. Instead of succumbing to his desires, however, he held his position. He wanted desperately to open his eyes, but at the same time he wanted to wait as long as possible. He wanted to imagine his freedom for as long as he could stand it. Finally lifting his hands from his forehead, he swung his legs over the side of the sandy mound, placing them squarely on the ground. He opened his eyes and looked everywhere in the cell of shadows. Nothing. No light at all. He had really fooled himself this time.

Then he swore he saw something. He felt his mind might be playing tricks on him again, but as he crawled across the cell he saw it clearly, a tiny sliver of light running up the side of the cell wall. It seemed to be measuring the height of the structure as it passed up one side, disappeared, and then took another slice, moving down another section of shadowy tiles. Conor backed away as he heard a familiar humming whine coming from the other side of the wall. He watched excitedly as his last minutes in the cell of shadows finally ran out.

A blinding flash of light scarred the far wall of the cell. It lashed in a precise line, from floor to ceiling, across the top, and then down again to the floor. The sizzling path of light easily sliced through the cell of shadows. With the tracking completed, a blazing corridor of brilliant energy beamed in front of Conor. The intensity of the corridor wall fluctuated briefly, and then held its power perfectly. The framework of the portal, once a separate line cut into the wall, now joined together with the main corridor. Flashing brightly one final time, the doorway to Conor's freedom stood no more than a dozen feet away.

The shadows in the immediate area had been obliterated by the appearance of the corridor, but the remainder of the cell would not give up its prisoner so easily. As quickly as the light appeared, the shadows from the other three walls and the ceiling collapsed violently onto the corridor. It looked to Conor like millions of shadowy tiles racing across the walls, hoping to overcome the light by sheer numbers. The corridor flared, holding the brighter focus of its power in order to repel the attack.

The boundless energies of radiance and darkness converged on each other in an explosion of light and sound. Conor shut his eyes and covered his ears to protect them from the intense battle. Thousands of shadowy tiles slammed into the bright corridor, only to be blasted into oblivion by the power of the creators. The corridor gained a manic strength as the battle wore on, determined to defeat any force in the struggle for Conor's safety. After what seemed like an eternity, the cell of shadows finally depleted itself. Every few seconds, a tile or two zoomed across the ceiling or along one of the walls, disintegrating into the beaming corridor. The portal burned stronger than ever, prompting Conor to lift his eyelids and look upon his savior. He fully expected the Lady of the Light to emerge. When he saw who entered what remained of the cell of shadows, he stood straight up with his mouth wide open.

"Well, Mr. Jameson," said the harmless looking man standing in front of Conor. "We've gotten ourselves into quite a predicament, haven't we?"

"Mr. Hikkins!" gasped Conor.

CHAPTER FOUR

"And how are you faring, Mr. Jameson?" queried Conor's mathematics instructor. "I see you've grown since last we met. I am pleased. The biomechanics of the cell of shadows worked precisely the way I believed they would."

"Mr. Hikkins," sputtered Conor. "What are you... How is it that... who *are* you really?"

"Let us say that I am a seeker," answered the man calmly. "For now, that is all you need to know. Let it be enough that I have finally found you after searching for a very long time. I assure you we will leave this place today, together. Your unacceptable imprisonment has officially ended, Mr. Jameson."

"I can't believe it," continued Conor, truly stunned by the discovery. It appeared he had forgotten all about his captivity for the moment. He grasped his teacher by the shoulders, squeezing tightly to assure himself of the reality of his benefactor. "Thank you, thank you, sir. I felt I might have stayed in this cell forever. I can never repay you for what you've done."

Conor released the seeker and took a turn around the small cell. "But how could it be you? Maybe Coach Rumsey, or the ROTC director, someone cutting a more menacing figure. Who would be afraid of a soft spoken math teacher?"

"Correct," stated Mr. Hikkins. "Who *would* ever suspect some-one like me? This is precisely why I volunteered to serve at the high school as your protector. After your journey with Maya, the leaders of the Circle of Evil took special notice of your abilities. After all, how could anyone be convinced that a small lad of twelve might defeat some of the deadliest assassins ever called forth by the shadow warriors? You nearly eliminated their leader, a danger-ous destroyer in his own right. Seefra will always be cunning and powerful; however, he will never be easily overcome."

"At first, the enemy merely wanted to destroy you. That is partly the reason why the creators allowed the Champions to pass some of their powers to you when you returned home after your journeys with Maya. We wanted you to be able to defend yourself should an attack come without our knowledge. You were extremely wise, Conor, not to reveal too many of your powers at Mountmoor High School. By doing so, you might have revealed yourself to the scouts of the shadow warriors. In the end, when they realized you lived under our protection as long as you remained within the confines of your own world, they waited patiently for your error in judgment."

Conor let his head fall with the weight of his shame and em-barrassment. He felt every ounce of guilt flood back into his soul.

"A grievous mistake, Conor," admonished his teacher. "One I dearly hope you never repeat. But where was I?"

Conor lifted his eyes.

"When the Circle of Evil witnessed Miss Cochran begging you for information regarding your past, they went to work im-mediately preparing for the opportunity to take advantage of any blunder on your part. Seefra himself directed the shadow warriors to their posts, promising every one of them a most unimaginable demise if they failed to seize the opportunity to capture or destroy you. The enormity of the operation astounded even the creators. The first councilor nearly summoned the Council of Seven. But in their wisdom, the creators opted to watch and wait. After all, you had yet to tip the scales in the direction of the enemy."

"The onslaught brought about by your transgression almost shifted control of the Crossworlds to the Circle of Evil for all time. After securing the realm, the creators scattered themselves throughout the system, trying their best to leave no trace of their intended destinations. Some fell into the hands of the shadow warriors; I fear they may never be seen again. Others we have no knowledge of, apparently their fear of Seefra keeps them in hiding. On a positive note, every member of the Council of Seven returned safely to the realm. The council chamber remains intact. The realm suffered no disastrous effects during the chaos. The creators are attempting to restore order to as many worlds as they can. This task proves difficult, though, without the five keys in their possession. They realize that at any moment Seefra could counter the Lady of the Light's magic. If that happens, I fear none of us will survive. The Crossworlds will become the domain of the shadow warriors. Chaos will be the order of the day."

The seeker walked over to Conor's makeshift bed. He touched the sand and dirt, judging it suitable for a moment of rest. Unsteadily, he lowered his tired body, sitting while he continued his story.

"The Champions, once thought to be nearly free of the cage of fire, have disappeared entirely, I'm afraid. When they vanished, their roaring cries of fear and frustration echoed in every corner of the Crossworlds. Our seekers have failed to locate them. We fear the worst since we cannot recover even the slightest indication of their existence. Many of the strongest creators have volunteered to penetrate the forbidden corridors to continue the search, but their requests have been turned away by the first councilor. Aside from your brief stopover many years ago, Conor, no one has breached the forbidden corridors in centuries. If the Champions of the Crossworlds were delivered there by the shadow warriors, I fear we may never see them again."

Conor had been standing at attention with his fists tightly balled as he listened to Mr. Hikkins detail the destruction brought about by his foolishness. He swallowed everything he heard without difficulty, but at the mention of the Champions of the Crossworlds, his body crumpled to the ground. He sat there repeating all of their names over and over, staring at the dirt floor of his cell. His teacher waited patiently for the young man to work through his grief. When he heard Conor's sorrows fade, he said the only words that might lift him out of his depression.

"Come come, my boy, every one of the big cats knew from the moment they claimed service to the realm that their lives were in danger. They defended the Crossworlds valiantly for millennia. We must focus on those who have survived. The creators need you more than ever now. The Lady needs you. She has been defending you in front of the Council of Seven for quite some time. She convinced them of your worth and swayed the council to allow my continued exploration into your whereabouts. Without her urgent request, you may have never seen the outside of this cell."

Conor stood slowly, brushing off his arms and legs. He raised his head and met Mr. Hikkins' eyes. He waited for his teacher to continue speaking.

"It was only because of her unfailing love for you, Conor, that the Lady of the Light found the strength to reach you in Seefra's chasm. Had she failed, I wonder where all of us might be at this moment. After convincing me to prepare the five corridors in my classroom and erect the barrier to entry for anyone but you, she disappeared into a corridor to find you. The resolve of her expression told me she would make short work of any shadow warrior standing between the two of you. As you saw by her condition when she located you, she fought many battles along the way. She led Seefra's warriors on a merry chase through the Crossworlds before leaving most of them behind. The rest she destroyed or incapacitated. After telling you of our plan for the five keys, she shocked the council members by releasing her powers to you. In the long history of the Crossworlds, no creator has ever bestowed such a gift upon anyone. I dare say she would give her life for you if she felt so compelled. In a sense she did, Conor, because after passing her powers to you she had to carefully pick her way through the corridors again. If the shadow warriors had found her then...," Mr. Hikkins' voice trailed off as he shook his head back and forth.

"I returned to our classroom without delay to carry out her instructions. I barely had time to cast the appropriate spells before fleeing back to the realm. I knew if you made it to the high school the enigma would unfold before you. Once you passed through Ajur's protective shield and located the first corridor, the remaining portals would be yours to discover. The corridor positioning and the placement of the five keys turned out to be exquisitely planned, if I may say so. You may find it intriguing that the strategy for the placement of the keys was based entirely on mathematics."

Mr. Hikkins allowed himself a brief pause while smiling to congratulate himself on his efforts. Conor stood patiently, waiting for him to continue. He knew from his studies that Mr. Hikkins would always let him know the appropriate time to speak.

"From their secret locations, the creators watched you progress through the journey for the five keys. They cautiously applauded as each key fell into Miss Cochran's possession. As you moved through the sequence of corridors, however, the shadow warriors slowly closed in. Once they relayed their information back to the master of darkness, it became too late for us to do anything to help you."

"Seefra has grown extremely powerful, Conor. With the destruction of Drazian and Loken, he has cemented his position as the leader of the shadow warriors. He also claims to be third in command of the power structure, although I doubt that those commanding the realm of darkness would agree with his lofty estimation. Be that as it may, he commands great energies now. I would estimate his abilities to be far greater than Drazian's, even at the zenith of his reign over the forces of evil."

Conor held his body rigid. Mr. Hikkins stood placidly in front of his student. He knew precisely the nature of Conor's concern, and he hesitated to deliver the news. Part of his reasoning lay in the difficulty of the message, but he also wanted to test Conor's ability to hold his tongue. At length, he began the most difficult part of his story.

"I presume," began Mr. Hikkins awkwardly, "that you are interested in the well-being of Miss Cochran."

Conor's eyes welled up, but he held himself steady. He nodded once to the affirmative.

"When you entered the final corridor, Seefra called off his army of shadow warriors. He commanded them to surround the corridor, but that was all. They were to make no move against you or Miss Cochran. He wanted to take her alone, without any outside assistance. Apparently your prior battles left a bitter taste in his vile soul. He wanted to destroy you in every possible way. First he would impersonate Miss Cochran. Next he would commit you to the cell of shadows for all eternity. Finally, after taking her away, he would use you to prompt the Lady of the Light to reveal the secret spell she cast on the metallurgy of the keys. Imagine a choice such as that, Conor; the life of someone you love over the potential destruction of the Crossworlds. You would think it a simple decision, but I assure you it would never be so straightforward."

Conor shuddered, letting the words fall from his lips. "Is she alive?"

"Yes," answered Mr. Hikkins. "However, we have no idea of her present whereabouts. We tracked Seefra for as long as we possibly could. Initially, he took her back to my classroom. After a fierce struggle with Ajur's force shield, he entered the room with her in tow. He must have been looking for some clue to the spell in the arrangement of the corridors. After finding nothing in the room, he took Miss Cochran on a duplicate journey, identical to the one you and she took to collect the five keys. We successfully watched his travels with her, but we could do nothing at that point to help her. You must understand, Conor, the creators at that moment stood helpless to even protect themselves. We could not intervene without risking more damage to the realm and to the Crossworlds."

"Upon finding no assistance with the spell on the keys anywhere along the path of your journey, Seefra commanded Miss Cochran to remove the five keys from her jacket. She refused, spitting in his face and calling him a coward for attacking a girl. The dark master must have used a dreadful form of coercion, because ultimately Miss Cochran produced the coveted items. Seefra's eyes blinked at the colorful brilliance of the keys. He reached out to touch them, and Miss Cochran turned her hand over, letting them trickle into Seefra's grasp. They fell harmlessly through the grip of the dark master, clattering on the floor of my classroom. Hissing in frustration, Seefra ordered her to retrieve the keys and place them in her jacket once again. She refused and kicked the keys with her boot. They flew in every direction, some banging up against the wall and others disappearing under desks or cupboards. Without a word, the dark master reached out with his mind, grabbing her nervous system and twisting it until she did his bidding. To her credit, Miss Cochran knew that as long as the secret to the keys eluded Seefra, she was safe. Painful though her lessons were, she knew he would not destroy her as long as she remained the keeper of the keys."

"We lost track of their movements after that. Our best seekers have been unable to locate her, Conor, and we fear he may have taken her into the shadow world. If that is true, then I must be truthful, it is altogether possible that you may never see Miss Cochran again. Even if she were to escape Seefra, she could never find her way back from that dominion. I can only say for certain that she is alive. As long as the five keys remain inaccessible to her captor, your companion will live, Conor. I assure you every force known to the creators will be used to locate and rescue her."

"I *have* to find her," said Conor as he walked toward the blazing corridor. "Take me to the entrance of the forbidden corridors. I don't expect you to come along. I know what's at stake for you if you cross that barrier. I'll go alone, as I always have in the past."

Mr. Hikkins stood quickly, reaching out for Conor's arm. His surprisingly strong grip stopped Conor in his tracks. Without looking at his star student, the teacher merely relayed his instructions.

"That will not be possible, Mr. Jameson. The first councilor and the Lady of the Light expressly stated that your immediate destination must be the realm of the creators. They wish to speak with you about your travels and imprisonment. The Lady in particular has expressed a fervent wish to see you alive."

Conor would not be placated. "She could be hurt or dying!

Seefra might be torturing her as we speak. She fell into his hands because of my mistake. She's been his prisoner for as long as I've lived in this cell. I have to find her and get her away from him. She's been waiting long enough."

"I will not be dishonest with you," answered Mr. Hikkins, "your estimation could very well be correct. Miss Cochran might be suffering unimaginable pain every day. Seefra would torture himself if it meant a solution to his problem with the keys. He certainly would not alter his strategy just for a meaningless detainee from another planet. But you must attempt to think rationally about this situation, Mr. Jameson. You have lived in the cell of shadows for just under two years. You are now sixteen and one quarter years old. When you entered the cell you were fourteen and a half years old. By some incredible form of biological magic, the cell has nourished you through your chronological development. But what do you think will happen when you exit this environment? Will you feel as you do now, or will the protective biomechanics no longer support your system? You may collapse the moment you leave the confines of this cell. You may not. However, if you do, you will be no help to Janine. You would rush blindly into the hands of Seefra and become lost to us forever."

"My instructions," continued Mr. Hikkins, "are to use this corridor to return you to the realm of the creators, and that I shall do. You would be wise to heed their counsel, Mr. Jameson. You need to reorient yourself with your powers. You need to confer with the creators and seek their advice. Most of all, young man, you need a lengthy period of rest."

Conor looked over at his teacher. He stood eye to eye with him now. He watched Mr. Hikkins turn his head and stare into Conor's eyes. *The man has never misled me*, thought Conor. *He has always been there for me, even when I acted like a fool. I don't see anything but the truth in his eyes, and he may be right about the cell of shadows.*

"Okay, Mr. Hikkins," said the young man. "I'll go with you on one condition: that we spend some time reviewing game theory during my convalescence."

Mr. Hikkins gave Conor a rare smile. "Excellent," he replied, turning to face the corridor. "I look forward to our exchanges. After you, Mr. Jameson."

Conor looked around the cell of shadows one last time. He couldn't understand how he had lived for so long in a place like this. Without light, food, water or companionship, he had lasted almost two years in a box prepared for him by the master of darkness himself. He glanced at all the holes dug into the bases of the walls, signs of his attempted escapes over the long months of captivity. He thought of his girlfriend, locked away somewhere with Seefra. According to his twisted logic, she remained the only obstacle to his supreme ascension in the Circle of Evil. He would keep her alive only as long as she served as the keeper of the keys. After exposing the secret to the Lady of the Light's magic, she would perish by an unimaginable technique. He swore on everything he knew and loved that he would save her and destroy Seefra once and for all. He would wait in the realm for as long as he felt it necessary and not one second longer. His reverie fell away at the sound of his teacher's voice.

"It is time," said Mr. Hikkins.

Without responding, Conor jumped into the light of the corridor. As he experienced the blast of freezing cold air upon entering the membrane, he sensed Mr. Hikkins following him into the portal.

THE CELL OF CRYSTALS

CHAPTER FIVE

Janine sat in the corner of her cell, rocking back and forth lightly. Her clothes, frayed at the edges, hung on her small frame like old, worn out rags on an abandoned scarecrow. She clutched the cargo pocket of her jacket, feeling the familiar weight of the five keys. During times when nothing made any sense at all, she grasped the keys for reassurance. Over the long months of her captivity, she had trained her mind to focus on this one reality. The motivation had nothing to do with the purpose of the keys, nor did she concentrate on their terrifying power. She had merely created a cause and effect relationship within her mind between the keys and her sanity. If she felt herself slipping past the point of no return, she grasped and shook the pocket containing the keys. This gave her a feeling of hope. She hoped that Conor and his friends might find her. She also hoped her horrible jailer would never be able to take the keys from her. As long as she kept grabbing her jacket and finding them in her pocket, she always had reason to hope.

When the creature's servants first placed her in this cell, she blacked out with fear. When she awoke, she screamed for so long she lost consciousness again. She opened her eyes the third time without moving a muscle in her body. Looking across the rocky crevasse, she measured the distance by placing imaginary yardsticks in front of her eyes. Roughly ninety if placed end to end. Then without moving her head, she rolled her eyes and looked up at the next wall, another sixty yardsticks away. Bringing her eyes forward again, she swept her right arm slowly across the floor of the cell. Then she moved her leg, very slowly, in the same direction as her arm. When the area appeared solid, she rolled over toward the wall. Using her left arm and leg, she determined the sturdiness of the cell on the other side of her body. Then, taking a deep breath and securing her fear the way her father had taught her, she cautiously rolled over and sat up. She did not lean back against anything just yet. She still had to decide whether any walls existed in these bizarre prisons.

The cell of crystals served as a torture chamber beyond compare. Completely clear and comprised of millions of transparent tiles, the cell gave the prisoner the impression of imminent peril during every second of his or her imprisonment. Similar to the cell of shadows, the cell of crystals possessed the ability to concentrate its power wherever it felt necessary. If a captive pushed too hard in one area, the crystals rapidly slid over to that quadrant, creating an impenetrable shield. The terrifying aspect of the clear cell, however, came with the unexpected disappearance of tiles at any given time. Over the length of her stay, Janine had the constant fear that her next step might propel her into oblivion. The fact that the cell remained utterly clear didn't help matters at all. She had never become used to the bizarre sensation of walking on nothing. On top of that, she had seen other prisoners accidentally fall through the floor of their cells. Because of a single moment of carelessness, they plunged into a pit and met their fate with something beyond horrible. She learned quickly to be extremely careful when she moved.

She certainly had no desire to see what lived at the bottom of the ravine. The others who fell to their doom had not screamed for long after reaching the bottom. They also never put up any kind of a fight. She would hear horrible shrieks followed by a punishing roar. An eerie silence followed – if the ripping and shredding of what once was a living being could be called silence. Each time it happened she huddled in a corner of her cell while looking in the other direction. She might be required to listen, but she would not watch. She rocked lightly back and forth asking anyone who might be listening to keep her from such a horrible demise.

Once a day the servants of the creature came to her cell with food. She never tried to fight them when they delivered her meals. Once or twice a month, though, she threw an apple core or a bone in their direction when they returned to collect the leftovers. The creature knew a little about sustaining an earthling, but not enough to provide a healthy diet. Janine felt her weight diminish by the month. As the time passed, she realized the sick humor in this aspect of her imprisonment. All the girls at Mountmoor High spent every waking minute trying to stay thin, or trying to keep their figures intact. As a captive of the creature, she lost all the pounds she could ever hope to lose. After six or seven months, she held her remaining weight. She felt weak but not depleted. If she had the chance to escape she felt she might be able to run at her best speed for three miles. *But three miles to where?*

About once a week the creature sent his minions to collect her. They walked into the cell of crystals without fear, dragging her out into a series of hallways cut into the chasm wall. After the identical number of turns, Janine counted nine each time, the creature's servants plopped her down in the corner of what seemed like a strange laboratory. A chair stood next to where they deposited her, and each time they left her there, she stood and seated herself. She had refused to sit many times in the past, asserting her right to stay slumped on the floor, but that had earned her punishment and pain, and she knew better now. So as she had done so many times before, she sat and waited for the creature to enter the room.

Seefra slithered into the laboratory. He never rushed anywhere within his complex, for he had an eternity to accomplish his task. The keys would be his no matter how long it took to decipher the magical code. Once again he had designed a new counter spell, one that he felt certain would work where the others had failed. Whenever one of his enchantments fell short of his expectations, he filed the information away in his mind while working on another spell. He would succeed; of that he had no doubt.

He commanded the girl to produce the keys. When she unzipped the front of her jacket and lifted the brilliant collection from her pocket, he smiled deliciously. These keys would propel him to the supreme position in the Circle of Evil. After he destroyed the creators he would eliminate his opponents here in the world of shadows. After that, he would destroy the girl and find his most hated adversary. He would bring Conor of Earth to this place and torture him for a thousand lifetimes. He looked longingly at the five keys of the creators.

Janine watched the creature fix his peculiar eye slits on the prize she held in her hand. She wanted to throw the keys in his hideous face and watch them pass right through his head. She held them for him to see, however, having learned her lesson from other more daring times. She watched Seefra's tentacle legs swirling slowly, like a freakish helicopter, keeping him in place while he prepared to cast his spell. She heard him whisper the incantations, and watched the keys crackle and spark as they rebuffed the spell directed against the magic. The creature continued his chant, hoping this time that the keys would become his to control. Finally the spell ended, and the sparks died away from the set of keys in Janine's hand. She knew before the creature attempted to touch them that the spell had failed. Saying nothing, she extended her hand toward her jailer. Seefra shifted his shape slightly, exposing a single arm with a peculiar little hand. He grabbed at the keys, but came away clutching nothing but Janine's hand. The keys fell to the floor, chiming beautifully as they bounced and scattered in every direction. Disgusted, Seefra whirled on Janine and left the laboratory. Seconds later, his servants entered, ordering her to pick up the keys. After she had deposited them back in her cargo jacket, they led her back to her cell. She braced herself when they threw her back into the crystal prison. The creature had a habit of directing the clear tiles to allow for a hole here and there that she could not see. Failure left a bad taste in his mouth, and Janine usually paid the price for an ineffective spell. When the creature's servants cast her into the cell, she splayed her arms and legs out as wide as possible. Unless the entire floor had been removed, she could be certain of finding some solid ground this way. When she collected herself and found a place to sit within the cell, she clutched the keys and thought of Conor. She wondered again whether he might even be alive. She had no idea of his present whereabouts, or if he suffered some form of torturous treatment similar to hers. She tried very hard to send him a mental message. She pleaded with him and any creator who might listen to come and find her. She sat alone in her cell, holding the five keys of the creators and her sanity in one tiny, trembling hand.

41

CHAPTER SIX

Conor stepped out of the corridor and promptly fell flat on his face.
He tried to break his fall with his arms, but they didn't respond any
better than his legs. The muscles of his body, now removed from
the cell of shadows, revealed their true condition. They had completely atrophied during his captivity. The biomechanics of the cell
had allowed him to function normally while imprisoned. Now far
away from that environment, he would have to rely on his own
power again. He struggled to rise and found that he couldn't even
turn himself over. He lay flat on the ground, his right cheek and
eye socket firmly planted in the dirt.

Mr. Hikkins had followed Conor through the corridor. Upon
seeing his student tumble to the ground in a heap, he calmly
stepped over him and squatted next to Conor's face. Flicking a
lock of the young man's hair from his eyes, the teacher appraised
the situation before remarking.

"Just as I had suspected," he said matter-of-factly. "Your musculature has diminished almost entirely. I fear your recuperation
might last a bit longer than we originally anticipated. Don't try to
move at all; in your state you could swallow your tongue or cause
irreparable damage to your eyes. I will deliver you to your destination myself."

Conor lay on the ground, completely motionless. He couldn't have altered his position if his life depended on it. Thankfully, his right eye remained closed and his left eye had landed clear of the ground. He saw only darkness through the open eye, a scary sensation for one recently freed from a cell as black as night. His optic nerves, shielded from the light for so long, had deteriorated along with the rest of his body. For a moment he became horribly concerned. After the emotion passed he remembered where he was and who accompanied him. The creators would see to his complete rehabilitation. He felt certain of that.

His mind racing, he began to wonder if he had fallen into a trap. Maybe the immobilization of his body had been a purposeful act. After all, Seefra's mastery of shape shifting was legendary. It would not be beyond his abilities to introduce himself as Mr. Hikkins and convince Conor that his cell now looked exactly like the realm of the creators. But his misgivings quickly evaporated as he felt his body rising gently from the ground. He became aware of his torso rotating in the air, turning around so he would face the sky. He sensed Mr. Hikkins standing next to him, directing the magic that held him aloft. While he floated silently, a solid white sheet roughly eight by three feet slid in place underneath him. Although the sheet seemed no thicker than a dime, when his body released itself into the soft material, Conor felt utterly relaxed for the first time in years.

"This sheet will carry you to a place especially designed for your rejuvenation," said Mr. Hikkins. The sheet floated alongside him, flanking the teacher effortlessly. The action occurred so fluidly that Conor hadn't even noticed the movement. Although he couldn't move any of his muscles, as he floated along, Conor felt the different parts of his body falling into place on the soft, flowing sheet. The heels of his feet, his calves, thighs, torso, shoulders and head all rolled into a perfectly comfortable position. He lay on his back, looking up at the breathtaking sky through the crowns of the trees. "Aside from providing a level of comfort beyond compare," continued Mr. Hikkins, "the fabric you currently reside on possesses medicinal qualities as well. Even now, your vital life statistics are being recorded and transferred to a team of healers here in the realm. By the time we reach our destination, they should already have designed a protocol for your complete recovery."

He looked over at Conor and saw the eyelids flapping up and down as Conor tried repeatedly to look up at the sky. Mr. Hikkins felt a pang of concern for the young man. Thus far, their association had lasted for less than a year's time. Even though he barely knew him, he had seen enough to understand Conor fairly well. Although very brave and solidly rational, Conor shared a similar trait with most of his human family. He cared deeply for his close relations. He loved his family and his friends, and he certainly showed a marked affection for Miss Cochran. He feared that Conor's emotional attachments might overwhelm the logical side of his faculties. He had been through a terrible ordeal, yet he knew that his companion was a captive of the master of darkness. It would not be surprising to hear of Conor insisting that he be released the first moment he felt healthy enough to find her. Whether he could muster the strength to do battle with Seefra would be another consideration entirely. But, of course, Conor would never think of that. He would be too eager to find and save Miss Cochran – a troubling quandary indeed.

"I do hope," Mr. Hikkins continued, "that you will allow the healers to complete their work with you here in the realm." He looked over again and saw that Conor's eyelids had closed completely.

His body lay motionless on the sheet. Mr. Hikkins smiled as he watched the fabric directly underneath his student's body caress and massage him. Not only would Conor receive the most tranquil sleep of his life, but the therapeutic qualities of his bedding would also begin performing their work even before they arrived at his chamber. When he awoke he would already feel a measure of fitness restored to his body.

The teacher and his student silently moved down the perfectly groomed path toward Conor's recuperation quarters. One by one, different residents of the realm came forward to have a look at the newest Champion of the Crossworlds. Tiny fragile birds, as colorful as a rainbow, fluttered softly down onto Conor's feet or knees. A brave bird or two even landed softly on his right shoulder, close to Mr. Hikkins. The birds tipped their heads a few times, looking at the features of Conor's face. After a second or two, they flicked their wings, retreating to the trees.

Four-footers, mostly deer and medium-sized cats, paced along side Conor's bedding. They looked and sniffed, trying not to disturb their newest hero. One particular cat looked at Conor, looked up at Mr. Hikkins for approval, and then jumped lightly onto the young man's belly. After sniffing for a bit, the feline walked right up Conor's chest until it stood face to face with him. Ever so delicately, the cat lowered its head and touched its nose to Conor's face. After a second or two, satisfied with its inspection, the cat jumped away from Conor and walked back into the forest.

One of the giant trees that lined the path bent over at midtrunk and brought its crown far down from the sky. It waved its immense branches and leaves directly in front of Conor, as if anointing him during his first visit to the realm. Without another sound or motion, the giant tree unfolded again, standing tall while protecting Conor's passage. Other interested flora and fauna crowded around the two travelers, but Mr. Hikkins waved them all away. Conor slept deeply now and he didn't want anything to disturb his repose. Disappointed but not at all resentful, the animals and trees merely lined the pathway, catching a glimpse of Conor as he passed in front of them.

Conor's escort guided his charge toward one of the smaller waterfalls in the realm. A jagged path cut away from the main trail, heading up toward the falls. Mr. Hikkins walked along the twisting path while Conor's bedding floated along above a lengthy formation of spindle ferns. The ferns formed an endless quilt of lime green feathers. They rolled out from the center stalk, spreading the fragile spindles out toward each other. The interwoven feathers formed a thick bedding that one could scarcely see through.

Upon reaching the falls, Mr. Hikkins uttered a quick chant before walking directly into the cascading water. As he entered the stream, the water spread out over his head, giving him a clear, dry passage. It seemed as though an invisible umbrella had opened up just above his hair, remaining open only long enough for him to pass through the falls. An identical phenomenon occurred when Conor's transport approached the waterfall. The streaming water opened up like a set of curtains in a windowpane. Conor passed under the powerful falls without so much as a fleck of moisture touching him.

Behind the roaring falls lay a rather ordinary looking cave. A rock formation roughly the size of a small apartment, the cave enjoyed no special additions to its environment at all. Mr. Hikkins guided Conor to the back of the cave and held the sheet in place for a moment. He looked at the wall of rock and whispered a lengthy spell. After waiting a few moments, he chanted another spell. Waiting another sixty seconds exactly, he bent down and scooped up a handful of dust from the cave floor. Voicing the last of the spells, he blew the dust from the palm of his hand toward the back wall of the cave. He stepped back two paces, moving the sheet and Conor back with him.

The cave shook from the force of three violent convulsions. Rocks and dust filtered down from above the back wall, first in small amounts and then with greater intensity. When the avalanche expired and the convulsions settled, the back wall of the cave shifted and transformed right in front of Mr. Hikkins. In the rock wall, it seemed the creators possessed their own version of shadow or crystal tiles. Thousands of irregular pieces of lava rock began rushing in all directions along the wall. They flew all around each other at incredible speeds, somehow never colliding once through all of the rapid misdirection. Like a mathematical formula dissecting itself, the wall obeyed the spell spoken to it by its smiling master. Mr. Hikkins waited patiently for the coding to become complete. As the last few pieces of the structure moved into their correct alignments, the wall pushed out from the side closest to Mr. Hikkins. A beam of soothing light – not exactly sunlight, but not entirely devoid of the sun's healing powers – poured into the cave from behind the wall. This particular light had been specifically arranged for Conor's arrival.

Mr. Hikkins passed through the doorway at the back of the cave. The nurturing fabric carrying Conor followed quietly behind him. After seeing the travelers through its portal, the huge wall of the cave slid back into place. Immediately, the rocks began dashing in all directions again, locking the wall into its original position. No one but a handful of creators knew the spells to find their way into these quarters. The Lady of the Light had commanded that Conor's convalescence take place here, with no disturbances whatsoever.

The sound of the rushing waterfall did not penetrate the back of the cave. This tiny portion of the realm held its own sounds, and these were very few indeed. Conor's "room" consisted of three massive water walls and one side was left completely open. When he awoke, Conor would experience the most breathtaking view in the realm of the creators, which poured forth from the empty wall of the chamber. A colorful glade, roughly fifty acres square, fell away from the small hill containing his quarters. Every hue in the rainbow stood out in the trees, pools of water, bushes and sky. Some said that the Lady of the Light herself drew forth the coloring in the sky. Depending on where one looked, they might see a handful of distinctly different hues. From purple to yellow, with blue, green, red and orange in between, the sky facing Conor's bed had no equal in the long existence of the Crossworlds.

The three water walls stood over twenty feet high, with equal distance between each. The wall at the foot of the bed shone a deep sapphire blue. To Conor's left, a brilliant purple, and on his right, a ruby red wall with softly trickling water fell at exactly the same pace as the others. Although the three walls glowed in a consistent manner, as soon as Conor's bed inserted itself between them, the colors began shifting rapidly. The sapphire wall changed its hue to a sky blue before changing back to its darker tint. The purple and red walls acted similarly, adjusting their moods to accommodate their new patient. After a period of inspection, the three walls settled into a harmonious rhythm of colorful consistency.

An Ezuvex, standing on its hind legs, studied Conor as he lay sleeping on the sheet. The guardian, an intellectual from the planet Wilzerd, had informed the Lady of the Light of his experience with

Homo sapiens. Having spent many years on Conor's home planet, he believed he might be able to assist in his recovery. After questioning him about the human body and hearing his tale about how his kind had avoided contact with humans on earth for centuries, the Lady placed him in charge of Conor's rejuvenation. The Ezuvex, who went by the name of Gribba, didn't lay a hand on Conor while looking him over the first time. Instead, he watched the coloration of the water walls change subtly, humming while they made their adjustments. Gribba never left the head of Conor's bedding; he always stood in a location that didn't impede any of the water walls. He merely watched the colors, looked at Conor's face from time to time, and kept his paws folded behind his back.

The Lady of the Light entered Conor's quarters without making a sound. Only the Ezuvex's superior hearing could have detected her wraithlike movements. Even though he heard her behind him, Gribba did not turn around. Instead, he kept his eyes and posture focused on his patient. He waited until the Lady stood next to him before speaking to her.

"The young man has suffered a great deal for all of us," he said softly.

"Yes," said the Lady of the Light. "If I could relinquish his responsibility I would do so without hesitation. I fear, though, that Conor's journey is far from over." She moved forward, holding out her left arm. She longed to touch his cheek to assure herself of its warmth.

"No, my Lady," said Gribba deferentially while holding her tiny arm in his huge, hairy paw. "If I may, he cannot be disturbed in the slightest at this point of the procedure. The bio walls have only recently centered on his physiological attributes. To disrupt them now could prove disastrous."

The Lady stopped in her tracks, but did not step back. She looked lovingly at Conor's face, allowing a single tear to glide down her cheek. She would take his place in an instant if the council would permit it. Still, she knew Gribba's counsel to be true, so she turned and placed her hand in the Ezuvex's giant paw. Squeezing it lightly, she asked the question she longed to ask since she heard of his release from the cell of shadows.

"Will he live, Gribba?" the Lady inquired softly. "Will he come to back to us?"

"Rest your fears, my Lady," answered the huge beast. "Purugama chose wisely when he found this one on the mesa many years ago. This young man has reserves even he cannot understand. I will not deceive you, however. His convalescence will be difficult. He sustained mental as well as physical damage during his last journey. His emotional scars from his long stay in the cell of shadows will be hard to erase. Even worse, the water walls have detected severe feelings of self-recrimination. He feels responsible for the loss of his companion, and he blames himself for the loss of the Champions. The walls also sense strong feelings of anger and revenge. They cannot precisely report them to me, but I would venture a guess that your young Champion cannot wait to avenge himself against Seefra and his shadow warriors. He knows he made a terrible mistake back on his home planet, but in his mind Seefra crossed the line by going after his companion. A burning desire for a confrontation exists within this young man. I fear it may be his undoing."

Without moving a muscle or even nodding, the Lady waited for a gap in Gribba's diagnosis. "His physical condition, will he recover fully?"

"The physical depletion of his human body will be less of a

challenge to correct, but there will be enduring damage to his biological system. Your Champion enjoys the strength of youth, however, something that will work to his advantage during his recovery. Although a few lingering problems will remain, his body should function normally. Of course this depends on how willing he is to stay here and complete his recovery. Creatures possessing feelings of responsibility and urgency usually do not fancy waiting for someone to tell them they are fully healed. At his age, this one will want to run off long before the process has been completed."

"Do not fret, my friend," said the Lady. "I will see to it that your patient stays here with us for as long as you desire." The Lady let go of Gribba's paw and stepped closer to the bedding Conor rested on. Folding her arms across her chest, she looked down at her young Champion's face. In repose, he seemed completely at ease. He looked like a sixteen-year-old high school student without a care in the world. "I would like to stay here with him for a while," she said to the guardian. "I promise not to disturb him in any way."

"My Lady," said Gribba, bowing his head slightly. "I am yours to command. You certainly do not need my permission, but I thank you for your consideration."

The Lady smiled slightly, turning her head so the Ezuvex could see her appreciation. After sensing Gribba's departure, she returned her gaze to Conor. How he had changed in two years, she thought. She recalled the first time she ever laid eyes on her young Champion. When questioned by the creators in the misty clouds, Purugama had remained stationary for a good five minutes. The Lady, without his knowledge, had taken a long look at the small boy riding on the great cougar's shoulders. At barely seventy pounds and skinny as a rail, he couldn't have looked less imposing. Yet he had grown into the young man in front of her in six short years. At almost five foot ten and one hundred seventy pounds, Conor looked like a grown man now. His sandy brown hair had grown quite long during his captivity, and it had darkened somewhat, obviously due to the lack of light. His face had matured as well. The round, soft face of a small boy had developed strong adult features with the passage of time. He looked handsome in a rough sort of way. The Lady smiled as she watched him breathing evenly. She almost couldn't believe he was here, safe at last in the realm of the creators.

"Don't worry, my young Champion," she cooed softly. "I will take care of you, and then we will work together to find Janine. I promise you that, Conor. I swear to you we will find her."

CHAPTER SEVEN

When the five keys of the creators fell within the grasp of the Circle of Evil, the Champions of the Crossworlds found themselves blasted across the limits of their dominion. They were propelled so far and at such speed that when they reached their destination, the cage of fire disappeared in a flaming blast of magical energy. None of the Champions sustained any serious injuries, but after scouting the area they believed they were desperately lost. Not one of them recognized any part of the world on which they had landed. The only fixtures they could clearly identify were the ancient corridors they found at the edge of a large desert. Maya had taken one look at the structures and denounced them as forbidden corridors. He would not allow any of the Champions to risk passage through one of the banned portals.

Although he hid his frustration quite well, it annoyed Maya that he could not call forth a functioning corridor. It should have been so simple; on any other planet the Lord of the Champions could easily have drawn the dimensions of a new passageway. The five of them could walk right through the portal to any destination he chose. For some strange reason his skills were stifled here. He had tried many times over the course of their confinement to summon a vehicle to help them escape. But every time his efforts came up short, and with each failure Maya's concern grew. He wondered if they might ever leave this place. He doubted that any one of them could conjure a magical spell of any consequence. He kept his speculation to himself, however, out of consideration for the other Champions. They all needed to cradle a fragment of hope, and he refused to douse their growing pessimism by delivering more bad news. The confinement to this strange world had left them quite irritable.

"Be silent, all of you!" growled Maya at his brother Champions. "We cannot escape our predicament by ridiculing each other's ideas. Now settle down so we can calmly discuss our options."

"Options?" snarled Surmitang, the huge Sumatran tiger. "We are finished, marooned here on this bizarre world. It would be the same had we been banished to the forbidden corridors. If we even knew where we are, we still wouldn't have any idea how to find our way back to the glade."

"That kind of negativity will assure our failure," replied Ajur, who hung loosely from a large tree branch directly over Maya's head. The black jaguar let his comment sink in as he stared icily at Surmitang.

Purugama flapped his wings, testing their utility for the hundredth time. "Ajur is correct, Surmitang," he said, "although you do make a valid point. We are lost to the creators, a condition we may never overcome. However, we must always hold out hope for deliverance."

A massive cheetah slept soundly on a pile of moss-covered rocks in the clearing where the Champions gathered. Every once in a while, he flicked an ear just to let his brothers know he was listening to their deliberations. Eha had never been one to worry much about anything. He knew that a good nap would help solve almost any dilemma.

Maya waited patiently for his brothers to finish their final remarks. Something in his mind told him that Conor no longer remained a prisoner of the shadow warriors. If that were true, and if the creators had freed Conor, then he and his brothers had some new options. What he proposed would seem irrational to the others, maybe completely insane to one or two of them. But he felt they might have no other choice. If he lacked the use of his powers here on this planet, then the only way out might be the riskiest path of all. On top of that, his strategy depended on successful communication with Conor. The big cat doubted his ability to reach the young man, but as Ajur and Purugama said, there must always be hope. He returned his attention to the group of formidable Champions he had known longer than he could remember. When their conversation cooled and they looked to him for guidance, he crouched down on his belly and spoke to the group.

"I propose that we use the forbidden corridors to make our escape," he said calmly to the group gathered before him.

Stunned into silence, the great Champions sat before Maya with mouths agape. They simply couldn't believe what their leader had suggested. The forbidden corridors carried the most bizarre and unpredictable magical forces known to the Crossworlds. The fact that Conor had entered a forbidden corridor and returned safely had never been fully understood by anyone. Even the creators didn't dare go near the volatile portals. Rumor had it that many centuries ago one of the Council of Seven stood before the oldest of the forbidden corridors, merely examining the exterior casing. The portal waited for the appropriate moment and then pulled the creator across the barrier. The corridor burst to life and dragged the council member into the void. She was never seen again.

When the Crossworlds Champions got over their cumulative shock, five voices exploded simultaneously in front of Maya. Even Eha, a prodigious nap artist, awoke to join in the protest.

"You must be joking," began Ajur, still hanging over Maya's head.

"Preposterous!" roared Surmitang, on his feet facing his Lord.

"I have no wish to enter the dominion of the forbidden corridors," said Eha. "If you command it, however, I will follow you there."

"Maya," Purugama calmly responded, "there must be another way."

"Unfortunately, there is no other way," answered the Lord of the Crossworlds Champions. "Would I ask this of you if another path existed? Do you not realize how acutely I sense the dangers awaiting us inside these portals?"

"I have spent many months trying to devise a method for our escape. I have tried many times, but I cannot call forth a corridor for our use. I cannot communicate with anyone in the realm of the creators. We are either on a world far too distant from the realm or the shadow warriors have erected a barrier against mental and magical correspondence."

"I have failed to reach Conor through traditional means. I fear these conditions will not change as long as we inhabit this world. I also fear that the five keys of the creators may be closer to Seefra's grasp than we care to admit. For as long as we have been imprisoned here, the master of darkness has been attempting to break the spell placed on the keys by the Lady of the Light. If he succeeds and gains control of the keys, then where we are and whether we can escape will no longer matter."

"You know as well as I that once Conor recovers, he will launch himself against Seefra and his shadow warriors. He cannot win that battle alone. We must accompany him in his charge against the Circle of Evil. The forbidden corridors are the only way open to us. If what I believe is true, then I believe Conor will be able to find us individually wherever the portals send us. We must give him that opportunity. Together we can defeat Seefra once and for all. Separately he will destroy us one by one and take possession of the Crossworlds for all time."

"I need not tell you that we will be taking a risk by entering the forbidden corridors. As certain as I am about my tactics, I could be completely wrong. We may never see each other again. We may all be destroyed. But I am willing to risk the chance if it means saving Conor's life. He is a brave Champion; he journeyed with his companion to a host of mysterious worlds. They collected the five keys of the creators with no outside assistance."

"Had he not opened his mouth," interrupted Surmitang, "he might not have needed to travel in search of the keys."

"You speak truth, Surmitang," answered Maya calmly. "The young man made a mistake. But have I not erred in judgment while leading the Champions from time to time? Was it in your best interest to irrationally jump into a forbidden corridor to save Conor from Therion's clutches?" The Lord of the Champions waited for a response. When they didn't come he continued his proposal.

"Have we not put our lives at risk many times in the past? Is that not our mission, our duty? I would gladly sacrifice myself for our brother Champion, but there are even more issues at stake. The creators will be at the mercy of the shadow warriors should Seefra crack the code of the five keys. Our Lady will be destroyed along with all the others, including the Council of Seven. The Crossworlds itself will be thrown into mass hysteria. Once the spell has been broken and the five keys fall into Seefra's possession, the shadow warriors will descend upon the Crossworlds like a plague. They will ravage world after world, some for vital resources, others for slaves, and still others for the sheer pleasure of spreading terror."

"If the five keys fall into the hands of the Circle of Evil, the damage to the system may be irreversible. Even if we were to defeat Seefra at some future date, we might never resurrect the Crossworlds again. Most of the planets may exist in a perpetual state of disarray. Others could float in the void forever, permanently damaged beyond repair. No, my brothers, I will not stay here if we have an opportunity to act. We must take our chances with the forbidden corridors."

The four other Champions sat silently for a moment. Surmitang, the bold one, spoke first, but with a question instead of an objection.

"Maya," he began. "I trust you. All of us here trust you. You have never led us astray before. But this seems like madness. It feels like the hopeless strategy of a desperate leader. How can we possibly know what to expect if we penetrate the forbidden barrier? You recall what I told you about my experience with Conor and Therion, do you not? That portal dropped all of us into the *Forest of Forever.* Conor was lucky to return at all, much less alive, from that sorcerer's madhouse. Like Eha, I will follow you, but I think we'd all like to know what that magnificent mind of yours has cooked up."

"Well said, Surmitang," stated Purugama, looking around at his brothers. Although alert and attentive, Eha and Ajur remained silent.

"Yes," answered Maya. "Well said indeed. Listen closely, my

brothers, and I will tell you what I think." The great cat paced in a circle for a few seconds, looking up into the trees. As softly as a breath of wind, he jumped into a tree and splayed himself among the branches. He looked like a prince in a natural wooden throne. He licked his right paw a few times and scraped it across his cheek. After examining the paw briefly, he continued speaking. "After our brave brother Surmitang rescued Conor from the forbidden corridors many years ago, I began to research the bizarre portals whenever I could. Without ever passing through the membranes, I stayed as close as I dared, trying to sense anything I could about their existence. I also tried to glean as much as possible about the nature of their function. I wanted to see if the forbidden corridors possessed any qualities that might be different from the corridors we've used so often.

I also spoke at great length with the Lady of the Light about the ancient portals. She referred me to the brightest engineers and scientists in the realm for extensive discussions about their nature. One of the physicists, an extremely aged creator by the name of Milton, returned to one of the forbidden corridors with me, and there we engaged in a most revealing discussion. He informed me that unlike our portals, which operate solely on the basis of location, the forbidden corridors contain an added element. They also operate as time portals, giving one the ability not only to travel from world to world, but from one time to another."

"Of course," said Ajur. "The creators would have to forbid their use. Anyone possessing the ability to travel through time could change the history of any planet within the Crossworlds structure."

"Precisely," replied Maya. "That's why they've been idle for so long. The mere notion of their unpredictability keeps us away from them. Even the evil ones would not risk sending the shadow warriors through the forbidden corridors. They could very well lose them forever."

"Milton gave me an extensive seminar about the time displacement characteristics of these corridors. If I manipulate the portal in the way I think I can, and if we are extremely lucky, we may be able to travel back to our original points of origin. Ajur, you and Purugama will return to the glade of Champions as small cubs. Surmitang will depart for the forests of Indonesia, where he will once again live with and protect his pride. Eha, you will go back to the Sahara where you can track game and lie in the sun."

"And what about you," asked the lanky cheetah. "Where will you travel to, Maya?"

"I will return to the woman who cared for me in a simpler life, to the yards I prowled and the home I occupied. Although I enjoy my travels throughout the Crossworlds, I look forward to seeing my former mistress again."

"And after all of us find our former selves?" asked Ajur. "What happens then?"

"Then," replied Maya as he looked at the giant jaguar, "we hope that Conor can find us. Once again, it appears he is the key to the security of the Crossworlds. If he can use the identical corridors the creators used so long ago to call us into their service, then he should be able to retrieve us one by one and bring us back to the glade of Champions. Once we are all assembled, the Lady of the Light can restore our physical and magical powers. After that, we can press the attack against the shadow warriors."

"What about Therion?" asked Purugama, causing all the cats to look his way. "If we truly wish to overcome Seefra and defeat the shadow warriors, we will need his strength and cunning."

"I have spoken to the Lady of the Light about our brother," said Maya. "She agreed to broach the subject with the first councilor. It is his choice, however, and we must abide by his decision. I agree that facing Seefra's armies would be much easier with Therion along with us. If Conor can pluck him away from his pride without angering him, he might be a willing participant in our cause."

Maya looked at his brothers. At a combined weight of roughly twenty thousand pounds of ferocious fury, they were a formidable party indeed. He knew what their response would be before he asked the question, but he wanted to give them a say in the uncertainty of their future.

"So now you know of my plan. I must go and try to communicate with Conor. But first I ask you, who among you will follow me into the forbidden corridors?"

"I will, and gladly," said Eha immediately.

"Try and keep me here," rumbled Ajur.

"Aye," chuffed Purugama. "And tell Conor not to drag his feet."

The huge Sumatran tiger looked at each of his brothers. He shook his large, shaggy head and then peered up at Maya. "Dangerous," he said. "Very dangerous, but how could you succeed without me along with you? Count me in."

"I am glad, Surmitang," said Maya. "For if we need the king of beasts with us to assure our success, then we surely need the brave tiger who stared him down to help in our quest to save our Champion."

CHAPTER EIGHT

Conor slept soundly inside the healing chamber. The water walls hummed quietly, maintaining their original colors as they worked to rejuvenate Conor's life force. Excellent progress had been made thus far – Conor showed significant improvement with all bio-physical and neurological human characteristics. His muscula-ture had gained substance and strength. His brain had returned to its peak processing power. His ability to conjure magical spells looked to be in top form. Still, Gribba had directed the water walls to keep Conor in a motionless state, almost in a light coma. He wanted the young man to heal as quickly as possible, and he knew that isolating his recuperative powers would yield the quickest re-sults. After only a few days Conor had shown remarkable results. Gribba would keep it that way; he wanted to share good news with the Lady of the Light every time she stopped in to check on him.

Gribba watched the young man breathe evenly, inhaling and exhaling, mimicking the movement of the realm. Even though he knew by the readings on the water walls that Conor's health im-proved every day, it disturbed him to look upon his inert form. The sight of a completely motionless patient troubled most caregivers, even if all signs pointed in a positive direction. The beasts from

Gribba's planet all shared this empathic trait. Conor couldn't have been in better hands.

Suddenly, Conor's brow creased. The fingers on his left hand twitched. His head rocked from side to side before centering itself again. The Ezuvex quickly rechecked the readings; no signs of any danger seemed evident. He stepped back and watched Conor closely. His large eyes flicked between the young man and the three water walls maintaining his biological functions.

Prior to the involuntary twitching, Conor had been dreaming of his first soccer match at Mountmoor High. The dream became so real that it resembled a highlight film of his dazzling play during the match. He became so involved in the excitement of the game that he forgot to conceal his newfound powers. Before the first half ended, he had scored four solo goals and assisted on three others. His coach clapped the freshman striker on the back as he left the field, but he did so with tempered excitement. In sixteen years of coaching, he had never seen anything like the skills young Conor Jameson displayed that afternoon. Athletic didn't do him justice. Superhuman maybe, if Conor had looked at all human. He hadn't, however. He had resembled an oversized cat playing with a marble amidst a group of small children.

The soccer game drifted away from Conor's mind, making room for the emergence of a new mental picture. Another dream or perhaps a vision floated into the forefront of Conor's mind. Wavy and blurry at first, the image took the form of an animal surrounded by some natural environment. It seemed to battle against some force as it tried to settle itself. It would come close to a finished image and then a wave of milky essence would blur the picture again. Conor's subconscious mind began reaching out to it. He shook his head, trying to clear the cobwebs. His hand twitched as he tried to grasp what lay before him. It was at this point that Gribba became alarmed at the sight of his patient's movements.

The vision finally crystallized. Maya materialized in front of Conor's mental line of sight. The Lord of the great cats sat quietly next to a calm pool in the glade of Champions. Swatting the water gently with his right front paw, he turned his gaze and looked deeply into Conor's mind. Greeting his newest Champion and congratulating him on his survival, Maya waved him over to the pool with his large tail.

Conor felt a part of him sit up and push away from the sheet cradling him between the water walls. He landed lightly on the ground and walked toward Maya. When he reached the north water wall, its color changed from a calm blue to sparkling silver. He stepped through the glistening monument and entered the glade of Champions. His body, so light in this form, seemed to glide over to the pool where Maya sat. As he approached his Lord, Conor extended his right hand to the big cat's left ear. He wished more than anything to scratch it and grasp the beautiful fur. Maya obliged him, lowering his head slightly to accept Conor's touch.

"Maya, Maya," said Conor over and over as he scratched the big cat's ears, head and neck. Maya turned his head to the left and right, giving Conor many different places to rub and scratch. He pushed his nose into Conor's hand time and again, hoping for a fingernail rub on the bridge between his eyes. After a lengthy greeting, Maya pulled his head away and addressed his newest Champion.

"Conor, I cannot begin to tell you how pleased I am to see you. We feared the worst, all of us, and we had begun making contingencies for a life without you. The seeker succeeded in his task, however, and now you are back where you belong, among the creators of the Crossworlds. One aspect of our resurgence is complete."

Conor took the first chance he saw to interject. "The other Champions. Are they all well? Purugama?"

"All alive at least," replied Maya. "However, we are lost to the creators. When the five keys fell into Seefra's hands, the Circle of Evil hurled the cage of fire to the extreme edge of the Crossworlds. Although the cage blew apart upon impact, the five of us have been marooned on an unknown world for a lengthy period of time. We have spent all of our energies unsuccessfully trying to return ourselves to the glade."

"But you are all well?" asked Conor. "None of you have suffered permanent injuries?"

"No physical injuries, Conor. But our spirits remain low. We are the Champions of the Crossworlds, and we can no more protect the creators and all of the individual worlds than we can assure the safety of one small cub." Maya let his gaze fall to the ground. He seemed to be looking at nothing.

"I'm sorry, Maya, truly I am," responded Conor. "I feel responsible for everything – the creators scattered, the Champions sent into oblivion, Janine's imprisonment. A Champion of the Crossworlds would never have acted so foolishly."

"Be silent," Maya said, softly but harshly. "The fool is the one who uses his energy chiding himself when he should be saving it for a return to glory. You erred, yes, but you are young, Conor. It is the destiny of youth to make mistakes, for you have many years yet to atone for them. Think of all the good you have accomplished. You captured the five keys. You vanquished Loken, a formidable former leader of the shadow warriors. Do not worry. The Crossworlds will find its way back with the help of the creators. We must prepare to assist them in their cause. Now, let me look at you."

Maya stood and circled around the young man. "Yes, you have

grown, and filled out somewhat as well. I cannot wait until Surmitang lays eyes on you again." He continued pacing back and forth, inspecting every little detail of Conor's physical attributes. "Excellent. You've matured well, Conor. This will surely help us when the time comes. How do you feel?"

"Tired, mostly," he replied. "Stronger than when I first stepped out of the corridor, but still fairly exhausted."

"That is to be expected. Gribba will give you the best care you could possibly receive. Obey his commands to the letter, and do not attempt to leave until he gives you his clearance. Do you understand me?"

"Yes, Maya, I do," Conor replied tersely, changing the subject immediately. "Have you heard anything about Janine? You must tell me, even if it's bad news."

"As I said," replied Maya, "we have existed at the most extreme boundaries of the Crossworlds for over a year. We've heard nothing about anyone or anything for so long we thought the worlds had been destroyed. I know nothing of your companion's whereabouts or well-being. I am sorry, Conor."

"I'm so worried about her I can't even stand it. The only thing I know is that she's alive. I don't know where she is, or what's happening to her. I do know that if he breaks the spell on the keys, then her fate is sealed. Every day that passes brings him another step closer to that goal. But I promise, Maya, I will stay here among the creators until I'm allowed to leave. As soon as that happens, I will use everything I have to locate and rescue Janine. I may perish in the process, but I won't leave her in his hands for one second longer than I have to."

"Seefra?" asked Maya.

"How did you know?" replied Conor with his own question.

"If all of you suffered such extreme isolation, how could you know that it was Seefra who captured Janine?"

"News of that caliber reaches even the most remote sections of the Crossworlds," answered Maya. "We knew of her predicament long ago. The news only increased our frustration because of our inability to do anything to help her. By rescuing her we could regain control of the keys. They are the link to a stable system, Conor. However important your companion is, the keys represent our most vital priority. More than anything else, we must work together to achieve that specific goal. We will help you rescue your companion, but you must assist us in our quest to recapture the five keys of the creators."

Maya continued. "I understand your impatience. Of all the vile creatures conjured up by the evil ones, Seefra is far and away the most loathsome. As you have no doubt gathered, he controls a vast array of powers. Not only can he manipulate himself and alter his environment as well, his command of shadow magic must be unparalleled by now."

"Neither you nor I, nor any of the other Champions, will be completely safe during this journey. None of us will ever be sure if the one we travel with or speak to is our companion or Seefra in disguise."

Maya let the shock of his statement settle in before continuing. "Seeing him again must have given you quite a shock, I'm sure. At least we know another of his many abilities – he can escape even the pummeling downfall of his own castle. He has become incredibly strong, and it will take every ounce of cunning we possess to overcome him."

"Maya," injected Conor. "How can you speak of destroying Seefra, or even of fighting him? I am a prisoner of my own depleted body, confined to the realm of the creators. You and the rest of the Champions sit hopelessly stranded on a forgotten world. The master of darkness thrives at the peak of his power, commanding a formidable army of shadow warriors. Even with your great powers you cannot free the Champions from their captivity. You currently exist in a world so distant even the creators cannot return you to the glade. What makes you think we'll ever find each other?"

"Because," said the Lord of the Crossworlds Champions. "I have a plan."

CHAPTER NINE

Janine huddled in the corner of her cell. She felt too terrified to stay anywhere else. Certain that she sat on a solid surface, she kept her hands in front of her just in case the crystals began to shift again. Over the last several hours, her small prison had experienced some frightening transformations. It seemed as though her cell and the hundreds of others around her reacted to Seefra's emotions. When he felt pleased with his progress, the floor of the cell firmed up and became whole. When he bellowed his frustrations at another setback, the crystals seemed to run for cover. This caused the cell to become very unstable, leaving Janine to guess where it might be safe to place her hands or feet.

During the last day at least, Janine had watched in horror as dozens of captives fell to their deaths. The floors in their cells must have disappeared entirely, leaving them nothing to grasp at but air. As they fell the first few feet toward their doom, the prisoners maintained an eerie silence. It seemed that in the shock of the moment they couldn't believe their time had come. The silence didn't last, however; it was soon replaced by the familiar terrifying scream of someone facing an indescribable horror. Then the roar of the beast came as it saw another intruder violating its space. Chaos followed, mostly from the movement of the giant creature

69

that lived below the crystal cells. It took a straight path toward its victim, knocking everything out of its way. Thankfully, the end came quickly, and all became silent again.

These last few hours had turned Janine's nerves into jelly. Not only had she watched many fall to their doom, but she also had to deal with the shifting crystals in her own cell. She couldn't count the number of times her hand or foot had fallen through an opening in the arrangement of the crystals. In some instances, she instinctively placed her other hand on the floor to brace herself, only to have that tile slide away as well. So many times her mind had convinced her it was her turn; that this time the floor would disappear and she would fall silently through the air to a horrible death.

Somehow she had managed to stay within the boundaries of the cell. She screamed at Seefra so many times and for so long that her throat burned. She promised him in no uncertain terms that Conor would come for her. She told the master of darkness that his days were numbered, that when Conor came for her he would bring with him the magic of the creators and a host of giant Champions. Together, they would destroy Seefra and tear down his fortress of torture. "The souls of every being that had perished here would join the charge of the Champions against his foul warriors," she had proclaimed.

"Then let them come," hissed Seefra, floating above the floor of Janine's cell.

Janine pulled her legs to her body, moving as far up the wall as she could. She treasured the feel of the solid floor beneath her, but seeing the master of darkness appear inside her cell unnerved her to no end. In her depleted spiritual state, she felt as though his presence might sap some of the crystals away from the cell. She felt completely impotent; she could do nothing except cower in front of him.

"They *will* come here," Seefra continued. "At some point in the future they *will* arrive. And we will meet and destroy them, all of them, including your precious Conor."

"NO!" screamed Janine loudly. She swallowed and felt the raw pain of her bruised throat. "He'll come for you, Seefra, and when he arrives he will bring destruction like you have never imagined. You will pay for every life you've taken here. He will exact punishment upon you while the Champions decimate your pitiful army."

"The boast of a desperate soul," said Seefra coolly. He slithered over to the far side of the cell, giving Janine a moment or two to digest his last biting comment. He let the remark settle in before shocking her with his next statement. "He has been freed. Did you know that? Conor has been released from the cell of shadows, rescued by a seeker in service to the creators. We held him for almost two years, waiting for our chance to destroy him. When he made the appropriate mistake, we would have crushed him like an insect. But the seeker found him before we could prompt an error out of him."

"Then he will be here soon," predicted Janine. "Conor will collect the giant cats and come here directly. Enjoy your last days, because he will come to save me. If you stand in his way, he'll flatten you like he did Loken."

"Your companion will never find the Champions of the Crossworlds, I assure you," replied Seefra. "When I snatched you away from him, we sent the Champions to the outer provinces of the Crossworlds. Even Maya, a formidable conjurer in his own right, cannot draw forth a corridor powerful enough to make good their escape. They have only one choice, and that is to use one of the forbidden portals. Maya is not as desperate as you or your foolish companion. Conor has tasted the abyss that exists on the other side of those portals. He would brave it again if he felt the slightest hope of finding you. Maya will find no great urgency to pursue that mode of travel. He possesses a rational mind, unlike your rash Champion. Even I would never tempt fate by passing through those treacherous membranes. The forbidden corridors are too unstable, too unpredictable; one could never determine the end result of such a journey.

"Unless Conor wishes to come alone and face a vast army of shadow warriors by himself, he will stay far away from this place. So you see, you have no hope of escape. None at all."

"The creators will help him," said Janine proudly. "The Lady of the Light will see to his safety and give him the power he needs to destroy you and your followers."

"The *creators!*" challenged Seefra. "The creators reside in their realm hoping that other beings might keep the Crossworlds safe for them. They have never lifted a finger in their own defense. After the protection forces learned of their treachery and left to form their own battle groups, the creators quickly assembled the Champions of the Crossworlds. Look at the history of the Champions. First Purugama lost his life defending Conor, and then Surmitang was destroyed performing the identical function. They lost Therion, the most formidable and fearsome warrior in their company during the same struggle with Surmitang. How many of the creators have given their lives for your companion's cause? Not one. They cringe in their realm while others sacrifice themselves."

"Liar!" screamed Janine. "The Lady of the Light came to us at great peril to herself. She came to tell us about the five keys. Then she transferred her powers to Conor so he could defeat Loken and the others sent to destroy us. She could have left us there to perish without any help at all. She even sent an immense bird of prey to help us escape the chasm after she left."

Seefra floated closer to Janine, leaning in to make his point. "Why did *she* not stay and battle Loken herself? Her spell would have prevented her from collecting the items, but she had you as keeper of the keys. Why did she not call an army of creators to follow her through the maze of worlds to collect the keys?"

"Perhaps she had her reasons," responded Janine weakly. "It is not for you or me to know. The creators should never be questioned by anyone but their own kind."

"And why not?" demanded Seefra. "Who proclaimed that their counsel stands above all others? Who ordained them to be masters of all the Crossworlds? Who placed them in such a position that they can order others to perish for their protection, when they refuse to fight for their own existence?"

Seefra whirled on Janine, swishing to the other side of the cell of crystals. He turned his insect-like head, glaring at her with the six eye slits, glowing in their precise rows. "Prepare yourself," he said with menace in his voice. "I am close to another spell. I grow weary of constant failure, and I will not be pleased should this latest effort fail. If I find out that you've had anything to do with the restrictive nature of the Lady's spell, you will wish you had fallen to the beast at the bottom of the chamber, I assure you. I will send my warriors for you soon." With that last comment, he turned abruptly and disappeared.

Janine huddled in the corner again. Wondering if the crystals underneath her would disappear, she touched the walls of the cell. She tried to grip anything she could – a handle, a scratch in the crystals, a loose tile, anything. The walls felt icy smooth, however, nothing emerged for her to grasp. She returned her hands to their strategic location on the floor of the cell and closed her eyes, breathing evenly and deeply focusing on one thought only. As she began concentrating, she reached up with her right hand and grabbed the five keys through her jacket pocket.

"Hurry, Conor," she whispered. "Please hurry."

CHAPTER TEN

"Are you nuts?" Conor asked, showing a little too much surprise. He respected Maya without reservation, but this suggestion took him completely by surprise. "You expect me to find the Champions somewhere within the forbidden corridors? What if the time displacement doesn't work correctly or the organic mechanism decides to hiccup the moment any one of us crosses the barrier?"

"It is a risky proposition," answered Maya. "But one I am prepared to take. The rest of the Champions have all agreed to support my plan. Two days from now we will enter the forbidden portals and begin our transformation. As soon as you are well enough, you must convince the Lady of the Light to accompany you to the proper corridor for your first attempt at reassembling our forces."

Conor stood next to Maya, almost staring eye to eye with the big cat now that he had grown quite a few inches. The Lord of the Champions calmly stared right back, saying nothing as he waited for his apprentice to speak. Conor felt uneasy about Maya's plan. It spoke of desperation, an emotion he had never known Maya to display. It also seemed extremely dangerous. Launching all of them into the forbidden corridors at the same time could prove disastrous. They might all be lost forever. He may never find any of the Champions; it would then be up to him to battle Seefra for the five keys all by himself. It didn't make any sense, but he felt as if nothing made much sense anymore. Instead of destroying him, the Circle of Evil had kept him alive in a pitch-black cell for almost two years. The Champions had been sent to a distant planet where even Maya couldn't devise a means of escape. Janine had been Seefra's prisoner for months, and who knew what kind of horrors he brought upon her every day. In the grand scheme of things, maybe Maya's plan had an element of logic to it after all.

"Go on," Conor said.

"Hopefully, the time displacement procedure will place each of us back in our original locations, where we existed long before we received our magical powers. Our lives will be as they were before the creators called us into service. It will be your task to reassemble the group of cats that ultimately became the Champions of the Crossworlds. To do this, you must enter the correct corridor in order to be transported, both geographically and chronologically, to each of our respective locations.

"You must remember, Conor," continued Maya, "that the Champions will not recognize you when you confront them. They will consider you an outsider, an intruder, and they will react as their instinct tells them to."

Conor felt a sliver of fear race down his spine. "How am I supposed to convince a tiger big enough to swat me like an insect that it's in his best interest to leave his pride and follow me?"

"You will find a way," replied Maya. "Of that I am certain. You possess an uncanny affinity with the animal kingdom, Conor, much like your uncle did before you. Use your instinctive nature when you find each of the cats."

Conor shifted his gaze from Maya's eyes. He knew it would be a sign of uncertainty, but he could not help himself. They were asking too much of him, *again*. He wondered when these journeys would defeat him. When he heard his mentor speak again, he picked his head up and met Maya's pale green eyes.

"There is another way to endear yourself to the Champions as you encounter them individually. Wild cats praise cunning and courage over all other qualities. If you can somehow gain their respect with a feat of bravery, something that benefits them or their pride, then I believe you will gain their trust. After that, it will be a matter of finding them alone and convincing them to follow you."

"I recommend you locate and draw out Eha before any of the others. Cheetahs by their very nature are easygoing and adaptable. He will be the easiest to call back to the realm. After you successfully collect Eha, I believe he might help you with Surmitang and Therion."

Conor felt a bolt of energy shoot down his spine. "Therion!" he gasped. "He tried to destroy me during our journeys to repair the corridors. Now you want me to travel back in time and perform the task that drove him away from you in the first place? Can you trust him after all this time?"

"To answer your question briefly, yes, I trust him. But it goes beyond that. We cannot win the battle for the five keys without him. His size alone will benefit us greatly. He is also a master strategist in the ways of war, and if we expect to overcome Seefra and his legions of shadow warriors, we will need his assistance."

"The Therion you will encounter during this voyage won't have any knowledge of the creators, or the Champions, or of you. He will be an ordinary lion, albeit the alpha male of his pride. Remember, Conor, you are traveling back to the origin of each of our respective lives. None of us will recognize either you or your quest. After you collect us and send us through the corridors, only then will we begin our transformation and become Champions of the Crossworlds again."

"You speak as though I will also be searching for you," said Conor.

"Yes," replied Maya. "In order to escape our confinement, I must tempt fate in the forbidden corridors as well. After you assemble Eha, Surmitang and Therion, you must make one final journey and find me."

Conor let his gaze flicker over Maya's hooded forehead. "If I am successful, am I to send all of you back through the forbidden corridors?"

"Thankfully, no," answered Maya. "I believe the creators will allow the Lady of the Light to call forth strong and dependable corridors for our use at each juncture. She will know when and where to construct the portals. Your job will be to convince the wild cats to jump through the membranes."

"And Conor," said Maya with the slightest hint of a smile, "you may have to use trickery to get one or two of them to cross the barriers."

Conor shook his head and smirked. He enjoyed seeing Maya smile, but he couldn't comprehend the humor in what they were about to attempt. The Champions had agreed to put their lives at terrible risk, and now Maya sat here asking Conor to do the same. Not only that, he expected Conor to travel to a host of unknown locations, face down a group of formidable wild cats, and talk all of them into gleefully leaving their homes and following him to the mysterious world of the creators. Every time a new journey presented itself, it seemed so much more difficult than the last encounter, he thought. He would gladly face a thousand Lokens instead of what lay before him now. His thoughts floated back to the Champions, and he met Maya's eyes once again.

"You haven't mentioned Purugama or Ajur," he said to his mentor. "Are they lost to us forever, or will they return to the glade by other means?"

Maya smiled at the thought of his two young cubs. "If my assumptions prove correct, as soon as we enter the portal they will instantly be transported to the glade of Champions. They will revert to their original selves and begin their lives as tiny cubs. If you find all of us quickly enough, you may get the chance to hold Purugama in your arms."

Conor almost laughed out loud at the thought of it – the enormous Champion of the Crossworlds, rocking in his arms like a helpless kitten. That he had to see.

"Alright, Maya," he said, "if you plan to brave the forbidden corridors, then I will do my best to find you. All of you. I ask only one thing, after we destroy Seefra's army, the Champions must accompany me in my search for Janine. I don't know how I know, but I have the feeling she's in great danger. She's under Seefra's control, and you know as well as I how vindictive he can be. If he sees the tide turning in our favor, there's no telling what he might do to her. I won't allow her to be destroyed because of my mistake. I'll help reassemble the Champions, but after we're done, I want you to help me save Janine."

Maya swatted the side of Conor's face with his tale. "As if any other course ever existed. We will find your companion, Conor. After all, she is the keeper of the keys, and a very brave young woman."

Conor examined Maya's furry countenance as it began to blur and fade into the background. As it had before, the view soon resembled an indistinct impression of something sitting in front a pristine, natural scene. Conor tried to say a few final words, but nothing came forth from his throat. He felt his body drifting backwards, away from the lake and away from Maya. The scene in front of him became nothing but a dull light as he continued to float away from his encounter with the Lord of the Champions. It felt as if a tiny cord had been placed around his waist. It pulled softly at his body, taking him back to where he began his bizarre journey. He felt rather than saw his body passing through the water wall in his recuperation chamber. He saw the coloring of the wall change from silver to the deep azure blue it previously maintained. As the small cord slipped away from his waist, he found himself sitting on the side of the soft sheet that served as the bed in his chamber. Looking to his right, he saw himself lying on the sheet. He could see the excellent work the creators had done so far. Compared to how he felt after leaving the cell of shadows, he seemed a good deal healthier. After gazing at his own face for many minutes, he finally floated down on the sheet, rejoining his corporeal body. He closed his eyes and fell into a deep sleep.

CHAPTER ELEVEN

Gribba stood at the head of Conor's chamber, slightly behind the Lady of the Light. They both watched as Conor's inert form twitched and jerked involuntarily. Lines of concern creased Gribba's bear-like face. The Lady masked her anxiety quite well, but the sparkle of her silver aura gave her away. She too felt concern for Conor. The fact that neither one of them knew why he was having spasms didn't help matters either. The water walls showed no evident signs of danger for their patient. Gribba's instruments could find no reason for them to be alarmed. However, both of them carried an instinctive concern about the latest developments in Conor's recovery.

Without any warning, Conor's body shuddered one last time and then lay motionless. His breathing fell into a deep, rhythmic pattern. Gribba checked the water walls with a flick of his fur-lined eyes. He noticed a minute change in their appearance. They reacted to the change in Conor's condition in a positive fashion. The Ezuvex relayed none of this information to the Lady; he preferred not to provide her with premature tidings. If his calculations proved correct, then Conor would be waking very soon. He would prefer to allow that occurrence to speak for itself. As he mulled these thoughts over, the Lady turned to leave the chamber. Gribba gently placed his huge paw against her shoulder.

"If I may, my Lady," said the Ezuvex softly, "I'd be most pleased if you'd stay just a little longer."

The Lady of the Light looked up at the guardian. She found nothing noticeable in his expression. Try as she might, she couldn't read anything in his thoughts either.

"Gribba," she answered, delicately. "What is it? Do you have unpleasant news? Is there something I should know about Conor's condition?"

Gribba said nothing. He merely peered into her eyes with a blank expression. Instead of telling her that his bodily functions had been fully repaired, he wanted her to be here when Conor opened his eyes. He could see the water walls winding down behind her, and he knew it was only a matter of minutes now. He focused his gaze back to the Lady of the Light, smiling broadly this time. He felt the Lady's body physically relax at the sight of his huge grin.

"My Lady, you may go to him now. Retrieve him from his deep sleep. He will answer to your voice easier than if another called out to him."

The Lady turned quickly, rushing to Conor's bedside. As she approached the sheet, she saw the water walls making their final adjustments, going dormant until they might be needed again. She gently stroked his left cheek with her smooth palm. She saw his eyelids begin to flutter and his body starting to move. It didn't twitch as before, though. This time his body evoked the look of someone waking from a long dream.

"Conor," she said softly. "Can you hear me?" She stroked his cheek as she called out to him. "Conor," she asked again, "do you recognize my voice?"

The young man's shoulders rocked back and forth, but still he did not wake. His lips formed into words, but nothing emerged from his vocal chords. Conor struggled to wake up, but it seemed as though he fought to rise from a deep place inside the soul of the Crossworlds.

"My Lady," urged Gribba, "he looms as close as he ever will. You must reach into his mind and convince him to come back to us. The creators are not the only ones battling for his survival. He fought for you, he respects you, and now it is your turn to fight for him. Find him and bring him back to us."

The Lady of the Light wasted no time. She revered Gribba's estimation of Conor's predicament. The Ezuvex stood alone in their intelligence among all the creatures of the Crossworlds. She closed her eyes, placing her palm directly over Conor's forehead.

With the slightest of incantations, she felt herself falling into Conor's mind. Once there, she stood still, taking in everything around her. Images flew in every direction. Everything a human mind could imagine existed in Conor's thought patterns. She wondered how anyone could maintain a sense of sanity with this much deliberation occurring at once.

She saw a perfectly still light glowing in the distance. She transported herself in that direction quickly and found her Champion sitting quietly inside of a ball of multicolored light. The perfect hues of the water walls had encased Conor in a globe of ruby, sapphire, and violet serenity. *This must be how they managed to cure Conor so quickly*, she thought. Any being would respond favorably to complete removal from an unhealthy environment. As she looked in on Conor, she witnessed a perfect example of that philosophy. He seemed completely at ease, without a care in the world.

He looked up to greet her, smiling broadly at the beautiful

goddess visiting him in his sanctuary. His expression soon changed when he heard her calling out to him, telling him he must wake up and rejoin the world around him. He fought against the suggestion, even turning away from her at one point. The goddess mentioned three words, however, and Conor turned back to face her again. He stood and stretched his arms, bursting the colorful bubble by expanding his essence. He took the outstretched hand of the goddess and followed her through the madness of his mind. After reaching her original insertion point, the Lady stopped and turned, facing Conor. She placed her hand on his forehead for a brief moment and seconds later felt the familiar sensations of cold and heat.

Conor opened his eyes and saw the Lady sitting on the side of his bed. She looked at him with a loving smile. "Welcome home, Champion," she said, brushing a lock of hair from his forehead. "We have eagerly awaited your return."

CHAPTER TWELVE

"Just lay back, Conor," soothed the Lady, *placing her lithe but strong* hand against his chest. "Gribba would like to perform a brief examination. Then I will help you stand, and we will go for a long walk together."

"Gribba?" asked Conor with a confused expression.

"Greetings, Champion," said the Ezuvex, introducing himself. "I have cared for you these last few days during your regeneration. I am honored to look after one of our most accomplished warriors."

Conor stared at Gribba for a long time. It seemed odd to hear such a distinguished voice coming from a creature such as this. The beast was huge, at least eight or nine feet tall. He must weigh close to six hundred pounds, and the weight didn't appear to be out of proportion. He looked like a bear for the most part, but his facial features seemed almost human. His expressions showed great intelligence, but Conor felt that this creature, if provoked, could revert to his instinctive nature in a flash. He blinked his eyes, filing that information away for future reference.

"Thanks for taking such great care of me, Gribba," said Conor with as much respect as he could summon.

"As I said," responded the Ezuvex while holding a peculiar

instrument over Conor's chest, "the honor is mine. I must defer to the structures you see stationed around this chamber, however. The water walls performed most of the restorative functions; I merely monitored their patterns and made minor adjustments when needed. If I may say so, the walls performed beautifully. Aside from a few minor limitations, your body will function normally again." Gribba shifted his stance a little, probing the young man's musculature with his large but gentle hands. "Tell me, Conor, how do you feel?"

Conor took a moment to prepare his answer. He focused first on his breathing, and then on individual parts of his body. He rolled his feet, flexed his legs, and brought his arms up over his head. He lifted his torso away from the sheet and turned it sharply from side to side. Then he lay back down on the sheet and glanced up at the guardian.

"I feel fine," he said to Gribba. "Never better, in fact. Please extend my thanks to the water walls."

The Ezuvex smiled broadly. "They will be pleased to hear of your well-being. I shall inform them of your progress during their next assignment." Gribba stepped over to the foot of Conor's bedding. From his great height, he looked down into Conor's eyes. After tucking his instrument back into a fold in his fur, he addressed his patient again. "I am pleased by your physical progress, Conor, but I have another question for you. How do you feel emotionally and spiritually? You've been through a terrible ordeal. You may feel responsible for what happened to the creators and the Champions, and to your companion. You may seek to take revenge on Seefra for imprisoning you and those you love. It is vitally important for you to give us an honest assessment of your emotional well-being."

Conor held Gribba's eyes as he spoke to him. As the Ezuvex delivered his question, Conor's eyes flicked to the Lady of the Light's face for a split second. Here he lay, in front of one of the creators of the Crossworlds and a creature whose powers Conor couldn't even fathom. If he told them anything other than the truth, they would see through it instantly. He sighed roughly and sank back into the sheet.

"I feel better than I felt when I lived in complete darkness for more time than I care to remember," he began. "No one can imagine what that type of existence is really like. To have one or two of your senses removed for an extended period changes a person forever. But now that I'm here I can leave the sensation behind me."

"Other feelings gnaw away at me every minute, though. I don't think it matters whether I'm awake or asleep. Every time I opened my eyes in that cell, the first feeling I sensed was always shame, and not just from telling Janine about my past associations with the Champions of the Crossworlds. I can't forgive myself for allowing Seefra to trick me so easily, because I *knew* something didn't feel right. I let the excitement of finding the keys carry me away, and along with my desire to return home, I allowed Seefra to trap us and take her from me. Every time I think about the torture she must be enduring I want to slap myself for being so foolish." Conor looked away from both Gribba and the Lady. He felt he couldn't face either of them while recalling his blunder.

"Please, Conor," soothed the Lady. "Continue."

Conor shaded his eyes, looking down at the floor to his left. He knew the Lady would cringe upon hearing his next remarks, and he didn't relish the thought of worrying her. As for Gribba, Conor somehow felt the Ezuvex might not mind hearing of his aggressive intent toward his former jailer. The giant bear-like creature had the look of a warrior, although he seemed many times removed from that part of his culture. As if oblivious to Conor's thoughts, Gribba stood stoically at the foot of the bed, waiting for him to speak.

"More than anything else, I'm fuming with rage right now. I've had enough of the Circle of Evil, the shadow warriors, and the struggle for the Crossworlds." He paused briefly to see if he could register any emotional tic from the Lady's expression. Seeing nothing but perfect composure, he continued. "I have given almost half my life to the cause of the creators, while others my age live as normal teenagers. I defeated powerful destroyers – first Gandron, then Fumemos, and finally Seefra, or so I thought. During the search for the five keys, the shadow warriors stalked us through the latter part of our journey. Even then, we overcame the strange creature in the forest and vanquished Loken during our search for the final key.

"How much more must we accomplish?" Conor continued, now sitting up on his bedding. "Will it ever end? Will evil continue eternally, or will we finally overcome the shadow warriors and cast their leaders into the forbidden corridors forever? Yes, I *am* angry. I'm angry that with everything we've done, there is still more ahead of us. I'm angry that I can't simply take Janine and go home. I'm angry because I don't know when all of this will end. If I knew of a spell that could show me a definite end to this struggle, maybe that might help me see things more clearly. There just doesn't seem to be any course of action that will bring these endless journeys to a close."

"Worst of all, I failed to destroy Seefra during our struggle in his castle. Now he leads the shadow warriors against us, and from what I've heard, his powers have grown beyond anyone's comprehension. If I'd known of his ability to survive, maybe I could have done something to..."

"To what, Conor?" interrupted the Lady of the Light. She appreciated his candor, but she would never allow him to punish himself for this. "You were only a boy, not even in your teen years. When Seefra first snatched you away from the glade, we gave you little chance for survival. You trapped the master of darkness in his own fortress, the very place where his magical powers originate." The Lady grasped Conor's wrist, holding it firmly. "How could you possibly know that he might survive the collapse of his castle? You fought bravely and nearly destroyed the most powerful servant the Circle of Evil has ever known. Believe me, you have nothing to regret about your confrontation with Seefra."

Conor uncomfortably accepted the Lady's praise, but none of it penetrated his deep sense of loss about Janine. He might forgive himself for everything up to this point, but he would never excuse himself for allowing Seefra to capture her. She had been under his care and he had failed her. He honestly didn't know whom he disliked more at this moment – Seefra for taking her captive or himself for letting it happen.

"Whatever else happens," he said. "Seefra is going to pay for what he's done to Janine. She didn't deserve any of this. It was my decision to tell her about the Champions and the creators. She didn't deserve to see her world ripped apart, or her sister frozen like a mannequin in her own school. She certainly didn't deserve to see all those gruesome sights during our journeys together."

"I'll do what I have to do here, but after that I want your help. I want you to call forth a corridor that will take me and whoever else will accompany me directly to Seefra. I will battle the shadow warriors with my own small forces, and then I will face Seefra myself. This time he will not survive. I promise you."

The Lady of the Light stood frozen in place. Without looking at Gribba, she communicated mentally with the Ezuvex. Both she and the giant guardian connected perfectly as they shared their reaction to Conor's last statement. Both of them smiled inwardly at Conor's bravery.

"Thank you for your honesty," said the Lady. "Gribba must attend other pressing duties, but I would be most pleased if you would honor me with a walk through the realm. Would you be so kind?"

"I am yours to command always, my Lady," responded Conor, "even in the midst of my rage."

The Lady held Conor's arm as he leaned forward and placed his feet carefully on the perfectly soft grass. Recalling his earlier entrance into the realm, he didn't feel the least bit chagrined about her assistance. He held the bedding with one hand as he tested the strength of his legs. After assuring himself that his muscles worked properly, he let go of the bed and took a few tentative steps. He grabbed the Lady's hand after he stumbled briefly, but once he regained his footing, he released it. His coordination quickly returned and he followed the Lady out into the realm. He stood at the top of the hill studying the breathtaking scenery all around him. He breathed deeply, inhaling the many aromas drifting through the realm. Then he stretched as far as he could, holding his pose for almost a minute. He looked over at the Lady and smiled.

The Lady of the Light watched his every move. She kept her silence until Conor looked ready to proceed. When he turned and grinned at her, she returned the expression with a dazzling smile of her own. "I am pleased to share your company again, Conor."

THE FORBIDDEN CORRIDORS

CHAPTER THIRTEEN

The big cats rested in different locations around the spot where Maya lay motionless. With Eha to his north, Ajur to his south, and Surmitang and Purugama covering his east and west flanks, the four Champions of the Crossworlds instinctively protected their leader. They knew Maya had departed from his physical body to try and confer with Conor. While exposed in such a fashion, the Lord of the Champions left himself extremely vulnerable. The four cats covered each potential avenue of attack out of centuries of habit. Nothing in the universe could have penetrated the barrier of security they provided. To an outsider, the scene might look quite innocent – five large cats peacefully sleeping the day away in the sun. If anyone threatened their perimeter, however, the observer would view another scene entirely. The four Champions would be up in a flash, ready to defend their Lord without a moment's concern for their own lives.

Eha lifted his head before any of the others. The golden eyes, framed by teardrop streaks of black fur running down his jowls, quickly scanned the immediate area. His small rounded ears twitched in a dozen different directions, taking in every sound for five hundred yards. He saw Maya's body move slightly, and then he watched as the fur around his leader's stomach began to steadily rise and fall. Without a sound, Eha stood and padded over to where Maya lay. Standing over the sleeping cat, his body dotted with dark spots from head to hindquarters, Eha swished his ringed tail back and forth above Maya's prone figure. He lowered his large head, sniffing Maya's body in several places, curiously assessing whether his Lord might truly be close to waking. After making his decision, the cheetah exhaled three quick chuffs.

Instantly the other three cats awoke, leaping into a fighting wedge around Maya. Surmitang and Ajur crouched menacingly on either side of their Lord, while Purugama stood tall in front of them, flapping his great wings in preparation for flight. All three of them kept their eyes moving, watching the surrounding environment for the slightest aberration. Their ears, pricked up to register any sound, never stopped moving while they monitored the area. After a minute or two, they turned their heads toward Eha and Maya. Sensing no danger, they finally lowered their guard. Seeing Eha in a relaxed pose next to their leader allowed them license to stand at ease. Each of them stared with guarded concern at Maya, who lay at their feet slumbering away.

"Has he stirred enough to speak?" asked Surmitang, always the boldest and first to inquire.

"Not yet," answered Eha. "A few sounds came from his lungs, but I would not classify them as speech."

"How long ago did he begin to show signs of reentering his body?" asked Ajur. The dark jaguar had advised Maya against traveling to speak to Conor in such a fashion. Too many inconsistencies existed on the astral plane. Creatures safely imprisoned in the corridors had been known to escape their confinement to travel spiritually in these dimensions. Whether they could do Maya harm was questionable, but Ajur did not care for the element of chance. In these dangerous times, he preferred absolute certainty. He looked at Maya longingly, almost willing his Lord to awaken.

Maya opened his eyes slowly, and found himself staring at two ebony forepaws. The muscular legs and feet stood strongly about two yards in front of his nose. He blinked a few times, focusing on the sight of Ajur's huge form. He stretched his limbs to their full length, holding the pose until his body embraced the joy of awakening from a long nap. He recoiled his limbs and sat up slowly, looking around at the other cats. He groomed his fur for a few moments before acknowledging his friends. Satisfied with his waking regimen, the Lord of the Crossworlds Champions looked at each of his protectors in turn, nodding his hooded forehead in appreciation.

"Are you well, Maya?" asked Purugama. "Do you feel any lingering effects from your journey?"

"Do you wish to rest here for a while?" added Eha. "We will stand guard for as long as you require."

"Thank you, my brothers," replied Maya. "My journey is complete. Although I could easily rest here for a few more hours, the time for relaxation is over. Everything has been prepared, and our task is at hand."

"You spoke to our brother, Conor?" asked Surmitang.

"Yes, and he understands the nature of my plan. He has agreed to search for each of us in the time before our association with the creators. He will escort the four of us back to the glade of Champions where we will join with Ajur and Purugama."

"With all respect," said the great tiger, "what if Conor fails in his mission to collect us?"

"He will not fail," answered Maya. "Even if he did, it would leave you for all time in the jungle of your birth, surrounded by your pride. Would you object to that possibility, Surmitang?"

"Not at all," replied the great tiger, "except for one sad fact. My pride was under siege when I left to join the Champions. Even though my siblings and I fought valiantly to turn back the invaders, they kept flooding our jungle with more and more hunters. Wave after wave of hungry men cut down my companions; there seemed to be no end to them. If I could do nothing but watch my family be slaughtered needlessly, then a life in service to the creators offers an acceptable alternative."

The five cats sat quietly, digesting Surmitang's comment. No one wished to speak and overshadow the importance of the tiger's feelings. The silence lingered for a few moments, finally begging a comment from someone in the gathering.

"Will Therion be joining us?" said Ajur. "Has Conor agreed to seek out the greatest Champion the Crossworlds has ever known?"

Maya turned to face the jaguar. "I convinced Conor of our need for a seventh warrior. He hesitated at first, remembering his last encounter with Therion. After assuring him that the great lion would not recognize him when he meets him on the veldt, he reluctantly agreed to include him in his travels."

"How I would love to be there when Conor first approaches Therion," laughed Surmitang. "He will look like an ant trying to convince an elephant not to step on him."

"Each of his journeys will be equally dangerous," said Maya. "Imagine a young man entering the forests where you and your kind roam, Surmitang. He will be fortunate to survive your sentries on his way to find you."

Saying nothing, Surmitang merely nodded his head once in agreement.

"Do not worry," continued Maya. "We have all seen the qualities Conor possesses. During our journey together to repair the corridors, he showed me a great deal of fortitude and conviction. While chance always exists within the vast reaches of the Crossworlds, I believe strongly that Conor will succeed. Besides, he has another source of motivation. Seefra currently holds the keeper of the keys prisoner. She is a close companion of Conor's back on their home planet. I believe if he could find a way, he would rush off to fight Seefra's armies alone if he felt he could free her. He feels responsible for his companion's imprisonment, and the thought of it burns in his soul every day. This will only feed his desire to reassemble the Champions of the Crossworlds."

Stretching one last time, Maya jumped completely out of the ring of protection, landing lightly on his feet beyond Ajur's reach. His tail twitched back and forth nervously. The other four Champions couldn't sense whether the motion signified eagerness or uncertainty, and Maya certainly wasn't about to give them any clues. Now that the decision had been made, the leader of the Champions wanted to be on his way. He looked back at the group of bold cats. He knew that while they offered to follow him on this latest adventure, they held cautious reservations about penetrating the forbidden corridors. Every one of them had heard troubling stories about entering the hazardous portals. Most that did were never heard from again. Some returned, permanently transformed by their experience. Others perished the instant they penetrated the barrier. Maya held tightly onto his own misgivings. He would lead them without reservation, giving them a strong beacon to follow. Nodding his head once, he turned toward their destination and trotted down the path.

The journey to the forbidden corridor lasted only twenty minutes. The five cats padded behind their leader silently, looking in all directions and listening intently, always prepared for any sight or sound that might threaten their Lord. Purugama traveled directly behind Maya, in order to fly him away from any danger the instant it appeared. Surmitang traveled in the middle of the pack, so his great fighting skills could be used quickly to guard their front or rear. Eha held the fourth position in their group. Not quite the last in the procession, his speed could be used to track down and attack enemies from both flanks. Ajur always traveled behind the rest. Anyone considering an attack from behind this group of traveling cats would think twice after seeing the muscular jaguar as their first objective.

They rounded a dusty, rock-strewn corner and stopped behind their leader. Maya's four brothers instinctively gathered around him again, protecting all four sides of their Lord's position. Maya sat down and stared at a great stone wall blocking the horizon in front of them. It seemed as though a huge flat boulder had emerged from the ground all by itself. Nothing else of any physical consequence accompanied the huge slab. How it stayed upright was anybody's guess, but for all they knew it might be the tip of an enormous granite mountain buried beneath centuries of dirt and dust. Alternatively, it could very well be the magic of the creators that placed the stone where it stood. After all, the immense boulder framed one of the earliest forbidden corridors. It held Maya's gaze as he sat calmly within the protective square of Champions. The big cat said nothing; he merely looked upon the immense passageway with a sense of awe.

The slab containing the corridor towered over the Champions at a height of over one hundred fifty feet. The rim of stone around the corridor teemed with life. Creatures of every description hung from the living rock surrounding the portal. These were the unfortunates who without knowledge of the inherent danger, came seeking transport. After hesitating a moment longer than the corridor deemed appropriate, they found themselves sucked into the stone by the organisms that inhabited it. Once attached to the rim of the portal, the magic of the corridor kept them alive for all time. They became immortal, nourished by the portal but always tormented by the organisms that lived among them. By the hundreds, they screamed at the Champions of the Crossworlds. They called out to them, encouraging the cats to run away as quickly as they could. *Nothing but an immortal existence of painful suffering awaited them here,* they cried. *Be gone and consider yourselves lucky,* they repeated over and over again. Maya and the Champions did their best to ignore the pleas.

The membrane of the forbidden corridor measured roughly eighty feet in diameter. Instead of the pure, consistent energy of a healthy portal, this membrane swirled with a yellowish, milky residue. Sparks flashed from different areas of the corridor, sending clouds of distorted elements shooting throughout the surface of the membrane. Reddish flames burst forth at irregular intervals, surging through small openings in the face of the passageway. *It looked,* thought Surmitang, *even more sinister than the corridor Therion tossed Conor into on his way to the Forest of Forever.* Even for a three thousand pound Sumatran tiger, jumping into this corridor seemed like a terrifying proposition.

Maya turned and looked at his brothers. "We must hurry," he said. "If we linger too long, we will end up like those on the perimeter of the stone. Before we enter the membrane, however, I wish to compliment all of you on your bravery during our years of service to the Crossworlds. If we should never find each other again, I want all of you to know that I consider you my family. I couldn't love a pride of my own kittens any more than I do all of you. May your journeys be quick and painless. I hope to see all of you again soon."

Before any of the Champions could answer him, Maya jumped straight into the forbidden corridor. The membrane flashed and a pillar of flame poured forth from the point where Maya pierced the portal. In an instant, he disappeared, leaving the other four cats staring mutely at the flaming membrane.

"I do not wish to enter this hideous corridor," said Purugama. "Maya has provided the example, however, and I will not turn away from it." With that, the giant cougar flapped his great wings, lifting himself up off the ground. After reaching a height of sixty feet, he flew straight into the membrane. Another eruption occurred when Purugama entered the portal. This time a shower of sparks exploded from his point of entry. The three remaining cats tried their best to shelter themselves from the rain of fire cascading down upon them.

Eha looked utterly terrified. Visibly shaking out of fear or excitement, the huge cheetah began running around the desert in wider and wider circles. When he reached his top speed, he turned toward the portal. At one hundred fifty miles an hour, the speeding cat jumped into the corridor. He entered and disappeared so quickly, the portal had no time to register an interruption in the membrane. No fire appeared, nor did any sparks flash from the surface of the corridor. The cheetah simply vanished in the blink of an eye.

Ajur and Surmitang stood in front of the forbidden corridor staring at each other. Neither one wanted to be the last cat waiting to enter the portal, for fear they might be sucked into the stone rim. Communicating this to each other without a word, both of the huge cats prepared to enter the portal. As they jumped into the sparkling, flaming membrane, Ajur heard one final statement rumble from Surmitang's lips.

"Mind of the creators," said the massive tiger. "I saved his life so we could jump into this madness?"

CHAPTER FOURTEEN

Conor walked slowly beside the Lady, adjusting his stride to match her regal pace. After leaving the recuperation chamber, she led him down a perfectly groomed pathway toward an open park in the middle of the realm. As they strolled along speaking to each other, dozens of creators and their servants came out to meet the young Champion. Some stood proudly in front of Conor, performing a gesture of greeting common to the realm. Others fell to their knees before him, asking to be touched lightly on their foreheads. Conor obliged all of them, but frequently looked to the Lady of the Light for some sort of explanation. Offering nothing, she merely smiled. The supplicants rose, thanking Conor respectfully before taking their leave. The young man absorbed as much of the experience as he could as he walked through the beautiful commons. Although he had many questions for the Lady, he would delay his inquiries until they found themselves alone again.

After leaving the park, the Lady escorted Conor to the base of an immense water wall. The dimensions of the wall were far greater than those in Conor's chamber. Conor had to stretch his neck as far back as he could to see the top. The sides spread so far left and right he could barely see the horizon behind it. It possessed another distinct difference as well. Instead of presenting a solid color similar to the walls in his chamber, this wall exhibited a vast array of tints and hues. Every color imaginable swirled within the trickling surface of the wall. Within a few moments, Conor felt transfixed by the thousands of hues gently blinking across his plane of vision.

The Lady of the Light raised her hand in front of her, drawing up an ornate marble bench from the ground. She gestured to Conor, who deferred, waiting for the Lady to sit and make herself comfortable. Afterward, the young man sat and placed his knees against his chest. He wrapped his arms around his legs and rocked slightly back and forth. He looked at the water wall for a few more moments, and then shifted his gaze to the Lady's eyes. She seemed content to sit and look into his soul, so Conor began their conversation.

"Tell me about this water wall," he said. "Why have you brought me here, out of all the places we might have spoken?"

"I felt this might be an appropriate place for us to reacquaint ourselves," answered the Lady. "For you see, Conor, this water wall cares for every form of life that exists in the realm. Not only does it look after the creators, it monitors every natural element you see around us. The entire ecosystem of our home rests within the hands of this capable wall. In fact, this ancient tablet maintains all life on every planet within the Crossworlds system, including your home planet of earth."

Conor didn't falter for a second. Nothing surprised him anymore. The more he learned about the Crossworlds, the less he felt shocked by its secrets. "How old is this water wall?" he asked the Lady.

"No one knows," she responded calmly. "It has always been here. I'm sure it stood in this location long before we came into being. We built the realm around its base, and as we began to occupy our new home, the wall teemed intensely with vibrant colors. We believe it lacked a symbiotic entity for many eons, causing it to lay dormant for millennia. When we arrived it returned to its natural course, caring once again for a civilization of beings. As the Crossworlds grew and more planets fell under our protection, the water wall added more and more colors to its surface. It appeared to regenerate itself, becoming stronger as the ecosystems of the worlds thrived. I believe it will always remain here, long after the Crossworlds and the creators return to their origin."

"Does it care for all beings?" asked Conor. "Does it also sustain the Circle of Evil?"

"We think so," said the Lady. "We have no reason to believe otherwise. The wall nourishes all life, and does not discriminate between good and evil. Perhaps it leaves that task for those who inhabit the worlds it watches over."

Conor looked up at the immense wall of gently trickling water. He could never count all the colors appearing in front of his eyes. It seemed perfectly symmetric, almost like an engine, but he knew better. The presence of so many biologics precluded a mechanical conclusion. This gigantic wall was alive; he could feel the emanation of life seeping down toward him. *Unbelievable*, he thought to himself, *yet another stunning facet of the Crossworlds.*

"So," he said, turning his gaze back to the Lady of the Light. "We are here, and I have been cured by your servant, Gribba. I am very pleased to be in your company once again, my Lady. I am also somewhat eager to get started on my journey. Janine haunts my every breath, and while she remains a prisoner of the master of darkness, I cannot rest here for one second longer than necessary."

"Which confirms our primary fear, Conor," stated the Lady. "You cannot defeat Seefra and his warriors with rash statements or tactical blunders. You must perform at the maximum of your physical, mental, and spiritual capabilities. Unless you vow to me right now, here in front of the source of all life, that you will not hastily throw yourself into the fire of Seefra's rage, I must refuse to assist you in your quest to reassemble the Champions."

Conor stared into the Lady's eyes without any emotion whatsoever. The Lady looked into Conor's soul with the steady gaze of someone who knows she has chosen the proper course. She would never back down; he knew it in his heart. She cared for him as she did all the Champions, but long ago she had dedicated her existence to the Crossworlds. She devoted herself entirely to the thousands of worlds and millions of corridors that made up the system. She would not place anyone or anything above that pledge, even herself.

"How long must I wait here?" asked Conor as he rocked gently on the surface of the bench.

"Not long," answered the Lady. "Please, Conor, let us converse for a while. I have just found you again after well over a year of waiting. You are one of my Champions, and I care deeply about your happiness. Can we not spend a few moments talking as friends?"

Conor melted at the softness of her plea. "Yes, of course, my Lady. Please forgive me, I'm worried about Janine."

"There is nothing to forgive, Conor. Do you not realize how special you are to me? Our paths first crossed over six years ago. With the passage of time, I have watched you grow from a small boy into a strong, handsome man. I have observed your transformation during all of your successful journeys in the Crossworlds. You have displayed abilities far beyond your years, my Champion." The Lady grinned at Conor during a small respite before continuing. "Let me ask you something, why do you believe you stayed alive for so long in the cell of shadows?"

"Because the cell continuously regenerated me," said Conor. "That's the way I understand it, anyway."

"That is true," continued the Lady. "But let me put the question to you differently. Why didn't Seefra destroy you while he held you captive? He couldn't have had a better opportunity. After all, you were helpless, a prisoner."

He thought about her question for a moment. It didn't make any sense for Seefra to keep him alive, especially since Conor had destroyed many of the dark master's most formidable warriors. It had to be so he could use him as a pawn to torment Janine, and he relayed this to the Lady.

"No, Conor," she replied, "although I could see Seefra acting in such an underhanded way if it served his purpose. He didn't destroy you because he could not successfully do so. He tried many times after first encasing you in the cell of shadows. Strangely enough, the same tiles that held you prisoner prevented Seefra from entering the cell to confront you. As you remember, each time you attempted to break through the wall of shadows, the tiles converged on you, making passage impossible. Seefra experienced the identical frustration every time he tried to gain entry to the cell. He called out dozens of incantations trying to gain access. None of them worked, however, so he dismissed you in favor of dedicating his energies to the five keys of the creators."

"It was Loken who originally designed and constructed the cell of shadows, with the help of the keepers, of course. Perhaps the bitterness over the loss of his position to the master of darkness prompted him to add one last element of design to the configuration. That is one possible explanation, although others have been offered in the council chamber."

"Such as?" asked Conor, clearly intrigued.

The Lady of the Light responded quickly. "That you are of royal blood, or you might be a descendant of nobility, or perhaps you claim a host of regal qualities from a long history of past lives. Perhaps you are the incarnation of one of the creator's ancient warriors, and this identification prevented Seefra from harming you in any way. You have become quite a topic here in the realm, young man. Those who greeted you in the commons paid homage to someone they believe to be quite extraordinary."

Conor stopped rocking and leaned forward, balancing himself on his feet. She spoke madness, he felt certain of it. Conor Jameson, the long lost progeny of the creators? Maybe he hadn't heard the last of her surprises after all. "When you first found me, my Lady, I was but a small boy. I am not much more than that today, only a teenager, still someone quite young in my world. I am not who you think I am, so please inform those who live here of my simple beginnings. I do not wish for anyone to be misled."

"Tell me something, Conor," said the Lady. "How is it that you wielded my magic so easily during your journeys to collect the five keys? How do you think you assumed the powers of the other Champions without any struggle at all? Do you honestly believe that a being from any planet in the Crossworlds system might have done the same?"

Conor thought for a moment. "If you delivered your magic to them as you did to me, then yes, I believe someone else could imitate my success."

The Lady of the Light placed her hand gently atop Conor's wrist. She leaned forward, looking up into his eyes. "Do you really believe that, Conor?"

The young man felt the power of the Lady's magic pouring from her hand into his body. The tingling fire and ice of the silvery surge flowed into his arm and rushed through his entire body. It gave Conor a sensation of strength, the likes of which he had never known. He looked down at the Lady's hand, which covered his with a sparkling silver luminescence. It looked similar to the emanation he saw coming from the final key of the creators after he and Janine vanquished Loken. Instinctively, he attempted to jerk his hand back. The Lady held it fast, however, speaking to him again.

"Conor Jameson, Champion of the Crossworlds, do you not feel the possibility that you might be more than an everyday teenager from the world called earth? Can you sit here staring into my eyes and deny the reality that you might indeed be more than you claim to be? Look down at your wrist again, young man. Does not the radiance of your skin suggest to you something more than a common background? Do you realize what could happen if one of the creators shared their power in this fashion with any other earthling?"

Conor watched the silvery glow inch its way up his arm. Although frightening to witness, the feel of it gave him an indescribable euphoria. Not only could he withstand the Lady's infusion of power, he seemed to thrive on it. With this much energy flowing through his body he felt as though he could overcome Seefra with a thought.

The Lady released his wrist. Almost immediately, the silvery radiance dulled and disappeared. Showing no ill effects from the exchange, the Lady folded her hands together on her lap. She smiled at Conor the way a mother smiles at a child who has been caught telling a lie.

"I suppose my judgment may have been rushed," said Conor, rubbing his wrist. "Perhaps you and the others are correct." Conor looked away from the Lady for the first time since they had sat before the immense water wall. He tried to wrap his mind around the Lady's comments but they were too overwhelming. He couldn't dismiss what he had always believed – that he lived a normal life on earth as a simple teenager. He decided not to wrestle with the idea right now; his voyages to reassemble the Champions would provide ample time for that. "I'd rather not consider that possibility right now. Let me focus my energies on finding the Champions. Maya recently came to me in a dream. He told me of his plan to lead the others into the forbidden corridors. Has he mentioned this to you or to any of the creators?"

"I am afraid not," answered the Lady, "although I'd suspect nothing less of him. Maya always displayed immense bravery and a keen sense of daring. We named him Lord of the Champions for that very reason. Please, tell me more of this strategy."

Conor turned slightly to face the Lady more directly. "He hopes to send each of the Champions back to their former lives. They will exist in their original form as they did before the creators initially contacted them. He asked me to use a specific corridor to seek out each of the cats. After contacting them, I'm to bring them through a portal of your construction, my Lady, and escort them back to the glade of Champions. Once I assemble all of them, only then can I travel through one final corridor to retrieve Maya. He will be living on earth with his former mistress, so he shouldn't be too difficult to locate."

"Tell me, Conor," questioned the Lady. "When you venture off to find the Champions, will they recognize you as friend and brother?"

"No," replied the young man. "Maya said something about their escape being connected to some kind of time travel, thus the need for the forbidden corridors. He said that once they assume their former lives, they will not remember anything about their service to the creators. They wouldn't recognize me, you, or even each other."

The Lady smiled again, this time with amusement and a light sense of shock. "Conor, if that is the case, you may find defeating Seefra to be a simple task after tackling the likes of Surmitang and Therion in their home territories."

Conor blinked at the mention of the giant lion. "How did you know that Maya planned to bring Therion back into the fold?"

"We always knew Therion would return," said the Lady. "His abilities are too valuable to be locked away for eternity. And if what you say is true, he will not remember anything about your interaction during your prior journeys. There is no chance of any danger arising from his former plans, because his life course will not yet have reached that moment in time."

The Lady of the Light rose and paced back and forth in front of the huge water wall. As she glided to and fro in front of the massive, sparkling surface, a brilliant, silvery hue emanated from the dripping liquid. The blinding radiance followed the Lady wherever she stepped, as if trying to embrace her as she paced slowly next to the wall. "I will gladly construct the corridors you will need to find and return the Champions to the glade. We will monitor your progress from the realm and call the corridors forth when you are ready. You must be quick, Conor, and never call for a portal unless you plan to use it immediately. It would be extremely dangerous to allow a passageway to remain in one place for too long. As you undoubtedly have heard, Seefra's powers have grown tremendously. We've no doubt that his shadow warriors could detect the energy of a corridor very soon after its activation. When you request transportation, you and the cat must be ready to move quickly."

The Lady came to a stop directly in front of Conor. She took his hands into her own, this time merely to hold them. No blast of unspeakable power passed between the creator and her Champion. She simply massaged the palms of his hands as she looked into his eyes. "Is there anything else I can tell you, or any other way I might assist you with your upcoming journeys?"

"Yes, there is," replied Conor, his hands hanging loosely in the Lady's strong grip. "What can you tell me about the Lady of the Shadows?"

The Lady of the Light wilted visibly. The brilliant silver reflection on the water wall behind her paled significantly. The Lady's shoulders crumpled, and suddenly the strength of the clasped hands emanated from Conor and not from her. She fell onto the bench in front of her, almost missing it completely. Conor grabbed her around the waist, helping her reseat herself next to him. He swept the hair from her eyes, holding her head in his hands. As she regained her breath, Conor gently released her, allowing her to resurrect herself. The color returned to her skin, and she reasserted her regal composure. She cleared her throat and looked up at Conor again.

"Where did you hear that name?" she asked with an obvious sense of alarm.

"From her own lips," answered Conor, watching the Lady's eyes go wide with shock. Apparently this development had not been expected by any of the creators, even the Council of Seven. "It was she who cast me into the cell of shadows. Seefra captured me, and after immobilizing me, he threw me into some strange type of void. I fell through nothing but dense air for so long I stopped trying to count the hours. Then suddenly I hit ground and began rolling down a long, rock-strewn hill. At the bottom I saw something that brought tears to my eyes. My old bed from my parents' home sat on the edge of the same cliff I landed on four years prior to that moment. I had returned to the exact spot where this adventure began. The shock of the experience rocked me to my bones. Seefra had taken Janine prisoner, the Champions existed in a cage of fire in a place I might never locate, and for all I knew, all of the creators had been destroyed. I knelt in front of my bed with my hands over my head crying like a baby, and that's when I heard her voice."

"What did she say?" asked the Lady of the Light, her mouth hanging open.

"She taunted me for crying the way I did, saying that a Champion of the Crossworlds would not carry on so. Then she asked if I recognized her, and after that she introduced herself as the Lady of the Shadows. Except for her clothing, she looked exactly like you."

Conor waited for his creator to collect herself before asking her directly. "My Lady, who is she, and is she really your twin? I feel I have a right to know, especially if I'm to encounter her again."

The Lady of the Light pondered this valuable bit of information. Conor's latest journey held enough challenges already. Throw in her twin sister, someone she hadn't seen since the last days of the equinox war, and things could get very complicated. Perhaps the vision appeared in front of Conor because of a spell cast by Seefra. It was entirely possible that the dark master wanted to confuse the forces arrayed against him as much as he could, thus giving him an edge in the approaching battle. As much as she wished to believe that, however, she knew she couldn't take that kind of chance with her sister. She had to inform the Council of Seven immediately, and she had to tell Conor the truth. He had certainly earned that much from all of them.

"The Lady of the Shadows *is* my twin sister, Conor," she said with as much strength as she could. "Raised by a warrior mother and a father who served on the Council of Seven, we lived on a world as distant as earth. Had our father not agreed to serve on the council, we may never have fractured the way we ultimately did. How my mother and father ever joined in the first place is beyond my ability to understand.

"Our parents saw to our early academic instruction. My father, being a diplomat and statesman, developed most of our educational criteria. As the years wore on, however, my sister tired of academics. She wanted to accompany our mother on her voyages of conquest. Our mother fought alongside the protection forces and then ultimately joined them when they attacked the realm of the creators.

As the years went on, my sister expressed a stronger desire to leave her studies behind and join our mother. Our father strictly forbade this, but our mother subtly encouraged her rebellion. You see, Conor, warrior civilizations value the development of the body more so than the power of the mind."

"In the end, our mother convinced our father to allow my sister to complete her studies while traveling with her. 'She could stand to learn a thing or two about protecting herself,' she would say to our father. He acquiesced, and this only fueled his desire to pour as much knowledge into my brain as he could. I certainly didn't object to his teachings. At that age I had no desire to visit distant worlds to fight for the preeminence of the Crossworlds.

"At the time of our ascendance, a right of passage that all off-spring of the creators experience, my sister and I had attained the rank of guardian. This is an important and vital position with the Crossworlds structure. Gribba serves the creators as a very formidable guardian. The position is the final stage before one receives the test for the bloodfire of the creators. The trial is absolute, one either possesses the true line and the power of the creators, or one doesn't."

"Your sister failed the test?" interjected Conor.

"Yes," replied the Lady. "And since that day I've spoken to her only twice. The first conversation occurred immediately following the test, the second after we defeated her in the equinox war."

"The equinox war?" asked Conor.

"Our ascension had been scheduled to occur on the threshold of the two thousandth equinox, a very important date in the epoch of the creators. Since her disappointment fell on that day, she chose to attack the realm of the creators exactly one year later. When the sun eclipsed the horizon and the equinox attained balance, her army descended on the realm. We marshaled our forces immediately, throwing her back into the shadows of the departing equinox. As we gathered up the remainder of her followers, she cursed us for fools and vowed one day to return with an indestructible army. She proclaimed herself the Lady of the Shadows, a false title she has retained ever since. Somehow she convinced the Circle of Evil of her validity. They took her in, giving her a position of great importance within their ranks. I imagine the appointment came about because of our mother's lineage."

"What happened to your parents?" asked Conor.

"Our father lived out the remainder of his years in relative comfort. He stepped down from the council not long after the equinox war. He loved both of us deeply, and he couldn't stand the thought of losing one of his daughters because of an ancient ritual."

"And your mother?"

The Lady of the Light closed her eyes slowly. The pain poured freely from her eyelids. She couldn't hide it no matter how hard she tried. "Our mother perished in the battle between our forces and my sister's. Even though they knew of her marriage to our father, the creators showed her no mercy at all. Her armies fell away like paper in a windstorm under the barrage of magical assaults called forth by our leaders. I saw our mother swept away into one of the forbidden corridors. I've never heard anything about her since that day. The memory of that day nearly destroyed our father. I believe to this day it is the reason he resigned his seat on the council."

"I'm sorry about your mother," said Conor. "I didn't mean to bring up a painful memory, but she's obviously loose again, your sister I mean. Will she cause me any grief or get in the way of my journeys?"

"She is capable of almost anything, I'm afraid," replied the Lady. "One of my greatest fears after she left to join the Circle of Evil was that she might learn the dark art of shadow magic. Apparently she has, and it allowed her to travel freely through the corridors again. She found you with Seefra's help, no doubt. And by confronting you before sentencing you to the cell of shadows, she used you to send me a message. She means to confront the creators again, I'm sure of it. She'll bide her time until she knows we are at our weakest, and then she will strike. This time, she will have with her the formidable army she spoke of on that terrible day. The shadow warriors represent one hundred times the force she brought with her during the equinox war."

"Maybe I should stay here, in the realm," said Conor. "You might need everyone you can find in case she attacks."

"No, Conor," responded the Lady of the Light, "your journey is more important than ever now. We need the Champions of the

Crossworlds returned to us as quickly as possible. More than ever, we need the five keys of the creators. If my sister joins with Seefra after he counteracts my spell on the keys, then the Crossworlds will be doomed. The realm will be shattered into a million meaningless spheres. The creators will never be able to withstand that much magical power."

The Lady stood, grabbing Conor's hand as she raced past him. Dragging him behind her, she ran as fast as she could toward the outskirts of the realm. Once there, she summoned a corridor and watched as it formed up in front of her and Conor. She began chanting in a bizarre language, and as she did so the corridor broke into a high pitched whine. The color remained static, a brilliant silver hue that gave the membrane a peculiar opaque quality. She finished her spell and turned to Conor.

"This portal will transfer you directly to the oldest of the forbidden corridors. We have no time to waste depositing you in one location so you can find another transport. Our time has just been cleaved in two, Conor. I apologize for asking this of you, but you are the only one who can help us now."

She embraced Conor, holding him tightly. The young man felt a tremendous surge of strength entering his body as the Lady transferred her powers to him again. When she released him, she kissed his forehead and smiled at him.

"Go with the creators, Conor," she said proudly. "Bring the Champions back to the glade. Use your love for Janine to do whatever you have to in order to reassemble the great cats. We need every one of them if we hope to defeat the shadow warriors."

Conor bowed to the Lady of the Light and turned toward the corridor. It sparked and hummed unlike any other portal he encountered during all of his journeys through the Crossworlds. His hair began flying in all directions as he stepped closer to the membrane. His clothing, once hanging idly on his teenage body, now clung to his back as it the corridor's energy pulled it forward. It seemed to be drawing him into the membrane, almost pulling him off his feet and into the portal. Conor felt a stab or two of biting fear upon feeling the strength of the passageway. In all other cases, he had initiated contact with the membrane. Now the twisted sorcery of the forbidden corridor seemed to call him forth with a vengeance. He looked back at the Lady of the Light, hoping to find a bit of comfort in those beautiful, serene eyes. She smiled and nodded her head, but didn't utter one word of encouragement. Still looking back at her, Conor felt one of his arms pull away from his body. The strength of the corridor increased greatly each time he inched closer to it. Now it pulled his entire body toward the membrane.

The droning whine seemed to increase in volume and pitch with every step closer. The noise became deafening when he came within five feet of the portal. Conor couldn't be sure if his imagination was playing tricks on him, but it appeared that the membrane changed shape before his eyes. Usually, the face of the corridor remained absolutely flat, like a mirror or a perfectly calm lake at sunrise. The membrane of this portal started to bubble lightly, and then small tendrils began emerging from the unstable mass. They reached out to Conor, attaching themselves to his clothing and skin. The touch of the strange fingers felt icy cold, much like the beginning of a journey through any corridor. The tendrils unnerved Conor, and he jerked his head around to find the Lady. She stood in the same location, hands folded together. Her aura seemed especially brilliant, as if she were focusing her complete being on Conor's journey. She smiled again at the young man, urging him forward. Her eyes told him that she would not allow him to be harmed during the transference.

Conor smiled at her nervously. He turned back to the corridor and swallowed a large lump in his throat. In one motion, he released his hold on the ground and allowed the membrane to pull him into the portal. As he flew toward the face, two small tendrils of magical energy fell lightly upon his eyelids. Before the membrane dragged him into the forbidden corridor, his eyes were gently pulled closed.

CHAPTER FIFTEEN

Conor felt the corridor encasing his entire body. It seemed strangely familiar, almost exactly the same feeling he had when he and Janine entered the last portal. He became paranoid and tried desperately to separate himself from the swirling blanket that covered him from head to toe. He prepared himself for the first punishing blast of electric shock he knew must be coming his way. When nothing of the sort occurred, he relaxed somewhat, allowing the membrane to perform its task. It wrapped itself lovingly around his body, not at all like the sloppy, buttery cocoon that took charge of him before he was taken prisoner. The velvety membrane even diminished the sensations of frigid cold and intense heat normally associated with corridor travel. Conor felt especially pleased about that because he sensed the cold and heat beating against him, trying desperately to penetrate the membrane. Normally he received two quick blasts before arriving at his destination. In this corridor, the sensations repeated themselves over and over again.

Conor felt the tiny tendrils fall away from his face. Before even considering whether it might be a good idea, he opened his eyes, looking straight ahead. What he saw before him caused his heart to jump into his throat. In a scene eerily similar to his own captivity, Conor looked upon his girlfriend alone and isolated in the cell of crystals. She seemed frightened but also resigned to her dilemma. At first Conor didn't even comprehend her imprisonment. The cell of crystals appeared so translucent that he thought he merely stared at her sitting on some outcropping in a deep chasm. The first time he watched her move he realized she was encased in some type of rectangular box, just as he had been. This cell, however, looked even more torturous than the cell of shadows. He focused on Janine as she moved about periodically, trying to avoid the shifting pattern of the floor crystals. Conor felt the weight of what he saw crush his soul. Even though Seefra had taken her prisoner, his own carelessness had placed her inside the bizarre chamber of cells. She had lived in that cell for close to two years, and she looked extremely frail. Conor could barely look at the changes in Janine's physique. As he stared at her, he wondered what might have happened to her spirit after all this time.

Suddenly the cell of crystals rocked back and forth like a gondola on a loose cable. Without clinging to anything at all, it traveled toward one edge of the chasm. Janine seemed to calm down as the cell moved; she lay down on the floor without a care for the placement of the tiles. As it approached a large cave cut into the rocky wall, two bizarre looking creatures appeared at the entrance. As they entered the cell, Janine let her body relax totally. They struggled to lift her lifeless form, as she knew they would. At one point, one of the creatures touched the back of her neck with a strange looking baton that seemed to grow out of its forearm. Janine jerked once and then lay flat and lifeless, causing Conor to shudder against the corridor membrane. He stood there, helpless, screaming Janine's name, but no one heard him. The creature pressed the baton against her neck again, this time holding the energy staff tightly against her skin. Her body convulsed a few times, and then she stood using her own power. She spit in the face of one of her escorts, not caring anymore about the consequences. The creature wiped his face and motioned for her to walk forward into the cave.

Conor watched all of this occur in utter horror. In impotent frustration, he wailed at the creatures hurting his girlfriend. Bellowing at the top of his lungs, he promised to repay them with suffering a thousand times more horrible after he finally caught up to them. In the midst of his verbal rampage, he noticed the cargo jacket hanging loosely over Janine's shoulders. Although ripped and tattered at the cuffs and collar, the main pocket in the front seemed intact. It looked as though it still contained the five keys of the creators. As Janine disappeared into the cave with her two escorts, Conor called out to her.

"Hang on, Janine!" he yelled. "Just hang on a little while longer! I'm coming to get you, and I'm bringing the Champions with me!"

EHA

CHAPTER SIXTEEN

The cocoon carrying Conor through the forbidden corridor unraveled without any warning at all. Conor felt his body rolling out of the membrane onto a grassy plain. After examining himself briefly, he stood and turned to look at the corridor that had delivered him there. The portal had disappeared entirely, departing without a single trace. Not one blade of grass or even a speck of dust had been displaced when Conor arrived. He shook his head and turned to look at his surroundings. The grassy area on which he stood was one of many such natural islands spread about in a vast desert. The grass grew very tall in these minor oases. Conor could see that if he knelt down it would provide ample cover in case of danger. The desert looked like a graveyard in front of him, nothing moved and no animals called out across the expanse.

Conor looked up at the sky. He had never seen so many beautiful, bright stars in his life. They seemed to cover every speck of the horizon. Although night still blanketed the area, Conor could see that morning would come soon. He knew he had to find a better place to conceal himself by the time the sun baked this barren desert, something better than these patches of tall grass anyway. He peered out into the endless sands, trying to see any sort of movement at all.

"Mind of the creators," he whispered. "Eha, where are you?"

He moved off toward a hilly area to his left, running at a slow jog through the soft grass. He held his arms out to his sides and let the thin reeds flick against his fingers as he ran. After a few hundred yards he exited the grassy area and instantly noticed the change in the texture of the ground. Inside the grassy islands, the soil felt soft and pliable. Out here in the sparse desert it became hard as stone.

Conor filed that information away for future reference. One never knew when a small fact like that would come in handy. He walked and ran for just under four miles, finally coming to the edge of an outcropping in the desert floor. A series of immense, flat boulders rose from the sand in front of him, piled on top of each other like a stack of stone pancakes. Conor found them easy to climb; he jumped and ran up the first group without any problem. He stopped for a moment to check the area for any overhangs he might use when the sun came up. He needed somewhere to camouflage himself, and soon. The stars, once so dominant in the desert sky, were fading fast as dawn approached.

Suddenly from far out in the desert, a series of wicked sounding cries echoed across the sand. Conor looked out in the direction of the sound but saw nothing. He relaxed his eyes, not focusing on any one feature of the landscape. Even with this technique he couldn't make out any movement at all. The succession of bizarre shrieks sounded again, this time much closer. *Hyenas*, thought Conor, *but not any kind of hyena he wanted to encounter without weapons or shelter.*

The wind began whistling across the plains as Conor stared

out into the coming dawn. He heard other animals calling out to the morning – predators signaling to the herds that another day of the chase would be upon them soon. The boisterous group of yelping creatures let out another round of terrifying cries, and Conor realized that the next time he heard them they might be right on top of him. He went to his knees and uttered a short incantation. After finishing his spell, he raised his hands to his forehead, cupping his eyes.

The spell rendered his eyesight into a sort of infrared vision scope. He scanned the desert once more, this time seeing everything that moved. He saw tiny swirls of sand kicked up by the wind, small rodents and insects leaving their warm nests, and a group of large four-footed animals heading his way across the steppe. They stopped suddenly, raising their heads and releasing another volley of horrible shrieks toward the sky. It almost seemed as though they wailed like this to intimidate any creature that might have the slightest intention of confronting them. They looked something like hyenas, but these animals stood taller and showed a more muscular physique than their earthly counterparts. Conor couldn't identify them from any of his readings. If Eha truly existed here, then this planet must be some sort of conglomeration of species from different worlds.

The first of the hideous creatures hopped up on the wide flat rocks. Conor watched but didn't move a muscle. He knew if the creatures spotted him he would have to act fast. At best they probably had caught his scent as soon as he arrived, and tracking it like bloodhounds, they would follow it until they found him. Conor looked around frantically, trying to find any cover at all. As he turned his shoulders to look back, the lead creature suddenly grunted and sprinted up the boulders. The remainder of the group reacted to his call immediately. Every one of them repeated his hearty grunt over and over as they scampered up the stone-covered shelf.

Conor took one good look at the lead creature and took off like a shot. The beast's face seemed be nothing but a series of harsh bruises and cuts. Blood and pus sprayed in every direction each time it took a step or jumped from one rock to another. The grotesque mouth looked fixed, like it didn't have a jaw that swiveled up and down. Huge, jagged teeth jutted out in every direction, horribly stained and filled with pieces of hanging flesh from its most recent kill. One large blood-stained eye peered intensely at Conor. No matter how the rest of the head moved, that one eye stayed locked on him.

By then, the rest of the creatures had caught up to their leader. They began fanning out in the true style of pack hunters. The largest creature, the one trailing Conor, kept persistently driving him forward. Another group closed in from either side to cut off any possible escape. Finally, the fastest members of the group circled around in front of Conor, trapping him inside the net. Once they closed the circle, nothing that couldn't defeat the group would ever escape.

Conor saw the pack of creatures using their numbers to press their advantage. He had jogged probably three miles to keep ahead of them, but now he understood their plans. He would have to defend himself within another mile of travel, he felt certain of that. Keeping well ahead of the lead creature, he saw the others keeping pace with his movements. Even though he felt like prey, he felt a keen sense of admiration for these wild beasts. Instinct may be their only drive, but any soldier would have been proud of their precision. The animals on either side never moved closer than they had to; they merely formed an impenetrable wall that no one could breach.

Cupping his eyes again, Conor used his enhanced vision to observe the last set of creatures turning around far out in front of him. They began jogging back toward him at a measured pace. Conor searched his mind for an appropriate spell to cast, either on the creatures or on himself. He didn't really wish to harm the pack. They were only acting as they always did on the hunt for their first meal of the day. He turned in every direction, watching them head toward him. As a group, they closed in on him at a perfectly measured pace. He could hear the cadence of their hooves as they calmly ran him down. He heard the raspy breathing of the creatures closest to him as they exhaled roughly when their hooves slapped the ground. The group coordinated their movements as they began to narrow the gap.

Conor began his incantation. As the words poured forth from his lips, an enormous howl startled every living thing on the desert floor. The deafening roar seemed to pour down from the entire sky, and if Conor had been shocked by his own magic, the pack of creatures chasing him visibly panicked when they heard the sound. Their hunting group scattered immediately, running in every direction at once. They forgot all about Conor on their haphazard way to finding protection for themselves. Even the leader, so huge and threatening, ran away like a puppy, peeing between its legs. Conor watched the group of hunters scatter off the boulders and run wildly across the desert. Their sharp hooves kicked up clouds of dust as they tried desperately to create distance between themselves and the sound of the menacing roar.

Relieved, Conor put one knee down on the stone surface as he scanned the desert again. Daylight had pushed the stars away completely, and now Conor enjoyed a clear view of a vast section of the region. He looked out upon bland areas with little vegetation dotted by sections of green grassy knolls. He spied a water hole far off in the distance, maybe three to five miles he reasoned. Even this early in the day, groups of animals converged on the precious water source. He saw both predator and prey warily exposing themselves in order to grab a drink of the life-sustaining liquid. Some of the animals he recognized immediately, others he didn't, but he imagined some might have the grotesque look of his earlier pursuers. He marked the location of the water hole by counting trees and grassy islands. He knew once he reached the floor of the desert he would need such landmarks to guide his way. Then he turned and scampered farther up the endless stack of flat rocks. He needed to find something before he joined the other creatures on the desert floor.

Conor climbed another half mile up the pile of stones. He stopped every fifty feet or so to quickly scan the area. Failing to find what he sought, he resumed his pattern of climbing and stopping. After reaching the additional half mile point of his climb, he looked over to his right and saw exactly what he needed – a large cave facing the rising sun. It had a huge opening and a large flat rock serving as a natural patio, with an area big enough to evade a predator. Conor estimated the sun would beam directly down on this area until a couple of hours past midday, which gave him plenty of time, provided he could find Eha sometime this morning. He stepped lightly across the rocks and ran over to the cave. He wanted to make sure nothing occupied the large cavern before he put his plan into effect.

He stood in front of the yawning entrance, roughly twenty-five feet across and fifteen feet high. He felt a brief sensation of fear as he stared into the darkness. Vivid images of his last voyage into a cave opening started dancing around in his mind. If Seefra really had become as powerful as they say, then what would prevent him from finding Conor and setting another trap for him?

He used the image of his imprisoned girlfriend to push the fear from his mind. He selected a large rock from the ground at his feet and lobbed it into the cave. He heard it bounce around a few times and then lay still. He selected another rock and advanced to the threshold of the cave opening. He threw it with everything he had straight into the darkness. He listened intently and heard nothing for quite some time. Then, in just about the amount of time it took for one of his throws to hit the ground, he heard the stone connect with a dense wall in the back of the cave. *It's huge,* he thought, *but how can I be certain of its vacancy*? He knew the answer before asking it. He had to enter the shadowy cave and check it out himself.

Walking to the far left side of the opening, he placed his hand on the wall, letting it glide along the surface as he stepped into the cave. He traveled ten feet and then stopped, holding his breath and listening for any sounds that weren't familiar. Hearing nothing, he traveled another ten feet and repeated the procedure. Soon he walked in total darkness, save the small circle of light back at the cave's entrance. As much as he tried not to, he couldn't help flashing back to his captivity in the cell of shadows. He panicked momentarily, almost running for the entrance. In the midst of his fright, he lost his hold on the wall. Dipping further into hysteria, he reached out wildly, trying to regain his grip.

Had he been able to see, he would have noticed the wall falling away into another large room, three times as big as the entrance cavern. Instead of exploring the area further, however, he took stock of himself and listened again for any sounds. Even though he heard nothing, he turned toward the light at the entrance and ran. As anyone would in a dark, forbidding place, he felt sure a hand or a set of teeth would clamp down on his shoulder as he sprinted for the safety of the light. Nothing of the kind occurred, but he did stumble over a group of small rocks on his way out, landing hard on his arm. He jumped up, more frightened than ever, and raced toward the entrance.

As he ran out into the warm sunlight, he glanced over his shoulder at the cave entrance. Seeing that nothing had followed him out of the cavern, he stopped and put his hands on his knees. Breathing heavily, he began to assess the damage from his fall. He had cut his right arm below the elbow pretty badly; blood dripped steadily from the scrape. He had torn his pants, but they had protected his leg. He saw a few scrapes but nothing like the oozing cut on his arm. He would have to watch himself. It seemed perfectly logical that wild animals out on the plains would be attracted to blood the same way sharks would sense it in the ocean. He didn't doubt the notion that they might be raising their noses into the air and sniffing his misfortune this very moment.

Trying to forget his injuries, Conor hopped down the successive layers of stone. Rock after rock skipped under his feet as he dropped his elevation by roughly a mile. He stopped at a point where he could easily view the animals on the steppe. He called forth another vision spell, one that would allow him to zoom in on anything he wished to bring closer. Cupping his hands around his eyes, he looked down toward the water hole. Large groups of different animals hovered around the water. Some members of a group dared to lower their heads to take a drink, while other members of the pack nervously watched for any danger. Almost all of the groups patterned their behavior this way, and for the most part it worked to their advantage. Every once in a while, however, a predator broke in on one of the younger, smaller members of a group while they focused their attention on the water. All groups scattered immediately when an attack like this occurred. Dust flew, water splashed, and after the ruckus died down, a fresh meal rested in the mouth of a hungry provider. Predators didn't always enjoy a successful charge, but the reaction of the group remained the same every time.

Conor turned his head slowly, scanning as much of the desert as he could. He didn't see any cheetahs, but he knew they lurked close by. Wild cats had the uncommon ability to sit like a statue for hours waiting for the opportune moment to strike. He scanned again, looking at every possible hiding place around the water hole, and then he saw them. Three males, sitting upright in a particularly thick clump of reed grass about thirty yards from the water. He blinked his eyes, activating the magical spell and bringing the cheetahs closer to him. There were three of them, most likely brothers – hunters who had stayed together their entire lives. He studied the trio intently, and after examining each one, he determined that the one in the middle must be Eha. He stood a good head taller than the other two, and his markings looked more complete, more defined.

Conor felt a pang of guilt shudder through his body. If he took Eha away from his brothers, how could they continue the hunt without him? They would never take an outsider, only direct relations hunted together in the cheetah's world. He couldn't worry about that, though. The two remaining brothers would have to fend for themselves. His main concern lay in how to coax Eha into the cave he found up on the hill. He had to separate him from his two brothers and lure him out of his traditional hunting territory, and that wouldn't be easy.

Taking his hands away from his eyes, Conor adjusted his vision back to its normal setting and began skipping down the rest of the rocky shelf. His arm had stopped bleeding, but it still looked like a gory mess. *The scent must be incredible,* he thought, *but that might help when the time came.* He hit the desert floor and stopped dead for just a second. Listening intently, he heard no sound of any approaching animals. He looked across the desert, spying the landmarks that would lead him to the water hole. Using the grassy islands for cover, he ran quickly from place to place. After reaching each new cluster of brush and grass, he would crouch down and hold his breath, listening for any movement around his hiding place. After a decent amount of time, he slowly stood and measured the distance to the next island. He also marked off the distance to the water hole each time he stopped. He wanted to keep track of how far he had traveled from the stone shelf. If he had to make a run for it, he wanted to know exactly how far he had to go, and at what point it would be futile to try and make it back to the rocks.

He peered over a tall stand of reeds and saw he still had roughly a mile to go. He counted five more grassy islands between himself and the water hole. If any creature hunting him made a charge after he had come that far, he would have to follow through with his plans to grab Eha. He wanted to maintain the element of surprise, but if everything hit the fan at once, he would have to think on his feet. He scampered away from his natural blind and ran toward the next island, feeling an odd surge of adrenaline as he closed in on Eha and his brothers.

Ten feet from reaching his final destination, one of Eha's

brothers turned his head in Conor's direction. Conor dove into the thick reeds in an attempt to escape its vision. From his prone position inside the grass and brush, Conor failed to see the cheetah calmly break away from his brothers and head in his direction. Eha and the other sibling paid no mind to their brother's investigation, except for keeping a wary eye on him and the water hole. It didn't appear as though they cared much about the third member of their group, but if anything made a threatening move toward the cheetah, Eha would be on top of it in less than a second.

Conor used his hands to push himself quietly off the ground. He went to his knees and checked his breathing. Something didn't feel quite right, but at this point he didn't know exactly what troubled him. While holding his breath, he listened to the normal sounds of the water hole. Had he been able to see through the thick reeds, he would have noticed a cheetah in full crouch, slithering across the hard packed desert on his way toward him. The cat had seen something as he sat with his brothers, and now he focused on the strong scent of a wounded animal. Conor knew nothing of this; however, because the cheetah's paws made no sound whatsoever as he padded silently across the soil. Eha had trained his brothers well. They were skilled hunters who rarely made a mistake in tracking or capturing prey.

Conor finally decided to part the reeds and have a look at Eha and his small pack. Adjusting his stance for a quick getaway, he kneed his way forward until he could press his hands into the grass. After squeezing his fingers through to the other side of the reeds, he opened his palms as they faced away from each other. With all due caution, he parted the tall grass very slowly and inched his face forward. As the last of the reeds separated, he found himself staring right into the eyes of a very curious cheetah. The two of them, man and beast, did not know exactly how to react to their unexpected meeting. They peered into each other's eyes for what seemed like an eternity before all hell broke loose.

The cheetah jumped fifteen feet straight up into the air. Every animal within fifty feet of the water hole scattered as if his or her life depended on it. Grass and leaves flew in every direction and a plume of dust the size of a football field exploded from the ground. Eha and his brother closed the distance to their sibling in two leaps, and almost immediately the three of them flanked the small grassy island. They didn't enter the camouflaged area right away, but they weren't about to let its occupant simply walk away after scaring their brother half to death. Eha took point at the location nearest the water hole. With a few quick chuffs, he ordered his two brothers to protect the left and right flanks. If the intruder managed to slip out the back door, well, Eha had been longing for a chase all morning.

Conor backed away from the reeds as fast as he could, frantically gulping large breaths of dust-filled air. He could see the frightened cheetah as it bounded straight into the sky, but after that he paid no attention to it at all. He tried to find another clump of reeds thick enough to conceal him, but this island contained a sparse amount of grass. The only protection lay in the direction he had just hustled away from, and he didn't feel safe moving forward again. He could hear the chaos around the water hole. He had no idea if Eha and his brothers had run for cover somewhere, or if they had stayed behind while all the other animals scattered. He figured Eha would do the latter, waiting silently for his prey to reveal itself.

He froze when he heard a large paw scratching at the area where he had parted the reeds. Apparently the cheetahs had waited long enough. Conor closed his eyes and summoned another of the Lady's incantations. He hoped the creators would guide his words, because he always had difficulty remembering this spell. He knew he had one shot at getting it right, because he saw a spotted paw step through the tall grass directly in front of him. He finished the spell but kept his eyes tightly shut. If he had made any mistake while reciting the words, he didn't want to see the reaction of the cheetahs when they saw him.

Eha stepped through the reeds, parting the grass with his nimble shoulders. After placing his forepaws on Conor's side of the barrier, the wise cheetah stopped. He sniffed everything around him – the ground, the reeds, even the air. He used extreme caution and appeared very patient. He wasn't about to allow any of them to be harmed by the strange visitor they had encountered. He chuffed a few times to notify his brothers that they could pass through the high grass and join him in the hunt. With perfect precision, the other two cheetahs slowly entered the island, bracketing Conor in a triangle of speed, power and extreme hunger.

Kneeling quietly, Conor finished his incantation and waited for the end to come. When he didn't feel a brace of claws or a mouth full of sharp teeth against his skin, he let his eyes flutter open. His nerves tensed briefly when he saw Eha pushing through the reeds less than five feet from where he knelt. It took everything he had not to jump and run. He looked at the sad, teardrop markings of the cheetah's face. He listened as the long nose inhaled and exhaled, trying to find a scent to follow. Then he heard Eha bark his commands to his brothers, and out of his peripheral vision he saw them entering the area.

Conor felt certain his time had come. Surely these excellent hunters could smell him from a distance of a hundred yards, and here he knelt just a few feet away. The wound on his arm should be drawing them in like a magnet. Maybe the spell he cast allowed for more than mere invisibility. Whatever had happened, he felt elated by the result. The three cheetahs appeared to have no idea that he shared the grassy island with them. Even so, they walked suspiciously around, sniffing everything and communicating with each other by sound, scent and touch. His brothers seemed to be satisfied with the lack of findings, but Eha would not be placated so easily. With a kind of supernatural sense, he kept pacing around Conor. He stopped here and there, sniffing Conor's back, his hands, and other body parts. Each time he examined a specific piece of Conor's body, he raised his head with a perplexed glare. He knew something or someone was evading him, and it bothered him that he couldn't locate the offender.

Conor sat as still as a gargoyle while Eha made his rounds. He could feel the cheetah's harsh breath on his body whenever Eha pushed closer to take a good sniff. The cat scratched at the ground next to Conor's knees, trying to dislodge whatever he believed to be there. Finally, with an abrupt blast of his nostrils, he looked as though he had finished his inspection. Instead of leaving, however, Eha walked around Conor until he stood directly in front of him. Standing there with his tongue jutting slightly out of his mouth, he looked frustrated but somehow satisfied. Conor could see it in his eyes; the cheetah knew something sat right in front of him, but he also realized he couldn't do anything about it. Then he lowered his strong head, letting his eyes fall to meet Conor's gaze. Less than an inch away from his nose, the inquisitive cat seemed to be telling Conor he had won this time, but that another round was coming soon. He wanted Conor to know that the three of them would be waiting for his next move. Most of all he wanted the young man to know he sensed his presence, which was enough for him at the moment. Eha blinked his large brown eyes once before signaling to his brothers. He leapt over Conor without any effort at all, joining the other cheetahs as they exited the grassy island. As they trotted back to their hunting spot, Eha turned around briefly, looking into Conor's eyes one last time.

Conor exhaled deeply, falling to the ground as quietly as he could. He didn't believe his good fortune. He couldn't count how many times he'd felt Eha had discovered him. What an amazing animal; no wonder the creators had taken him to serve with the Crossworlds Champions. The cheetah just knew by instinct that Conor had knelt right in front of him. He would have to be very careful with his next move. He understood now that Eha's intelligence could overcome even the most carefully conceived plans.

Conor moved to the edge of the small oasis. Still wearing the cover of invisibility, he walked calmly out onto the desert. He stood one hundred feet from the water hole, and approximately the same distance from Eha and his two brothers. He noticed the water hole's residents had returned to their morning routine. The commotion only a few minutes past faded into history. The desert animals had resumed their normal activities. *Curious*, thought Conor, *even in the face of extreme peril, these animals knew that once a chase or a kill had been completed, a certain measure of safety would return to the water hole.* Either that or they simply had to brave the predators to drink their share of the precious water every day. Looking off to the left, Conor saw the pack of crazed hunters that had given him a scare earlier in the morning. They seemed sated as they lounged around on the dirt. Hopefully their lack of hunger would keep them from joining the cheetahs in the pursuit.

Conor turned and walked toward Eha and his brothers. They had resumed their casual stance, each of them watching a different section of the water hole and the surrounding area. Conor marveled at the sight of Eha surveying his kingdom in the wild. To look at his face, you'd think he didn't have a care in the world. Conor had seen those eyes up close, however, and he knew differently. Eha didn't miss a thing, and he judged every movement as a possible source of food or threat. He might look relaxed and indifferent, but he could react instantly if something interested him.

Stopping about thirty feet from the cheetahs, Conor remembered the distinct difference in the texture of the ground around the grassy islands. The variation of the soils held the key to separating the three brothers. If his plan failed at that juncture, he might as well throw himself into the jaws of one of these hunters. Either way, it would be over very quickly. He looked up at the rocky ledge about two or three miles from where he stood. He estimated it would take him about four or five minutes to cover the distance. He would have to outwit and outrun three of the fastest animals on the planet for that long at least. Turning to face his rivals, he reversed the spell of invisibility and revealed himself.

Eha's brothers tensed immediately, ready to strike out after Conor without thinking. Their elder sibling merely turned his head and stared at the intruder, looking at Conor for a full minute. His body language instructed his siblings to hold their ground. This was a human being after all, the most dangerous predator of all. Who knew what this young man kept hidden away in his clothing? Even with their incredible speed, they could not outrun a bullet. So he sat there for a while, staring, certain that he was the same creature that bewildered him just a few minutes ago. He saw what his brothers saw as well, a deep gash in one of the young man's arms. He had lost blood so he must be weakened. This would cut down his reserves when the chase began.

Eha didn't figure there would be much of a chase anyway, not between a cheetah and a human. He gave one brief chuff, ordering his brothers out onto the perimeter. They were to flank the human and not allow him to break free of their hunting ring. When he saw them executing his command perfectly, Eha calmly stepped out into the desert. He moved slowly, but assuredly, never taking his eyes from Conor. He didn't make a threatening move toward the young man, but he inched closer with every cautious step. Without giving himself away, he flicked his eyes toward his two brothers, making sure they held their positions. He went low, crouching down in a perfect stalking position. The other cheetahs followed his example and soon all three were closing in, executing a triangulated attack.

Conor waited until the last possible moment. He wanted the cheetahs as close to each other as possible, so when the time came, they wouldn't be able to coordinate their patterns so easily. As soon as he saw Eha lower his body to the ground, he reached deep into his soul and recalled the gifts Eha himself had bestowed upon him for his battle with Gandron. Summoning the Lady of the Light's power, he felt his body charging up with the astounding energy of a cheetah preparing to run full speed. He took one last look at his path toward the stone shelf and then exploded in a cloud of murky dust.

One of Eha's brothers had somehow anticipated Conor's strategy. Taking a chance, he had started his sprint a split second before Conor took off running. Legs pumping, he passed Eha and the other cheetah swiftly on his way to intercept his prey. Kicking his legs into high gear, he caught up to him in seconds. He reached out with his right forepaw, trying to trip Conor up in mid-step. After trying three times, he dropped that tactic and focused his strength on running again. The human seemed to be pulling away from him, and he spent a few bewildered seconds wondering how that could possibly happen.

Conor couldn't believe the speed of the cheetah chasing him. It seemed like he had barely started running when the animal fell right in behind him. He whizzed past the first grassy island without even seeing it. His attention lay focused on the cheetah trying to swat one of his legs out from underneath him. Conor felt a bolt of fright race down his spine as he turned his own speed up a notch. He had seen shows on television about how big cats killed their prey. This recollection only helped his legs kick for more speed. He saw the second oasis coming up fast. He ran at a perfect angle towards the left edge of the reeds. If he cut to the right just inches in front of the soft dirt around the grass, his plan might work. With the cheetah in full pursuit, he ran as close to the edge as he dared and then bolted to the right.

Eha's brother hadn't anticipated such a strange maneuver. He expected the human to run straight into the brush looking for cover. He turned to follow his prey and sensed his claws giving way. Instead of the hard packed ground of the desert, he had planted his pivot foot right into the soft, forgiving dirt of the oasis. At close to seventy miles per hour, he went down in a twisted heap of dirt, grass and fur. His spotted face smacked the ground right in front of a stand of reeds. He rolled through the grass, arms and legs flailing through the air trying to gain purchase on anything. When he finally stopped moving, he had traveled almost fifty feet on his sides and back. He lay there, dazed, knowing that his part in the chase was over.

Conor raced around the perimeter of the grassy island. Without a second to applaud himself for his first maneuver, he saw Eha's other sibling coming toward him at breakneck speed. The cheetah covered all possible escape routes in a flash, cutting off any hope of turning back toward the water hole. Conor left the grassy oasis, speeding toward the last of the islands leading to the rocky shelf. Without any idea about how to free himself from his pursuers, he focused on maintaining his distance from the two remaining cheetahs. Conor hoped to leave both of Eha's brothers behind at the oasis, but the first had gotten such a jump on him that his plans had changed in an instant.

As he observed the last grassy island rushing up to meet him, Conor seized upon an idea. It might be the only disturbance that would tear his pursuer away from him. He turned his head just enough to see Eha's second brother following closely behind him, just a little off to his right. The line of vision should be perfect. As he passed the boundary of the last oasis, Conor murmured a quick spell and pointed his hand in the direction of a thick stand of reeds.

Eha's brother sensed the end of his pursuit, partly because he was tiring, and also because his prey seemed to be weakening. As they approached the last grassy area before the end of the desert floor, the cheetah prepared to pounce onto the back of the young man. Just as his legs tensed for battle, the cat spied something out of the corner of his eye. After all the intense fighting he and his brothers had engaged in to secure their hunting grounds, he couldn't believe what he saw standing there in the middle of the oasis. After Eha, the largest cheetah in the entire region, had chased off every competitor for hundreds of miles, a pair of strangers had taken up residence right in the center of their coveted territory. Forgetting

Conor completely, the cheetah darted to the left, a menacing snarl emitting from his lithe form. He made a beeline toward the strangers, careful not to make the same mistake his brother made. He planted his forepaws squarely on the ground at the edge of the grassy island and vaulted straight into the alien cats.

The invaders didn't move a muscle. If that affected Eha's brother in any way, he certainly didn't show it. The cheetahs simply sat there staring out onto the desert. They never looked toward their attacker, never growled or snarled in response, and never tried to get out of the way of the attack.

He hit the first cheetah broadside, driving it into the other invader in an attempt to knock both them down. They did fall over, but Eha's brother received quite a surprise when he impacted the cat nearest to him. The first cat exploded in a shower of thick, gelatinous water. The second cheetah burst open as well, but instead of the watery substance, it contained a compressed assortment of feathers and sand. The two phony cheetahs contained enough material to cover Eha's brother in a wet, sticky mass of feathery goop. He reacted with shock and disgust, flipping around to face any further threat, scratching and licking vigorously. The hunt had ended for the second brother as well.

Two down, thought Conor, *with only Eha left*. He smiled momentarily as he hopped up the first few shelves in the stone staircase.

Eha had paced himself, running along with brothers but content to let them perform most of the heavy pursuit. He wanted to observe the young man, maybe anticipate his strategy, and hopefully catch him when he made a fatal mistake. He hadn't suffered any setbacks, however, and as a matter of fact, he had taken out the only hunting partners he had ever known. Eha's brothers were not fools; if this human had overcome their shrewd nature, then he knew better than to take him lightly. He trotted by the final oasis, watching the young man bounce up the steps above the desert. Instead of blindly following him, Eha approached the first step and calmly sat down on the hard packed sand beside it.

Conor watched the bizarre series of events unfold. He expected Eha to be smart enough not to expend his energy in the chase, but this tactic went beyond mere instinctive planning. It validated once again the choice made by the creators when they brought Eha into the fold of the Champions. This creature was thinking the same way a human would.

As he stood on his perch looking into those calm, intelligent eyes, Conor thought twice about his ability to lure Eha into the cave. He half expected the cheetah to turn and walk away at any moment. The stakes in the game were about to go a lot higher.

Conor slumped to the surface of a rock. Acting like a wounded, sick animal, he held his arm gingerly as he sniffed the caked blood that coated his wrist. He began breathing heavily and erratically; giving off the impression that he might be close to passing out or even dying. He let his wounded arm drop to his side as he rolled over and put his head against the warm stone. He let his face fall against the stone surface so he could watch Eha through hooded eyes. Then he waited for the cheetah to act upon thousands of years of instinct.

Eha sat calmly at the base of the rocky shelf. With keen eyes, he watched a light breeze spin tiny clouds of dust across each series of steps as they rose ever higher. He kept Conor in his peripheral vision at all times; he watched him faltered on a shelf not too far above him. Instead of immediately investigating, however, he held his ground, waiting for another of the young man's tricks. He sat there for a good ten minutes before placing one paw gingerly upon the first step. He hopped up onto the shelf, never taking his eyes from Conor. *The human looks asleep or maybe unconscious*, he thought, as he skipped lightly up another dozen steps. He stopped again and sat down, observing his adversary. The pungent odor of caked blood tickled his nostrils, almost forcing him to abandon reason and charge up the stone shelf. Instead, he climbed in a wide arc around Conor. He wanted to remove the one advantage the human had – his ability to see his pursuer. As he passed twenty feet from the crown of Conor's head, he sensed a twinge of fear coming from the young man.

As Eha changed direction, Conor chided himself for not anticipating the strategy. The big cat was pressing his advantage by walking around behind him. He wouldn't even see him until the cat had his neck locked in those powerful jaws. *Think fast*, he told himself. *Think of something, and do it quickly.* He could hear the soft click of the cheetah's claws coming up behind him.

After walking around to Conor's rear, Eha stared at the motionless form lying on the ground in front of him. The smell of the blood overpowered him, causing instinct to replace reason. He walked right up to the young man, muscles tensing with every step. If Conor moved a muscle, Eha would be off the shelf and back down to the desert floor in three quick hops. He bent his head down, sniffing Conor's back. He let his nose drift toward the injured arm. After two quick sniffs, Eha's tongue fell from his mouth. He wanted more than anything to taste the crystallized blood from the young man's injury. He could wait for that, though. First he would have to make certain his prey had expired. He moved his head along Conor's arm until he reached his shoulder, and finally his neck. He opened his jaws preparing for the strike, and then jumped back in surprise.

Conor disappeared from right under Eha's nose.

Conor sat up from his new perch, twenty steps above his previous position. He watched Eha briskly sniffing around the area where his body lay only seconds ago, and he went to work preparing the next temptation. While watching Eha, he took a twig from the ground and dragged the pointed end across the dried wound on his arm. Fresh blood oozed from the split in the caked skin, no doubt sending waves of delicious smells down the shelf toward Eha. He squeezed his arm, forcing fresh droplets to litter the stones around him. Then he stood and scampered up another twenty steps. He could see the cave now, although it was still some distance away. He figured that wouldn't matter though. Once Eha caught the scent of fresh blood, he would come after him without hesitation.

The big cheetah surveyed the scene before him. The young man had vanished without a trace. The enticing scent of caked blood remained, however, and only fresh blood could smell more tempting. Eha lifted his head toward the higher steps. He didn't see Conor, but he sensed his premonition exactly – the smell of fresh blood. He looked down at the desert floor, then back up toward the rocks again. By all rights he should go down and collect his brothers, but he didn't want to wait. He couldn't allow such a prize to escape him. He turned and bounded up the next series of steps, letting his nose guide the way. When he reached the rock containing the droplets of blood, he eagerly lapped up a sample of his prey's fluids. He lifted his mouth, now crimson red with the blood of the wound, and saw Conor staggering up the stone shelf above him. He seemed very weak; he had to halt his progress more than once to care for his drooping arm. Bathed in the duty of ten thousand years of inbred instinct, Eha jogged up the rocky steps in pursuit of his target.

Hunched over while struggling up the steps, Conor turned his eyes to look under his arm from time to time. He saw Eha taste his blood and then follow him up the stone steps. *So far so good,* he thought, but he would have to be quick. The sounds rising up from the desert floor worried him more than his skirmish with Eha. The pack of bizarre alien animals had obviously become hungry again, and they had set about gathering at the base of the rocky shelf. No doubt they had smelled Conor's blood and were assembling in preparation for the hunt.

Eha also heard the sickening sound of the droccan calling its pack together. He glanced down at the base of the shelf. At least half of the hunters had already assembled and the others would join them soon. He would never allow such a disgusting creature to claim his prize. He could not battle a dozen of them together, though, so he would have to take the young man down immediately. He looked past the stumbling human at a large cave some distance ahead. If he caught him on the stone shelf and hid the body inside the cave, perhaps he wouldn't have to face the hoard of droccans.

Eha galloped up the stone steps three at a time. He could be on top of his prey within seconds at this pace. After cresting one particularly large rock, he noticed the young man lying prone on a wide shelf directly in front of the cave. *Good,* thought Eha, *the human will make the chase all that much easier.* He stared at Conor for a moment, and then the call of the droccan hoard forced his hand. He jumped to the peak of the large rock and began hopping and jogging toward the cave.

Conor watched Eha with eyes barely open. He heard the call of the strange beasts, but he decided he couldn't do anything about them at this point. If they came over the rocky hill, he would have to abandon his plans for Eha and save himself. Without him, the creators might not have anyone else to send on these missions, so safety remained his primary concern. Turning his attention to Eha, he noticed a sense of urgency in the cheetah. He obviously had heard the cries coming from down below as well. Maybe the beasts would end up serving a purpose after all. When Eha was within fifty feet of him, Conor staggered to his feet holding his arm. With a grimace wide enough for the cheetah to see clearly, he limped into the dark face of the cave and disappeared. He whispered a silent message to the creators, hoping Eha would enter the cave behind him.

Eha followed the human all the way to the mouth of the cave and stopped. He paced deliberately back and forth in front of the dark entrance. The cries of the droccan hoard would not force him into the unknown. He sniffed purposefully, seeking the familiar scent of a large predator, something that could easily call this cave home. Sensing nothing, he leaned forward, dipping his head into the shadows. After his eyes adjusted to the darkness, he saw Conor's limp form hunched over a small string of rocks. He lay motionless only twenty feet from Eha's position. Capturing and stowing him somewhere wouldn't take more than a minute or two. He heard the cry of the droccans again. They were much closer this time. Their proximity convinced him to penetrate the interior of the cave. Just as he had stepped through the reeds almost an hour ago, Eha split the darkness with his shoulders and stepped quietly toward Conor.

Conor shivered with excitement. He had but two things left to do – call for the corridor and scare the living daylights out of his brother Champion. As he saw the cheetah's face peering into the darkness, he called to the Lady of the Light for a portal and uttered a very familiar chant.

The deafening roar that had scared the pack of creatures earlier today now reverberated around the cavern like a sonic boom. Eha reacted so quickly his paws shot out from under him as he tried to flee. Regaining his balance, he ran for the light as if shot out of a cannon. Conor opened his eyes wide and watched as the opening of the cave flashed and became a silvery membrane of pure energy. Frightened beyond reason, Eha hadn't even noticed the difference in the light. He shot through the opening like a bullet, frantically disappearing toward his new life. Conor wondered if the cheetah had even felt the intense cold and heat as he passed through the portal. He rose, wiping the last of the crusty blood smears from his arm. He walked over to the corridor membrane and stood inches from its glowing, vibrating surface. *How different these portals were*, he thought. The forbidden corridors seemed so damaged, so distressed, so temporary. These portals exuded such incredible power and life, and he wondered if this one would remain here forever if the Lady deemed it so. He shook his head, stretched long and hard, much like a cheetah might after an afternoon nap. He took one last look at the cave, listened to the pack of enraged animals dancing around on the other side of the membrane, and walked through the corridor.

After the flash of cold and heat, which Conor had somehow grown to enjoy, he exited the portal, finding himself walking beside the lake in the glade of Champions. Everything was beautiful here, completely peaceful. While smiling up at the sun, he heard the melodious purring of a large cat off to his right. He turned and saw Eha lying across the lap of the Lady of the Light. She sat calmly next to a beautiful stand of palm trees, cooing softly to the large predator. She spoke gently to him, telling him he would be safe here in the glade.

"You have done well, Conor," said the Lady, still brushing the cheetah's rough fur. "You have brought the first of the Champions back to the glade, as I knew you would."

Conor walked toward the Lady. Eha tensed, letting his lips rise in a silent snarl. The Lady cooed to him again and he relaxed back into her lap. He never took his eyes from the strange magical human who had transported him to this bizarre place.

"I have yet to reconcile with Eha," said the Lady. "Although bonded to me, his wild qualities still remain. He will not be approachable until later on this evening, and I'm afraid you will be far away from here by that time. I have prepared a corridor for your next journey."

Conor looked around the glade and saw another portal on the far side of the lake. He turned back to the Lady, smiling at the cheetah. "Will Eha remember me when I return from this journey?"

"Undoubtedly," answered the Lady. "But you must go, and quickly. The hunters are coming for Surmitang and his pride. They mean to exterminate them, and our great Champion will perish before he allows that to happen."

Conor opened his mouth to ask for a breather so he might attend to his wound and clean himself up. He didn't fancy walking into a den of tigers with a bleeding arm. As he lifted his hand to show the Lady, he saw that his injuries had disappeared. He felt as if he had eaten a full meal, and his clothing had been replaced as well. The Lady had dressed him in a bizarre type of camouflage, one that changed as he moved between different backgrounds. He smiled at her, nodding his head once. Accepting her encouragement in return, he tipped his hand to Eha and jogged toward the far side of the lake. He watched his clothing change patterns as he moved from sand to brush to water. Then he looked at the strange corridor growing larger and larger as he rounded the curve of the lake.

CHAPTER SEVENTEEN

Seefra cackled with glee as he held the sapphire prize in one of his small, misshapen hands. After thousands of failed spells, his latest concoction had given him command of one of the five keys of the creators. He stared greedily at the intense hue of the sparkling blue key, his six eye slits blinking with delight. He knew the remaining keys would be his with slight variations of the spell he used to transmute the first one. It was only a matter of time now; he knew the keys and the Crossworlds would soon be in his possession.

Janine sat in the corner of Seefra's laboratory, plucking the remaining keys off the floor. Her heart stopped when she saw the sapphire key come to rest in Seefra's hand instead of falling to the floor with the rest. The Lady's magic was truly powerful, but with this achievement the dark master had peeled back the corner of the safe. He had figured out one of the numbers in the combination of the Lady's spell. It would not be long before he deciphered the remaining codes, and when that happened, she was doomed. He would throw her down into the pit and watch the hideous creature that lived below the crystal cells consume her. She shook the thought from her mind as she placed the other four keys back into the pocket of her cargo jacket. She zipped the pocket closed and waited for Seefra's minions to escort her back to her prison. She wondered if she might enjoy a complete floor in her cell tonight. Seefra seemed overjoyed with himself. Maybe he might allow her some comfort after all.

The dark master massaged the beautiful blue key with his tiny hand. He turned to Janine with a glint in his eyes, and gestured for her to come to him. He watched as she came forward, defiance blazing in her eyes.

Janine kept her gaze locked on the single key rolling back and forth in Seefra's hand. She wanted to snatch it away from him and throw it as far as she could into the cave. She knew it would be a fruitless gesture, however, and his retribution for such a display would be extremely painful. Stopping in front of the dark master, she raised her eyes until they met the six small slits that gave Seefra his vision. She didn't like looking at his eyes because she never knew which pair was glaring at her. She switched her gaze from eye to eye and back again, wondering if he saw the hatred she held for him.

"You got lucky, that's all," she said boldly. "You'll never figure out the spells for the remaining keys." She jiggled the pocket of her cargo jacket in a mocking gesture. She even smirked at Seefra, laughing silently in his face.

"Your time is short," hissed the dark master, showing little emotion. "I will decipher the combination to the other four keys, and quickly. Now that I have the first, the clues to the others will emerge with very little struggle." Seefra held the sapphire key in front of Janine's face. "You have failed, Conor of Earth has failed, the Champions and the creators have failed as well. Soon I will have all of you begging for your lives."

"You may win in the end," said Janine into her jailer's face, "but none of us will ever beg you for anything! We'll all perish proudly and happily rather than give you any satisfaction at all!"

"An arrogant boast," replied Seefra icily. "One you may indeed regret." He turned toward the door of his laboratory. When he reached the opening, he looked back at Janine. He stared at her for an uncomfortably long time and then glanced at his two servants. As he left the room, the shadow warriors entered and escorted Janine back to the cell of crystals. They threw her roughly into the clear box, and as she had done a hundred times before, she splayed her arms and legs out as wide as she could. She felt solid crystal underneath her body for the first five feet. After that the floor of the cell simply disappeared. Hugging the edge with the toes of her boots, she reached up and plastered her hands against the wall closest to her. She stopped her momentum just before going over the edge. She gulped for breath, trying to calm herself. She looked down into the foggy abyss, feeling tempted to just let her body tumble into the hole and have it all be over. She wanted so desperately to let the tears come, but she had cried enough because of the dark master. Certain he was watching her every move, she would not give him the pleasure of seeing her shed more tears. She turned around and saw the shadow warriors laughing at her predicament. She jiggled the keys in her pocket as she stared at them.

"Keep it up, you bozos," she said spitefully. "When Conor gets here with the Champions, you won't be laughing then." She looked up through the crystal ceiling of her cell. Somewhere through the miles of rock, the sky shone with a brilliant sun. Conor could see the same sun, and he was working his way toward her. She kept that thought in her mind as she relaxed her breathing. She tried to calm herself so she could hopefully get some sleep. She hoped no one displeased the dark master during the night; she didn't want to hear the agonizing screams when one of the other captives suddenly found themselves dropping down into the pit.

"My compliments," said the Lady of the Shadows. She stood in front of a view screen watching Janine struggle with her accommodations. Seefra swirled back and forth next to his mistress, pleased with himself. His plans were coming together perfectly, and soon he would take his rightful place among the inner element of the Circle of Evil. The Lady of the Shadows had served him well, and he would continue to act with all due deference toward her. Some day, however, he would sit in the first chair of the circle, and the Crossworlds would be his to command or destroy. The worlds that obeyed his orders would exist in relative peace, but those that defied his authority would vanish from the Crossworlds forever.

"The key, dark master," the Lady of the Shadows insisted. "I should like to hold it."

Seefra shook himself from his reverie. His daydreams had almost revealed his plans to the Lady, a most painful error if she ever suspected him. "The key rests in a secure location, my Lady," he said, bowing subtly. "Since its value is beyond estimation, I would like to keep it locked away until the others are within our grasp."

"I understand," replied the Lady of the Shadows. "But I advise you not to assume this attitude with Shordano should he ask to see the key. He's likely to put you in one of your own cells."

Seefra bowed again, this time more deeply. His posture may have suggested submission, but his thoughts certainly did not. He would bide his time. One day the Circle of Evil would be his to command. The Lady of the Shadows would become a most interesting subject indeed. He turned and bowed one last time to his mistress before returning to his laboratory. He wanted desperately to resume his work counteracting the spells placed on the keys. He could feel victory within his grasp and he refused to waste any more time with pleasantries.

"With your leave, my Lady," he said, deftly touching the sapphire key through the pocket of his waistcoat.

SURMITANG

CHAPTER EIGHTEEN

Conor exited the second corridor and found himself in a dense, humid forest. After stepping through the membrane, he held his hands up to keep from being slapped by an endless succession of thick leaves. He tried walking straight ahead for some distance but found it to be too much of a struggle. The jungle seemed to grab at his limbs every time he tried to take a step. He stopped, holding his body stiff and his breathing steady. Listening for anything he could recognize, he finally heard the sound of crashing water that could only come from a high waterfall. Judging as best he could the direction of the falls, he extended his hand and spoke softly. The incantation worked immediately, for directly in front of him as far as he could see, the forest began reshaping itself. Large, leafy trees raised their branches, leaning back from the trail summoned by Conor's magic. Endless chains of tangled roots and branches groaned while straightening limbs that had matured into their curved shapes for hundreds of years. An infinite number of leaves and twigs fell into the vacated area, inviting Conor to walk upon the freshly groomed pathway. The young man watched as the forest reformed itself for his personal use. *One could become comfortable with this type of power,* he thought, witnessing the awesome display.

After listening to the surrounding area again for a few moments, Conor took to the path and proceeded through the lush forest. Without the ability to reshape his environment, he might have been lost in this tropical jungle for the rest of his life. The *Forest of Forever* seemed endless, but at least he could remember being able to see more than a few feet in front of him. Even with his freshly cut path Conor felt claustrophobic. The jungle seemed to close in on him every time he so much as glanced at the trees. *No wonder tigers flourished here,* he thought. One of the big cats could be standing within the branches of the rainforest ten feet away and he wouldn't know it.

His magically produced trail died out after about a half mile, and Conor found himself looking directly into the jungle again. He refocused, listening for sounds he could comprehend. The waterfall seemed much closer. Conor heard another sound far off in the distance. It was so faint he couldn't really determine its source, but he felt certain he recognized it. At some point in the past he remembered hearing something very familiar, but for the life of him he couldn't figure it out. He dismissed it, knowing he might come across it again, and instead focused on the waterfall. He considered the distance for a moment and determined the falls to be no more than a hundred yards away. Instead of creating another lengthy pathway, Conor decided to press the branches aside as he walked through the jungle. This way, if something lived around the falls, he would not give away his location by displacing too much of the flora.

Using a constantly repeated spell, Conor walked toward the waterfall. The jungle divided in front of him as he moved forward, pressing the leaves and branches to either side as he approached. He heard the falls crashing down into a large pool roughly ten yards ahead of him. He stopped one last time and listened intently. Hearing nothing but water, he continued forward until he reached the wall of the rainforest. Beyond the stand of trees and branches loomed an immense waterfall and an even larger pool. Conor stepped through the jungle and out into the clearing.

Surrounded by an umbrella of lush tropical rainforest, a tall stream of water fell along a rocky cliff into a glistening pool below. To Conor, it looked like a scene from someone's idea of paradise, almost as striking as the realm of the creators. He stood so transfixed by the natural beauty that he almost missed the massive Sumatran tiger standing in the pool next to the falls. The cat made no move toward him; nor did he make any threatening sounds. He just stood there, staring at the strange human who had disturbed his bath.

"Surmitang," whispered Conor to himself. There was no mistaking it. Without seeing any other tigers from this jungle, Conor knew instantly that this one was the Champion who had saved him from Therion. He wore the same proud, majestic bearing, as if questioning any other beast's right to inhabit his jungle. He stared at Conor with supreme confidence, daring the young man to make any move forward or backward. He dipped his great head down into the pool, slowly extending his tongue for a lazy drink. Never taking his eyes from Conor, he allowed himself to enjoy a long, refreshing series of swallows. After satisfying his thirst, the handsome tiger lowered his furry torso into the cool water, allowing the pool to rise up and wash over most of his back and haunches. The ripples highlighted his vibrant coloring. Gleaming rows of black, gold, orange, and white fur collapsed into the glistening water.

After resting there for a moment, the cat rose and padded over to the edge of the pool. He stepped gingerly onto the bank and hopped out of the water. He shook himself two or three times, licking his fur in various places. Then he glanced over at Conor again. Without a growl, chuff or groan, the big cat turned away toward the jungle.

Conor couldn't believe his good fortune. He had literally walked out of the corridor right into Surmitang's jungle. All he had to do now was communicate with the Lady of the Light and ask for a portal that would take the two of them back to the glade of Champions. Walking briskly, he kept his eyes fixed on the huge tiger as he made his way into the thick bush. In his eagerness to capture Surmitang, however, he made a critical error. Before moving forward, he should have forced himself to remain motionless, listening for any threatening sounds around him. Had he done so, he might have heard the sound of branches bending behind him.

Two female tigers emerged from the jungle in flanking positions behind Conor. Just as Eha and his brother's had done in the deserts of their world, these two tigers, on Surmitang's orders no doubt, had silently positioned themselves behind him. They followed him from the moment he began thrashing through the jungle, and now they had him dead to rights. He couldn't move back into the bush, and he certainly couldn't move forward toward Surmitang. Trapped in the middle of nine hundred pounds of formidable Sumatran tigers, Conor began to tremble involuntarily.

Surmitang exited the trees and brush of the jungle, moving deliberately back into the clearing. He calmly paced toward Conor, sending peculiar sounding commands to the females of his pride. Humans had nearly decimated his entire family, almost every tiger in these lands, and he wasn't about to allow this one to join in the hunt. Believing he had the young man penned in, he began snarling and growling with great menace. The two females behind Conor added their voices to the chorus, and he soon found himself surrounded by three very angry tigers.

Conor waived his hand across the front of his camouflaged outfit. Reaching behind his neck, he pulled a flexible hood over his head, zipping the enclosure all the way over his face. He could see the jungle and the tigers well enough to move about, but he knew they could no longer see him. He rolled the sleeves of his jersey down, covering his hands completely. He stood absolutely still, totally invisible to the snarling tigers stationed around him. He knew the cats had astounding senses of hearing and smell, so he wasn't out of the woods yet. For now he would simply stay calm and see how Surmitang reacted.

When Conor vanished into thin air, the three tigers stopped their vocal intimidation in unison. They simply couldn't believe that their prey had eluded them. The two females looked to Surmitang for guidance, but even he hadn't a clue about how to proceed. He crouched down low to the ground, signaling for his pride to do likewise. He sniffed quietly as he listened intently, but aside from the crashing waterfall, he didn't hear another sound. He hadn't seen or heard anything entering the jungle around the clearing, so he assumed that the human had not moved very far. He chuffed at his two hunting partners, ordering them to close ranks and seal off the jungle behind them. Then in a classic tiger's crouch, he began creeping forward in a direct line right to the human's last known position.

Conor watched with terrified awe as Surmitang crawled straight toward him. He would be on top of him in seconds, and the two females had efficiently cut off his only escape. Even though he knew Surmitang couldn't see him, the big tiger seemed to be looking right at him. His colorful, furry lips flared up in a menacing snarl, exposing a rack of thick fangs that would tear Conor to pieces if he caught hold of him. He had to admit it was an awesome sight – a huge predator coming straight at him.

Conor bolted from his spot, shedding his protective camouflage as he ran for his life. The three tigers pursued him in perfect formation, leaving a shower of leaves and brush floating in their wake. Working with the precision of a thousand generations of training, they separated into a tight circle as they slowly closed in on their prey. All three tigers converged on Conor when he reached the edge of the jungle. They jumped into a mound of snarling rage, ripping at anything that seemed to resemble the human. Their frenzied attack even inflicted serious injury upon themselves. Surmitang and both of the females suffered bites and scratches in the ferocious melee. When they finally broke off the attack, the jungle had been reduced to confetti. A large, open area had been cleared away, and not a single trace of the young man remained. A puzzled Surmitang lowered his great striped head and sniffed the area of their attack. He smelled nothing of the human, and he lifted his open mouth and roared his frustration to the heavens. It was bad enough that hunters with rifles could get the better of them. This human carried no weapons of any kind and he had gotten away without a scratch.

Conor watched the carnage from his hiding place about twenty-five feet above the jungle floor. When the three tigers took off after the image he had created, he moved quietly to the nearest tree and scaled the knotty branches. He sat there, completely camouflaged, watching Surmitang and the two females press their attack. As they lay waste to what they thought was the human in their midst, Conor gulped down huge breaths of air trying to calm himself. It was bizarre watching himself being pounced upon by three enormous tigers. The savage attack reduced everything within their reach to rubbish. Even large branches disintegrated under the gnashing teeth and ripping claws of the big cats. When the tigers realized they had been duped, the frustration on Surmitang's spectacular face tore at Conor's insides like a knife. He saw nothing but supreme intelligence in that expression. No one would ever convince him that animals such as these couldn't command the ability of reason.

They're so powerful, thought Conor. *How am I supposed to do battle with such immense strength and cunning?* Surmitang had figured him out before Conor even saw him relaxing in the pool beneath the waterfall. He had heard his approach, dispatched his soldiers, and simply waited for Conor to walk right into his trap. A brilliant tactic; he would have to be extremely careful from now on. After all, how many other males lived in this forest? Surmitang may indeed be the alpha male of the group, but in times of peril even the unlikeliest foes band together. The hunters had produced something in this region never before seen in the wild. Casual groups of Sumatran tigers were undoubtedly coming together to fight a common enemy. There might be fifty, even a hundred tigers roaming around this forest, and every single one of them would destroy Conor without hesitation. The mere thought of it made his heart pound forcefully in his chest.

He watched as Surmitang led the two females away into the forest. He tracked them visually for as long as he could, and then stayed in the tree for another thirty minutes. He heeded his own warning this time, listening for any sounds of tigers creeping through the jungle back toward the waterfall. After assuring himself that he sat alone overlooking the dense jungle, he unzipped his hood and exposed his head. His hair gripped his skull tightly and his face glistened with sweat. The humidity in the jungle felt oppressive enough without an enclosed head covering soaking his face and hair. Shaking his head vigorously, he removed as much of the irritating moisture as he could. Then he checked his breathing and listened to the sounds of the jungle.

As he quieted himself, he heard the strange but familiar sound again, far off in the distance. He closed his eyes, concentrating as hard he could. He tried desperately to pinpoint the source. Just as he felt ready to give up and tread through the jungle again, it hit him square between the eyes. Machines. The sounds he heard far away came from machinery – the machinery of mankind. *Of course*, thought Conor. Humans had come to this forest to extract resources and develop what remained. Surmitang and his pride were merely defending their habitat from the unstoppable force of human industry. He remembered the great tiger recalling his experiences with the hunters of his pride. Conor had been transported to the exact place and the precise moment in time when these events had occurred. He smiled as he pulled the jersey back over his head. He may become a meal for one Surmitang's siblings, but not before he paid a few visits to the other humans in this jungle. The Lady said he might have to win the Champions over with feats of bravery and cunning, and Conor knew just what he had to do to gain Surmitang's confidence.

Conor adjusted his protective clothing and climbed down from the tree. Since he had no frame of reference, he decided to head in the same direction as Surmitang. As long as he carefully protected himself, he would not fall into another of the tiger's traps. He dropped from the trunk of the tree to the ground, a distance of ten feet, and began making his way through the jungle flora. Instead of carving through the leaves and branches with a magical spell, Conor decided to find his own path. Using his arms and legs, he slowly twisted his torso through and around the dense jungle. The scents from various plants wafted into his nose as he passed through different sections. He grasped the larger leaves, holding them for a second or two, feeling the textures of the different plants. Looking up from time to time, he redirected his route according to the tall trees he had selected as guides. Although slick with sweat, Conor enjoyed his informal stroll through the dense rainforest.

After walking for about thirty minutes, he heard the machinery quite clearly. As quick as any monkey in the jungle, he scaled another tree for a clearer view of what lay ahead of him. Standing a hundred or more feet above the jungle floor, Conor caught a clear view of the equipment off in the distance.

It was exactly as the Lady had said. Without any consideration for the natural world of the tigers, the workers decimated the jungle of Surmitang's pride. Conor could easily see the path cut through the jungle by the men and their machines. He estimated they had been here for quite some time, judging by the pattern of the destruction. He didn't know when they might leave, but he imagined it would be when nothing remained of the forest.

An uproar down by the earthmovers grabbed Conor's senses. He heard the distinct sound of tigers roaring, no doubt trying to frighten their prey into a submissive posture. The horrible screams of men followed as the tigers dragged away another pair of victims. The machinery came to an unplanned halt, and gunshots echoed through the trees. Conor saw small puffs of smoke rising into the air, obviously the discharge of the weapons. A few of the men, no doubt hunters, ran ahead of the machinery, chasing after the tigers and firing their weapons as they penetrated the curtain of the rainforest. They didn't travel very far into the jungle, however, because they knew that other tigers could be waiting for them. They had learned that lesson the hard way, when six of their best trackers had been taken in an ambush.

After that particular encounter, the hunters, sitting around a fire that evening, commented repeatedly on the cunning nature of the attack. The tigers seemed to work as a coordinated team, and their strategy had not remained static. The attack and counterattack had flowed according to a plan laden with contingencies. Only humans allowed for modifications like these, and the big tigers acted exactly like they possessed far more than mere instinct. They had planned the campaign perfectly.

During the first attack the tigers had seized two of the workers, dragging them into the jungle. The hunters and their trackers immediately followed, hoping to drive off the big cats and save their comrades. Their impatience became their undoing, and after running hastily into the jungle they found themselves surrounded by a dozen very angry males. The hunters put down two of the cats during the skirmish, but the huge predators decimated the group of men. All six trackers perished in the jaws of different tigers, and two of the most experienced hunters had been taken as well. The intelligence displayed by the tigers unnerved the men working in the rainforest; they had almost decided to leave Indonesia altogether. The company won them over, however, with huge bonuses and hefty pay raises, and the work commenced. The tiger attacks continued, but at greater intervals. From that day on, the men always worked with one eye looking over their shoulders.

Conor watched the entire scene play out below him. He

followed every move made by the men, especially the hunters. He wanted to know their tactics, because he understood his own kind very well. There would be a hunt this evening, he felt certain of it. More of Surmitang's pride would be destroyed in retribution for today's attack. This was his chance to prove himself to the great Champion. Somehow he had to thwart the attack and save the tigers. If he pulled it off successfully, he could almost guarantee leniency from Surmitang. Either that or he would initiate the biggest slaughter of mankind in the history of these jungles. Without the protection of the hunters, the tigers would end the confrontation quickly, and he doubted he would be spared either. He was counting on the noble quality inherent in all great beasts – a respect for strength, cunning, and loyalty.

Surmitang had throttled him when they first met in the glade of Champions. Almost every time he came across the great tiger, he had belittled him, questioning the value of his service to the creators. Partly because of his belief in his own fantastic qualities and partly because of his distaste for the human race, Surmitang made trouble for Conor at every stage of his journey with Maya. But that had not kept him from providing Conor with the abilities and advice he needed to overcome Fumemos, the hideous being that had used the ocean in an attempt to destroy him. Although waiting until the last minute and still questioning his utility, Surmitang had helped Conor slay the being in the waves. He also defied the forbidden corridors and gave his life to save Conor from Therion. The gigantic lion had planned to abandon Conor in the *Forest of Forever* and then destroy him outright, and it was Surmitang who challenged a much larger and stronger cat to a battle for Conor's safety. He felt a strange sort of kinship with him, and even though he wouldn't allow that bond to get in the way of his good judgment, he hoped it would carry the day when the time came.

Conor marked the path leading to the human camp and then worked his way down out of the tree. Looking up at the sky, he decided he might have two hours at most to head off the attack on the tigers. Although he wanted to walk through the jungle using his own power, he knew he'd lose too much time that way. After adjusting his camouflage suit and listening for sounds of large cats stealing through the jungle, he uttered a spell that allowed him the quickest route toward his objective. From this point forward, until he reversed the spell, anywhere he looked would be free of foliage. The jungle would simply vanish in front of him and reappear after he had gone his way.

Checking his markers one last time, Conor started off toward the camp. At first his new power made him feel awkward. Watching the dense foliage disappear in sections in front of him made him overly cautious. He paid too much attention to everything else he could see as he stepped forward. After a while, however, he became accustomed to it and began making good progress. He did find it fascinating to watch what emerged as the trees and bushes disappeared before him. He saw an endless variety of creatures silently resting all around him. Had he known of their existence beforehand, he might have taken greater care where he placed his feet and hands. He noted that none of the creatures made any threatening move at all. They probably shared his sense of shock at the strange development in their environment.

As he approached the human camp, Conor heard the low, droning hum of the heavy earth-moving machinery. Although not presently in use, the colossal machines sat idle with their engines running. Apparently it took too much effort to start the behemoths, and the process remained unpredictable at best. If one the huge machines failed to start, it took five days for a mechanic to come to the island and see to its repair.

Conor began to see the pale orange coloring of the machines through the apron of the forest, so he stopped long enough to secure his camouflage. After making certain of his invisibility, he dismissed his spell, stepped through the leafy curtain and into the human camp.

He hadn't realized how big the encampment was until he began walking through the clearing. A dozen mammoth earth-moving machines sat abreast of each other like a row of metallic whales waiting to dive into the rainforest. Close by, a series of roughly two dozen structures had been erected throughout the camp, no doubt to house and care for the men. The smell of roasting meat and vegetables drifted through the camp. Conor surmised that the men planned to eat a hearty dinner before heading out into the jungle in search of their prey. The fools didn't realize that a predator's sense of smell could pick up the scent of the meal far easier than if they entered the forest without eating beforehand. *All the better*, he thought. He wouldn't have to walk far before the tigers found their prey.

A group of strange looking scarecrows circled the outer barrier of the camp. They stood upright on metal poles and resembled human men in height and weight. Conor walked up to one of them for a closer look. He heard a peculiar humming noise and almost touched the dummy to ascertain its source. He pulled his fingers away after seeing the electrodes attached to the wires encircling the scarecrow. These decoys were designed to give a considerable electric shock to any tiger that attacked them. The men hoped to convince the predators that attacking a real human would bring about the same result. Conor shook his head at this realization. Surmitang would never be so stupid, and besides that, he would figure out the ploy in a short time anyway. *How much of a fool did they take the great tiger for anyway?*

He watched as groups of men left their individual tents and walked in the direction of the mess hall. The delicious scent of the food tore at Conor's stomach. He hadn't eaten since before he left to find Eha. Somehow the creators had provided the necessary nourishment, but it could never be the same as eating real food. He could almost taste the steaming beef and chicken swimming in a large bed of grilled vegetables. Closing his eyes, he let the aroma float into his nostrils for a few seconds.

When he felt certain that all of the men in the camp had entered the mess hall, Conor quietly stepped inside. The room itself looked quite simple, a hastily fabricated shelter that comfortably housed fifty men. A long table running down the center of the room served as the main dining area, and a few smaller tables sat here and there around the hall. The jungle provided the flooring for the room. A few swamp coolers tried their best to pump frigid air into the shelter. It did little good; the men sat around the table sweating into their shirts anyway. Everything about the mess hall looked completely normal to Conor until he looked past the main feast at the smaller tables. What he saw on those tables and on the floor around them caused a lump of bile to surge into his throat.

In the same room where the men ate their food, they also slaughtered tigers they had shot during their skirmishes. Huge tiger skins lay stretched out on the floor crudely fastened down to the extreme limits of their fur. Whole paws, drained of their fluids, lay about the floor of the mess hall as if tossed about by children. Most repulsive of all were the trophy skulls of the great tigers, severed cleanly at the neck and lined up in a row of mute protest. The eyes of the skulls had been removed in preparation for the insertion of glass marbles. For now, though, the striped faces stared at nothing. Conor stared back at them as an uncontrollable rage built up inside his body. *I could take this entire encampment and all of the men residing in it,* he thought as he tried to control his anger. He wanted to tear off his camouflage and destroy the mess hall and everyone in it. He wanted to call forth a spell that would remove the jungle floor from beneath this place. He wanted to watch as the defeated hunters and all of their equipment fell screaming into the center of the earth. He tamped down his fury, trying to find a sense of reason somewhere within the madness. Surmitang would not be impressed by something he could not witness. He would never follow him even if the threat to his kind vanished. Conor knew that he had to wait until the confrontation climaxed later this evening. Only then would the great tiger witness his feat of bravery.

Drawing in measured breaths, Conor's thoughts lapsed in importance as one of the men in the mess hall spoke up.

"So, what's our strategy for the hunt tonight, Baker?" asked one of the hunters, shoveling heaps of chicken and vegetables into his mouth.

"Watch your arse, and everyone else's," answered a tracker while nervously lifting a forkful of beef into his mouth. "Especially mine."

"Maybe we should put you out on one of those scarecrow poles, Flynn," said one of the more callous hunters in the group. He took a flask from his safari jacket and dropped a quick swig.

A round of applause and laughter rose up from all but one chair at the table. The lead hunter for tonight's expedition sat in front of a shiny, unblemished plate. He hadn't touched the food even though he felt very hungry. He understood something about a tiger's terrific senses the rest of these men did not. He also realized that out of the twenty men, five trackers and fifteen with automatic rifles, only a dozen would be coming back to the camp.

Baker had been quietly disturbed by the intelligence of the tigers for some time. Maybe the isolation of the island distinguished them from other species of tigers, or maybe his men just plain got lazy, he couldn't tell for sure. But in thirty-three years of hunting big game for profit, he had never encountered anything like this group of animals. In the first place, tigers never banded together, especially male tigers. They certainly never attacked or defended themselves in coordinated teams either, and never with any sort of appointed leader. But more than once he had spied one particularly large male, always up in the hills looking through the foliage of the jungle. On a few occasions the lead tiger had joined in the battle, but only after the hunters had taken one of his comrades. It scared him, watching wild animals work together this way. More than once he had almost cancelled the entire contract, but the owners of the project threw so much money at him he couldn't help but stay. And now the hunt was on again, and his men were acting like fools. He wondered how many of them knew that this hunt might be their last.

"We go as we always have," said Baker sternly. "Five rifleman in an arrow formation up front, with our trackers pulling in right behind them. Five men with rifles covering our rear, and five floaters. I want the best we have in the floater positions tonight. That means Simmons, Parham, Heller, Komick and Wolfe."

"I'm always floater," said the hunter with the nasty disposition. "I could outshoot any two men you picked tonight and you know it."

"You're off the hunt, Jeffries," responded Baker. "Any man foolish enough to drink while holding a rifle is foolish enough to shoot himself, or maybe someone else. You'll stay behind and guard the camp."

Jeffries sat in his chair, chewing on Baker's comment. He could barely stand the insult. He felt half-tempted to fire on Baker and take over the hunt himself. He looked into those icy blue eyes and thought better of it. Instead, he tried his best to hide his embarrassment and act casually.

"When we return from the hunt, those of us who do return," added Baker, "I want these carcasses cleaned up and cleared out of this mess hall. It's bad enough having to destroy such remarkable creatures. I certainly won't have their remains strewn about the floor like we're a bunch of savages."

Baker stood and slid his chair back from the table. "Alright, get your gear and meet me out by the front gate. Five minutes. Jeffries, you help the mess crew clean up this table."

Jeffries knocked his chair to the floor as he stood. He held his tongue, however, as well as his plans. He backed away from the table as the men filed out of the mess hall. He gave Baker a challenging glare as the hunt captain walked through the door. After everyone had gone, he huffed around the table a few times and then left the tent.

Conor sat in the corner of the mess hall watching everything transpire. He liked Baker because even though he made a living hunting animals, the man seemed to respect wildlife. He also respected him as a leader, and he saw that the other men did as well. Everyone except Jeffries, anyway. With Baker leading the expedition, Conor felt that his plan might just succeed, leaving very few casualties behind. If there were any others like Jeffries out on the hunt, then things could get dicey. He couldn't worry about that right now, though; the men were assembling at the gate. Conor hustled through the door and joined the line of men crowding around Baker.

"I don't want any heroes tonight," said the hunt captain. "Stay in formation, follow my orders, and shoot with purpose. With any luck we should be back in camp in less than three hours. Hopefully the only trophies we'll be carrying will be striped."

The men gave a rousing cry of support for their leader and broke out into their respective teams. The pattern of the expedition formed exactly as Baker had ordered, giving the men eyes in every direction. Should the tigers charge the group in anything but a sophisticated pattern, the men would cut them down like kittens.

Conor followed along behind the large group of men. He didn't bother to mask his footsteps since he walked around so many other pairs of boots. *The men did not act foolishly*, he thought as he watched them step through the jungle. *They moved like experienced hunters, every one of them.* He looked ahead of the group and into the rainforest. In another hundred yards they would all be deep into the jungle. The advantage of seeing every one of their comrades would be absent once they stepped into the forest, unless they tightened their formation. Conor felt oddly fascinated by the group of hunters, the tigers ahead in the jungle, and his role in the coming encounter.

Baker held his right hand high up in the air, fist closed. Every man in the expedition halted his forward progress. Wherever their feet touched the ground, they instantly froze there. It happened so quickly that Conor almost gave himself away by taking another step. He watched as Baker called one of the trackers forward, sending him into the brush. The group remained completely silent for the longest time. The only sounds Conor could hear came from the jungle. After a few minutes, the tracker emerged from the branches, shaking his head at Baker. The hunt captain opened his hand, extending his fingers out straight. Then he crossed his index and middle finger, signaling to the men that they should close ranks as the entered the rainforest. The group followed his instructions without a hitch in their step. Conor watched all of this with an increasing sense of dread. He harbored the terrible feeling that things would go badly for Surmitang on this night. The men were too disciplined, too purposeful. Baker knew his business too, and he looked like a man on a serious mission.

Conor decided to move ahead of the group and check on the tigers. He wanted to put some distance between himself and the hunters as well, so he decided to make as much noise as he could as he ran away from them. He let all three teams enter the jungle before he started traversing around to their right. When he saw all the men fighting their way through the thick brush, he called forth the spell he had used before, the one that pressed the foliage aside as he moved forward. After adjusting his camouflage suit, he started running by the group at a fairly good clip.

"Movement!" shouted one of the trackers.

"I hear it too, three o'clock," answered another tracker.

"I'm after it," shouted one of the hunters as he chambered a round into his automatic rifle. He broke through the foliage with amazing agility. Had he been able to see Conor, he might have had him cold.

"Simmons!" barked the hunt captain. "Back in formation, on the double! The rest of you men keep your eyes and ears open. The footsteps you heard were way too light to be a tiger's. Mind of the creators; use your heads, men! I won't lose one of you before we even find our targets. Now form up and follow the front wing."

Conor dashed ahead of the group of men, with trees, branches and roots bending out of his way as he moved along. He traveled quickly for about fifteen minutes before backing off to a brisk walk again. He felt the jungle becoming thicker as he traveled farther into the brush. He also noticed the ground rising slightly, as if he were moving up into a hilly area of the rainforest. Out of sheer instinct he decided to climb a large tree to see if he could scout out Surmitang's camp. Silently uttering the words to release the spell on the jungle, he jumped onto the base of the nearest tree. Climbing up the trunk like a leopard, he lifted himself high into the branches. The vantage point gave him an excellent view of the entire rainforest. He could hear Baker's men in the distance behind him. He kept his eyes focused forward, however, watching for any movement in the brush.

Trying not to look too hard for creatures that blended in perfectly with their surroundings, he finally spotted three tigers sleeping in the evening shade of a large tree. He let his eyes fall over the adjacent area and other tigers began popping up from the thick foliage. In a short time, he had spied two dozen tigers, all dozing in the leafy bedding of the rainforest. He panicked for a moment, wondering if the tigers had posted any sentries to their front or rear. It didn't seem so, and if Baker's men found them unprotected they would slaughter every last one of them. Conor squinted, trying to find Surmitang. The tigers looked so similar from this distance, he couldn't really tell the difference between the males. He had to do something, but what? If he woke the tigers then some of the men would perish. *But if he didn't wake the tigers?*

Without thinking he moved through the trees in order to

be closer to the big cats. Instead of climbing down and running through the forest, however, Conor merely jumped through the trees like a flying squirrel. Sailing from branch to branch and enjoying every second of it, he moved through about thirty trees in a matter of minutes. Without making a sound he had positioned himself right over the tigers. Even at this range he couldn't recognize Surmitang. Then he heard the sound of a single twig snapping, down on the ground and a little behind him. He turned his head and saw Surmitang standing on a small ridge overlooking the leafy valley where his pride slept. When Conor turned and looked down at him, the great tiger looked right into his eyes. The big cat didn't make a sound, because he couldn't be sure that anything was in the trees. Conor's camouflage kept Surmitang from making a positive identification, but the tiger knew he was there. He had purposely snapped the twig to see if anything would move in the tree. Conor smiled inside his camouflaged hood. He applauded the big cat for his intelligence, and at that moment he realized just how smart Surmitang had been. The other tigers in his pride weren't sleeping at all; they were setting the oldest trap in the book for Baker's men. Surmitang had probably scouted out the hunt from the time the men had left the encampment. Conor figured he had about ten minutes before he had to put his plans into effect.

Baker raised his hand again, fist closed. He expected his men to halt their progress, so he didn't look back to check on them. The jungle kept getting thicker as they moved forward, and he didn't like that at all. Every time the brush closed in on them, the tigers gained more of an advantage. There was still plenty of light, enough to hunt for another hour at least. Still, a nagging feeling irritated the back of his neck. Something didn't feel right about the hunt. They should have seen something by now, anything; even some of the tigers' normal prey would have made him feel better. So far, nothing had disturbed their progress through the jungle.

"What is it, chief?" asked Carrillo.

Baker almost jumped out of his shirt at the sound of his tracker's voice. Carrillo could sneak up on his own shadow his movements were so silent. "I can smell the tigers," answered Baker. "I can actually smell them, but we haven't seen any yet. Doesn't that seem a little odd to you?"

Carrillo answered without glancing over at his captain. "The cats, they are always crafty, Jefe, and this jungle is very thick. I think they will find us before we find them."

Baker looked over at his lead tracker. The man understood the jungle better than anyone he knew. He also understood the minds of large predators. Although the hunt captain had known this would be a bloody battle, hearing confirmation from a man he trusted sent a chill down his spine.

"Pass the word, Peter," instructed Baker. "Two lines, loose columns, not too deep. Tell the men to click off their safeties."

Carrillo left so silently Baker wondered if he had ever been there in the first place. He heard his men falling into their new formation and listened as the automatic rifles clicked into their ready positions. He turned his head once for a quick head count and then used his rifle barrel to pull a large leaf out of his line of sight. He looked at everything he could see for a full minute and then stepped further into the brush. His men followed behind him as quietly as they could.

Conor could see the hunters now. From his perch high above the ground, he watched as Baker and two of his men picked their way through the thick jungle. As he spied the rest of the expedition team coming through the foliage, he estimated they were roughly two hundred yards from the sleeping tigers. Conor gave them six or seven minutes until they reached the first of Surmitang's pride. The hunt captain, Baker, took no chances with his men. He and his two lead trackers eyeballed everything before taking the team another step. Once again Conor felt a measure of respect for the man whose mission was to hunt down and destroy a respected adversary.

He switched his line of sight back to the tigers, saw them "sleeping" soundly in the bed of leaves. He glanced back at Surmitang to make sure he still watched over his pride. The great tiger had disappeared; Conor searched the area frantically trying to find him. With a pang of horror, he saw the big cat crouched in the rainforest, creeping toward the group of men. He was heading straight for them, and looking for all intents and purposes like he planned to attack the column alone. Conor fought the urge to call out to him.

"Tiger tracks, chief," whispered Carrillo as he touched Baker's shoulder. "Big cats, males for sure, and a lot of them."

Baker closed his fist and held it high into the air. After a moment he folded in his middle fingers, leaving only his index and pinky raised. His men moved silently and efficiently. The hunt was on; the tigers loomed close by, and whoever ended up as prey depended on who could be sneakier, man or beast.

Conor watched the men break out into a circular formation. Nothing could penetrate their perimeter unless it fell down from above them. The trackers shouldered ten-gauge shotguns in case the tigers broke through the first line of defense. They served only as comfort sticks, however, because if a tiger made it through the automatic weapons they would be on top of the trackers before they raised the shotguns an inch.

Conor flicked his eyes, watching as Surmitang crept closer to the group of men. He stopped his forward progress suddenly, roughly fifty feet in front of the hunt captain. Conor strained himself trying to figure out what the great tiger had on his mind, when suddenly it came to him. Surmitang wanted to wait for the group to close to a certain distance. Only then would he give up his position and reveal himself to the hunters. Waiting until the last moment, he would lead the frantic band of men right into the largest pack of males they had ever seen. He planned to massacre them once and for all. Conor could not let that happen, but he wouldn't allow the tigers to be slaughtered either. Sailing amongst the branches of the trees again, he positioned himself directly at the midpoint of the battleground. He had the men to his left and the tigers to his right. If the mêlée didn't become too disorganized, he might be able to keep most of the combatants safe. He watched Surmitang's body tense while the tip of his tail wriggled back and forth quickly. *Only seconds left until he bolts,* thought Conor.

"Baker, BAKER!" a voice roared from within the rainforest. "I told you I was the best floater in this group! The best hunter, too, and the best shot by far!"

"Mind of the creators!" whispered Baker to a tense but unruffled Carrillo. "It's Jeffries, and he's drunk out of his mind. The idiot's going to get us all killed. If we survive this, I swear I'll dip him in syrup and bury him in an anthill!"

Jeffries crashed through the forest using his rifle as a machete. He fell many times, swearing as he kept pushing his body off the ground. Covered with a stinky coating of whisky-smelling sweat, the inebriated hunter bellowed again, calling out for the hunt captain.

"BAKER! I'm here to rescue the team. Put me on the tip of the wedge and I'll shoot the first five of those miserable cats we see. Bakerrrrr!"

Conor couldn't believe what he was seeing. As if he weren't juggling enough potential outcomes, now this drunken fool walks right into the middle of everything! He looked pretty far gone, too, which only complicated matters further. He offered a silent wish to the creators for this man's life, because he knew he would lose it, and soon. Then he checked Surmitang one more time. The great tiger had shifted his focus away from the larger group. He now aimed his huge, three hundred pound frame directly at Jeffries. Conor gripped a large branch as he waited for what he knew would happen next.

"BAKER! How far are you going to make me walk? I know you fools are out here somewhere! BAKER!"

The next phrase collapsed silently on Jeffries' lips. After ripping aside a large leaf and stepping over a thick, twisting root, Jeffries jaw dropped and his eyes went wide. The biggest Sumatran tiger he had ever seen stood no more than five feet from him. For a second, Jeffries examined the beauty of the regal tiger, with its huge colorful face close enough to touch. Then he regained himself, realizing his life lay in his ability to kill the beast before it slaughtered him. With his movements slowed by alcohol, the intoxicated, terrified hunter raised his weapon as quickly as he could.

Surmitang reacted with a swiftness bred into every wild cat since the dawn of time. He recognized Jeffries instantly. This man had not only taken two of his prime females, but he had mutilated them in plain sight of the pride. Firing repeatedly into their lifeless carcasses and roaring with deranged laughter, the man had set himself up as the number one target for every tiger in the jungle. Surmitang bared his huge fangs and loosed a menacing snarl into

Jeffries' stunned eyes. Every muscle in the huge tiger's body tensed as he prepared to tear the man to shreds.

Surmitang launched his massive bulk into Jeffries with a passion born out of months of increasing frustration. The proud tiger had done everything he could to protect his pride from the invading horde. Now, with this one strike, the big cat would release his pent up rage once and for all. He hit Jeffries on the shoulders simultaneously with both enormous paws, knocking the man twelve feet through the air. The man's weapons, his rations, and most of the sweat clinging to his pores flew forward as his body left the ground. A drunken wheeze followed his implements as the tiger knocked the wind out of him with his attack. Surmitang landed on all fours directly on top of a stunned and whimpering Jeffries.

Remarkably, the hunter found enough sense to unclip a large knife from his belt. He ripped the blade from its sheath and stabbed wildly at Surmitang's flank. One of the blows seemed to penetrate the striped fur on its way to the rib cage, but Jeffries failed to force the blade in at the correct angle. The last lunge of Jeffries' life fluttered into heavy fur and skin, damaging nothing except the great tiger's pride. Surmitang roared wildly as he stamped down onto the arm that held the knife. As the thunderous call died away, the big cat slammed his powerful jaws over Jeffries' throat. With all oxygen to Jeffries' brain cut off, the man perished in the iron grasp of Surmitang's death grip.

"Mind of the creators," said Carrillo. "Look at that!"

Baker had given the men a sign to hold their positions during the attack on Jeffries. He knew the man was finished as soon as he heard him coming through the jungle, and he didn't want his men needlessly harmed as he tried to rescue him. The man had violated the cardinal rule of hunting, paying the price for his stupidity. But Baker couldn't believe what he saw happening now.

"Jeffries must weigh close to three hundred pounds," said Carrillo. "That huge cat is dragging him off somewhere. Fool or not, we can't deny him a proper burial."

Nodding once to his lead tracker, Baker lifted his hunting rifle, sighted into the wide scope, and took steady aim at the retreating tiger. He fired one shot slightly over the big cat's head and stood stunned as it turned and stared right into his eyes. It seemed to be taunting him. *Tigers never do that*, he thought, *no animal does that but humans, because they were the only mammals capable of reason.* He lifted the rifle again and prepared to sight directly into the big cat's shoulder. He lowered the weapon, however, when he saw that the tiger now carried Jeffries' limp body on his back like a protective cloak. He had seen enough and he called for his men to follow him.

"After him, men!" he shouted. "Hold your formation and fire at will. This will be the last hunt one way or another; it's either them or us! Remember the other ambushes and keep your wits about you. The man who bags that big one gets a free weekend off the island."

Conor watched from his perch high in the air as the hunters broke into a slow run. They whooped and yelled after the hunt captain cut them loose and allowed them to approach the tigers freely. He watched the men with an instinctive feeling that many of them would share the same fate as the big man wriggling within Surmitang's powerful jaws. As if confirming this last thought, every tiger in Surmitang's pride rose and shook the leaves from their striped fur. They watched as their leader dropped the carcass of the arrogant hunter at their feet. With a few quick chuffs of instruction, he sent the restless group of cats into battle against the invading horde.

"Show them no mercy," said the big cat, in a language only they could understand. The pride turned and disappeared into the rainforest. Conor couldn't see even one of them inside the heavy cloak of the jungle. He stood on his perch wondering what in the name of the creators he could do to stop the carnage.

Rapid-fire gunshots reverberated around the jungle. The men were shooting wildly, firing at anything that moved. Wicked sounding snarls and bristling roars preceded the sounds of huge cats crashing through the jungle toward their prey. Horrifying screams were cut off in mid-breath as the enormous tigers pounced on their prey with feverish intensity. The men kept firing into the jungle, hoping to catch a flank or a leg by random luck. For the most part they missed their targets entirely, but every once in a while, the pained squeal of an injured cat echoed through the jungle. This only fueled the fury of the rest of the pride, sending them into an even more murderous rage. They focused their anger at the hunters wherever they found them, dragging them down and holding them until another cat jumped in to finish them off.

Surmitang waited until the last of his pride flew into action before entering the rainforest. He wanted the entire team of hunters occupied so he could sneak up on his adversary unannounced. Confident that his pride held the upper hand, he silently stalked in a wide path around the battleground. Sensing his prey more than seeing him, the great tiger poked his huge, furry face through the brush behind his foe. Surmitang spied the lead tracker holding a shotgun in quivering hands, and stepped gingerly through the brush and padded up behind him. He knew that if the tracker was stationed here, the lead hunter must not be far away. He wanted the lead hunter more than any other man in the group, and if he had to take this other one as well, then so be it. He smelled the tracker now, and just as he peered over the man's shoulder, he heard the unmistakable sound of a rifle bolt locking a bullet in place. Surmitang's body froze; only his head moved to turn toward the sound. Baker stood less than a dozen feet away, bracing a large hunting rifle against his shoulder. He had foolishly fallen into the hunter's trap, and while the tracker shivered with fear, the lead hunter stood steadily, rifle in place and fully prepared to fire.

"Carrillo," said Baker without emotion. "Turn around slowly and don't make any quick moves. Whatever you do, don't use your shotgun on this tiger. It won't hurt him. It will only anger him, and I don't want him any hotter than he already is." Carrillo turned his head and froze. A big male, the biggest Sumatran male he had ever seen, had walked right up behind him without his knowing it. He kept his eyes on Baker, however, and didn't seem interested in anyone else at the moment. He felt raw, icy fear as he listened to the rest of the hunters and some of the tigers perishing in the jungle. In the midst of all the killing, this cat had come specifically for them; he knew it all the way down to his bones. He didn't even know if Baker's rifle could stop it either. A cat this big could be on top of you before you even thought about reacting.

"Take it easy, big fella," said Baker softly to the massive tiger standing between him and Carrillo. "I know why you're angry, and I don't blame you. Humans can be pretty darn stupid when it comes to nature. I only work for them."

As if trying to swallow Baker's words, Surmitang snarled menacingly. He didn't seem to care for the hunt captain's remarks.

"Chief," said Carrillo, "you'd better shoot him. I don't think he's here to socialize."

Baker pressed the stock of his rifle against his cheek and sighted through the scope. Looking at the great tiger standing only a few yards ahead of him, he whispered softly under his breath. "I know you can't believe this, but this is the last thing I want to do." The hunt captain curled his finger around the trigger and squeezed it gently.

The bullet left the rifle barrel just as Surmitang pounced toward Carrillo. A split second later, the bullet, the two men, and the big cat stopped as if captured in some sort of bizarre photograph. Baker stood motionless with his rifle propped up against his shoulder. Carrillo cringed with his hands held in front of his contorted face. Surmitang's hind paws still touched the ground, but the rest of his impressive bulk stood frozen in mid-pounce. With his huge fangs bared in a horrifying grimace, the great tiger was a study of ferocious intent. Only the golden eyes showed any motion at all as they tried to find some sense in what had just occurred.

Conor held onto one of the tree's sturdier branches as he looked down on the frozen carnage below him. In an area roughly the size of a football field, men and tigers stared at each other in mute horror as they tried to figure out why they suddenly couldn't move. Human and feline eyeballs jerked back and forth and up and down, looking anywhere for a possible explanation. No one – cat or human – could call out to their fellows. They remained in whatever position they found themselves, wondering what kind of crazy magic had descended upon their field of combat. Conor counted the number of live participants from his perch high in the trees. He calculated that four men and one tiger had lost their lives so far. If he could keep the damage to that level he would consider his part in this tragedy a success.

Keeping his camouflage suit in place, Conor climbed down

through the branches and hopped onto the ground. He walked through the battlefield, looking at individual hunters and tigers as he passed by them. Every time he walked by one of the hunters, he murmured a quick spell causing the man to lose control of his rifle. After discharging their clips, the weapons followed Conor as he strolled through the rainforest, trailing after him like beer cans behind the car of a newly married couple. Soon he had almost a dozen automatic rifles and a handful of shotguns tagging along behind him. He also had quite a few pairs of eyes following him as well. Every human and every tiger kept their eyes glued to the strange pack of weapons bouncing along on the floor of the jungle. Fury and anger vacated their eyes as they saw this bizarre scene unfold before them. The emotions were replaced by bewilderment and fear, for neither tiger nor hunter had ever witnessed anything like this before.

Feeling quite certain that he now had control of every weapon in the hunters' arsenal, Conor took a straight path toward the outer edge of the jungle. He wanted to confront the hunt captain directly, and he wanted Surmitang to witness it. He walked purposefully, dragging the strange menagerie of weapons behind him. As he approached the break in the rainforest, he could see Baker and the tracker frozen solid in the clearing. He saw Surmitang as well, or at least parts of his magnificent striped coat. He marveled at the tremendous strength in the tiger's body. The cat had huge, muscular shoulders that looked extremely impressive. Surmitang's frozen leap had not only extended the massive frame to its fullest, but it had also flexed nearly every muscle along the graceful body. He looked absolutely beautiful, and Conor felt a familiar surge rising within him. He couldn't understand how anyone from any world could harm such a creature. He wiped away the anger with a thought – he would not jeopardize Surmitang's safety with emotion. Pressing a wide cluster of branches aside, he stepped into the clearing. The rifles followed, much to the dismay of the tracker, Carrillo.

Carrillo tried to swallow as he saw the automatic weapons and shotguns bouncing through the trees toward them. He couldn't move his throat, however, so he just flicked his eyes over to Baker. He watched the hunt captain's eyes follow the weapons as they came closer to the tiger. When they came abreast of the big cat, they rose into the air and then crashed down at its feet. Even the tiger looked at the freakish scene with fear in his big, golden eyes. Carrillo could tell it wanted nothing to do with this strange occurrence.

"Mr. Baker," said Conor, in a voice that seemed to come from nowhere. "I'm here to inform you that your hunt is over." Without waiting for a response, Conor removed the hunting rifle from Baker's hands. Recoiling the bolt, he dislodged the bullet currently loaded into the firing chamber. After securing the weapon, he threw it roughly onto the pile of rifles. He stared at the stack of firearms, beating back the fury trying to fight its way up into his mind. He despised these men and their mission. Every time he glanced at Surmitang the fire became even hotter.

Conor uttered a single sentence as he looked at Baker. The hunt captain almost fell after Conor released his body from the immobilizing spell. Instead, he stood completely still, wondering how he and his men might live through this frightening ordeal.

"Who are you?" he asked. "What are you, and where are you?"

Conor unzipped the camouflage hood and rolled it back over his head. He wiped the sweat from his eyes and slicked back his hair. Saying nothing to Baker, he checked Carrillo and Surmitang for any signs of movement. He wanted to be certain that the discharge spell had affected only the hunt captain.

"A t-teenager," Baker stuttered. "You couldn't be more than eighteen years old!"

"Sixteen, actually," responded Conor. "But I hardly see how that matters. Before you say anything else, I want you to watch something, Mr. Baker." Conor pulled the camouflage jersey over his head and tied it around his waist. Extending his right arm toward the loosely stacked pile of rifles, he drew a sparkling, silver corridor directly above them. When the corridor membrane settled, Conor lowered the portal over the rifles. Baker stood there with eyes wide, watching the weapons disappear from the rainforest. After the corridor swallowed them completely, it folded itself up and vanished into thin air. Conor walked over to the spot where the rifles lay just a second ago. He swished his leg through the leaves and grass, confirming the fact that they no longer existed. Carrillo watched the young man perform his supernatural feats with a growing sense of fear in his eyes.

"Okay," said Baker. "Now you've removed our weapons. I don't know who you are or where you came from, but I strongly suggest you leave this jungle immediately. We have a contract to fulfill here, and as much as I don't like it, I mean to see it through. What's to stop us from securing additional weapons and coming back another day?"

Conor couldn't hold his anger back any longer. The image of these tremendous animals being slaughtered for material gain was too much for him to bear. He wheeled on Baker, stepping toward the hunt captain.

"Watch your words, Mr. Baker. I can freeze you again with a thought. If I feel so inclined, I might release every one of these tigers and let them finish you and your men off at their leisure."

The hunt captain kept his mouth shut. He had tried to bully

the stranger but it hadn't worked. The young man's eyes told him all he needed to know. That and the fact that he believed what the kid said about letting the tigers run wild on them. Whoever he was, Baker wasn't about to trifle with him. He couldn't possibly imagine where he got them, but he obviously wielded tremendous powers.

"Alright," said Baker. "Release my tracker and then we'll talk."

"I don't feel like chasing a rabbit through the jungle right now," Conor replied. "Your tracker will bolt the instant I set him free. I've seen the communication between you two. Now if you don't mind, I'd like to tell you what's going to happen here today."

"Please do," said Baker, folding his arms.

Conor gestured toward the rest of the battlefield. "You, your men, your entire camp and all of your machinery are leaving this rainforest permanently. I will guarantee safe passage back to where you came from. Make no mistake though, if you ever return to this island, or disturb these animals in any way, you'll be making the biggest mistake of your life. I don't want to harm anyone, Mr. Baker. I sensed your apprehension about destroying these tigers, and that impressed me. As a matter of fact, your men can thank you for their lives. If you had been like that oaf Jeffries, this day might have turned out quite differently.

"In the next fifteen minutes you will find your entire encampment transported to wherever you'd like it to go. Your men will not be harmed during the transition, I assure you. When you arrive at your destination, it will be up to you to convince whatever authorities you deem worthy that this island is off limits."

Baker scoffed, cutting Conor off in mid-statement. "What do you expect me to tell them, that a high school teenager with supernatural powers has sealed off an entire region of our world?"

"You can tell them whatever you like," answered Conor. "It will be on your conscience, Mr. Baker. Be assured, though, that anyone who returns to this island with the intent of destroying these magnificent tigers will never leave this place alive."

Baker and Conor eyed each other for the longest time, both of them waiting for the other to blink.

"Do you doubt my ability to enforce this threat?" pressed Conor.

"No, no I don't," replied Baker. "Although I can't for the life of me figure out your motive. Why in the name of the creators would you be so protective of an anonymous group of tigers on an island in the middle of nowhere?"

"If I told you, you'd never believe it," said Conor. "It's a worthwhile cause though, Mr. Baker, I promise you. But you must leave now, because my time grows short. I'm going to release your men, but first I want you to set a clear image in your mind of where it is you'd like me to send you. It must be a place large enough to accommodate all of your equipment, your entire camp, and all of your men, do you understand?"

"Go ahead," said Baker, not really convinced that the event could occur.

Carrillo crumpled to the ground the instant Conor released him. As he scrambled back to a standing position he heard the other men on the team shouting and running toward him. He stared at the strange young man standing between him and Baker, but he did not charge him or threaten him in any way. He turned his eyes to the hunt captain, who had his eyes closed in a look of intense concentration.

Then something happened to Baker that caused Carrillo's breath to stop dead in his throat. A bizarre looking filament seemed to emerge from his chest. It grew into a large rectangle of silvery light that rose up over his head. Just as Carrillo was about to warn the hunt captain about the weird light, he noticed the same type of silver light rising up from his own body. It morphed into a square above his head, just as Baker's had done. If he moved, the pattern of light followed him, always maintaining its position directly above his head. He turned at the sound of almost a dozen men running toward them. He saw every one of them shadowed by the same bizarre halo of silvery light. Carrillo turned back to look at the strange young man who had caused all this to happen. He looked at Conor and uttered the last words he would ever say in this rainforest.

"Hijo loco!" whispered the lead tracker.

Back at the camp, a monstrous event occurred that paralleled the emergence of the individual corridors. Those left behind by the hunters ran from hut to hut trying to find some sort of protection from the immense silver walls growing out of the ground. Coming from nowhere, the gigantic pulsating corridors grew to a height of seventy-feet before joining together at the sides. They formed a huge rectangular box that enveloped the entire encampment. After connecting with each other, the sound of the walls increased mightily, emitting a deafening whine that caused everything in the camp to tremble. The makeshift huts fell apart one by one, causing the cooks and attendants to rush to the center of the encampment. They huddled there together, grasping each other for comfort. Their heads turned continually, looking at the mammoth walls now sliding toward them. What happened next caused all of them to scream in terror.

Directly overhead, another huge silver sheet began taking shape in the sky. First, the texture of the image solidified. Then, the sheet expanded rapidly, finally stretching to the exact size of the four walls surrounding the terrified workers. The silver ceiling lowered itself down onto the four walls, creating a massive box-shaped corridor. The glowing container swallowed the entire encampment. Everything the hunters brought with them lay within a surging rectangle of pulsating energy.

The workers at the camp watched as the walls slowly slid toward them. They saw some of the rubble around the camp disappear as the walls moved closer. They gasped as the giant earthmovers were swallowed by the corridor. The huge machines finally disappeared altogether, leaving only a few structures. As they screamed prayers to their individual deities, the walls rolled over the camp workers. As if cleansing the jungle of the encampment once and for all, the immense sheet that served as the ceiling dropped down onto the floor of the rainforest.

The pulsating walls vanished and the silver ceiling disappeared into thin air. The jungle looked as it always had, long before men came to destroy it. As if waiting for a pathway to open, a mild wind began to retake the area where the encampment formerly stood. Small blades of grass and leaves began to dance around the floor of the rainforest. Trees extended their branches toward the sunny sky, hoping for an afternoon rain. No sounds of human occupation disturbed the jungle. It looked and felt as if the hunters and their party had never been there.

Conor watched as the corridors overtook Baker and Carrillo. Within seconds, the hunt captain, his lead tracker and the rest of the hunters vanished, hopefully on their way to a safe place. Conor had read disbelief in Baker's eyes as the hunter visualized a destination for him and his men. He hoped that Baker at least had the sense to give him the benefit of the doubt. After dwelling on it for a moment, he turned his attention to the reason he came here in the first place.

Surmitang was still in mid-pounce. The great tiger rolled his huge eyes from Conor to the jungle and back again. The big cat had never felt fear in his life, but these events had nearly peeled the fur right off his back. Returning his eyes to the strange young human, Surmitang wondered how the other tigers in his pride had fared.

"Don't worry," said Conor as he stroked the gorgeous striped fur on the tiger's cheek. "Can you understand me, Surmitang? Do you know what I'm saying when I tell you that I came here to save your pride? Do you understand that the price for my intervention is your service to the creators for the rest of your life?"

Surmitang rolled his eyes. He wanted desperately to know about the other tigers in his group. He had a strange feeling about this young man standing in front of him. He couldn't pinpoint it exactly, but something seemed very familiar about him.

Conor released Surmitang's cheek and stepped back a few feet. "I'm going to reverse the spell now. I need you to come with me, Surmitang, but I'll understand if you'd rather cut me down and tear me apart. After what you and your pride have been through, I will certainly understand." Lowering his voice to an almost imperceptible level, Conor uttered the words that released the spell on the great tiger. Surmitang fell lightly on his feet, completely balanced and ready to strike. But he did not lash out at Conor. He snarled in confusion and paced back and forth a few times, but he made no threatening move toward the young man. Conor stood perfectly still. He didn't say anything to his brother Champion. He didn't try to convince him to leave with him, he simply did nothing. He wanted Surmitang to believe he posed no threat to him at all.

All around them, huge trees and branches strained forward as a dozen furious tigers crashed through the jungle to save their leader. Every one of them turned their eyes and their intentions toward Conor after bursting into the clearing. Two of the larger tigers slowly approached him with the worst of intentions. They stopped, turning toward their leader when Surmitang growled a stern warning to leave the young man alone. One of the big males immediately backed off. The other, the largest of the pride next to Surmitang, maintained his position but did not threaten Conor directly. This particular tiger had challenged Surmitang for leadership more than once in the past. For him, this could be an opportunity to establish dominance over the pride. After looking back at Surmitang, the big cat snarled horribly and vaulted toward Conor.

Having anticipated the tiger's move, Surmitang met him in mid-air less than a yard from Conor. The impact of the two tigers colliding so close to him nearly knocked him off his feet. Although the cats growled and snarled at each other, the struggle lasted only a few seconds. After knocking the wind from his opponent, Surmitang rolled him over, securing his submission. The large male offered a few insubordinate chuffs, but he didn't challenge his leader again. Surmitang moved away, looking at each member of his pride in turn. He seemed to be conveying orders so that no one would lay a paw on this human. None of the cats disobeyed him, and Conor felt safe for the first time since he released the immobilization spell on the pride.

Feeling uncertain about what to do next, Conor attempted to speak to the group of tigers. Some of them lumbered down to a resting position, and a few even began cleaning their fur. Secure in the knowledge that Surmitang would handle the situation from this point forward, the rest of the pride placed their attention on other matters.

"The hunters will never bother your pride again," said Conor to a bewildered Surmitang. "I've arranged it so they can never return to this jungle. Your brothers and sisters are free to live out their lives in peace."

As Conor expected, Surmitang looked right through him. He could no more understand the young man's words than he could understand the voice of the rain or the wind. The great tiger stepped forward and nudged Conor with his huge, furry head. When Conor tried to move aside or get out of the way, Surmitang adjusted his direction, nudging him again and again. He seemed to be attempting to move Conor away from the pride, or maybe out of the rainforest altogether. When Conor darted around the big cat and returned to the pride, Surmitang let it be known that he wasn't the least bit amused. The human had performed a great deed, and Surmitang's actions were meant to repay the debt. By gently forcing him out of the rainforest, the big cat was essentially allowing him to leave the jungle alive. He would not be humiliated in front of his pride, however, and if Conor didn't take full advantage of his generosity, then he wouldn't be responsible for what might happen to him.

Conor waited for Surmitang to return to the center of the pride. The great Champion of the Crossworlds met the young man head on, trying again to convince him to leave the jungle. Instead of resisting this time, Conor allowed himself to be manhandled by the huge cat. Surmitang lowered his head, using it like a battering ram to push the human farther away from his pride. With his eyes looking toward the ground, the big cat never noticed the glistening corridor that had appeared between two of the larger trees in the jungle. While altering his path slightly here and there, Conor let Surmitang drive him forward so they would eventually intercept the portal. The young man focused his thoughts toward the Lady of the Light, asking for her assistance with Surmitang. He would need her help if things went awry before they reached the portal. If the big cat looked up even for a second, he could shy away from the strange silver wall in his path. Conor kept backing up toward the shimmering corridor, using a small part of his mind to measure the remaining distance before they penetrated the membrane.

With less than ten feet separating the young man from his goal, Conor heard a mighty roar echo around the jungle. The tiger that tried to attack him earlier, the one that Surmitang punished, signaled a clear warning to his pack leader. A few harsh chuffs followed the initial blast, just in case Surmitang failed to hear the message.

The leader of the pride lifted his head slowly. He took a long look at the brilliantly lit corridor directly in front of him. Then he turned his huge head, shifting his gaze toward Conor. A low, thick, menacing rumble circled the inside of the tiger's belly. Surmitang peered into Conor's soul; the tiger's golden eyes seemed to flare when he finally roared his disapproval. Bristling with apprehension, the great tiger didn't quite understand the meaning of the corridor. He did, however, view it as a threat to his pride. Long ago, he learned that anything peculiar or unique might prove to be terribly dangerous, and this strange, glowing doorway certainly seemed curious. Glancing at the strange portal again, he stepped away from the young man. Aside from an occasional glance at the corridor, he kept his eyes locked onto Conor's gaze the entire time.

Trying to look very relaxed, Conor moved closer to the corridor. Standing right next to the glistening membrane, he extended his arm directly into the sparkling wall. He retracted it, showing the great tiger he had received no injuries by establishing contact with the portal. He watched as Surmitang's jowls rose up into a snarl, exposing his huge fangs, and he tried his very best to calm the big cat with a few soothing words. While speaking softly to his fellow Champion, Conor kept inserting different appendages into the membrane. After removing them, he would make an exaggerated attempt to show Surmitang that he had not been harmed by the massive silver screen. Conor smiled as Surmitang took one step toward the corridor, and then another. He smiled, signaling to the tiger to come closer. He almost thought his journey had been completed, when he heard the rest of the pride approaching through the jungle.

The group of majestic tigers burst through the leafy passage one at a time, with Surmitang's rival leading the way. When everyone had assembled around the corridor, the large tiger that had previously tried to attack Conor swept the ground in front him with a large, meaty paw. After scratching out a suitable place for himself, he lowered his great bulk to the ground, placing his forepaws directly in front of him. The other tigers in the pride followed his lead, and soon every male from Surmitang's family sat comfortably around their leader. They seemed to be waiting for a final decision about what to do with the strange human.

Conor watched as Surmitang calmly walked over to his rival. After staring into the golden eyes for an uncomfortable amount of time, the great tiger lowered his head and touched the whiskers of the next leader of his pride. He seemed to be conveying confidence in his brother. By doing so, he let the males of the pride know that he would serve as their leader from this point forward. After emitting a few soft chuffs to his fiercest rival, Surmitang turned and padded over to Conor. Although he made no move toward the corridor, Conor knew that the big cat had finally understood him. He knew his destiny lay beyond the shimmering screen of silvery light.

"As they did when selecting Eha," said Conor softly, "the creators chose wisely when they asked you to fight for the Crossworlds. Come with me to the glade of Champions." Conor walked into the membrane with his head turned sideways. He watched as the great tiger kept the pace with him. Without showing any fear at all, Surmitang left his former life behind and marched into the sparkling portal.

The Lady of the Light sat upon a ring-shaped stone by the lake. Her hair fluttered in a gentle breeze curving through the rusty hills and out over the crisp, blue water. Always wide open and alert, her silver-coated eyes, highlighted with multicolored hues, stared at something roughly twenty feet away. To anyone else, the place where her eyes rested might have revealed nothing. She alone could see the exit channel of a corridor called forth by her magical powers. After hearing Conor's silent call for assistance, she had produced the shimmering wall in the jungle of Indonesia. After providing the method of transportation for her two guests, she calmly seated herself at the foot of a rocky hill in the glade. Waiting patiently for something she could neither hear nor see, the Lady focused her mind on Conor's journey. If she could help him, she certainly would. Amazed by his progress so far, the council allowed her a certain amount of latitude with her capable Champion.

She smiled as Conor and Surmitang stepped through the membrane and into the glade of Champions. They appeared to materialize out of thin air, and, although they looked somewhat unkempt, neither of them looked terribly bad. She looked at Conor feeling a strong surge of pride. The young man kept completing journey after journey, always successful and ready to serve the Crossworlds without complaint. She thought of the young boy who had penetrated the barriers between worlds so many years ago. During his journey with Purugama, the ten-year-old had clutched the cougar's fur with a glazed expression at every turn. Yet, even at such a young age, Conor had thrown himself into the fray to defend his new friend and mentor. Barely six years later, after surpassing everyone's expectations, he sauntered casually into the glade alongside a beast that only hours ago would have gladly torn him to shreds.

She turned her attention to the big cat, who suddenly forgot all about Conor. After coming through the corridor unscathed, Surmitang took one look at the Lady and sprinted briskly in her direction. Stopping just a few feet in front of her, he crouched down and dropped his belly lightly on the ground. Extending his forepaws out in front of him, he looked up at the Lady as he released a soft chuff. His large golden eyes held her exquisite silvery gaze.

"Surmitang," cooed the Lady of the Light, extending her right hand toward him. "Will you not honor me by allowing my fingers to stroke your luxurious fur? After all, has it not been many months since we have had the pleasure of seeing each other?"

The great tiger bounced up from his crouched position. Shaking his ample coat, he walked the last few steps toward his mistress. Instead of letting her close her hand around a fistful of striped fur, however, Surmitang nudged his head against her arm. He slid his three hundred pound bulk gracefully along her knees and shins, letting her feel the bristling muscles underneath his silky fur. Emitting a soft chuff every few seconds, he continued rubbing his shoulders, flanks, and haunches back and forth along the Lady's body. When she finally grasped his fur, scratching and massaging every part of his huge frame, Surmitang purred so loudly that the Lady and Conor smiled broadly at the big cat. Conor could tell the great tiger was truly happy to see her.

"Thank you, Conor," said the Lady. "I know these are not simple journeys. Surmitang has always held a special place in my heart, and I want you to know how appreciative I am. You are now half-way to your goal, young Champion. You look exhausted, however. Even though our need to continue is urgent, I believe a rest would do you good."

Conor immediately straightened his posture. "I wish to continue, if that's cool with you. I can't allow Janine to be hurt; I *won't* allow it. If I take time to rest, will that be the interval Seefra needs to break the spell on the keys? With all due respect, my Lady, throw the next corridor in front of me. Let me move on to collect Therion."

"Our greatest Champion will not simply walk into a corridor for you," replied the Lady, "nor will he be tricked into a rash decision. You will need to be at your very best when you walk into his territory, Conor. I highly advise an afternoon's rest. We cannot afford any mistakes at this stage, for Seefra has already reversed the spell on the first of the five keys."

"*What?*" said Conor with shock and surprise. He advanced as he spoke. "Then I must leave now! Who can say how long it will take for him to discover the code for the remaining keys! My Lady, call the corridor! Let me go now!"

The Lady of the Light stroked Surmitang one final time, dismissing the great tiger momentarily. She rose elegantly, brushing off her robe in a precise, graceful gesture. Her steps were so soft she seemed to float over to Conor. Touching him lightly on the forehead, she caused his eyelids to fall. His body slumped, and she caught him in a blanket of sparkling silver. After placing his sleeping body in a prone position, she waved her hand over the ground beyond his right shoulder. A glistening silver water wall emerged from the soil, rising up next to the young man. It would provide shade, nourishment and medical care to Conor at a highly accelerated rate. Within an hour or two, the Crossworlds Champion would be fully restored. The water wall would supply all of the important nutrients, the appropriate care, and the equivalent of an entire day's rest. The Lady dropped her own eyelids as she uttered a few chosen incantations. The healing waters began trickling over the top of the wall. Hundreds of silver-coated lights began flickering all over its face. The Lady of the Light stood next to Conor, chanting softly and adding her strength to the recuperative powers of the wall. Surmitang had walked away, presumably with instructions from the Lady to find Eha. He would join his brother Champion and wait for the Lady to return to them. With Purugama and Ajur already somewhere in the glade, the Crossworlds Champions were very close to their original company. They lacked only Therion and Maya, and somehow, as he padded through the glade looking for Eha, Surmitang believed that Conor would succeed in bringing both of them home.

CHAPTER NINETEEN

Janine felt the floor of her cell solidify with a sensation of shifting underneath her body. She hadn't slept in two days due to the instability of her cell tiles. She could sense the frustration seeping out of Seefra's laboratory during the last week or so. He had convinced himself that the other keys would be easy to capture after successfully reversing the spell on the first, and as a result, he exploded in rage day after day with each failure. She heard the vicious way he treated his servants after each defeat in his laboratory. Rather than accepting the blame, he would lash out at the closest shadow warrior. Sometimes he would simply annihilate them, leaving the others standing in fear. At other times he would disfigure entire groups of soldiers, turning all of them into grotesque creatures. Some would find their legs missing, only to see them attached to another warrior. They in turn might have four arms but no way to transport themselves. On occasion, the dark master would reverse his cruelty and return the shadow warriors' bodies to them. Sometimes, however, he would incinerate them rather than have their ugliness tarnish the perfection of his laboratory. It became clear to everyone that Seefra was quickly losing control of himself. The drive to uncover the secret to the keys had utterly consumed him.

The one constant around Janine's cell was the ceaseless

destruction of Seefra's captives. There seemed to be no end to the number of creatures coming into the chamber of cells. She had tried on occasion to count the number of crystal cells dangling in the chasm just to keep her mind occupied. Even after many attempts, however, she couldn't come up with a constant figure. The cells would disappear and captives would fall from the dizzying heights, and then more prisoners would arrive. They slid into the chasm as if gliding along some invisible cable. Hundreds of crystal cells crowded into the chasm on any given day. There might have been over a thousand at different times. Every day, Janine could always depend on a number of hopeless creatures meeting their doom in the jaws of the horrible creature that lived at the bottom of the chasm.

Every time she saw a captive falling to the depths of the chasm, she screamed to smother the horrible shrieks that rose up from the murky mists below her. Sometimes she slammed her hands over her ears and sang as loudly as she could, hoping to drive out the sound of another creature's demise. At other times she slumped against the crystal wall of her cell, watching in horror as the poor creature fell to its doom. The end always occurred in the same fashion; the captive disappeared into the mists, a few seconds went by and then she would hear the echo of the terrified cries. Janine would lay there, wailing for another creature she didn't even know.

But a different sort of scream pierced through the silence this morning. After realizing her cell contained a complete floor for the first time in days, Janine stood and looked at all the other cells in the chasm. Creatures of every kind rose in their cells as well, walking gingerly at first but more confidently after a few steps. Something had happened in the laboratory – something positive for Seefra – Janine felt sure of that. If he treated his prisoners this well, there had to be a reason. She clutched the remaining four keys in her coat pocket. Hoping for the best, she didn't act surprised at all when two of the shadow warriors appeared at the opening of the chasm wall. Her cell slid toward them on its invisible cable, and soon she found herself walking through the labyrinth of hallways alongside her guards.

They entered the laboratory together, and after a swipe from inside Seefra's waistcoat, the two guards backed away. They posted themselves at the entrance, awaiting Seefra's next order. The master of darkness turned from his work and swished over to confront Janine.

"The keys," he said without emotion. The dark, unblinking eyes never left Janine's cargo jacket. The constantly swirling tentacles accelerated slightly, as Seefra anticipated unlocking the code of another key. His tattered waistcoat floated about his midsection, around a torso that did not exist. The soulless emptiness underneath the coat unnerved Janine.

She unzipped the pocket of her cargo jacket and produced the four remaining keys. Seefra ordered her to lay them on a small table he had prepared. When she complied, he stood directly in front of them. A peculiar vial of syrupy liquid floated over to the master of darkness from the main laboratory table. Hovering a few inches above the keys, the vial awaited its instructions. Seefra closed his six insect-like eyes and uttered a lengthy spell. The liquid in the vial reacted to the words Seefra spoke, changing colors and consistency every second or two. Janine watched the transformation occur with a frightened admiration. Something inside her kept screaming that the dark master had succeeded this time. She fully expected to see him scoop up the keys and storm out of the lab when this experiment concluded.

Seefra completed his incantation. He waved a frail, bony hand above the four keys, and then touched the vial of liquid by exhaling a mist from his tiny mouth. The vial tipped itself over directly above the first key in the line. A few drops of the thick substance fell from the lip of the vial. The liquid spread out, covering the entire key. The ruby red luster immediately changed to a disgusting rusty reddish-brown. The gleaming beauty of the key blinked out forever, and when Seefra saw this occur, his eyes squinted with delight. Another key had fallen into his possession.

He ordered the vial to move to next key in the row. Repeating the same procedure, the vial distributed its liquid along the length of the purple key. The brilliant color faded instantly, causing Janine to gasp with surprise and fear. The purple coloring changed its hue to a sickening yellowish-white. Seefra blinked his eyes, trying to clear his mind, as he watched the transformation. His ascension to the inner element of the Circle of Evil was all but assured. With all five keys in his possession, he would command the first chair and the Crossworlds would fall under his power forever.

With a thought, he ordered the vial to proceed to the next key in the line. The vial slowly tipped itself over, allowing only a single drop to fall from its lip to the brilliant golden key. The droplet of heavy, multicolored liquid seemed to hang in the air for a lifetime. When it finally made contact, Janine threw her arms in front of her face and covered her eyes. The tiny droplet of liquid seemed to collide with the surface of the key. The magic of the creators repelled Seefra's spell violently, disintegrating the liquid in an explosion of sparks and fire. The coloring of the key flashed into a brilliant hue, causing even Seefra to wince and turn his head away. When he turned back to look at the key, the coloring of the metal remained unchanged. The perfect golden tint looked as if nothing had touched its surface.

Janine slowly dropped her arms and opened her eyes. When she looked at the key, she wanted to jump up and down with joy. She wanted to scream at Seefra, telling him that his plans had failed again. Even though he had taken three out of the five keys so far, Janine had braced herself for the worst. Now, at least one key would remain in her pocket. She could relax, at least for a little while. She knew better than to show any outward emotion, however. Containing herself, she merely looked at the golden key along with Seefra. She said nothing as she waited for him to test the fifth and most powerful key in her possession.

"Ordaxa!" spat Seefra as he looked at the shining golden key. He hissed and stared at the tiny vial floating in front of him. The tube instantly obeyed his orders, floating a few inches to the right until it hovered over the ebony box containing the final key. Seefra motioned to Janine to unlock the casing. As she did so, the dark master gasped deeply as he saw the blinding light emerge from the sheath. Janine opened the final flap as she held her other hand in front of her eyes. She drew back her arm, holding both hands up to her face. The key shone like the sun in the sky above her world. It didn't even seem like an object to her. It appeared to be a container of the most powerful magic in the Crossworlds. She swallowed hard at the scene unfolding in front of her.

Seefra commanded the vial to distribute a few drops of the elixir onto the surface. He watched as the liquid reached the tip of the vial and then dripped down toward the table. The liquid impacted the key without any result at all. The brightness prevented Seefra from seeing the reaction, but it seemed as though the key just absorbed the liquid without incident. The master of darkness nodded his head, and the vial tipped again. He watched the droplets more intently this time, disregarding any damage to his eyes from the brightness of the key. They fell directly into the surface of the metal, with no reaction whatsoever. The droplets simply vanished. Frustrated, Seefra commanded the vial to upend itself. A rush of liquid fell from the opening, heading straight for the shining key. Seefra grinned in anticipation, hoping beyond hope that the larger dose would turn the tide. When nothing happened, he spat his rage toward the vial. The small cruet sailed across the laboratory, crashing into a million shards against the far wall. The master of darkness turned toward Janine, rage exuding from his six tiny eye slits.

"The last two keys stay with you, for now," he hissed, staring at the table. He bent down and snatched the second and third keys away, quickly depositing them into his waistcoat. "I have deciphered the code for three of the keys, and soon, my dear, I shall have them all." He watched as Janine folded the dark flaps of the box over the fifth and final key. She took the golden key, which was placed on top of the box, and inserted it lovingly into her jacket pocket. After closing the zipper, she lifted her eyes until they met Seefra's squarely.

"You've done well, jailer," she said viciously, "and I believe you might capture the fourth key with a little time. But you will never have the fifth key. Your magic is weak against the supreme power of the creators. Did you not see how your elixir passed into nothing as it touched the surface of the fifth key? You will never decipher the code of *that* spell, because it isn't a spell at all. It is the raw power of the creators, inserted into the key by the Lady of the Light. Nothing you can conjure up will ever compete with the elemental power placed in that key."

Janine felt herself being rapidly propelled backwards. She slammed into the wall of the laboratory with a sickening thud.

The back of her head smashed against solid rock and the whip-lash nearly knocked her cold. She bounced violently off the wall, crashing down onto the floor, cutting her lip and chipping two of her teeth against the hard stone surface of the laboratory. With what remained of her conscious thought, she scolded herself for losing control. She had angered Seefra before and paid the price. It served no purpose at all and usually made her cell all that more uncomfortable. In a twisted way, though, she felt good about defying him, and it certainly demonstrated that her little theory might prove to be true after all.

Something gripped her hair, ripping her off the floor like a rag doll. Her feet dangled a few inches from the floor while her scalp screamed for relief. She tasted blood in her mouth and she could tell that parts of her teeth were missing. She opened her eyes to find Seefra swishing calmly in front of her, his six beady insect eyes staring at her without blinking. He came closer, as close as he could without touching her. After looking at her for a few seconds, he said something that sent chills down her spine.

"Perhaps I should focus my efforts on finding another prisoner who might be able to hold the keys for me. Then your usefulness would be at an end, my dear."

He turned without another word, signaling the shadow warriors. As they walked toward Janine, Seefra released his hold on her hair. She fell to the floor in a crumpled heap, but did not shed one tear. As the guards picked her up and roughly set her on her feet, she heard Seefra's command to them as he left the laboratory.

"No nourishment for three days! Give her only minimal amounts of water! Sustain her life, but do not renew her strength!"

Janine ripped her hands away from the shadow warriors and

walked out of the laboratory under her own power. Wiping away the blood on her lip, she spat a bloody tooth on the floor as they escorted her back to her cell.

CHAPTER TWENTY

Conor sat up abruptly, screaming and looking everywhere for Janine. He had dreamed repeatedly of her imprisonment, and although the images appeared dim at times, she seemed so close to him toward the end that he found himself reaching out for her again and again. Finally realizing it had all been an illusion, he jumped up from his resting place and ran toward the lake in the middle of the glade of Champions. His movements came so instinctively to him he didn't even notice the silvery water wall sinking slowly back into the ground. He hadn't even sensed the change in his physical condition until he had run more than a hundred yards. Stopping suddenly, he realized that his breathing came easily; he didn't feel tired or winded at all. Then he noticed that the aches and pains in his body had disappeared, and that he felt completely refreshed. Wondering how long he had been sleeping, he called out to the Lady of the Light, hoping to find her waiting for him alongside another corridor. The images of Janine's suffering and torture kept hammering in his mind, and he ran again in a frantic search for the Lady. Seeing no sign of her anywhere, he decided to return to where he found her before. As he turned around, he almost stumbled at the sight of Eha. The cheetah had been restored to his stature as a Champion of the Crossworlds, all twenty-five feet and two thousand pounds of him. He looked spectacular, lithe and powerful, ready to face any danger for the Crossworlds and for his Lady.

"Eha!" shouted Conor a little too hastily. "The Lady of the Light, I must see her at once. Can you take me to her?"

The giant cheetah ruffled his fur all the way back to his tail. "She is in council, Conor. She and the other members are working to restore Surmitang as we speak. I am afraid that will take some time, for once the transformation begins, none of them may be disturbed."

Conor grasped his knees and leaned over in disappointment. The images of his girlfriend swirled inside his head. He wanted to scream his frustrations, but he thought better of it. "Eha, did she leave any instructions for you to take me to a corridor? Did she at least tell you that the next portal had been constructed?" "I'm sorry, Champion, but she relayed nothing of the sort to me. I believe if you wait just a little while, she will accommodate you in your quest. May I extend my thanks for bringing me back to the glade of Champions? I'm certain it must not have been an easy task."

Conor smiled, thinking of their encounter. "You trained your brothers well, Eha. I'm sure they'll have no trouble keeping your pack well fed."

Eha smiled at his friend, noticing Conor's growth for the first time. The boy had grown quite a bit since last he saw him, almost to full manhood. "May I show you something, Champion? I'm afraid you might be too large to ride on my back, but I imagine you might be able to keep pace with me as I run."

"What is it?" Conor asked distractedly. "Will it take long? I have to be here the second the Lady returns."

"She will join us at our destination. Come, I wish to show you something that will make your heart sing."

Eha sent clouds of dust and small pebbles flying in his wake as he sprinted away from Conor. The gigantic cheetah ran like a locomotive, kicking into high gear within seconds of his departure. Even with his great size, he looked almost tiny as he rounded a distant corner by the sandy edge of the lake.

Conor raced after him. It felt good to run, and in seconds the young man had turned the corner and was gaining on his brother. His legs churned like pistons, and in a playful gesture, Conor reached out, trying to grab Eha's tail when he came up behind him. At fifty miles an hour or better, this proved to be a difficult task, and soon Conor was laughing uproariously behind the cheetah.

Eha looked around to his left and saw Conor grasping at his tail. He flicked it away from the young man's grasp, and with a simple kick of his hind legs he broke ahead of him. The cheetah accelerated to almost ninety miles an hour, and then stopped suddenly.

Conor almost tripped over his own feet when Eha stopped. He ended up sprawled out on the dirt next to Eha, soiled arms and legs splayed haphazardly underneath him. He grinned at the cheetah as he unwrapped himself. Finally standing, he brushed himself off and prepared to speak to Eha. When he looked up at his friend, however, the ability to speak momentarily escaped him.

A cougar cub, no larger than a small dog, stood next to Eha. A pair of dainty wings, partially formed at best, grew out from the shoulders of the golden beast. The tear lines, clearly formed along the snout, gave the cougar its familiar expression. Conor ran over to embrace his mentor. As he approached, the small cub squared its shoulders, snarling at Conor. Small he might be, but this future Champion was all heart even at this age.

"Eha, is this really him?" asked a delighted Conor.

"Yes," answered the cheetah. "It is really Purugama, as a young cub of course." Eha lowered his furry head and spoke to the cougar in a language only the large cats understood. The two Champions exchanged a few remarks, and then Purugama flapped his tiny golden wings a few times. He stepped away from the cheetah and chuffed in Conor's direction. Then he stood his ground, inviting the young man to approach and introduce himself.

Conor walked slowly toward his mentor. He watched Purugama gently move his wings back and forth as he came closer. The golden eyes never left Conor, and although the cougar cub felt slightly nervous, he didn't show a hair of it to the young man. When Conor reached out with his right hand, Purugama lowered his head without taking his eyes from him. Conor placed a closed fist over the top of Purugama's right ear and began rolling his knuckles in a tight circle. He remembered how the cougar, even as a giant Champion of the Crossworlds, enjoyed the gentle scratching just as much as Conor's own cats. Today proved to be no exception, because the small cub began purring almost immediately after he started to massage his forehead. Conor moved his fist around the cougar's face, scratching under his chin and on the bridge of his nose. Purugama accepted every second of the attention, for it was a new sensation for him. Many of the creators had attended to him, even one or two of the other Champions had done so, but this sensation seemed very different. Wherever this young man came from, he obviously retained some rare knowledge about the receptive areas of wild cats.

Pushing past Conor's rolling hand, the cougar stepped forward, brushing his flanks against Conor's legs. Conor immediately knelt down and began petting his mentor's shoulders and hindquarters.

He cooed to Purugama, almost giggling at the sight of the magnificent cougar in miniature. Every aspect of his development appeared to be perfect, just smaller in stature. *Even the wings seemed built for flight*, thought Conor as he softly stroked the golden, fuzzy appendages. They just needed to grow out before they would be strong enough to support his eventual bulk.

A beautiful voice resonated from behind him. "Are you enjoying your reunion with Purugama?" asked the Lady of the Light. "As you can see, he has always been a very handsome Champion."

Conor stood immediately, assuming a posture of respect and deference. Purugama held no feelings of propriety, however, and he continued to rub Conor's legs as he walked back and forth in front of him. The young man reached down, trying to halt the cat's progress, but Purugama would not be put off. He had tasted Conor's scratching talents, and he wanted desperately for the young man to continue.

"He is exquisite, my Lady," replied Conor, as he tried to hold the cougar cub in one place. "How did he come to be here, and at so young an age?"

"Both he and Ajur are Maya's descendants, and as such, they were transported here the instant they passed through the forbidden corridor. It would have been impossible for you to find them had this not occurred, and the only price we've gladly endured is watching them mature through their young years. You should see the tussles he and Ajur engage in. If not for Eha's quick feet, we might have had to separate them for good."

Just as she said this, a jaguar cub, black as a starless night, hopped around from behind the Lady's feet. Conor's jaw sprang into an involuntary smile at the sight of Ajur as a small cub. Not yet an imposing figure, Ajur lacked the bulk he would eventually pack on as he grew to his full size. For now, he looked like a sleek, oversized black cat with a coating of fur so dark it seemed to shine with a soft, blue sheen. The glowing, dark brown eyes missed nothing, and as he stood next to the Lady's legs, he flicked those intelligent orbs over the entire area. He looked up at Conor, his jowls crinkled into a silent snarl. Then he glanced up at the Lady of the Light before finally glaring at Purugama, who crouched low behind Conor's legs. The golden cougar awaited his own opportunity to strike at an unsuspecting foe.

Upon seeing Purugama, the jaguar charged the cougar. The two of them clashed together like a pair of cymbals. They rolled down the hill toward Eha, biting, scratching and snarling the whole way. The two combatants barely noticed when they bounced roughly off of Eha's strong legs. They kept after each other until Eha released a threatening snarl from deep within his lungs. The two cubs broke away instantly, both assuming a fighting stance and looking around for intruders. Conor laughed so hard he had to bend at the waist to regain his breath. Even the Lady of the Light giggled softly with a delicate hand over her mouth. Purugama heard her soft laughter, saw who stood facing Conor, and ran headlong for his mistress. The Lady crouched, gathering him in and saving one arm for Ajur, who followed closely behind Purugama. The two cubs, in a struggle for supremacy just moments ago, now snuggled together in the arms of their mistress, oblivious to any prior differences.

Conor came forward to embrace Ajur, but the fierce jaguar turned him away with a frightening growl. Jumping from the Lady's arms, he placed himself between the young human and his mistress. He did not know this stranger, and he would give his own life to protect the Lady from any danger. Conor stopped in his tracks, gazing at the formidable young jaguar. Even as a cub, Ajur proved himself to be a very capable warrior. He may not have been able to seriously injure Conor, but any encounter with him would certainly leave some painful reminders.

Deftly lowering herself next to the young cub, the Lady took one of Ajur's ears between her thumb and index finger. She rubbed the ear lovingly as she spoke to her diminutive Champion. "Calm yourself, Ajur," she cooed. "This is a friend. You have already become his companion in battle, and I assure you, you will be brothers for the remainder of your lifetime."

Ajur looked up at the Lady one more time before springing forward and knocking Conor off his feet. The jaguar took Conor down without any effort at all, and as he stood on his chest sniffing and nipping at Conor's face, he failed to hear the sound of a certain cougar running up behind him. Soon a rolling ball of dust containing one human and two young but very strong cubs careened off the trees and rocks around the glade. The two cubs snarled happily, toying with their new friend, carefully biting at his hands every time he tried to gain an advantage. Conor finally threw off his two attackers and jumped to his feet. He managed to scamper about ten feet before the two cubs attacked again, happily growling and purring as they toyed with their new playmate. Conor laughed as he kicked and called out their names, and after a few tactical moves, he stood with a cub in each hand, holding them above the ground by the scruff of their necks. Each one, now hanging in the tranquilized hold, looked to their mistress for aid.

"I never instructed you to start a tussle with him," said the Lady to the coal black jaguar. "This is Conor Jameson, Champion of the Crossworlds, slayer of some of the most formidable warriors of the Circle of Evil. He has brought two of your brothers back from where the forbidden corridors sent them, and now he will venture forth to collect the final two, including your sire, Maya. The two of you had no chance against a Champion of his capabilities."

The two cubs cowered in submission. Their formidable expressions dropped into a pair of wide-eyed pleas for help. After Conor set them down, they purred and brushed up against him vigorously. They seemed to be asking for another round of play already. Conor walked them over to the Lady's loving hands, watching as Eha came forward to take charge of the two cubs. The intelligent cheetah knew precisely when he should step in and resume his custodial duties.

"Thank you, Eha," said the Lady with a smile. She turned back to Conor, taking his arm and leading him away from the playground. Her expression shifted to one of mild concern as the two of them walked briskly toward the glimmering lake. Conor glanced over at the Lady, but did not question her about her troubles. He knew the information would be forthcoming, so he merely kept pace with her as she marched along the rim of the lake. After walking close to a mile, a break appeared in the rock-strewn hills that bordered the gently lapping shoreline. The Lady of the Light steered Conor into this small grotto, finally pushing him into a tall but shallow cave. Less than ten paces away stood a sparkling silver corridor. This, Conor suspected, would serve as the passage between the glade and whatever jungle Therion occupied. Reaching out to grab the Lady's arms and thank her for the portal, Conor almost jumped back when she took his hands in a very strong and almost frightened grip.

"Conor," said the Lady, very seriously. "Something has happened to Therion."

"Then I should go immediately and find him," answered the young man hastily. "Has he been captured by hunters? Have they injured him? Did he not survive the journey through the forbidden corridor?"

"No, nothing of the sort," replied the Lady. "We simply are unaware of his present whereabouts. He did not journey to his original location, as the others did after entering the forbidden portal. He is lost to us, and even our seekers cannot locate him. We do not fear his demise, but we cannot be certain that following him will result in a safe journey for you. In fact, the council is debating whether to delay your final two journeys until we can determine his fate."

"No," said Conor firmly. "I'll not wait another moment. With all due respect, my Lady, every second we wait might make the difference in whether Janine lives or dies. I must go, and right now. Give me your blessing, your powers, your protection, and anything else you'd care to bestow on me, but I am going through that corridor right now."

Conor gently twisted his wrists out of the Lady's hold. Not knowing what else to do at that awkward moment, he bowed slightly to the Lady, and stepped through the beautiful, glistening corridor.

"You have everything I can give you, Conor," said the Lady to the blazing corridor, "including my love."

THERION

CHAPTER TWENTY-ONE

Conor tumbled out of the burning corridor. Instead of landing on a solid surface, he was launched into a free-fall toward an unknown destination. He flailed away with his arms trying to turn himself upright, but no matter what he did he couldn't correct his flight. He could sense the ground rushing up to meet him, but he couldn't tell where he might land or on what type of surface. Floating through a thick, spongy cushion of air, he entertained a passing thought that he might never even meet Therion at all. If he hit a hard surface at the wrong angle he could be killed.

With a mighty effort, he wrenched himself around and saw that a rude arrival loomed a few seconds away. Closing his eyes tightly, he covered his face with his forearms and prepared to collide with whatever lay below.

The impact knocked the wind from Conor's lungs but did no other damage. After picking a few dozen strands of straw from his hair and clothing, and remembering how to breathe again, Conor pushed himself to his feet. Standing on the large bales of hay that had broken his fall he peeked over the side of the container.

He partially recognized the bizarre surroundings, but he

couldn't really be sure. Amidst the dirty paths and rock-lined walkways, he saw horse-drawn wagons and standing refuse containers, odd-looking brooms and huge vats of water. The area reminded him of something, but he couldn't recall exactly what it was. He saw various areas cordoned off into smaller venues, and small outbuildings attached to each adjoining area. He finally calmed down enough to soak up the smell of the place, which gave him the final identification he needed. It smelled decidedly primal, like the smell of a barn where horses congregated. This scent was quite a bit stronger, however, and very different from the corrals he remembered as a young boy. He had landed in some sort of public zoo. He knew he had traveled back in time quite a bit as well, maybe to the turn of the twentieth century. Wherever and whenever he had arrived, if the keepers of this era had managed to find Therion, they were going to have their hands full when they brought him back to their zoo.

Conor climbed over the side of the wagon and brushed off the rest of the dirt and straw from his clothes. He looked up at the dark blue sky, estimating by the slightest tint of pink on the horizon that dawn might be an hour away. *Good*, he thought, *I have an hour before daylight to find Therion and get back to the glade of Champions.* He began jogging through the zoo, looking for the painted wooden signs directing visitors to the various exhibits. In short order, he found the first of the signs with a large cat painted on the surface. The edge of the sign ended in a smart looking arrow, pointing toward a tree-lined path that rose slightly as it meandered away from him.

As he started walking toward the pathway, he heard a tremendous ruckus far off in the distance. The upheaval appeared to repeat itself over and over again, and it seemed to be coming from the far end of the walkway leading up to the big cats. Suddenly concerned, Conor hurried his pace and began jogging up the path. When he heard another explosion of sound coming from further up the trail, followed by the distinctive roar of a terrified and very irate lion, he broke into a full gallop. He ran as fast as Eha's cheetah speed could carry him. Within seconds he came upon the source of all the noise.

About a dozen strong men wrestled with a large covered wagon close to one of the enclosures. They tried again and again to successfully back the wagon up and fasten it to the large double-door of a building connected to the exhibit. Each time they attempted another coordinated effort, the immense beast inside the wagon began thrashing around, throwing off their ability to work together. The wagon invariably fell off the tracking they had designed for the job, leaving the men exasperated and exhausted. After each failure, it took them at least thirty minutes before they were able to make another attempt. Even worse, the beast in the wagon had more than once managed to rake its giant claws through the seams in the paneling, causing injury to three of the men charged with his safe delivery. Although not serious, the injuries had lessened the patience of the whole group. As they began routing the wagon back onto the rails again, the huge paw raked the sides of the paneling. No one was injured this time, but the beast let out a roar that caused every man in the group to back away in fear.

"Therion," whispered Conor quietly. Standing behind a large wooden fence, he watched the men struggle with the king of beasts. He wondered exactly how he would rescue Therion and bring him back to the glade of Champions. He couldn't charge this many men, throwing magic in every direction, and expect there to be no unfortunate consequences. He certainly couldn't fool this many into believing he had the answer to their problem. He thought about using the spell of immobilization, but then Therion might not react as calmly and wisely as Surmitang had. He decided to watch and wait, because, after all, it might be amusing to see these men trying to overpower something they couldn't possibly understand. By the newness of the signs pointing to this section of the zoo, Therion was probably the first large cat ever brought into captivity here. As frightened as the big lion felt at this moment, Conor knew that his captors were ten times more afraid of the snarling, growling cat they had in their wagon. He focused on their next attempt as the men began to position themselves against the wagon again.

Six of the keepers wedged large poles into the ground behind the wagon. As they systematically pushed it forward, three keepers worked on both sides to keep it on the rails. They made good progress, pushing the wagon halfway toward their goal. One of the men on the left side let up a bit as they closed in on the double doors.

"Maybe he's finally tired out," he said, wiping his forehead with one hand and holding the pole with the other.

"Don't bet on it," said his mate. "I got a good look at his eyes a second ago, and they didn't look promising. I think you'd better start leaning on that pole again."

"Maybe you're right."

Just as the first keeper started to tighten his grip again, the massive lion hurled his entire body against the left side of the wagon. With the decreased amount of resistance on the left, and the increased pressure from the three men on the right, the wagon tipped up on two wheels, teetered for a moment, and then crashed onto its side. The huge banded crate collided with the ground in a violent spray of straw and dirt. The keepers scattered away from the wagon, every eye planted on the roof of the rolling structure. Determined to escape, the lion bashed his huge frame against the top of the wagon repeatedly, growling his hatred of confinement for the entire world to hear. Even with his great strength, however, Therion could not free himself from the enclosure. The men slowly crept back toward the wagon, every one of them ready to bolt if the top popped off unexpectedly.

"Why don't we just shoot it and be done with it," one of the keepers remarked. "He obviously isn't going to take to captivity, so why waste the manpower. Three of us need to see a doctor already."

"Yeah," chimed in another keeper. "We can always say he broke out of the wagon and we had no other choice."

After the last comment passed into the thick, morning air, a long, painful roar peeled out from inside the wagon. It seemed as if Therion understood the nature of their discussion.

Two of the keepers had gone to their trucks during the short conversation about the big lion's fate. Both of them returned carrying three Springfield bolt-action rifles in their arms. They passed four of them off to other keepers around the wagon and then positioned themselves at precise angles roughly a dozen feet from the swinging doors.

"Hall," said the one directing the operation. "After we've loaded our magazines, I'll give you a signal and I want you to unbolt the door to the wagon. After you throw the lock, roll around to the backside of the cart and get down. The rest of you find shelter inside the exhibit. If this thing gets away from us, anyone waiting around to introduce himself is going to have a very bad morning. Everybody clear?"

"Aye!" the men returned.

"And good shooting," sounded a lone voice.

"Load your rifles, lads," said the leader, "and for the sake of the creators, keep the firing pin on single and don't miss. We've got thirty rounds between the six of us, so we shouldn't have a problem."

Conor couldn't believe what he was witnessing. The idiots had the greatest prize their zoo would ever see and because they suffered a few failed attempts at securing it, they were going to destroy him. *The sheer stupidity of the lot of them!* Conor began to feel his rage building. He began to feel an intense dislike for these keepers, if they could even merit the name. He wanted to cast a spell that would force them to turn the rifles on their own kind. He wanted to take the weapons as he had done in the jungle of Indonesia, and let Therion have his way with the men. He wanted to call forth the power of Surmitang and deal with the men himself.

He let the fury run its course and then called his rational mind forward again. When he heard the sound of the bullets being inserted into the individual magazines, Conor walked around the fence and jogged quietly toward the keepers. He kept to the heavier brush around each of the enclosures, hoping to keep himself concealed until the last moment.

"Alright, Hall," said the lead keeper, "throw the lock and get the heck out of there."

Hall stood as far from the wagon doors as he could. He looked at his mates gripping their weapons firmly while bracing them against their shoulders. When he saw them aiming the rifles directly at the doors, he reached around with shaking hands and placed a key into a large lock.

"Mind of the creators, Hall," said one of the riflemen. "Stop your shiverin' and throw the doors!"

Hall tried to insert the key completely into the rusty iron lock, but he couldn't find the right angle. Two things slowed his progress. One was the silence inside the wagon. The lion hadn't made a sound since the rifles came out of the trucks. The other mildly unnerving incident happened when Hall had moved by one of the creases in between the large boards on the side of the wagon. He had made the mistake of glancing inside, and when he did, he came eye to eye with a very angry lion. He could see the purpose behind that huge golden eye. He could see his own destruction in the gleaming bronze orb, and he suddenly decided he didn't want to be anywhere near the whole scene.

"Blast you, Hall," said the lead keeper. "Throw that lock or I'll do it and toss you inside with the lion!"

Hall jammed the key into the lock and turned it clockwise. As he felt the tumblers fall into place, he saw the lion stand and assume a crouched position at the back of the wagon. At a level only Hall could hear, the lion spit out a threatening snarl when the doors wavered on their hinges. Hall removed the lock, threw up the latch and crawled twenty feet on his hands and knees in about two seconds. He dove behind the wagon and waited in a pair of soiled trousers. The last thing he saw, he would later relate to others, was the strange sight of a teenager walking up behind the keepers.

Therion exploded from inside the wagon with a thunderous roar that ruptured the dawn's peaceful serenity. The wagon's two heavy doors flew off their hinges, one splintering into a shower of kindling and the other flying through the air in one ragged piece. The oak door with its metal plating and hinges must have weighed over fifty pounds. When it crashed into two of the keepers on its way through the exhibit, the number of remaining riflemen fell to four. The unfortunate pair who happened to be in the way of the door now lay unconscious on the dirt path to the left of the destroyed wagon. Therion, with a burst of uncanny strength and speed, had escaped the ring of keepers and their inadequate weapons. The lead keeper managed to get off one shot, but that came more from fear and surprise than anything else. He missed the big lion completely, almost taking out one of his own men in the process. He watched as five hundred pounds of wild cat bounded off into the main section of the zoo.

Conor shook his fist and silently screamed encouragement to his friend and fellow Champion. *Therion had escaped*! He allowed the keepers to think they had depleted all his reserves, and at the key moment he surprised them and made a clean getaway. The keepers looked to be in a state of mindless disarray. They didn't have the slightest idea what to do. Therion was probably three enclosures away by now and the man in charge finally looked to be establishing some semblance of order. Conor waited by a large stand of trees to see what their strategy would be as the lead keeper stood by the mangled wagon barking out orders.

"Mason, Whitney, see to those two men by the gate. Pick up their rifles and give them to Jensen." He turned his attention to the new recruits. "Jensen, you and Peters are now part of this rifle company. The six of us are going to track that lion down and destroy it. No matter what happens, we all stay together, is that clear? None of us are professional hunters, so I want our strength to come from numbers. This animal is obviously intelligent, it's loose in an environment that can easily camouflage it, and it's fuming mad." The keeper checked the magazine on his rifle one more time before ordering his men to do the same. "One more thing before we go. I want the rest of you men to prepare another wagon, and bring up a team of horses as well. When we get this lion, I want him out of this zoo fast. Every one of our jobs is on the line here, gentlemen, so I want this taken care of quickly and quietly."

"What about calling the police?" asked one of the keepers.

"Not yet," answered the lead keeper. "We can handle this ourselves. Everyone knows his job, so we should be able to get on top of the situation. Let's move out."

Conor shook his head as he listened to their conversation. Even after Therion's escape, they still didn't understand what they were up against. The lead keeper appeared ready to walk his men into a terrible confrontation. If Therion had eluded them while locked in a wagon, what made them think they could have any chance against him out in the open? How could he hope to save these men from their own stupidity if they didn't have the sense to do it themselves?

After watching the group of riflemen walk off in Therion's direction, Conor decided that finding the big lion himself would be his best course of action. He climbed the nearest tree in seconds, passing branches from hand to hand as he sailed to the top. Once there, he watched the keepers for a moment again, and then began scanning the zoo for any sign of Therion. Although he never saw him, he realized that the area of the zoo with the most animal activity was most likely where Therion would go. He saw a large area with six to eight enclosures, all with antelopes and gnus of some sort. The animals appeared to be very agitated, so Conor decided to head in that direction. Instead of descending and running for the enclosure, however, he used the agility and steady feet of a jaguar to move through the trees. He walked his way through the branches in tree after tree toward his destination.

Therion padded silently through the foliage. He felt as though he had returned to the place of his birth, but with an added bonus of thousands of new trees and bushes to conceal him. He smelled a veritable smorgasbord of animals all around the zoo. Every direction he lifted his nose gave him another scent of helpless prey. He wanted to give in to his hunger, but he knew better than to attract attention to himself. If he attacked now, the men would find him in seconds. He could wait to gorge himself, but first he had to find a way to throw off the keepers. Just as his pride did when protecting a fresh kill or a water hole, drumming up some sort of distraction would give him the time he needed to get away from this place. He moved through another exhibit, quiet as a ghost, and then he found his answer. He watched as a small gazelle, terrified by what she saw walking through her enclosure, tried repeatedly to jump the moat that separated her home from the main walkway. Once or twice she nearly leapt over the wide chasm, but the keepers knew their business. Only the proper encouragement or the right piece of lumber would allow her to escape.

This gave Therion a very devious idea indeed. If he could free all of the animals, or as many as he could, the ensuing chaos would throw the keepers off his trail. They would be so busy with the other zoo residents, they might never find time for him again. He watched the terrified gazelle smacking its front legs and chest into the rough cement of the moat as it tried again to escape. He looked to the left of the exhibit and saw exactly what he needed – a large group of bushy trees clumped together, separating four different enclosures. He crouched down and crawled around the back of the exhibit, entering the thick branches of the trees as silently as a small breath of wind.

The lead keeper had his men flared out in a tight pack. They walked quietly up the wide, leafy trail that brought visitors toward the African plains exhibits. The keepers heard a strange commotion coming from the enclosures in this area, and they held their rifles steady as they approached. As they crested a small hill, a scent-filled breeze ruffled their uniforms. The lead keeper stopped in mid-step, sniffing the air again and again. He had worked in zoos all his life, and he knew which smells belonged and which didn't. He couldn't tell for sure, but he sensed the lion lurking close by. The conclusion came from intuition as much as the scent that filled his nose, but he had learned to trust his instincts after many near misses with wild animals.

"Check your rifles one more time, men," he commanded. "I want single shots only. Don't waste the whole clip shooting at nothing. He's here, somewhere close, so stay together and stand ready."

None of the men answered in the affirmative. They were too frightened, too nervous, or both. Going up against a man-eater didn't sound like fair duty for men making a few bucks a day in compensation. Nevertheless, they stood by their leader. He was a good man and they felt safe with him. The six keepers walked slowly around a large stand of dense, bushy trees as they entered the gazelle enclosures.

Conor raced through the trees, grabbing branches with his hands and bouncing off the higher portions of the trunks with his feet. When he found nothing but small, feeble branches at the end of one tree, he pushed off with all his might, vaulting across the expanse toward the next trunk. Sometimes he made the jump cleanly, at other times he scraped his arms and face bloody while sliding down a section of the tree, trying to gain purchase. A few times he had to halt his progress completely because the keepers were right below him. He didn't want one of those fools taking a shot at him out of blind, uncontrolled fear.

He reached the gazelle enclosures just ahead of the keepers, and just in time to see Therion's tail disappearing into the brush underneath a particularly large stand of trees. From his high vantage point, he could tell that the scruffy branches served as a hub connecting four large enclosures. Each of the exhibits contained a family of gazelles, maybe sixteen to eighteen animals total between all four areas. Therion could attack in any of a dozen directions and have a kill between his huge, toothy jaws in seconds. Conor couldn't believe that the big lion would be so desperate, though. If he attacked, the noise would bring the keepers right to him. He wouldn't be that foolish, no matter how powerful his hunger. Conor decided to stay where he was and watch from a high branch in the trees. He could be on top of any occurrence in a flash if needed, or he could fling a spell or two down onto the men if the situation became dangerous. Either way, he wanted to see exactly what Therion would do, because the keepers had climbed the hill and were now rounding the corner right where Therion lay hidden. He watched as the lead keeper raised his nostrils and sniffed repeatedly. *The man knew about animals*, thought Conor, *and he understood the power of scent.* If he smelled Therion inside those trees, the men might open up with their rifles any second. Conor shifted his feet and grabbed a slender but firm branch in each hand. He readied himself for anything, in case his brother Champion might need his help.

Squinting his golden eyes, Therion stared through layers of multicolored leaves. He saw the group of men walking just beyond his natural shelter, and he paid close attention to the one leading the group. He watched the man stop and sniff the air, trying to pick an unusual scent from the breeze. Therion remained perfectly still, for he knew by the way the man's head tilted into the wind there might be trouble. He knew the keeper smelled him, and he didn't want to contribute to any more of his senses until he felt ready to do so. The tall man with the frayed, worn hat held his position for an uncomfortable length of time, and then finally began walking again. He must have cautioned the others in the group, because they all checked their weapons before continuing up the pathway. Therion watched them disappear around the corner as he rubbed his thick, sensitive whiskers against the leaves and branches. He picked out his exit through the trees and prepared to execute his plan.

Conor watched the men as they vanished around the corner. For the first time since he had ventured to this world, his tensed muscles relaxed. He felt his grip on the branches relax, and saw the coloring and small pieces of bark attached to his palm when he turned it over. He shook his hand silently, tossing off the remnants of the branch's skin. He looked at the dried blood streaking down his forearms. He raised his hand and gently touched the right side of his face just above the jaw line. He examined his fingers after drawing them across his cheek. No fresh blood had escaped from the cuts. After checking his other cheek he returned his gaze to Therion's hideout. If he had waited another second before doing so, he might have missed one of the most dramatic scenes ever witnessed by anyone at a public zoo.

Instead of bursting out of the trees right away, Therion hissed and moaned a few times from behind his wall of leaves. The gazelles in their enclosures pricked their ears and lifted their heads immediately. The larger males chirped a few times in rapid succession, ordering the others in their respective groups to huddle closely together. The zoo may have never housed a lion before, but the gazelles knew those sounds and understood what type of animal made them. They had no idea exactly where he was, but they knew the deadly king of beasts lurked nearby. They couldn't do anything about it except put on a brave face, so the males of each group did exactly that. Out of pure instinct, they moved their groups toward the moats that offered their only means of escape. Every single gazelle in all four enclosures kept their head up and their large, dark eyes wide open while they waited for the impending attack.

Therion crashed through the thinner branches of his refuge, making as much noise as he could. The leaves from the thick stand of trees blew outward as he entered the first enclosure. To the wary animals inside, it must have sounded like an entire pride coming in for the hunt. The huge cat dropped his massive, furry jaw and released a roar that raised the hair on the backs of every animal in the zoo and sent a surge of gripping fear through the gazelles around him. His immense mane, almost coal black and a sign of his impressive lineage, waved back and forth as he turned his great head from side to side. Sighting a group of five gazelles to his right, he pounced and roared again, covering the distance in one leap. The sight of the gigantic predator surging toward them produced the effect Therion hoped it would. The five gazelles bolted for the moat, and all but one made the jump cleanly. With pure adrenaline coursing through their bodies, the gazelles leapt higher and farther than any of their kind in recorded history. The smallest, obviously younger than the rest, couldn't quite clear the distance, and the other members of the group were not about to return and offer assistance. Therion took one look at the small animal and leapt over the wall separating him from the next enclosure.

The keepers needed no encouragement from their leader to turn around and run back toward the gazelle exhibits. They did heed one command from the lead keeper, and by so doing they kept themselves in a tight pack. As a group, they advanced up the hill toward the enclosures. Even as a team, however, they couldn't possibly have been prepared for what they encountered once they arrived.

The enclosures looked completely deserted. Except for a few smaller residents, dozens of gazelles ran freely, leaping in every direction at once. One of the keepers shot one in the rump out of sheer confusion, earning a swift and loud reprimand from the lead keeper. The gazelle went down momentarily, but when it heard another booming roar from the lion, it forgot all about its pain and ran for cover again.

"Maintain your wits, men!" the lead keeper yelled. "Save your bullets for what we came here for!"

The chaos seemed to be gaining in intensity. The gazelles had no idea where to run. Each time they dashed off in a certain direction, a mysterious snarl would drive them back toward the keepers. It sounded like a large pride of lions had circled the area. The sounds of angry wild cats seemed to be coming from everywhere. Adding to the disarray of the moment, other animals started escaping from their enclosures as well. Zebra, tapirs, warthogs, and a giraffe joined the gazelles in their mad rush to freedom. The keepers found themselves huddling together for their own safety now, dodging crazed animals large enough to knock them off their feet. The lead keeper wouldn't let them waste their ammunition on anything but the lion, but none of them saw Therion running wild in the middle of the melee. The big lion simply disappeared once the madness had begun, and there was nothing the keepers could do about it. They couldn't move away without risking injury, so they went to their knees and huddled close together while they waited for the animals to calm down.

"Smart boy," said Conor from his perch high in the trees. Fearing that the big cat would pounce on one of the smaller prey animals for a quick meal, he had readied himself for a quick encounter with the keepers. Once he saw the true nature of Therion's plans, however, he sat back against the trunk of his observation post and watched the action unfold. *The Lady of the Light was right*, he thought, as he watched Therion execute his strategy. *We do need his brilliant mind to successfully overcome Seefra's forces*. It all looked so simple from up in the trees; the zoo animals occupied the keepers so completely that Therion simply waltzed around the perimeter of the action. Not knowing precisely where the zoo entrance was located, or where he might find a fence low enough to scale, the big cat took the best course and headed in a straight line. Conor gave him a tiny head start and then followed him, again using the trees as his pathway through the zoo.

"Peters!" screamed the lead keeper as the chaos began to die down. Most of the animals had run off to different sections of the zoo. The others stood just outside their enclosures, eyes wide with fear. "Hustle over to that paddock and get on the phone to the local police. Tell them an African lion might be loose in the city. Tell them that he's hungry, afraid and very pissed off. They're to take whatever measures they can."

Jensen looked over at his boss in disbelief. "It's our jobs if we let this get out, chief. What if he's still around here, inside the zoo? If he's hungry, there's no better place for him to find a meal."

The lead keeper shook his head while responding. "That big bastard knew exactly what he was doing. He threw all these animals at us to create a diversion. While we've been sitting here protecting our butts, he's been making his way toward the nearest fence. He's a smart lion, that one. He had our number from the moment we started working with him today. Now listen up, men. I'm sorry to ask this, but we're going to have to split up. I want each of you to find a different tower as quickly as you can. Scale it, scan the fences and the entrance to the zoo. If you see him, or any sign of him, yell out the location as loudly as you can. If you hear any of us sing out, get over to where that lion is and blast him to the outer realms. Don't wait for the rest of us, we'll be coming as fast as we can. Just shoot and hope you don't miss. If that lion gets out of this zoo and into the city, we're going to have one heck of a mess on our hands. Now go on, and hustle. We don't have much time."

The lead keeper cursed as he ran toward one of the six observation towers located around the zoo. If he could get up high enough, he might be able to find the big cat. As he started to climb the freshly painted rungs of the ladder, he shook his head, cursing himself for agreeing to the zoo's demands. He had voiced strong opposition to bringing this animal here in the first place. Large cats were just too unpredictable, too proud. They'd never be happy in a confined environment, and this little "experiment" of theirs had proven his point. Stepping out onto the observation platform, he cupped his eyes and began scanning the perimeter of the zoo. *Never again*, he thought while squinting. He would never allow some silly bean counter to tell him his business again.

From a distance, Conor watched Therion approach the main entrance of the zoo. The gates, sixteen feet tall and curved inward at the top, were comprised of slick cylinders of blue-plate steel. Therion bounced his head off of the thick chain holding the heavy gates together, seemingly frustrated because of their ominous stature. He backed away from the entryway and took a long look at the small kiosks with bamboo walls and thatched roofs stationed next to the entrance, which housed the offices for certain zoo essentials, like security, lost and found, and the tourist shops. Conor studied them along with Therion, guessing that the construction of the kiosks were very basic.

To Conor's amazement, Therion reached up and began pulling the sidewall of the first kiosk with both front paws. The booth fell apart easily, landing in a heap at the big lion's feet. The pile of rubble stood about four feet off the ground, and Therion hopped up onto the small stack with ease. He immediately began pushing against the wall of the second kiosk with his head, sending the four walls and the roof crashing down around the first. This increased the height of his stack of disheveled booths by another three feet. The big cat climbed up on his stack of lumber and palm fronds, steadied himself, and vaulted to the roof of the main administration building located next to the entrance gates. A solid brick and mortar building, it was the only structure in the entire zoo that interrupted the fence line. Therion padded noiselessly over to the far side of the roof, lowered his great bulk as far as he could over the edge, and then dropped down into the parking lot. He heard sirens blaring quietly in the distance, shrill sounds that seemed to be heading in his direction. He looked back toward the zoo where he saw a young teenager standing high in the trees by the entrance, and then sprinted across the dirt expanse. The slumbering city, still fighting off the first rays of the approaching dawn, was about to receive a very surprising wake-up call.

Conor pleaded with the creators to give him more speed next time. He had missed Therion by only seconds, and all he could do now was watch the big lion jump off the building into the parking lot. He should have done something sooner, because now Therion could make his way into the city. He might never find him in that concrete maze. Even worse, he could be hurt badly in that environment, or mortally injured by a car or a policeman's gun.

Conor dropped thirty-five feet straight to the ground. He didn't care who saw him at this point because he had to find Therion quickly. He bounded across the expanse between the tree and the main entrance in two huge leaps. Ignoring the toppled kiosks, Conor jumped to the roof of the administration building in one nimble attempt. As he ran across the wooden thatch tiles, he heard the sirens from at least three police vehicles charging across the parking lot. Without caring for his safety, Conor jumped as far and as high as he could away from the administration center and onto a long walkway bridging the parking lot. After a few more high jumps, he settled into a fast walk. Scanning everything around him, he frantically looked for any sign of a large, carnivorous cat hiding in the brush.

"Jensen," ordered the lead keeper. "Take these keys and unlock the gate for the police. Don't open it until they arrive. Just unlock it and wait." Turning to the others, he asked if any of them had seen the lion from their observation posts.

"I never saw the cat," said Lee. "But I did see something even stranger. I kept my eyes on the entrance the whole time, figuring that the lion might remember the scent from when we brought him in last night. I must have gotten topside too late to see him, but I did see the kiosks lying in a pile next to the main building. As I stared at that trying to make sense of it, I saw a kid, a teenager, fall out of one of the bigger eucalyptus trees near the front entrance. He must have fallen fifty feet. After he landed, he skipped forward and hopped up onto the roof of the admin building like he had bounced off of a trampoline. Weirdest thing I ever saw."

"Well," said the lead keeper. "We're never going to forget this night. Here come the officers. Let's give them the bad news."

Conor walked hastily through the parking lot. He'd seen no sign of Therion yet, but that certainly didn't convince him of anything. A lion as brilliant and crafty as Therion could walk up and stand right behind you and you wouldn't even know it unless he knocked you on the shoulder with a beefy paw.

What Conor worried about most now was the fact that Therion might be frightened. He had been taken from his home, forced to leave his pride. His captors had tried to push him into a ridiculous cell in their zoo, and now he was all alone in a strange environment. He couldn't possibly know where to go or what to do in a city setting, even one as old as this. Conor had to find him fast, and get him away from here and back to the glade of Champions. But how could he find one big cat in a thousand square blocks of concrete metropolis? He hadn't even the slightest idea which way Therion had gone.

A blast of sound gave Conor a good idea of which way to turn first. Therion's unmistakable snarl echoed down the streets and alleys from about three blocks away. A horrendous growl followed his warnings, and Conor took off like a shot in his big friend's direction. Racing around a half dozen brick and mortar walls, Conor finally came upon a scene so amazing he had to chuckle a bit when he first saw it. Therion, finally unable to control his raging hunger any longer, had attacked a meat truck out on its early morning delivery schedule. The three meat cutters, outfitted in their bloody work shirts and aware that they stood a good chance of losing a month's profits, tried their best to stand fast against the ravenous lion. Therion would have none of it, however. He held the men against a grimy brick wall with continued swipes of his large, imposing claws. In his other paw he held a side of beef that must have weighed two hundred pounds. Finally believing that the men would give him no more trouble, the big cat loudly cracked off three of the larger ribs. He scampered away down the alley, tearing the frozen meat from the bones as he ran. Conor laughed so hard he almost allowed Therion to leave him behind. He knew those men wouldn't move from that wall for another hour at least, and they would always have an unbelievable story to tell their grandchildren.

Therion ran through the streets with the renewed energy of a recently sated predator. With the city completely awake now, screams and gasps of surprise could be heard rising up from each alley or cobblestone street he visited. The human sounds seemed to blend in with each other after a while, because Therion couldn't seem to find any way to escape the unfamiliar surroundings. Two or three times he attempted to scale the walls of the buildings by running up stairs and jumping for the higher balconies. He never benefited from these attempts; he always ended up dropping back down into the filthy street.

People began throwing random objects at him as he sped by, and when he stopped to voice his boisterous disapproval they increased their onslaught. He began to wish he had never left the zoo grounds. At least there he had ample places to hide. Here there was nothing but dirt, buildings, and noise. He pricked his ears as he heard a familiar whine coming toward him. He heard the same sound when he left the zoo, and something instinctively told him the siren bore nothing good for him.

The police cars wheeled their way through the streets, sliding around corners and barely staying on four wheels. The reports kept coming in; a lion was running loose in the city. It had already attacked a meat wagon, and over three dozen people had seen it passing their homes on its way to who knew where. People even stood in the street pointing in the direction they had last seen the big cat. The policemen on the running boards of the cars half thanked them and half yelled at them to get back into their homes for their own safety. After thirty minutes of aimless driving, they cordoned off a six block area, enclosing the big lion inside a wide net of cars and paddy wagons. Every man on the force seemed to be somewhere within this concrete net, and each one of them held a Springfield rifle. There was a difference between the keepers in the zoo and the policemen out here in the city streets. These men knew how to fire these weapons as a team. They would be extremely lethal when the altercation between their forces and the big lion finally occurred.

Conor watched everything from the top of a radio tower twelve stories above street level. He could see Therion's time growing short. The police, running haphazardly at first, had now coordinated their vehicles. They had cut off virtually every avenue of escape, and Therion, caught between the large buildings and tight streets, had no way of knowing this. He tore through the slick, dew-coated streets like a madman, dodging debris and snarling at anyone who stepped out from within the safety of their homes. He looked in every direction for a safe haven, and, finding none, he ran even faster. *At his rate of speed*, thought Conor, *he would run right into the arms of the police within minutes.* Conor switched his line of vision and glanced over at the column of police cars waiting for Therion. The men looked a great deal more determined and capable than the keepers back at the zoo. They would hold their lines until the big lion had been taken or destroyed. Conor felt sure of that. He blinked his eyes and looked back at Therion again. Suddenly a thought jumped into his mind, a memory about something that occurred over four years ago, something that Therion himself had called forth in the *Forest of Forever* to defeat Surmitang. *It might work*, thought Conor. *It just might work.*

"Ready yourselves, lads," Captain Murphy called out to the line of uniformed officers. "I've been told the big beast is coming right toward us. I don't know what to expect from a wild animal like this, but your Springfields will put him down, I guarantee it. Just hold the line and fire at will, and remember, lads, keep your nerves steady. There's a lot more of us than there are of him. We have a clear advantage, so let's use it and go home early today." The beefy, red-faced police captain turned at the end of the column of men, walking back the other way toward his car. He shouted a little, just to make sure every man heard his next comment. "I've a box o' cigars and a dozen pints for the one who lays him low."

After the captain voiced his encouragement, the entire street where the policemen sat waiting turned into a tomb of silence. Only the soft creak of new boot leather disturbed the quiet as the men adjusted their positions one last time. Caps off and hair slicked back by cotton-coated palms, the men waited to see something they had only ever seen in books or silent movies. A few turned their heads, eyeing the rest of the lads on the line, but most of the two dozen riflemen kept their eyes glued to the street, waiting for their target to emerge from either corner. As the sun peeked through the alleys between the waking buildings, they heard the scraping of claws on the smooth cobblestone streets and the echo of the lion's heavy breathing. A few times a chuff or a light growl escaped the beast's lungs, causing the men to check each other once again. When they finally saw the shadow of the lion decreasing in size as it raced by the last building it would ever see, every one of them curled their fingers around their triggers. Pressing their cheeks against the stock of the rifle butts, the men peered down the street through the precision Springfield sights.

"Here he comes, men!" called out Captain Murphy.

A dark mane appeared from the backside of the building on the right. It shifted slightly as the lion leaned hard to his left as he rounded the corner. Each of the men began to squeeze their triggers, when something in their sights caused them to stop and pull back. A few seconds later the alley erupted with the sound of gunfire. The policemen fired in every direction at once, even bouncing a few rounds off the walls close to their captain. True to their training, they had in fact held the line, but they fired indiscriminately all the same. Captain Murphy hadn't said a word. His men were doing their level best against overwhelming odds, and unless he was still in bed dreaming, the captain told himself he would swear off the Irish whiskey for good.

A split second after Therion appeared in the officer's line of fire, hundreds of Therions poured into the street from every possible direction. They followed him around the building's brick corner by the dozens. Large groups emerged from every window in every home, and on every street visible to the officers. They sent manhole covers flying through the air as they piled into the street from the sewer lines below. Therions fell from the sky into the street, landing with a cascade of roars as they bounded off in every direction. If anyone had the opportunity to count them, they would have tagged close to a thousand crazed lions running wild in front of the line of bewildered officers.

Clearly frazzled, the men shot at everything that moved. When they hit one of the lions, it would flash and disappear. The same thing would happen when the big cats broke through the line, which happened with increasing frequency as the bizarre event unfolded. A lion would roar its displeasure, attack one of the officers on the line, and at the precise moment of impact it would flash brightly and vanish. The terrified policeman would peer out from beneath folded arms to find his body intact, his blood still inside his veins, and his rifle lying on the street by his side. After a few moments of shocked disbelief, the officer would take up his rifle again and return to the fight.

A few of the men tried to shout encouragement to their fellows, sharing the news that the lions before them were all fake images. They told them to keep shooting, and not to worry if they broke through their defenses. The brave words fell on deaf ears, however, as the men continued fighting for their lives against the snarling horde sent to destroy them.

Captain Murphy sat in his car with the windows rolled up tightly. He looked upon the mayhem with eyes as wide as baseballs, wondering how so many animals could have gotten loose in his city. Every once in a while a lion would fly toward his police car, smashing against the side or the windshield in a blaze of silvery light. The animal would disappear or bounce off and retreat to a safer location. He couldn't be sure of anything at this point, except that his men continued to fire their weapons. He felt a twang of pride in that; he would have to recommend all of them for a letter of commendation if he ever made it back to the station.

The huge group of angry lions kept pounding away at the officers. With a maximum of only five bullets to a clip, the men on the line had exhausted their rifles in a matter of minutes. Without the necessary amount of time to reload, the officers used the rifles as clubs and began swinging wildly at the approaching cats. Whether they were shot or impacted by a thick rifle butt, the lions flashed and disintegrated instantly, leaving one less predator to harass the policemen.

"They're not real!" shouted an officer at the far end of the line.

"One of them sure is," answered another over the din of the action, "and I don't want to be the one who catches it!"

"Keep swinging!" said the first officer. "The captain has a full clip, once we find the real one he'll put him down for sure!"

The officers fought valiantly, swinging their rifles like war clubs as dozens of gigantic, golden lions fell upon them from every direction.

Conor followed Therion down a dark, shadowed alley. All alone and far away from the officers and their current problems, the big cat calmly padded down the cool, damp side street. He didn't know where to go at this point, but he knew that the street teeming with officers was not a healthy option for him. As soon as he'd seen the insane rush of lions flood the street from all around him, he had quietly excused himself from the area. He had no idea where all the others of his kind had come from. He knew male lions never traveled in huge groups, so he felt the safest course of action would be to get out of there fast. The whole thing made no sense at all.

To think that a few weeks ago he rested comfortably with his pride, basking in the sun and waiting for his females to return from the hunt. He had sired nearly a dozen cubs, and as they played and wrestled with each other, he had wondered which of the female cubs would stay with the pride. He had also scrutinized the male lions, wondering which of them might someday come back to challenge his position as patriarch.

He swallowed heavily. The memory left him with heavy pangs of regret. He had no idea what had become of them. The hunters had captured him so swiftly that he hadn't even had time to say goodbye or give any directions to the females and the cubs. For all he knew, another male had come along soon after his departure. Sensing an easy conquest, he would have claimed ownership of the females, destroyed all of the male cubs, and began staking out a new territory for his pride. Therion moaned softly at the thought of his sons coming under attack by another large adult male. They wouldn't stand a chance against him, and the females wouldn't oppose his rule, for he would put them down without a backward glance. Other females would arrive soon enough and would be happy to join his pride for nothing more than the protection he would give them.

Therion began fixating about his capture. After shooting him full of tranquilizers, the men had transported him halfway around the world to be displayed on a pedestal like some living stuffed animal. Those foul-smelling men who worked for the zoo had hired a crew of hunters to scour the deserts in Africa looking for one of its favorite sons. After removing him from his natural environment, his home, they boxed him up like a piece of meat and threw him in the hold of a gigantic ship. Keeping an eye on their prize so they wouldn't lose their investor's money, they checked on him every few hours, just to make certain he was still alive. If they saw his stomach rising and falling, they heaved a sigh of relief and returned to their cabins. Never mind what the lion's large, golden eyes told them. Never mind if the horrible sadness and stress from the intolerable situation dripped from those eyes onto the light brown fur around the bridge of his nose. Never mind that the big cat seldom moved at all, or had any interest in the food given to him. The only thing that mattered to the hunters was that they delivered a living specimen to the zoo.

As he padded slowly around the corner of a building, Therion thought of his small male cubs again. The image of their destruction sent jolts of powerful anguish through him. The golden fur twitched along his spine. He grew more furious with every step, thinking about what the keepers who worked for the zoo had done to his pride. They were all he had, and as their sire and leader, he had taken excellent care of them. No other male had ever successfully challenged him for dominance, although many had tried. But all that seemed like a distant memory now. He was in a strange place with no idea how to escape, and as he softly stepped around the holes in the street, he became more and more angry. The thought of one of the keepers at the zoo made him snarl involuntarily, and he held that image in his mind. The particular cut and color of the tan uniform, the work boots and the high knee socks, and the implements that every one of them kept attached to their work belts. They all looked exactly the same, and if he could go back to the zoo and find just one of them, he might be able to exact revenge before the men with the guns finished him off. *Yes*, he thought, *that is something I can focus my energy on.*

As the big lion settled on his determined plan, he briskly padded around another corner in the city. Shining brightly in the gleaming morning hours, the sun illuminated a figure standing at the end of a dead-end street. Therion stopped so suddenly his huge mane bobbed forward before resettling again. He looked down the street, perhaps a distance of fifty yards, sharpening his golden eyes at the human figure wearing the outfit he knew so well. He examined the tan shorts and shirt along with the work boots and belt. Surely, thought the big cat, he couldn't be this lucky. Directly in front of him, with no means of escape, stood one of the zookeepers. He seemed rather young, not quite a man, but older than a boy, with a swatch of sandy brown hair swimming atop his head. Holding his hands on his hips, the keeper stared at him with a defiant smile on his face. He said nothing, but his posture mocked Therion, and the great lion was not at all amused.

With a roar that shook the bricks from the aging buildings lining the cobblestone streets, Therion surged forward. All of the rage, frustration and pain boiling in his soul ever since leaving his home raced through his body, turning it into a manic locomotive. The big lion covered half the distance to his prey in seconds, and as he closed in on the keeper, he saw the young man dash along the gutter toward the brick wall at the end of the street. This only increased Therion's craving, and with another ear-shattering roar he increased his pace. He smelled the fear in his prey, and he wanted to collapse his mighty jaws around the human's neck more than any other animal he had ever faced.

With only twenty yards to go, and seeing his prey looking hopelessly for an avenue of escape, Therion pounced. He sprinted a few more feet and then jumped as far and as high as he ever had in his life. He saw the young man in the keeper uniform growing larger as he fell down toward him. At this moment, however, the human didn't appear to be very afraid. In fact, he held a strange sort of relaxed smile on his face.

Therion reached out with his forepaws, claws fully extended, ready to shred to pieces the being that had caused him to become separated from his pride. The last thing he saw before landing directly on the zookeeper was a bright, bizarre-looking silvery light. It seemed to occupy the entire street. As a matter of fact, it took up his entire field of vision. He wanted to stop his progress, for he felt that something was strangely amiss here in this dead-end alley. However, he could no more control the laws of gravity than he could turn back the ship that brought him here to this strange city. He drifted down toward the young man, who stepped lightly through the silver barrier, just out of his reach. The befuddled lion threw out his right paw in a futile attempt to contact the zookeeper before he sensed his own body entering the silvery barrier. He felt an odd sensation of icy coldness, and then fiery heat.

Conor and Therion crashed through the corridor, landing roughly on the pebbly lakefront of the glade of Champions. Neither of them noticed any of the onlookers sitting quietly around the lake. Conor rolled to a standing position and looked at Therion, who from years of battle experience had righted himself in the same way. The big lion glanced over at the young keeper. Without any hesitation at all, he charged Conor, emitting a furious snarl. Clumps of dirt and oversized pebbles flew from beneath the lion's feet as he exploded toward the zoo employee. Conor barely had time to roll underneath the bulk of Therion as the huge lion passed over him in mid-pounce. Conor knew that his brother Champion had attacked out of fury and would not make the same mistake again. He prepared to jump for the trees the next time Therion came at him, but neither he nor the big cat had a chance to execute any further moves. The Lady of the Light, watching her two warriors from the edge of the lake, called out to the huge predator.

"Therion!" she said forcefully with her arms folded gracefully across her torso.

The ferocious lion, confused at first, looked over at the glorious creator standing by the lake. She seemed to glow with a bright, silvery radiance, a luminescence promising something extraordinary. She would provide Therion with a sense of peace, something he presently lacked. The big lion forgot all about Conor and sprint-ed happily toward the Lady. He fell at her feet, turning over in case she might want to scratch his golden belly.

"Therion, my handsome Champion," cooed the Lady as she knelt to rub his rib cage with her outstretched fingers. "Words cannot express the joy I feel upon seeing you again. You are as strong and beautiful as ever."

The lion rolled from side to side, scratching his own back while the Lady focused on his stomach and ribs. His huge burnt gold eyes, squinting slightly from the smile on his huge, furry face, nev-er left the Lady for an instant. It seemed as though he regarded her as some form of motherly figure. Either that or he thought of her as exactly what she was – a goddess and one of the creators of the Crossworlds, someone to whom only reverence could be given.

"My Lady," asked Conor, now standing only a few feet from Therion, "how is it that each of these magnificent predators, who would take my life without hesitation, see you and become as doc-ile as a four-week old kitten?"

"Must you ask such a question?" she responded without ad-dressing him with her eyes. Still scratching the lion's belly, and tak-ing his whiskered face into her hands, she continued. "Do you not remember, Conor, the morning I came to you in your bedroom at your parent's house, how I offered you the opportunity to accom-pany us on a great and perilous task? Do you remember what you said to me after I explained what might be in store for you during your travels with Maya?"

"I agreed to go with you to meet Maya at the glade of Champi-ons," replied Conor without delay.

"Yes," said the Lady. "A twelve-year-old boy, not quite a teen-ager, not quite five feet tall, not even close to one hundred pounds, accepted the challenge to face a group of the most terrifying destroyers ever assembled by the Circle of Evil. You accepted in the name of your departed mentor, Purugama, as a tribute to your love for him."

The Lady raised her head and looked directly at Conor. The silver eyes, glistening with multicolored flecks took the young man's breath away. He almost stepped back a pace, but held his ground instead.

"Why did you answer our call on that morning so long ago?" she asked.

Conor licked his lips twice as he thought. "It was for Purugama, that's true. But I also agreed to go with you out of a sense of duty."

"Was there no other reason?" the Lady of the Light asked softly.

"Yes, of course," said Conor directly. "You provided the first proof of a race of beings greater than my own. You seemed all powerful, but gentle at the same time. You also struck me as a virtuous goddess, someone who would be on the side of good. A savior, if you will, which we sorely needed on earth."

"And there is your answer, my Champion," she replied. "These wild cats look upon me with the same eyes. They see me as a savior, a custodian, someone who will never allow harm to come to them. Upon realizing that, all of their instinctive protections fall away, and they come to me freely, uninhibited."

Conor couldn't help but smile as he watched Therion, a fierce five hundred pound man-eater rolling around at the Lady's feet. Even though he looked as harmless as a cub, he didn't dare try to touch him or approach him in any way. He knew that the docile behavior was reserved for the Lady of the Light alone.

As he pulled his gaze away from the scene directly in front of him, he caught sight of Eha running wildly around the edge of the lake. The cheetah kicked up large piles of sand with every spring of his huge hind paws. Every once in a while the streaking spotted cat would stop and turn so quickly that all Conor saw was a wall of sand arcing toward the water. It would fall and dissipate onto the surface of the lake and then Conor would see Eha again, happily racing away in the other direction. He smiled as he watched his friend enjoying himself. When he turned back to the Lady his smile broadened even more, so deeply his lips almost split wide open.

From out of nowhere, Ajur and Purugama had joined the Lady of the Light on the shore of the lake. Therion had disappeared, no doubt to begin his transformative process, a procedure the other two cats had obviously completed. Even as he sat, Ajur towered over the Lady. His coal black muscular shoulders braced against the ground like a pair of massive stone pillars. Rippling against his beautiful fur, they stood ready to protect his Lady from any potential threat. His huge, broad face, massive jaws and immense fangs projected absolute strength. Ajur looked exactly like what he was – a ferocious brute who would give any Champion a run for their money. Conor knew that the Lady loved all of the Champions without limit, but he could tell she held a special place in her heart for Ajur. The jaguar retained a deep cache of magical powers, seldom speaking of them to anyone. He exhibited a rare combination of cunning and intelligence that one could easily detect in his dark, brooding eyes. The huge cat heard Conor's initial step toward the Lady and craned his strong neck around for a look. Saying nothing to his fellow Champion, he merely winked once and smiled ever so slightly. Then he turned back to address the Lady, while Purugama held his wings high over her, sheltering her from the bright sunlight.

Purugama was the first of the Champions to come into Conor's life – a gigantic golden brown cougar, with wings any dragon would envy. He was a powerful addition to the glade of Champions, and an indispensable mentor and friend. Conor stared at the big cougar with an enormous amount of admiration, recalling the adventures they had shared together. *If not for this magnificent creature*, Conor thought, *what other course might my life have taken*? He watched Purugama protecting the Lady of the Light in a loving way, and he realized again that he would never change what had happened to him over these last six years. He felt a warm sensation swimming around in his head. He let it wash over him completely.

Taking all the good and bad, even the fact that he had not seen his home for more than two years, he began to understand everything now. His involvement in the fate of the Crossworlds was as necessary and important as any of the other Champions, indeed, maybe as important as any of the creators. He belonged here among these fantastic creatures, alongside the Lady of the Light. He let the rhythmic sensation play itself out inside his body before joining the Lady and the cats by the shoreline of the lake.

"Ajur, Purugama," he said as he approached. "I am glad to see the two of you faring so well."

"It is you who gives us pause," answered Purugama. "You certainly have grown, Conor. You are not the small boy I met on the mesa many years ago. I wonder if you might be too large to sit comfortably on my shoulders."

"I'll never be that big," replied Conor as he collapsed into the cougar's huge, furry chest. He grabbed a thick tuft of hair in each hand and rubbed vigorously. He felt Purugama slightly listing to the left. The huge Champion had no desire to have others see how vulnerable he was to a good scratching. He nudged Conor away with his monstrous forehead, swatting him lightly with the crown of his tail.

"I am pleased that you are well and safe," said the giant cougar to his longtime friend. "You have done an excellent job of locating and reassembling the Champions. Once you deliver Maya to the glade for his transformation, we can begin making final plans for the assault on Seefra's chamber of cells. We are anxious to face him, Conor, and I know you are as well."

"Only a fool would be anxious to face such a being," injected Ajur. "Your magic is formidable, Purugama, but never forget that Seefra's primary powers allow him to shift his form at will. He can alter his form and everything around him. You may find yourself facing Drazian again, in an unknown location where your powers could be neutralized."

"Ajur is correct," added the Lady. "No one among the creators knows how powerful he has become, and his ambition is the only force greater than his magic. He imprisoned Conor, kidnapped his lady friend, and as we speak he holds three of the five keys of the creators. He means to bypass the Circle of Evil and rule the Crossworlds. We will be careful, Ajur, but we haven't the time to be too cautious. We will need some of Purugama's passion for this engagement."

Ajur bowed his heavy, dark head in deference to the Lady. Instead of commenting further, he stepped closer to Conor, almost pinning him in between himself and Purugama.

"I am pleased the seekers found you and freed you from the cell of shadows, Conor," he said sincerely. "The shadow tiles represent the most despicable of Loken's creations. I wouldn't wish that type of captivity on my worst enemy."

"The loneliness became my greatest struggle," said Conor to the big, black jaguar. "I fear very few things, but the lack of companionship for so long began to wear on me."

Ajur nodded his wide head. "I apologize for our failure to destroy Seefra in his castle during our previous encounter. Perhaps if I had been more perceptive, we would have crushed him completely, and your companion would be with us instead of in his clutches. For that, I am truly sorry."

"Then we will work together to destroy Seefra once and for all," said Conor as he reached up to rub the bridge of Ajur's nose. "You have nothing to apologize for, Champion, for without your powers and counsel I might not be standing here today. Let us pool our knowledge and abilities to make certain he does not escape us again."

Conor made certain to address the great jaguar with the plural pronoun, "we" or "us." He did not want Ajur or any of the Champions taking responsibility for anything that had occurred over the course of their association. He didn't understand these animals completely, but he did feel a strong kinship with all of them. "It is I who should be making amends to all of you, for my transgression back on earth. Without my lapse in judgment, perhaps none of this would be necessary."

"Rubbish," inserted Purugama. "A human mistake, that is all. How many in the history of your planet have made similar blunders? Is it not in your nature to forgive? Then let it be ours as well. No one among the great Champions of the Crossworlds bears any ill will toward you, Conor. You have proven yourself worthy of our trust many times, and I speak for every one us. We hold you as dear and as valuable as we do each other, and that will never change. You are bound to us, Champion, as we are to you, forever."

"He speaks truth," added Ajur, nodding his head.

The Lady of the Light merely smiled. She scratched both Ajur and Purugama lightly, and then turned to address Conor.

"Come," she said as she guided him away from the two immense cats. "It is time for you to locate Maya."

MAYA

CHAPTER TWENTY-TWO

It was a pleasant, sunny afternoon in the tranquil neighborhood of Tierra Mesa. The long, sidewalk-edged streets slumbered, hot and silent, with no automobile traffic to disturb the few leaves resting in the recently swept gutters. The calmness of the area perfectly set the stage for a leisurely afternoon nap. The neighborhood was always quiet, free of unnecessary traffic or visitors, for Tierra Mesa was a closed community. When residents and guests entered, they had to leave the same way they came in. The designers of the community valued seclusion above all else.

The neighborhood sparkled with its prim detached homes. The architecture of each structure looked unique and inviting. The one and two story wood-framed homes gave off beckoning warmth. Each residence seemed to want to outdo its neighbor, for every yard was professionally landscaped and meticulously tended. Tierra Mesa was a dream neighborhood near the coast in Southern California; every family of middle class means wanted to live there, and those that did never dreamed that anything horrible might happen to them or those they loved. It truly was an ideal community.

Maya loved his new home in Tierra Mesa. He and his mistress had come from a townhouse community – with few places for a cat to enjoy himself – and Maya didn't expect to find anything promising in their new neighborhood when they first arrived. But when his mistress opened his transport box, he knew the rest of his years would be spent happily hunting and exploring the vast canyons and yards in his new neighborhood. After jumping from his container, he sprinted to the door of his new home demanding to be released into the wild. The moving van stood in the street, barely unpacked, and Maya was already making demands. At first, frustrated and tired from a demanding move, his mistress refused his request. She admonished him for his selfishness, telling the big black and white tabby that he had plenty of rooms in the house to explore. Maya won her over in the end, and after a few more insistent yowls, she gave in to his demands and slid open the patio door.

His new backyard gave him ample opportunities for exploration. His old house hadn't even had a backyard; the grounds of the townhouse complex left much to be desired. A multitude of possibilities existed here in this yard; different colored bushes of every size and shape lined the fences. Burrows and holes seemed to pop out of the ground everywhere as he prowled quietly underneath the foliage. The fence that closed off his yard from the rest of the canyon seemed very high and quite impassable. That would be overcome – far too many things waited for him in that canyon to allow any sort of barrier get in his way. As soon as his mistress began to pile boxes up on the patio in that area the journey would begin. He would wait patiently as he always had, for the world always delivered its secrets to a persistent cat.

Maya couldn't wait to find out who lived in the homes along the street. He easily scrambled up the six-foot wooden fence separating the backyard from the front yard. He stood at the top of the fence, straddling the stakes and taking in everything. He smiled as he gazed upon yard after yard for as far as his eyes could see. He had really hit the jackpot; he could spend the rest of his years investigating this neighborhood and never tire of what he found. He dropped down to the ground and began crawling through the fern bushes in his front yard. Crouched down like a tiger pursuing his dinner, Maya took his time seeing, sniffing and touching everything that crossed his path.

He decided to stay in his own yard for the first day. As tempting as it might be to run next door or across the street, he knew his mistress would fetch him back into the house if she saw him that far away on their first day here. So he happily played in the front yard of his new home, eating a few mouthfuls of grass, marking a rock or two, and just relishing the beauty of his new surroundings. He knew he would enjoy it here – every day, every hour, and every minute – for the rest of his life.

So it was that Maya became everyone's favorite on his street in Tierra Mesa. It was not uncommon for a neighbor to walk out into their backyard and find Maya sleeping soundly in the branches of one of "his" trees. He seemed as comfortable there as any jaguar in the wild, and he expertly placed himself within the branches so he wouldn't tumble out in mid-nap. If he awoke to find the neighbor watering their trees or performing some other duties in their yard, he simply smiled and closed his eyes again. At peace with his domain, Maya enjoyed the neighbors as much as they enjoyed him. He certainly never turned down a treat if it happened to be placed before him. He was rather selective though – only fresh chicken, fish, or perhaps beef liver would cause him to wake from his nap or run to a hand extended out of an open screen door.

255

Maya had lived in Tierra Mesa for close to a year. He knew the neighborhood better than the mailman did. He had a host of favorite hunting spots, he knew every tree in everyone's backyard for three blocks, and he knew precisely when his mistress and her consort returned home from work every day. He knew which homes contained other cats, and of those, which were playful. He knew which homes contained dogs, and of those, which ones he could easily outrun or intimidate. He knew where he could sleep safely, and where he would have to keep his eyes open for trouble. He loved his surroundings, and he loved his mistress for bringing him here. Her consort seemed like a decent enough fellow, even if he competed for his mistress' attention, but he did have a bad habit of coming to collect him at the most inopportune moments. Invariably, he would come to fetch him back to the house just when Maya stood ready to catch a prize or have a tussle with another cat. But he wasn't a bad sort really, and he cared for his mistress quite well. Maya had decided long ago to allow him to stay in the family.

Conor exited the corridor and landed on a sidewalk in a strange neighborhood he didn't recognize. It appeared to be more developed than the areas he remembered from back home, yet it seemed like a nice quiet place. He started running down the sidewalk, looking for any signs of Maya.

The Lady's words rang in his ear again and again, causing Conor to increase his pace every time. The creators had received a message from one of their most advanced seekers. Seefra would have the fourth key in his possession by the close of the final month before the equinox. With only one more key in Janine's possession, Seefra would be able to press his efforts more efficiently. His spells would be directed toward one specific type of magical energy. The odds of his finding the counter spell for the final key increased with each passing day.

Conor pushed those thoughts from his mind as he searched right to left and jogged up and down the perfectly tailored streets. He felt a momentary tug of fear when he realized that he might be miles from Maya. He shook the apprehension from his shoulders and picked up his pace a bit.

The three dogs, penned in with no one home to assure their captivity, pushed against the flimsy chain link fence that held them in their yard. Each of the powerful animals took their turn pounding away at the thick wire, sometimes digging with bloodied paws, sometimes biting at individual links, and even turning on the other dogs if they crept too close. The dogs knew the fence would ultimately lose the battle, as it had so many times before. They would be free to roam the neighborhood and terrorize other animals. They had already destroyed an innocent dog after freeing themselves once before, and the police had been called numerous times by terrified neighbors trapped in their homes by these repulsive animals. The owner of the dogs claimed ignorance after their repeated escapes. Their owner locked them in his yard before going to work, and that was all anyone could expect of him. Indifferent to his neighbors suffering, and downright rude when anyone suggested he might take more serious precautions with his violent animals, the owner of the pit bulls never bothered to mend the existing fence or buy a new one. The animals would break free again, of that his neighbors felt certain, and the owner would do nothing at all to prevent it.

The three dogs pressed their powerful bodies into the fence at one of the most flexible joints. The huge, slobbering jaws bent the links out until a few of them snapped cleanly. One of the dogs pushed its head through, receiving a nasty scrape across its ears. The other two, seeing their freedom so close at hand, began growling and clawing at the open links. In a rush similar to a bitch giving birth, the three snarling animals poured through the small opening in the fence.

After stopping to address their wounds, they scuffled a bit in the side yard before rolling out to the sidewalk in front of their master's house. Endless adventures awaited them, for he would not return home for many hours. They started down the sidewalk toward the canyon at the end of the street. One of the dogs chased a cat over a fence. Upon seeing the brutal threesome, a neighbor quickly gathered her gardening tools and hurried inside her house. She knew those dogs well and wanted nothing to do with them.

Maya stood by the sliding glass door in the living room, signaling his displeasure at not being released into the wild. After all, his mistress had taken the day off, so he should be allowed to roam freely while she was home. He bellowed his most dramatic meows, and eventually she came and pulled the door back. Maya zoomed over the threshold and ran out onto the deck. He soaked up the sun, rolling over onto his back to give his stomach a good dose of penetrating warmth. After a quick sunbathe, he jumped up and raced over to the fence. Up to the top in a flash, the big tabby walked his paws down the other side until he had to drop down onto the pebble-strewn asphalt. He walked out into his front yard – his domain – sniffing everything that floated past his nostrils.

After checking the area for any new inhabitants, and marking his territorial boundaries again, Maya silently padded out onto the sidewalk. He lifted his beautifully patterned head to the sky, sniffing the air for any signs of trouble. Sensing nothing out of the ordinary, he moved onto the sidewalk and out into the street. After checking for cars, he sprinted across the street and jumped into the yard directly across from his mistress' house. Mr. Richards was always home, and he usually had some delicious leftovers. Maya supposed he could act cute for the sake a healthy piece of chicken breast. He scaled the fence and in seconds he had placed himself outside of Mr. Richards' back door.

Conor was getting close to calling upon the Lady of the Light for assistance. The corridor she had drawn forth for him hadn't placed him anywhere close to Maya. He felt more frustrated with every empty street he inspected. She had told him Maya would be clearly visible, but Conor had yet to see anything more than a newspaper left on a front porch. He became more worried with every passing second. He didn't know how he would explain it if he arrived too late to save the leader of the Crossworlds Champions.

CHAPTER TWENTY-THREE

Seefra looked up at the ceiling of his laboratory and howled with glee.
The sound of his triumphant shriek pressed against the boundaries of the lengthy room, spilling out into the cavernous chamber of cells and beyond. The shadow warriors, stationed just beyond the doors of the laboratory and ordered never to even flinch unless by the command of their master, did their best to stand perfectly still under the vocal onslaught. Without even turning to look at each other, the guards knew that the sound coming from within meant either their promotion or their doom. If the master of darkness had scored a victory, they would live another day. If he had suffered another defeat, however, their lives would end at the bottom of the chasm, pummeled to a pulp by the beast within the fog. They stood their ground, unmoving, awaiting their fate.

Inside the laboratory, Seefra held the fourth key of the creators in his tiny, spindly hand. In the other, with an equal amount of force, he held the sleeve of Janine's cargo jacket. He focused all of his attention on the key – the second to the last key he had worked so diligently to recover. Now only one remained, and even with the incredible mystery fused into the metallurgy of that brilliant instrument, he would decipher the code in very little time. He could focus his experiments acutely, toward one goal, instead of five, or three, or even two. The five keys of the creators would soon be his to wield. He felt a tug against his left hand, and turned his six eyes toward the young woman who wore the coat.

"You were correct, my dear," he said while drilling Janine with his pinched eyes. "I have defeated the spell placed on the fourth key. But that is where your prophecy ends, for I *will* decode the magic placed on the final and most powerful of all the keys."

Janine struggled against his grip. For one so slight, Seefra clenched an amazingly powerful fist. She could not break his hold on her.

"Let me go!" she demanded. "You have completed your tests. The fourth key is now yours to command. Send me back to my cell where I can be free of you."

"I will grant your wish, my dear," responded the master of darkness. "But I wish to show something first. Something I believe you will find quite interesting."

Seefra reached into the pocket of his tiny waistcoat and produced a small crystal. He shook it in his hand, watching it expand until it matched one of the crystal tiles in the cell where Janine slept. After a short incantation, Seefra shook the tile again and then tossed it lightly into the air. The tile stopped immediately in front of them and began expanding. It stretched first lengthwise and then vertically until it resembled a huge viewing screen. Seefra passed his tiny hand in front of the panel, causing it to spark and glow with a soft, dark texture. The border of the frame solidified, and the membrane within became soft and wavy. It began changing colors, and before long a picture emerged within the solid borders. It looked like a movie of a contemporary neighborhood. It showed a long row of homes warming themselves in the bright sun. A young man jogged quickly along the far sidewalk, turning his head now and again as if looking for something, or someone. The picture crystallized, finally allowing Janine to recognize the runner on the sidewalk.

"Conor," she said with utter shock. "CONOR!" she screamed while trying to rip her jacket away from Seefra's grip. She knew the look of a corridor when she saw one. All she had to do was break away from her captor and jump into the screen. She could be with him in seconds. She began thrashing wildly against Seefra's grip. When she felt him losing purchase, she fought even harder.

"Zof!" commanded Seefra. "Adzico!"

The two shadow warriors broke their stances and ran into the laboratory. They immediately took charge of Janine, roughly tearing her from Seefra's grip. They assumed positions on either side of her, grasping her underneath each arm. Almost holding her up off the ground, the two warriors waited with blank expressions for their master's next command.

"Yes," began Seefra, now swishing comfortably in front of the screen. "Conor of Earth, alive and free, and searching for the Champions of the Crossworlds. He has done rather well, all things considered. He has collected the entire group with the exception their leader, and under sometimes strenuous circumstances. You are watching him as he searches for Maya, the leader of the Crossworlds defenders. He runs through a very average neighborhood, much like those you and he resided in before becoming involved in matters beyond your comprehension. "Before allying himself with the creators as the leader of the Champions, Maya spent his days frolicking along this street as a common housecat. His true lineage had been hidden from the creators by forces even we do not understand. Be that as it may, after reassembling most of the Champions from their natural surroundings,

Conor has traveled through one final corridor to collect the last of the enemy that will oppose us. They will come here together to free you and reclaim the five keys of the creators. Maya is the key to their success, an immensely powerful warrior in his own right. But I have prepared a small surprise for both him and for Conor of Earth as well."

Janine twitched at the sound of Seefra's threat. She watched the image on the screen change. It showed a peaceful front yard with a lush variety of trees and bushes. A light breeze wafted through the branches, pecking at the smallest of the leaves. One particular wispy bush moved more than the rest, drawing Janine's attention to it. There, hidden beneath a leafy umbrella, crouched a black and white housecat. Janine squinted slightly until she felt sure and then softly uttered the name.

"Maya."

The small cat sat crouched within the thick brush, unmoving, except for the few strands of fur displaced by the wind. He looked straight ahead, eyes locked on a point across the front yard. No one, not even the birds playing in the low branches in the yard, could see Maya's tail rapidly swishing back and forth under the brush.

"Look at him, in all of his innocence," said Seefra in a sarcastic tone. "The leader of the greatest group of warriors ever arrayed against the forces of the Circle of Evil. Here, in this reincarnation, however, he stands alone, completely helpless."

Janine opened her mouth to respond, but before she could utter a sound, the image melted away, shifting again into another vision. In obviously the same neighborhood, but on a different street, a small group of animals rumbled down the street. Janine couldn't make them out at first, but after the screen solidified she sucked her breath deep down into her lungs. Her heart jumped into her throat as she watched three medium-to-large pit bulls scurrying along the sidewalk. With their huge, powerful jaws jutting out in front of them, the three predators slobbered their way through the neighborhood. Anything that came within their field of vision was immediately chased away or attacked. They even assaulted each other from time to time if one pushed another one off the sidewalk or tried to take the lead. They were hideous animals, bred to kill anything they managed to run down, and they were running loose in Maya's neighborhood.

"Take a close look, my dear," remarked Seefra as he swished contentedly in front of the screen. "Take a very close look at the three animals. You might notice that they are not so ordinary after all."

Janine stepped closer to the screen, following the three muscular dogs with her nose as they tramped down the sidewalk. She looked again and again, failing to see anything abnormal about their appearance. She finally backed away, turning toward Seefra.

"I see nothing fascinating about those dogs," she said with a note of irritation in her voice, "except for the fact that they should all be put down."

"An interesting aspiration," answered Seefra. "You might feel quite a bit more enthusiastic about your assessment momentarily."

The master of darkness leaned toward Janine, moving his tentacles in her direction. After positioning himself next to her, he leaned in with his insect-like head. He turned and looked at her with his six dark eye slits.

"For, you see, my dear," he continued, "the minds of these three dogs, as you refer to them, have been taken over by three of my

most accomplished shadow warriors. They have the physical features of dogs, but my warriors control their thoughts and movements. They may look like a bumbling group of stray animals, but I
assure you, these warriors know precisely where they are headed."

"Maya," said Janine softly, for the second time.

"Yes," replied Seefra. "The leader of the Champions will soon
find himself confronted by overwhelming odds. Just one animal
with this much power could destroy most anything else of equal
size, but I want to make an example of Maya. I want to embarrass
Conor of Earth as well, for he will come upon Maya just a few
seconds too late. My shadow warriors will then attack him with
an equal measure of vengeance. They know Conor of Earth's story,
about how he nearly destroyed their master, and they seek retribution. They will fall upon him in those animal forms like a group of
rabid tornados. Believe me, my dear; there will be nothing left for
the creators to save this time."

"CONOR!" screamed Janine as loudly as she could. "RUN! RUN
FOR YOUR LIFE!" She struggled hard against the two guards, but
they held her fast. Seefra swished on the ground next to her.

"Scream as loudly as you wish," said Seefra, gloating. "There is
nothing you can do, and neither of them will escape the trap I have
set. See for yourself."

Janine lifted her head and looked at the screen. The image shifted again, this time pulling the street scene with the three pit bulls
back away from her field of vision. The layout altered its dimension,
with the image now presenting a view from high above the neighborhood. Janine could see the street with the pit bulls. She could
also see Maya's street, and she could see Conor sprinting down the
sidewalk of another street, seeking his objective. The images looked
quite a bit smaller, but there was no mistaking the outcome.

"They will converge on one another in matter of minutes," said the master of darkness. "Conor and the three warriors travel on two different streets toward the same destination. Maya sits at that point; completely unaware of the fate that awaits him. It should be an interesting encounter. Shall we stay here to witness the slaughter?"

Janine could think of nothing else to do. She spat in Seefra's face with all the force she could muster, calling him names she had never used in her life. She practically pulled her two guards out of the laboratory as she tried to get back to her cell. The shadow warriors, after Seefra gave them permission to leave, finally fell in line with Janine. The master of darkness wiped away the spittle by activating a stiff breeze in front of his face. He watched the screen for a few more moments, tossing about the idea of staying behind to watch the massacre. As his thoughts floated to other duties, however, he turned to leave his laboratory. With a wave of his tiny hand the corridor screen shrunk back down to the size of a single tile. It followed him out of the laboratory, finally dropping into a pocket of his waistcoat as he rounded the corner by the hallway.

CHAPTER TWENTY-FOUR

Moving at a fairly good clip, Conor jogged around yet another street corner in Tierra Mesa. He had covered at least a dozen blocks during his search; so far he hadn't seen hide or hair of Maya. As he ran down the lengthy avenue with the perfectly groomed lawns and manicured gardens, he began to drink in a sense of familiarity. *Something about this particular street just felt right,* he thought. The homes seemed to exude a comfortable friendliness. The sun, formerly quite hot on his forehead and shoulders, appeared to have lost some of its intensity. The perfect warmth of the environment signaled to Conor that he had finally arrived at the right street. This must be where Maya lived, or at least where he liked to roam. The young man smiled with the realization that he might indeed be close to the end of his journey. He slowed his pace, not wanting to miss any sign that Maya might be near. He kept his attention riveted on his side of the street, almost forgetting that a whole different section of homes existed across the avenue. Unfortunately, he looked for Maya so intently, and with so many of his senses, that he never saw or heard the enraged group of pit bulls as they rounded the corner after him. The dogs ran together roughly ten yards behind Conor. Their pace allowed them to keep up with him, but not overtake and pass him as they rumbled down the sidewalk.

The pit bulls were tired, hot and angry. So far, they had unsuccessfully chased three cats, one dog, and two homeowners. They had received nothing for their efforts. No food, no water, and no challenges. As a matter of fact, the only scuffles they found themselves in all day were with each other. Those were no fun, however, because they always ended up in a draw. The muscular dogs wanted to satisfy their bloodlust; they wanted something to put up a fight, even if only for a few seconds. They certainly didn't want to have to go home without getting something out of their illegal freedom.

The lead dog stopped dead in its tracks. Its head reared up roughly, causing a severe strain to its neck and shoulders. The other two pit bulls stopped sprinting momentarily to watch the strange occurrence, and then they also began to contort and twitch. The three dogs whimpered for a few seconds, both from pain and fear. Something was taking over their bodies and their minds, and their limited intelligence simply could not deal with it. They didn't cry out, however, they simply whined as the transformation took place.

The lead pit bull recovered first. The other two followed within seconds. They looked into each others' eyes, communicating in some bizarre fashion. They did not attack each other or scuffle at all anymore, because they now had a group objective. Each of them knew about a cat at the end of the street, a cat sleeping in his favorite tree, a cat comfortably wiling away the afternoon without a care in the world. It was the cat, they knew, whose world was about to change radically. They turned together, as a group, and began running toward the house at the end of the block.

Maya shifted his position slightly, removing a small nub from his back. Of all the places to sleep in his neighborhood, this tree provided the most restful slumber of any of them. He loved to come out here late in the afternoon and hang in the branches like a wet towel, surveying the neighborhood as he waited for his mistress to come home. After taking a long look at his domain, he enjoyed curling up amongst the leaves and sleeping the afternoon away. Sometimes he would awaken after dark to the sound of his mistress' consort coming to call him home. He would wait silently, usually until the last minute and then give away his location by emitting a strained groan at the end of a huge stretch. Thinking about these moments, he adjusted his position one last time and fell back into a deep sleep.

Conor examined every yard closely as he walked down the sidewalk. He looked under every car, bush, awning, deck, and anywhere a cat might be hiding. It was only because of a break in his concentration that Conor heard the small pack of dogs running across the street. He looked over absentmindedly and saw what type of dogs they were.

"Pit bulls," he whispered.

Pit bulls running loose in a pack could only mean bad news. He watched them for a second or two, trying to get a fix on where they were heading. He wanted to know where, in the middle of this fine afternoon, three pit bulls could be headed together. He watched them run for about ten yards, and then turned his head in the direction of their objective. The three dogs, now running flat out toward their goal, began to snort and snarl as they smelled fear dripping down from the sky all around them. When Conor saw what they were after, his whole body shook as if blasted by an electric prod.

"Mind of the creators," said Conor, out loud this time. "It's Maya."

Without even thinking, Conor roared his frustration at the three dogs as he took off running. Even with his increased powers, he couldn't seem to catch up to any of them. They ran with an almost superhuman speed, kicking up chunks of asphalt as they darted across the street toward Maya. Conor saw the lead pit bull, bigger and stronger than the other two, pull into the lead as it jumped up onto the sidewalk and raced into the yard where Maya slept.

Maya lay in his tree, completely comfortable and dreaming about his old neighborhood. A woman had lived next door to his mistress for quite some time, and she seemed to enjoy an unnatural affinity with cats of all types. He could sometimes count on her for a good scratch or a small treat, but only every once in a while. She could not be repeatedly persuaded as so many others in the neighborhood could. Although it irritated Maya to no end, he felt a grudging respect for her.

After some years she took on a consort, just as his mistress had done. Maya enjoyed waiting for him to arrive home from work or the beach or wherever his world took him. He gave Maya a great deal of respect, only petting him so long as Maya wished to be touched. He did something that Maya found most attractive as well, something that no other human had ever done. He talked to him as if he were another person, asking him about his day, his girlfriends, and his hunting adventures. Maya felt an affinity with this human whenever he came home. It made him feel oddly wonderful, as much as any cat could feel honored about sharing a pedestal with a human. He smiled, thinking back to those times as his dreams faded. As he emerged from sleep he began to hear the snarling sounds of the charging dogs. Maya shook his head and opened his eyes, irritated that the neighbors had left their animals outside again.

When he caught sight of the first pit bull sprinting through the front yard like a small locomotive, Maya came wide awake in an instant. The adrenaline of flight or fight surged through his body so rapidly he lost his footing in the tree. He scrambled to regain his hold on the branches, but it was no use. He felt the hand of gravity pulling him from the safety of the tree. Turning as he fell, he directed his body as best he could toward a thick stand of sprawling ground firs. If he could manage to land within those burly roots, he might just be able to stay clear of the savage dogs.

Conor lost sight of the first pit bull as it dashed into the yard ahead of him. In his peripheral vision, he saw Maya struggling in the tree. He knew somehow that the lead dog was heading straight for him. He couldn't concentrate on that, however. He would have to take the other two down if he could and let Maya tackle the first one. If he could manage to get away from one, Conor felt certain he could delay the other two long enough to make good on Maya's escape. Running as fast as he could, he rounded the corner by the front door of the house and bolted across the lawn. He heard the hideous sound of a dog closing in for the kill. Immediately following that grotesque snarl, he heard Maya issue a warning of his own. That loud and angry hiss made one thing clear: come closer and pay a horrible price.

Luckily, Maya landed exactly where he wanted to – in a hole between the fir plants at the far end of the yard. Crouching low within the roots, he lifted his hooded head only high enough to see the huge pit bull charging straight at him. He puffed his fur up as wide as it would inflate and let loose a hiss that would have turned back almost any living animal. Maya could never handle a pit bull one-on-one, but he was no lightweight either. He had defeated or scared off almost every dog in the neighborhood at one time or another. At sixteen and a half pounds of lanky muscle, Maya could throw the lumber if backed into a corner.

The pit bull crashed headlong into the ground fir. Its momentum took its body deep into the branches, trapping its muscular frame inside dozens of very strong and deeply buried roots. Its powerful jaws could do nothing to help regain its freedom. The dog lay frozen within the roots, snarling at its prey, which stood only twelve inches away, staring in fascination.

Maya attacked immediately. He pounced on the trapped pit bull, grabbing onto its body with all four paws. With his razor-sharp claws fully extended, he latched onto the perplexed and frightened animal. Maya bit down on the dog's left eye with a rage that surprised even him. He ripped the eye from the socket, spewing blood and sinew all over himself, the dog, and the sprawling fir. Instead of feasting on the other eye, Maya clamped down on the bull's neck, digging his fangs deep into the skin and muscle. When he found what he sought, he chomped down on the carotid artery and pulled with every ounce of strength he had.

The pit bull screamed and yelped even louder than it had upon losing its eye. It somehow knew that it was going to perish at the hands of a cat, making its rage much more intense than the pain. He felt the cat releasing his grip, and out of its good eye, watched as the big black and white tabby backed up toward the fence. The pit bull smiled inwardly with its last breath, knowing that its two brothers would tear this foe to shreds in mere seconds. The pit bull turned its mangled head and watched the other two dogs jump cleanly over the sprawling firs, heading toward the fence line and the cat.

Conor powered through the yard, placing his last step on a tree trunk to propel himself toward the two snarling dogs. He dove at them head first, leading the two bulls by enough space so he would take both of them out like a blocker clearing the way for a running back. The dogs never saw him coming; their complete attention stayed with Maya the entire time. Conor hit both animals simultaneously, knocking them into the fence about five yards from where Maya sat crouched and ready. The bulls sprang up instantly, still completely intent on destroying their prey. Conor tried desperately to stop their progress, but his right ankle had caught up in the roots of the fir. He had also sprained his left knee and ankle when he dove into the two pit bulls. He lay there, helpless to do anything against the two remaining dogs. He pleaded with the creators under his breath to give him freedom of movement again. He looked over at Maya, now backing away from the advancing pit bulls. The fence line would provide no means of escape for him; the top of the spears were covered with a thick line of standing firs. The branches of that particular tree would not support a cat of any size. If he tried to climb the fence and escape, he would fall back down into the jaws of the waiting dogs. Conor watched as the two slobbering, snarling pit bulls bracketed their prey against the fence.

"I'm sorry, Maya," screamed Conor, as he struggled with the entangled roots. His heart was racing and his entire body was overtaken with rage. He couldn't believe it was going to end like this for Maya and he would have to sit here helplessly watching. "I failed you."

Suddenly, the bright, sunny sky over Tierra Mesa exploded with a pair of immensely powerful lights. The huge frames of blinding luminescence surfaced in mid-air, forcing Conor to turn his head away quickly. Two expansive corridors, mirroring each other's positions on either side of the street, unwrapped themselves to dimensions taller and wider than a pair of motion picture screens. The sky bracketing the tranquil street looked like something out of a special effects movie. The neighborhood appeared abnormally calm in stark comparison to the two huge dominating corridors, hovering a dozen feet off the ground on both sides of the street.

Another bright flash of light and a powerful gust of wind hit Conor squarely in the face. He looked at the two openings and to his amazement and utter relief, Therion and Surmitang, fully restored to their lethal sizes, fell from within the corridors to the street below. They hit the asphalt running as they rushed forward to save their Lord. The massive cats, each weighing between one and three tons, bounded across the street toward Maya and the two pit bulls. As they ran, they both emptied their lungs, throwing deafening roars at the three animals in the yard ahead of them.

The two Champions worked together in perfect precision. Surmitang guarded Therion's flank as they raced onward. No animal would be able to slow the big lion's progress without first fighting their way through an angry tiger. Therion kept his eyes focused on the target, always ready for any switch in strategy or tactics. Working together this way, the two warriors would blast through any defense on their way toward their objective. Without even acknowledging each other, these two very different cats joined together in a hunting team as formidable as any in history. When they saw their Lord crouching by the fence line, the two Champions let their voices explode again.

The confrontation between Maya and the two pit bulls ceased when they heard the approaching Champions. When the first of the snarling roars heralded across the yard, the two dogs forgot all about Maya. They looked in every direction, streaks of panic and terror racing up and down their spines. The fence line shuddered under the sound wave blowing through the neighborhood. Two shattered stakes flew through the large fir at the top of the line, smashing against the wall of the house next door.

After they watched the fence wobbling under the assault, the animals yelped and whined as two massive shadows fell upon them. The apparitions loomed over them, gigantic and menacing. The bodies of the two Champions blocked all light from reaching the yard, the fence, or even the neighbor's home. The pit bulls visibly shook now, petrified by what they saw coming for them.

Maya saw two things happen at the same time. First, he saw angry purpose change to absolute terror in the faces and body language of the two dogs. There was something sharply distinctive about the roar of a wild cat, or of any cat for that matter. Maya could tell the two bulls knew their time was up. They saw their demise in the huge shapes coming through the yard. Instinct became a powerful communicator, and in these dogs the message came through loud and clear.

The other thing Maya witnessed almost made him faint away. Two wild cats, handsome and incredibly huge, came around the corner of the house toward the two pit bulls. Different from any cats he had ever seen, the massive felines deftly ducked under the eave of the house. One had a gigantic mane, beautifully cared for, and dark like the dirt from his mistress' garden. He appeared to be quite a bit bigger than the other cat, although both were immense. The other cat wore a coat the likes of which Maya had never imagined. It seemed as though every color of the rainbow lent itself to the fur. The face of the cat looked threatening all by itself, with the streaks of white, black, and orange flying in every direction. They ran together as if they hunted in a pack every day of their lives – quite serious and very determined.

After a moment Maya realized that they had come to save him. For what reason, he could not fathom, but he saw what they focused on and why they had come. Their eyes never left the two dogs, and their body language emitted a single message. Maya blinked once just to make certain of his observations. If he blinked again, he might miss what was about to happen, so he crouched low into the pathway by the fence and kept his eyes wide open. He watched as his two giant saviors performed their duty.

The two pit bulls took one look at what was coming through the yard and immediately scattered, leaving two puffs of rising dust where they had previously stood. They tried to give yelps of terrified fear but found their vocal chords to be temporarily inoperative. The only parts of their bodies that worked seemed to be their legs, and both dogs pumped them frantically. Clawing, climbing and pushing their way past each other, the pit bulls zoomed out of the yard toward the street. The terrified animals left all sense of brotherhood behind, kicking up dirt and rocks and debris trying to get away from Therion and Surmitang.

The two Champions attacked the pit bulls without mercy. Surmitang pounced on the bull closest to the street, landing next to it with a thunderous crash. Rearing up on his hind feet, the huge tiger swatted the dog like a fly with a swipe of his forepaw. The impact sent the bull rocketing toward a small car parked across the street. Smashing against the metal door panel with a sickening thud, the dog rolled around on the ground like a drunken sailor for a few moments. Finally shaking what remained of its brains back together, the pit bull stood on four wobbly feet and found itself staring directly into the golden eyes and striped face of a Sumatran tiger. The giant cat made the car he stood next to look like a baby carriage. The enormous tiger licked his lips as he walked toward the dog. At the sight of the approaching tiger, the pit bull lost control of all bodily functions and peed all over itself as it anticipated the end.

Therion caught the second animal as it tried to cut away down the fence line. Soaring out of the sky like a huge golden angel, he landed flush with both front paws on top of the scampering dog. The sprawling fir that had trapped the first pit bull exploded into a hail of green and brown confetti. With almost five thousand pounds of bulk behind his limbs, Therion drove the shrieking animal straight into the ground. The fence line, structurally sound only seconds ago, erupted, sending a volcanic spray of wooden splinters about the yard. Sixteen feet of fence disintegrated immediately, and the rest came out of the ground as if plucked like a row of toothpicks. The crater underneath Therion, some twenty feet in diameter and six feet deep at its center, contained a mixture of landscaping and pieces of what used to be one of Seefra's shadow warriors.

Surmitang returned to the yard, holding a squealing, wriggling pit bull in his huge jaws. When he saw what Therion had created while destroying the other bull, Surmitang used his great height to slam the dog down into the center of the crater. The dog whimpered while staring up into the gigantic faces of its tormentors, but did not try to escape. It just lay there, injured and horrified by what had happened. Oddly, the one thought that repeated itself over and over in the dog's mind had to do with the fenced yard in which it lived. The pit bull decided that if it survived this ordeal, it would never, ever sneak out again.

"Perhaps Maya would care to finish this one himself," said Surmitang, kicking a mound of dirt at the terrified animal.

"Apparently," answered Therion, "Maya defeated the largest of the pack before we arrived." Therion motioned to the one-eyed pit bull with most of his neck ripped out. The big tiger took a step forward, sniffing the lifeless animal. He nudged its ear lightly, making certain it was dead. He chuffed at the bull, believing without hesitation that it got exactly what it deserved.

Surmitang looked up at Maya, bowing his head slightly. "Surely he was meant to lead the Champions as our Lord. Look at what he overcomes even in his natural state. The dog he faced was three or four times his own size; a remarkable feat, even for one as advanced as Maya."

Conor lay only a few feet from the carnage caused by the Crossworlds Champions. He had watched them defend their Lord with a savage vengeance unlike anything he had ever seen. Surmitang had shown an amazing capacity for cunning and ferocity in the forests of his home world, but this was something else altogether. If this was how the Champions fought when one of their own faced mortal danger, then the coming war with Seefra and the shadow warriors didn't frighten him at all. It was Therion and Surmitang who had just scared the wits out of him. These immensely strong cats had shown him a side of their nature that he would never forget. Even now, after the short battle had been decided, he had to work to collect himself. He breathed as normally as possible as he tried to free his foot from the twisting, binding roots.

Maya hopped over the gigantic paws of his saviors, moving to Conor's side as soon as he felt it safe to do so. With a delicate touch known only to cats, he inspected his foot and the remains of the sprawling fir that entangled it. He looked with concern first at the mangled, twisting roots, then at Conor, and finally back to the roots again. He nosed around for a bit, pawing at the thick cords of wrecked foliage. At length he looked up to Surmitang and Therion as if they were just two ordinary cats in the neighborhood. Even after the slaughter he had just witnessed, Maya didn't seem the slightest bit daunted by his new benefactors. His only interest lay in freeing Conor from the painful trap that presently occupied his limbs.

Surmitang looked at the pit bull cowering below him. The dog's fierce nature had been frightened away; it sat there swimming in its own excrement at the bottom of the crater. It was no more going to move than speak in tongues; the animal was that scared. Surmitang snarled at the tiny dog, baring his teeth slightly. Then he turned his attention to Conor, who pressed his hands against the ground as he stared up into the huge golden eyes of his brother.

"And what did you plan to do, young one?" asked Surmitang in a booming, baritone voice. "Did you hope to convince these disgusting animals to join you in your self-made prison?"

Conor smiled as he grabbed a handful of dirt and rocks. He flung the mess at Surmitang's face and watched the big tiger turn his head away. Knowing him as Conor did, his only concern would be his perfect appearance. The great cat shook his striped fur vigorously, returning his eyes to Conor for a brief moment. As he prepared to lower his head and break Conor's bonds, a massive golden snout moved past Surmitang's multicolored grin.

Therion took the bulk of the root system in his mighty jaws and clamped his huge teeth around it. The base of the tangled fir split into a large group of severed chunks of kindling. This gave Conor the opportunity to tear away most of the heavy branches encircling his foot. Once free, the young man took stock of his injuries. He tried to stand on his left foot and almost fell forward into the pit with the panicked dog. He could stand briefly on his right foot, but not without some assistance. For this he grabbed a large handful of the fur on Surmitang's cheek along with one of his ears. He tugged downward as hard as he could as he watched the great Sumatran tiger grimace under the pain and embarrassment of having to serve as Conor's nurse.

"You did well, Conor," said Therion, crouching low to the ground. "You delayed their progress just long enough, and you sacrificed your own well-being in the process. The Lady of the Light will be pleased."

"Agreed," added Surmitang tersely. "Without your interference these foul animals might have had their way with Maya. I am pleased by the outcome, and I am not the least bit regretful about disposing of these horrid creatures." Surmitang looked around and snarled at the lone pit bull.

Maya ignored the conversation playing out in front of him. He seemed to realize and accept that something remarkable had occurred in his neighborhood. He knew this strange young man and these gigantic cats had come here to save him from a horrible death, and he felt he owed them something in return. He also understood that these events would result in an amazing journey for him, and he wanted to prepare himself for travel. He had two things to take care of before leaving, however, and being an orderly cat, he wanted things left just right. First he wanted the last of the pit bulls dispensed of, so he walked past his two massive brothers and into the crater. He padded quietly right up to the nose of the shaking dog, looking directly into its eyes the entire time. Maya gruffled once, then twice, and then actually nudged the frightened pit bull with his nose. The terrified dog, too scared to even breath a moment ago, took a step toward the far edge of the crater. When he didn't hear any warnings from the huge cats standing at the other edge, he took two more steps. Maya nudged him again, gruffling with a bit more emphasis now. The dog finally concluded that its life might indeed be worth running for, and took off like lightning through the yard and down the street. Therion, Surmitang and Conor watched this strange interaction unfold with confusion burning in their eyes.

With that complete, Maya started his second task. He lowered his head to the ground and placed his forepaws on his collar. Grabbing the band on each side of his neck, he backed himself up with his hind legs until the collar inched itself over his head. After freeing himself of his identification, he grabbed it in his mouth and carried it over to Conor. He dropped the collar and tags at Conor's feet and looked up and the young man with a purposeful stare. He yowled at Conor once, jumping into the same tree he had occupied before all of the madness began. When he reached his favorite branch he called out to Conor again while scratching the end of one of the larger twigs. When Conor didn't immediately respond, Maya became more insistent, meowing and scratching the branch in question.

Conor looked at the two Champions and shrugged his shoulders. He bent down to pick up the collar, and when he lifted it off the ground Maya became even more adamant. He watched him call out to him as he slapped the tree branch with his right forepaw.

"Place the collar on the branch, Conor," instructed Surmitang.

Conor lifted the collar and set it on the branch. Maya immediately walked to the end of the limb, inspecting Conor's handiwork. He yowled impatiently upon seeing how the collar had been hung.

"Hang it so the information on the tags points away from the tree," said Therion, truly fascinated by the bizarre ritual.

Conor did as instructed, and when Maya observed that the collar was hung in the appropriate fashion, he cooed and purred loudly. Without any warning at all, he jumped from the tree into Conor's arms. Conor nearly toppled over as the heavy cat hit him in the chest with all four paws. He managed to steady himself, and he set Maya on Therion's broad back. The black and white tabby crawled forward into the thick mane, pushing his head out near the top of Therion's neck. He meowed loudly, signaling to everyone present that he felt ready to go wherever they wanted to take him. Conor pulled himself onto Surmitang's back. Grabbing the great tiger's ears a little too forcefully, Conor smiled at the sight of a tiny housecat riding on the back of a huge lion. He even chuckled a little while smacking Surmitang on the cheek.

"Maya's right," he said as he looked at the curious faces peering through the windows of the homes on the street. "We'd better go, and right away. I'd hate to be here if the wrong people show up, and the creators help us if the idiot television stations get here before we leave."

Therion took the lead and jumped over what remained of the bushes in the yard. Surmitang followed close behind, running and jumping roughly just to see what it might take to throw Conor off his back. His antics proved worthless, however, because Conor held on tightly with both hands and his one strong foot. Maya seemed to be having the time of his life, hunkered down inside the huge furry mane of his personal transport. Every few seconds he would bark out a command or two, as if he captained the gigantic lion's course.

When they reached the broken asphalt in the center of the street, both Champions focused on their respective corridors. They walked to the middle of the avenue, facing the mammoth picture screens sitting quietly above each sidewalk. The corridors sensed the close presence of their passengers and began activating themselves. A few sparks and stray bolts of energy flashed across each of the screens as they systematically arranged their membranes. Then all became quiet again. The soft, rippling surface of the silver portals invited the Champions into their midst.

The two cats quickly checked on their passengers before embarking on their journeys. Therion smiled broadly as he rolled his eyes up to his forehead, in an attempt to see if Maya needed a moment to prepare. When he finally spotted the leader of the Crossworlds Champions, he saw a very small cat with his paws forward and his face pointed in anticipation directly at the portal. The look on Maya's face told Therion everything he needed to know. Even at this stage, before any transformation had taken place, Maya knew exactly where they were headed, and he looked as if he couldn't wait to get there.

Just then, the two Champions sent warning growls in the direction of a van from the local news station as it careened around the corner, almost on two wheels. A neighbor, obviously watching from the safety of a locked window, must have called in an eyewitness report.

"Look at that!" exclaimed the reporter as he locked eyes with a lion that stood taller than the van. "Stop the rig and get the equipment now! We've got to get a shot of this before anything else happens!"

The news crew scrambled out of the van. They fell all over themselves trying to get everything in place. In less than three minutes, they stood camera ready, waiting for the first sound and light test.

Therion and Surmitang felt uncomfortable with the intrusion, and Conor quickly reaffirmed their suspicions. "We need to go *now*," he said quickly. "If those jerks get a picture of us, these poor people living on this street will never be left alone. Make the jump. Let's get out of here."

The two giant Champions wasted no more time. Surmitang leapt first, carrying Conor into the flowing mist of the membrane. Therion ascertained their safety and then followed through his own corridor. The giant screens, after receiving their passengers, zipped themselves up until nothing at all remained. Aside from the terrible mess in the front yard of one home, the quiet street in Tierra Mesa looked as it had only a few hours earlier. The only remaining observers were the news crew, now openly gawking at the street in front of them, and one very frightened pit bull cowering underneath the deck of a home across the street.

"Mind of the creators," said the camerawoman. "Did you see that?"

"The question is," answered the reporter, "did we get it on *film*?"

"Sorry, Denny," said the man in the van checking the monitors. "We missed it clean. Not a frame."

"Let's get the neighbors anyway," said the frustrated reporter. "Set up for a pan shot with that one house as center focus. What was the name of the guy who phoned it in?"

CHAPTER TWENTY-FIVE

Conor lowered himself from Surmitang's striped shoulders as soon as the four travelers landed safely in the glade of Champions. Although always ready to tease Conor at every opportunity, on this occasion the great tiger stood strong and firm while Conor disembarked. When the young man finally placed his injured legs on the ground, Surmitang did his best to help him stand.

"You'll give everyone the wrong impression, brother," said Conor while thanking the big tiger with a rough scratch behind the ear.

"What impression might that be, Conor?" asked a voice as beautiful as dawn on a spring day. "That he might care about you, or even feel love for you?"

Conor turned his head and smiled broadly. The Lady of the Light stood amongst the other three Champions – Eha, Purugama and Ajur. Therion strolled over to join his brothers. Maya didn't move a muscle as he rode inside Therion's mane. He watched the Lady's every movement, but did not approach her or make a sound.

The Lady left her group of Champions and walked over to Conor. She removed a lock of hair from his eyes, moving it across his forehead with a graceful pinch of her fingers. As she touched the strand of hair, Conor felt the pain of his latest journey leaving his legs. A rush of powerful strength returned to his limbs, allowing him to relax and stand in a resting position. The Lady of the Light stood quietly, staring into Conor's eyes. He could see the smile in her soul highlighted in those hypnotic silver eyes. He smiled back to her but stayed silent, preferring to reserve comment until after she spoke again. Surmitang, convinced of his brother's restored health, moved away from Conor's side, joining the other Champions a short distance away.

"You have surpassed everyone's expectations, Conor," said the Lady softly. "The council has asked me to invite you to their next session so they might thank you personally for your brave service to the Crossworlds." She looked around at the assembly of Champions gathered before them. "The group of seven has been restored to us, thanks to you. The next phase of our journey may now begin."

Conor bowed deeply before her, accepting her praise humbly. Without hesitating, he mentioned the essential contribution of his brother Champions.

"I appreciate your confidence in me, my Lady, but Therion and Surmitang should receive an equal measure of praise. Had they not burst forth from the corridors when they did, I doubt Maya would be enjoying the glade right now with the rest of us."

"You speak truth, Champion," she responded while looking over toward the big cats. "We owe a large debt of gratitude to both of you. Maya is very important to our plans, as are all of you. Only with the group of seven intact can we hope to successfully engage and defeat Seefra's forces."

Therion and Surmitang bowed their heads before the Lady of the Light. After accepting the praise of their benefactor, Therion took a few paces forward and crouched down before Conor and the Lady. At this level, it became easy for them to spot Maya within the huge, dark mane. Almost playfully, but still filled with respect and awe, Maya crawled forward out of the bushy fur. He looked like a mouse creeping along the back of a giant. He kept coming, however, boldly walking out of his hiding place on Therion's head. Once there, he sat up in an erect position and stared directly into the Lady's eyes.

"Maya," said the Lady, smiling broadly, "will you not greet me, formally or informally after so long an absence?"

A gentleman as always, Maya had been courteously waiting for an invitation. Upon hearing her request, he jumped from the point between Therion's eyebrows into the Lady's arms. She caught him gracefully, wrapping his tail underneath his hind legs and cupping his rump within her supportive arm. She held her left forearm out gracefully in front of her body, giving the great leader of the Champions a bench where he could place his forepaws. Maya did so with the expertise of a thousand lifetimes. He began purring quite loudly, rubbing his cheek against the Lady's chin, hands and breast. Any of the others gathered in the glade could clearly sense the love Maya and the Lady shared. Conor and the other cats respectfully allowed their reunion to continue, standing in silence while two old friends caught up on many months of lost time.

After a few private moments together, the Lady brought Maya forward, placing him on the ground in front of the others. As gingerly as if they were greeting a baby for the first time, the gigantic Champions of the Crossworlds bade their leader welcome. With a paw that could easily have crushed him, Purugama brushed a single toe against Maya's shoulder. He rubbed him lightly while voicing his great pleasure at seeing him again. Ajur, the muscular jaguar, crouched low in front of his master, throwing chuffs against Maya's happy mewling. As the rest of the Champions greeted and played with Maya, it became clear that he was reverting back to his true self. His countenance changed. His demeanor calmed and became more regal and calculating. Even the sounds that came from his throat became less feline and more human. A bizarre language began to pour from Maya's lips, something not quite cat-like yet not altogether understandable.

Then Maya's body began to change. His physical dimensions expanded right before the eyes of everyone gathered in the glade. From the size of a normal housecat, he grew to the height and weight of a golden retriever or a husky in little time. Conor and the other cats backed away, giving Maya the room he needed to complete the process.

The leader of the Crossworlds Champions paced back and forth as he grew, sometimes even circling the area provided for him by the others. Now roughly the size of a large pony, Maya began speaking again, this time in a language the others could clearly comprehend. Although making little sense, everyone could tell that the cat had departed and their leader had returned. Maya kept growing until he finally reached his regal dimensions. He stopped pacing and began stretching his huge frame. Muscles tensed and bones popped as the huge Lord of the Champions inspected his own body. After a lengthy grooming session he finally turned to the others standing in the glade. He stared at each member of his party in turn, including the Lady of the Light. Returning his gaze to Conor, he walked slowly and purposefully over to the young man he had met nearly five years ago.

"Another journey ahead for us, my friend?" he said without expression.

Conor left all decorum behind him as he jumped into Maya's black and white fur. Standing with his head barely touching Maya's breastbone, the young man fought back tears of joy. The rush of what he had accomplished finally overtook him. He had gone into a host of dangerous environments and brought his friends back from the abyss. Here they stood together, safe and ready to unite in a savage battle against the one enemy that had vexed Conor for years. Danger lay ahead for them all, but for now, they could spend a few moments together enjoying the reunion of each other's company.

"Maya, I can't tell you how glad I am to see you standing here before me," Conor said into the warm fur against his face. "I thought those dogs were going to tear us both to pieces."

"Champions of the Crossworlds fight as one," replied Maya. "After all, did you not protect me as I repaired the corridors on our prior journey?"

"Did you not risk your life to reassemble the force you see before you now?" asked Eha, nosing his way in between Conor and his master.

"We would never allow you or our leader to come to such an end," said Therion, settling down on the ground for a short rest.

"Yes," added Surmitang. "Maya is irreplaceable. A human is a human. We find you mildly amusing, so we saved your hide as well."

Conor pulled his face from Maya's thick fur and looked directly at the great Sumatran tiger. He walked the few steps it took to confront Surmitang, gently pressing the legs and faces of the other Champions aside as he approached him. When he reached the big black and orange tiger, he raised his hand as if to strike him. Instead, he merely combed the cat's eyelashes with his separated fingers.

"You gave me the biggest challenge," he said softly. "You could have destroyed me easily any number of times, and yet you chose not to. Of all the journeys, yours posed the greatest danger. Your prowess is as great as your pride, Surmitang, and I am glad for that. We will need your arrogance when we face Seefra. I for one am glad you returned to the glade."

The Lady of the Light and the other Champions stood stone silent as they awaited Surmitang's response. They honestly had no idea what to expect from one so egotistical.

"I," stuttered the great tiger. "I thank you for bringing me home, Conor. I consider it an honor to have come to your aid." He turned his gaze and addressed Therion. "I believe in the value of the great lions as well. What is in the past is erased, Therion. I look forward to fighting alongside you again."

"So be it," added the Lady of the Light. "The Champions of the Crossworlds are once again assembled and ready for battle. Surmitang speaks for all of us, Therion. The past is forgotten. You are once again a trusted member of the group of seven. Let us away to the realm of the creators, where we can plan our strategy for the conquest of Seefra's shadow warriors. Together, we will crush the armies of the evil ones and return the Crossworlds to those who created the covenant for the good of all beings."

CHAPTER TWENTY-SIX

"Only a fool would arrange all of his forces for a frontal assault on Seefra's tower," said Ajur softly. He respected his fellow Champions, but he wanted his message to ring clear. "Seefra would allow you to scale half of the mountain and then transform it into molten lava. We would be slaughtered needlessly.

"You must remember," he continued, "Seefra can change form at will, and he can also alter his physical environment. He might change the look of a single room to provide cover for himself, or transform an entire planet to hide the bulk of his forces. Once we cross over into the dominion of the shadow world, everything changes for the worst. You must never accept the identity of anyone you see. Conor can testify to this reality, for Seefra nearly destroyed him in battle. Without shame or hesitation, Seefra shifted into the image of Conor's uncle. He used Conor's love as a weapon, and he will use any weakness we have as an edge against us. He can even assume the form of a creator. Even if you find yourself fighting alone, and our Lady appears to assist you, be on your guard. Remember the codes we used during our imprisonment in the cage of fire. Use them after we engage the enemy; they may just save our lives. These are traits of his magic I remember from our confrontation many years ago. His powers must be far greater now than what they were at that time. Shape shifting was bad enough, I cannot even conceive of the magic he now wields."

"Ajur speaks wisely," added Gribba, the Ezuvex, who was sitting outside the group of seven. The Lady had asked him to leave his healing stations and lend his counsel to the gathering at the realm, which he agreed to do. He maintained a respectful position, however, always deferring to the Champions and their station. "In the time it took Conor to bring all of you back together, Seefra deciphered the protective spell placed on all but one of the five keys of the creators. Only a seasoned shadow magician with tremendous skill could break the codes placed in the metallurgy of those keys. We have to assume that his powers have grown enormously. We must also believe that Seefra is spending every second available trying to crack the code of the final key. We feel he will not be able to do so, but I caution you that his achievements thus far have taken every one of us by surprise."

"What are you saying, Gribba?" asked Therion.

"I am saying expect the unexpected at all times. Use your magic as a weapon, as well as a defensive shield. Don't wait for Seefra to press the issue. Instead, be proactive and attack imaginatively and without mercy."

"What do you suggest?" asked Purugama, sitting quietly with his wings at rest. The big cougar moved aside, giving enough space for the Ezuvex to join in the circle. "Come, Gribba, sit among us and give us your counsel." The other Champions bade Gribba welcome as well, making room for the huge bear with the human features. The Ezuvex smiled shyly and settled in among the Champions.

"When the armies of Seefra overran my planet," he began, "we saw four distinct types of opponents: keepers, slayers, shadow warriors and destroyers."

Gribba described each of the soldiers intimately, as only he or any of his kind could do. Shortly after the equinox war, the Circle of Evil delivered its vengeance to the race of Ezuvex on their home planet. They unleashed their remaining forces against Gribba's tribe, nearly extinguishing them from the Crossworlds for all time. The attack was payment for the Ezuvex taking the side of the creators and battling the shadow warriors in the main confrontation of the equinox war.

Gribba's village had been obliterated during the assault. When it was finally over, everyone close to him had perished in the merciless onslaught.

The slayers and keepers had come first, softening up the fortifications the Ezuvex had erected. After the slayers scattered the population, the shadow warriors landed in force. They raced across the surface of the planet like a plague of mystical death. They destroyed entire cities with hideous magical spells. What remained after the magic had run its course was cut down by the shadow warriors themselves, sometimes visibly but mostly under the cloak of transparency. The Ezuvex fought bravely, but they were deeply outmatched.

When they thought that small pockets of their kind might be gaining an advantage here and there around the planet surface, the arrival of the destroyers changed that notion with severe finality. Seefra and others of his rank decimated the remainder of the planet. Those who could found safety underground, but they were not many. All told, when the battle had finally ceased, a race of five billion Ezuvex had been reduced to ten thousand.

Gribba described the tactical abilities of the shadow forces as specifically as he could. The largest among all sectors of Seefra's armies had to be the slayers, he reported. Gribba could never tell the gathering how many slayers had descended upon his world during their attack. Even if they had been fully prepared, the sheer numbers would have eventually overwhelmed them. Although they possessed superior battle skills, the slayers held few other abilities. They had access to corridors and could use them freely. They held a marginal amount of control over dark magic, they could move extremely fast, and they seemed to have limitless energy. No matter how many times the Ezuvex turned them back or cut them down, if they still lived they would return to the battle with a vengeance.

The slayers' limited intelligence would provide one advantage for the Champions. Even with a tactician like Seefra coordinating their movements, once the slayers found themselves engaged, they fought recklessly and without direction. A superior force with the right magic, following a preset battle plan, might be able to hold the slayers at bay. They might, Gribba advised, be able to overcome their careless attitude and defeat the slayers before other forces arrived to assist them.

"It might be to our advantage to lead them away from the tower," offered Conor. "If we could separate the battle groups, perhaps we could defeat them in sections."

"You will have no idea of their numbers," said Gribba. "They came to our world following the main confrontations of the equinox war. You will face them at full strength, *and* in their own territory. You must assume that their numbers will negate any hope of sectioning them off from the other warriors."

"Continue, Gribba," said the Lady of the Light softly. "Tell us of the other battle groups."

"As you wish, my Lady," said Gribba, bowing his head to the beautiful creator. "The next group fighting for the Circle of Evil is the keepers. These beings present the most benign threat to the Champions of the Crossworlds. They are primarily imprisonment specialists. They will follow the slayers, erecting crude but service-able detention cells for any beings not destroyed in the first wave of the attack. They can follow the slayers through any corridor, and they can build a cell of any type known to us in seconds. The keepers constructed the cage of fire that kept the lot of you at bay for the better part of two years. They also constructed Conor's cell of shadows, using instructions left by Loken during his time as supreme commander of the shadow warriors. The keepers built and maintain the crystal cages in Seefra's chamber of cells, such as the one containing your companion." The Ezuvex gestured toward Conor as he said this. "Other than this one unique and valuable capability, the keepers are essentially harmless. The have a narrow command of dark magic, limited battle skills and a decent mental ability. If you can, as Conor suggested, split these two initial hosts and take the slayers away from the keepers. They will be easy to dispense with."

Gribba surveyed the gathering for any questions before con-tinuing. "Shadow warriors will provide your next objective. They will not be easily overcome. These are the premier soldiers in See-fra's army. They can travel through any corridor and they possess superb battle skills. Unlike the slayers, these warriors will fight as a coordinated unit. They have a superior level of intelligence, and they command an exceptional amount of dark magic. They are masters at on-the-spot weapons construction. They will assess a situation and within minutes manufacture a weapon to overcome any obstacle. You must take this into consideration when marshal-ing your offensive strategy. You must be prepared to shift focus and change tactics immediately and without reason. If these talents weren't enough, they also possess the gift of invisibility. They can render their forces undetectable in the blink of an eyelash."

"Tell us," said Surmitang, suddenly very much awake. "What must we do to defeat such a foe?"

Gribba bowed his furry head before answering. "I am sorry, but I cannot suggest a way. By the time the shadow warriors descended on our planet, the fight had been taken out of our forces. We couldn't put up any visible challenge against the shadow warriors, so they decimated our world without resistance. Had we been able to successfully engage them, I might have more information. Forgive me."

"There is nothing to forgive, my friend," replied Surmitang. "Take heart, for I will bring one of these warriors back to the realm so you can exact your own vengeance against it."

The Ezuvex stared at Surmitang, unsure of how to take his comment. At length, he smiled and bowed his head in appreciation. He kept a very real sentiment tucked away in the recesses of his mind, however, one that welcomed Surmitang's offer with open arms. He packed it down and continued.

"The last beings you will encounter are the destroyers – powerful entities very similar to Seefra in capability and ferocity. The master of darkness created this rank after defeating Loken for the principle leadership of the shadow warriors. By doing so, he produced an impenetrable layer of protection for himself. From time to time he would elevate one of the shadow warriors to the status of destroyer, providing them with a host of new powers and a better command of dark magic. Those promoted to these new, dominant positions became Seefra's private security force. He even speaks of the destroyers as the mirror image of the protection forces that served the creators before your time."

"Pah!" said Maya in a rare break with decorum.

Gribba continued without a hitch. "Conor erased two of See-fra's strongest destroyers during his journey with Maya. With the magical and physical assistance of the Champions, he annihilated Gandron and Fumemos. Even Loken, in an attempt to reclaim his throne, battled Conor in the quest for the fifth key. He has also been eliminated, due to Conor and his companion's astounding efforts. We are fortunate those three have been defeated, but I caution you, other destroyers will gladly take their place. The opportunity to gain Seefra's favor will not be lost on any of them, nor on any of the shadow warriors."

"Can we fight the destroyers in their own battlefield, Gribba?" asked Ajur. "What powers do they possess that we should be aware of?"

"Yes, you can fight them," answered the Ezuvex. "The question is, 'can you defeat them?' Look at it as fighting a dozen beings as powerful as Seefra at the same time. You can rest assured that the master of darkness has provided them with every ounce of power available. They may very well be able to do what he himself can do. This includes identity transfer, or shape shifting, as you call it. They can transfer their own powers to another, in much the same way that the Lady has transmitted her powers to Conor from time to time. They can also alter or animate their immediate environment. If it suits them, they can change the formation of the flora and fauna to something that benefits their style of fighting. It you encounter a being that finds water to be its most formidable arena, prepare yourself to be submerged. If it prefers fire, or wind, then plan for that eventuality. You cannot delay or hesitate when battling a destroyer. You must be prepared for any possibility, *any* possibility, and you must press the attack instead of simply reacting to what they throw at you."

Gribba stayed silent for a moment before continuing. He wanted the group of seven to absorb what he planned to say next. "A destroyer's magic is impenetrable in their own territory. You cannot overcome their power as long as you fight on their terms. This is why the cage of fire held all of you for so long. The cage existed in an environment that Seefra created, and after he took Conor and his companion prisoner, the cage followed a preset course to a distant location well within the confines of the forbidden corridors.

"Of all the shadow forces, the destroyers possess the greatest intelligence. This aspect of their existence, combined with their tactical brilliance on the battlefield makes them the most daunting enemy indeed."

"After the assault on my world, Seefra visited our planet to congratulate his shadow warriors on their resounding victory. He commands awesome power, abilities that today must be even more astounding. Just remember that the key to the destroyers' magic is in their control over the environment. If Seefra hasn't deciphered a way around that limitation, you might be able to use that against them."

The Ezuvex stood and brushed off the few leaves that had settled into his fur. He bowed to the Lady of the Light, and then walked to the center of the circle. Looking at each Champion individually, he bade farewell to those who would decide the future of the Crossworlds. When he finally met Conor's eyes, Gribba smiled at the young man. He walked over to him, extending a huge furry arm in his direction. He took Conor's hand in both of his big paws, embracing it warmly.

"That is all I can tell you, my friends. I wish you the wealth of the creators' abilities, and a speedy return to the glade of Champions. My brothers and sisters will tend to your medical needs when you return. All of the remaining Ezuvex, what is left of my race, will be with you in spirit."

The Lady of the Light rose gracefully from her floating position next to a large stone shelf. She walked over to Gribba, embraced his paws in her delicate hands, and thanked him for his counsel. The Champions of the Crossworlds, already on their feet when the Lady stood, gave their own variety of thanks to the brave Ezuvex standing in their midst. After all farewells had been declared, hugs and clasps exchanged, the Lady walked from the informal circle holding Gribba's forearm. When the two of them reached a ridge in the pathway leading back to the center of the realm, the Lady turned and spoke to her Champions.

"Make whatever arrangements you deem necessary," she commanded. "Hail whatever deities you claim allegiance to, and most importantly, take rest and sustenance before nightfall. We leave at peak moon on this night."

"*We?*" asked Maya, surprised but not entirely alarmed.

"You heard me, Lord of the Champions," she responded. "Someone is waiting for me in the area beyond. I believe it is time a creator fought alongside her protectors. Remember. Peak moon. Tonight."

Conor and Purugama walked along one of the more peaceful and beautiful pathways of the realm. The young man, although strapping for a sixteen-year-old human male, looked again like the small boy who had met the great cougar roughly six years ago. Conor may have been close to six feet tall, but Purugama, whose strong golden flanks and huge, leathery wings towered over his companion, overshadowed him completely. They walked slowly through one pathway after another, stopping periodically to gaze upon a series of tumbling waterfalls and the breathtaking view of the grounds. The two companions padded through the leafy walkways in silence, each pondering what lay ahead in the coming battle. After close to an hour of silent assessment, Purugama finally queried his longtime friend.

"You are troubled, Conor. I can sense it," he remarked. "Even during our first journeys together, as a frightened young boy, you rarely kept silent this long."

Conor stopped walking, but held his tongue. He wanted to confide in his big friend, but something kept him from saying what was on his mind.

"You can always speak freely around me, Conor," added the big cougar. "I would be honored to hear your thoughts. I remind you that we have only a few hours left before our departure time."

Conor tried to relate the thoughts racing around in his mind. He couldn't verbalize what troubled him, however, so he decided to show the big cat instead. He walked over to Purugama, lifted his great wing and put both of his arms around the great cougar's chest. He grasped two large handfuls of his soft, golden fur, pulling himself close to his big friend. He leaned strongly against him, listening to the cougar's powerful heartbeat. He inhaled the wonderful scent of the big cat's fur. He listened with his heart to the soft purr emanating from his best friend's soul.

"I watched you die once, Purugama," he finally said with his face pressed against the heaving chest. "I don't want to see it happen again. I fear for us, for all of us. Even with the Lady of the Light joining our company, I fear what we might face once we encounter Seefra's armies. I can't bear to lose any of the Champions, even Therion, who once tried to destroy me. All of you have become so important to me." The young man shifted his head, turning it to one side so he could speak more freely.

"I haven't seen any of my family for over two years, or my friends for that matter. The Champions are my family – you, the Lady of the Light, Janine – that's who I consider most important to me now. I don't want to see any of you get hurt, but you most of all, Purugama. If not for you, I wouldn't be part of the Crossworlds, nor would I have met the other Champions. If not for you, I would never have become your apprentice. I said it before many years ago, Purugama, and I still mean it today. You're the best friend I've ever had. Promise me you won't allow yourself to be hurt."

The huge, mystical cougar stood quietly for what seemed like an eternity to Conor. Breathing evenly, Purugama looked out onto the vast gardens of the realm of the creators. He felt the young man clinging to his body, providing a sensation unknown to him for so long he couldn't readily describe it. He knew he loved Conor deeply, and it didn't matter in what context the connection presented itself. Be it father, brother, son or friend, the great cougar didn't think the nature of their relationship really mattered that much. What counted was that two beings had formed a strong bond from their close association. He had known Conor for almost half of the young man's life. He had watched him grow from an insecure, troubled boy into a capable, strong young man. He made mistakes along the way, as all humans do, but he felt more than a twinge of pride in Conor's achievements.

The two of them formed an attachment all those years ago, and that link had intensified over their many journeys together. He always strived to build on that foundation. He wanted to be his primary mentor during his growth as a Champion. He decided long ago to watch over him during the upcoming battles, and he knew only one way to accomplish that.

"Conor," said the great cougar, drawing his companion away from his body with a strategically placed wingtip. "With the Lady's permission, I would be honored if you rode with me when we attack Seefra's forces. I believe there is enough strength in my shoulders to carry you. At least that way we could surely watch over each other."

The young man stood quietly for a moment, not quite sure what he had just heard. When he realized what Purugama offered him, he immediately scrambled up the side of the giant cougar. He settled himself around Purugama's shoulders, checking the fit of his larger body as a passenger on the great cat. Unlike before, where his small stature had created an unstable seat on the giant shoulders, as a young man his body seemed to fit Purugama's neck and shoulders perfectly. His feet hung lazily alongside the great cougar's jowls, but his legs seemed to fit in a tight groove around the thick, muscular neck, almost like sitting on a horse back home. He felt so comfortable, as a matter of fact that he believed he could ride without the use of his hands. If this proved to be true, the pair of them would present a formidable enemy to the shadow warriors. Purugama would use his own magic, flinging it forth with his eyes and mouth, and Conor would have his hands free to hurl his own mystical destruction down on the opposing forces.

"Take us up, Purugama, just for a short while," said Conor. "I want to get the feel of flying together again."

"Only for a few passes around the realm, young one," answered the great cougar as he began flexing his wings. "We both need a period of rest before the departure time arrives."

Purugama unfolded his fur-lined, leathery wings and brushed

them against the wind. He took a few long strides and jumped into the air, pounding his wings furiously. He and Conor soared into the sky, higher and higher, until they found a jet stream well above the realm of the creators. Purugama cruised along in the rushing wind, dipping here and lifting there so Conor could get a feel for the ride again. He thought the young man might need some time, but he realized the opposite was true. Conor leaned into every turn, holding tightly with his thighs and feet. Now that his arms were longer, Conor was able to hold on to a number of different areas when he needed to secure himself. If Purugama was merely coasting along, then the young man could easily keep himself steady with only his legs and knees. If the big cat flew in an attack pattern, Conor could still leave one hand free for his own purposes. This would, as Conor had thought earlier, provide a heightened measure of offensive power to their alliance.

Conor let out a loud roar as they circled around the far perimeter of the realm. As Purugama lowered his great head and tucked his wings into his flanks, Conor also lowered his shoulders and head, leaning into the cougar's fur. They streaked toward the center of the realm. Conor roared again, this time with one fist raised triumphantly in the air. Purugama, not one to get easily excited, got caught up in Conor's emotions and cut loose with a roar of his own. *It seemed*, thought the great cougar, *as though the young man's fears had been soothed.*

After a few more passes over the realm, Purugama set himself down close to one of the water wall treatment areas. He walked quietly toward a tight grouping of walls scattered here and there around the area. The rest of the Champions lay about in various degrees of rest, with a healing wall standing close by.

As Purugama entered the area, two walls, one small and one

quite large, rose up out of the ground. Without a word, the great cougar crouched down next to the large, organic structure. With a nod of his head, he bid Conor to do the same with the smaller wall. The young man plopped down on the emerald grass, where a soft bed rose up underneath him. The bed transported him to the wall, or the wall moved closer to him, he couldn't really tell. Instantly, however, a serene, rejuvenating feeling washed over his face, shoulders, chest and stomach, and finally his legs and feet. He fell asleep immediately, and as soon as the wall sensed his state of repose, it began fueling his body, mending any remaining aches and sores that might hinder his ability in battle. All of the Champions were undergoing similar treatments, even Purugama, who lay on his side with his right wing tucked under his huge, golden body. When the departure time came, every one of them would find himself completely refreshed and free from hunger or injury. The impending battle was for the Crossworlds itself. The Champions would be in premier condition and ready for combat.

CHAPTER TWENTY-SEVEN

At fifteen minutes before midnight, the group of seven gathered in the chosen spot to await the Lady of the Light. All of the Champions, each and every cat, wore a look of poised concentration. Eha appeared to be the only one in a cheerful mood. He walked among the Champions, licking their flanks or their foreheads for a few seconds before moving on to the next cat. He said nothing to any of them; he merely loosened them up while they awaited the arrival of their mistress. He approached Conor last, and instead of licking him, he let his head fall into the young man's grip. Conor took up the request and scratched Eha's nose and ears vigorously. The gigantic cheetah began purring in unison with Conor's attentive hands. Eha enjoyed the attention, undoubtedly, but the big, furry Champion knew the human in front of him would glean a measure of comfort as well from this brief interaction. He continued to purr as he pushed his head farther toward Conor's body. He rubbed his cheeks against the young man's breastbone, allowing the soft hum of his song to bore deeply into Conor's soul.

The Lady of the Light stepped gracefully from a corridor. She walked purposefully into the ring the Champions had created in preparation for her arrival. She looked at each of the cats, noting their condition and spiritual readiness. As she moved her eyes around the circle, each of them rose in turn. They presented themselves to their mistress in all their muscular, magical glory. Therion's dark mane flowed softly in the breeze, but his eyes locked onto the Lady's gaze like a steel vice. Surmitang puffed his fur out to its fullest volume, looking as menacing as possible. Ajur maintained a fighting stance, muscles bristling, ready to protect his mistress against all of the shadow warriors in every quadrant of the Crossworlds. Purugama, wings extended and teeth bared, chuffed lightly a few times, letting the Lady know he felt ready for battle. Eha, still showing the lightest attitude of the entire group, sat calmly licking himself as he waited to cross over into the shadow world. Maya had reseated himself, apparently taking every last second of rest before their departure.

The Lady took a particular interest in Conor. The young man looked ready to depart except for one small detail. He still wore the clothes he recovered from the Mountmoor High School gymnasium more than two years ago. Although serviceable, it certainly wouldn't do to have one of the most important Champions fighting for the fate of the Crossworlds in rags. She walked over to him, holding her finger to her lips in a sign for Conor to keep silent. Gazing into his blue eyes, the Lady touched his shoulders lightly, then his hips, and finally his feet. She stepped back and uttered a simple spell that only she and Conor heard.

A silver tornado, as tall and wide as Conor's body, swept up from the ground around his feet. The wind of the twister circled around his legs before rising quickly to surround his entire body. Only his hair remained visible as it danced madly over the top of the small whirlwind. As quickly as it appeared the funnel vanished into thin air. Conor, unaffected by the small tempest, stood quietly in the same position he held before the disturbance began. From his own vantage point, he felt completely unchanged. He looked at all of the Champions, however, who stalked toward him, and he knew that a meaningful transformation had occurred. Before the first cat moved within sniffing distance, Conor looked down at his new clothing. Lifting his hands, he pressed his palms against the strange material. He gasped when he saw what the Lady of the Light had given him.

The boots, made of a golden material Conor could not recognize, fit as comfortably and as functionally as a pair of tennis shoes. It almost felt as if he wore a second skin around his feet. The pants, also of a golden color but darker than the boots, fit snugly but moved amazingly well. They seemed to attach themselves to his body somehow, moving perfectly with every ripple of his muscles. Along the seam of both legs ran a series of small pockets. Each held something, he could sense that, but what they contained he could not decipher. The shirt, sleeveless and short in the midriff, allowed for maximum movement. Its color matched the color of the boots perfectly, and while it held no attachments like the pants, Conor knew the material of the shirt would serve as protection against the evil ones. For that matter, the pants and boots would do so as well. Conor knew this in his heart.

He looked up into the Lady's glistening eyes. Just as he tried to speak, the Lady of the Light touched his forehead lightly. She brushed back a lock of his hair, and as she guided her delicate finger around his temple a band of golden armor circled Conor's head. After completing the revolution, the band joined with itself directly over the bridge of his nose. An ornate emblem formed amidst the two ends of the material, creating the letter "C" in the center of Conor's forehead. The headband fit tightly, but not painfully, and Conor could feel a mix of blended energy surging through the material. A great power existed within this crown, though he had no understanding of its purpose. Just as with the items encased along the seams of his pants, though, he knew that when appropriate, he would know how to use it.

"My Lady," said Conor, touching the headdress. "I am honored by your gift. I only hope to prove myself worthy of your generosity."

"You have already done so, Champion," answered the Lady. "Many times, in fact, and I believe you will again." She turned him around, glancing at the fit of the material. Adjusting his stance so he faced forward again, she touched the insignia above his eyes. "Do you know what the "C" stands for, Conor?"

"I can take three guesses," he replied. "Conor, Champion, or Crossworlds."

"You would be mistaken if you chose any of those," said the Lady. "Before your journey is complete, you will understand the meaning of the letter. For now, however, let the power of the band join with you. The symbiosis between you will increase in magnitude the longer you wear it. Once we cross over into the shadow world, never make the mistake of parting with it. Do you understand, Conor?"

"Yes, my Lady, I understand."

"Good," she said with a smile that tore at Conor's heart. She turned, addressing the Champions. "Purugama, step forward to the center of the circle."

The great cougar flapped his huge wings and strode powerfully forward. When he reached the middle of the gathering, Conor saw something he couldn't comprehend at first. He walked forward toward his mentor and best friend. He extended a hand, feeling the soft but durable nature of the material the big cat wore about his shoulders and wings. It resembled the fabric of the clothing he was wearing; in fact it was a perfect match. Conor felt so awed by this development he began glancing at all of the other Champions. He wanted one of them to step forward and explain everything. He needed someone to convince him of the necessity of his role in this bizarre but heroic journey. He grasped the foothold of the huge golden saddle Purugama now wore.

There was no mistaking it; the great cougar's outfit matched Conor's clothing for a reason. Without asking the Lady of the Light for permission, Conor pulled himself up into the grooved saddle fastened around Purugama's neck and shoulders. He slipped his boots into the sleeves without even looking, and grasped the thick, leathery strap in front of him. He pushed into the foot sleeves with his toes, making one final adjustment to his posture. Then he looked around at the rest of the group gathered before him. He looked down at the faces of the five other Champions, and finally over to the Lady of the Light. He suddenly felt very much a part of this amazing, mystical group. In these clothes, sitting atop the one creature he had always treasured, he felt invincible, even dangerous. He was Conor of the Crossworlds, a Champion among Champions. With Purugama underneath him, there were no limits to what he could accomplish.

The Lady of the Light walked to the center of the circle, smiling broadly. She looked up at Conor, sitting so majestically astride his brother Champion. The creator felt a strong rush of emotion as she gazed upon the last of the Champions, so confident and intimidating. She wanted to call the council forward so they might see firsthand what she had promised. She looked at the rest of Champions briefly. Every one of them stared at Conor in a bizarre state of wonder. It seemed as though they were looking upon him for the first time, even though they had known him for almost five years. He looked both oddly different, and exactly the same. One thing they all noted without question, however, was his determination to confront Seefra and his shadow warriors.

The Lady of the Light stood before Purugama, addressing him and the other cats. "Behold," she announced proudly, "he has returned, just as the oracle promised." She looked up at Conor, this time not as a creator, but as an equal. Her hair freshened by a soft whistling breeze, she spoke again. "After two times ten thousand settings of the equinox, *he has come home to fight for the Crossworlds again.*"

The realm exploded with a chorus of deafening roars. Even Purugama, who held the young man on his shoulders, joined his brothers in the booming snarls. All six of the gigantic, mystical cats bared their huge fangs while scraping the ground with their razor-sharp claws. Ajur and Surmitang began to spar lightly, slapping each other on the cheeks with their powerful forepaws. Eha jumped from an overhang and landed on Therion's backside, riding the massive lion as he dashed around the realm. Therion roared powerfully with every attempt to throw him off, but Eha would not be shoved aside so easily. He held on, claws extended, until Therion bounded back into the group. Only then did he leap from the huge golden haunches, landing on all fours less than a foot from Maya.

Instead of acknowledging Eha's presence, the Lord of the Champions sat quietly watching the aggressive displays. He knew the Champions needed this session of battlefield foreplay to excite them into a stage of readiness. Over the eons of serving the creators, he had watched this drama play itself out many times. Although they were pressed for time, he allowed them to banter with each other and prepare for the assault. He looked to his left and saw Conor and Purugama playing a peculiar game with each other. Conor would lower his hand just enough so that Purugama had a chance to bite his fingers. At the last moment, after the great cougar struck, Conor would snatch his hand away. Seconds later, he would drop the opposite hand within Purugama's reach and repeat the procedure. Maya smiled at the interaction, it certainly didn't replace a joust or two with another cat, but it wouldn't hurt their reflexes one bit. The Lord of the Champions sat by content-edly while his warriors prepared for battle. He never made a move the entire time, save a very active tail, which flicked back and forth kicking up a considerable amount of dust.

After the activities died down, the Lady of the Light walked again to the center of the gathering. She summoned the group of seven, commanding them to form up behind her. They immedi-ately complied, standing in a ready position – first Eha, then Sur-mitang, followed by Conor aboard Purugama. Therion came next, by far the largest in the group. Maya stood next to the great lion, with Ajur closing out the line. As always, Maya situated himself between the biggest and fiercest Champions. The Lady glanced over her shoulder once, and then threw her arms out in front of her body.

The corridor boundary began at the left-most edge of their viewpoint. It drew a line across the landscape, completely eclips-ing the scenery in front of the group of seven. The beam of organ-ic energy sliced through the air at a precise speed and direction, drawing out the perimeter of the portal perfectly. The Lady had summoned a massive passageway, at least two hundred feet across and fifty feet in height.

The internal membrane appeared ready to materialize within

the border, and then the mist would flash convulsively, almost fighting the command to come forward. The perimeter remained solid, however, and after an intolerable amount of waiting, the portal began to emerge. Swirling colors of every sort, dominated by a silvery luminescence, filled the corridor as the group of seven and their mistress quietly watched. The membrane seemed to fall into the center of the passageway from every corner, filling the corridor like sand falling into a timepiece. The other colors eventually vanished, leaving a glistening silver film sliding to and fro within the walls of the massive portal. The Lady dropped her arms, taking in a few badly needed breaths of the realm's fresh air. Then she turned her head, once more glancing at the row of warriors awaiting her signal. She smiled and nodded her head slightly, and then walked nonchalantly into the membrane. Before she took her second step, the group of seven had advanced toward the portal. As one, the huge column of Crossworlds Champions passed through the corridor, leaving the safety of their world behind.

CHARGE OF THE CHAMPIONS

CHAPTER TWENTY-EIGHT

The filmy membrane on the far side of the corridor shuddered violently as it came to life. Huge waves of distorted energy coursed through the surface of the portal. The first forepaw broke through the membrane, causing the energy mass to shatter. A million particles of silvery liquid glass shot through the air, preceding the group of seven as they exited the massive corridor. After all of the travelers had entered the shadow world, the membrane congealed again. The corridor reclaimed every splinter, no matter how small or insignificant.

The Champions watched as the portal fell into itself, regrouping before making its way back to the realm of the creators. Considering itself completely restored, the perimeter silently secured itself. In a matter of seconds, their only path back to the realm disappeared entirely. The group stood alone on the plains of the shadow world.

"Cortez and his ships, eh Maya?" offered Therion.

"Precisely," answered the Lord of the Champions. "There's something to be said for motivation."

"My Lady!" shouted Conor, alarmed. "She didn't pass through

the corridor with us. What if Seefra diverted her passage and sent her directly to the chamber of cells?"

"He would be painfully sorry he did such a thing," answered Ajur, still standing guard at the rear of the Champions.

"But where is she?" asked Conor again. "Perhaps Purugama and I should go aloft and look for her."

"Our Lady is fine," inserted Maya. "She has duties that even we don't know about, but I assure you, she passed through the corridor without incident. Some of us will see her during the remainder of this journey, and some will not. We must trust her to fulfill her unique obligation, as we must also perform ours."

The group of seven accepted Maya's explanation without question. They turned as one, staring at the bizarre land before them. Dead didn't do it justice. The scene was empty in every sense – it offered no sounds, nothing to look at, smelled only like ash, and could not be touched or tasted. It was a horrible sight to look upon.

"You would think Seefra might be glad to surrender and leave this disgusting place forever," muttered Surmitang.

"This is the result of the last stages of the equinox war," said Maya as he shook his furry black and white head in dismay. "The lands have never recovered. Believe it or not, this world was once the garden spot of the Crossworlds. Centuries later, it still reeks of destruction and oppression." Maya turned his head slowly to the left and right, scanning both horizons for any movement. "Do not be completely convinced, however, because this could be one of Seefra's transformative models, specifically designed to throw us toward an expected course of action."

"I do not think so," said Ajur. "I have seen Seefra's work personally. There is always some flaw, no matter how minute, that tips his hand. This scenery, although repulsive, carries a certain amount of perfection with it. I believe we look upon exactly what you previously mentioned, Maya, a decimated world."

Not another word of conversation escaped their lips while they gazed at the endless vista of destruction. To a cat, and to Conor as well, dead seemed to be the best way to describe this land. Scarred violently and ashen gray in color throughout, the land stretched for hundreds of miles in front of them. Not a bush, tree, or blade of green grass grew anywhere. Conor straightened in his saddle and turned to look behind him. He saw a mirror image of what lay in front of them – nothing but dark gray destruction. He turned again to share the view with his brothers.

Severe cracks streamed along the broken, scarred ground. They shot forward in a thousand different directions, cutting the landscape into a series of distorted jigsaw pieces. The lines appeared to go on forever, all the way across the endless valley until they hit the base of a mountain range many miles away.

Even the mountains had not escaped the wrath of the equinox battles. In some locations, the peaks maintained their original height, extending high above the horizon like impassable sentinels. At other sites, however, huge gashes tore apart the magnificence of what once towered over the valley. It looked as if a giant of incomprehensible size had stepped through the mountain range, kicking down anything he couldn't easily climb over.

Here and there a lonely stalk of some form of plant life managed to reach through the dust and destruction. At one point it actually might have lived for a moment or two. But as surely as this valley had died, the stalk and any other brave plants had long since perished. The acidic state of the graying soil destroyed anything attempting to come alive in the valley. The brave flora met a quick death in the dusty air surrounding it. Some trees still stood at odd locations along the valley floor, but they too had suffered from the horrible destruction this world had endured. Only a dead trunk and a few crooked branches stood above ground. They seemed to act as a warning signal to anyone unfortunate enough to find themselves stranded on this world.

The Champions looked out upon the shattered land, stunned and speechless. After an eternity, the winged cougar broke the silence.

"Ajur speaks truth, Maya," said Purugama. "As much a truth as any of us could know and more of a truth than we can dispute. If he claims the lands before us to be real, then I believe him."

"Aye, he speaks truth," said Therion and Surmitang.

"Yes," added Eha. "Let us proceed."

"So be it," said Maya. "We will move forward, but with the greatest caution. If any of you sense the slightest change in the environment, call out immediately. Purugama, I suggest that you and Conor take flight and scout the valley floor. Scan the entire region and look for any abnormalities. Check the mountain ranges, both whole and broken for any potential hiding places. I imagine that Seefra will call forth a corridor when he wishes to descend upon us, but we may as well be prepared for a traditional attack as well. Eha, take a position roughly a hundred yards ahead. Therion, you must guard our rear, not at quite the same distance behind, but give yourself enough room to see any approaching forces. Ajur and Surmitang, you stay with me. We will walk three abreast protected by our front and rear defenses. Does everyone understand?"

Maya's question had already been answered. Eha quickly sprinted out to the point position. He turned his massive head around to wait for the rest of the group. Therion stood his ground waiting for the remaining three Champions to march ahead of him. Purugama and Conor could be seen flying high above the valley, crisscrossing back and forth along the horizon. Maya and his two compatriots stepped out onto the harsh, crusty ground, beginning their endless journey into the unknown.

The ground of the dead world fought against their footsteps. Although completely lifeless, the crusty dirt and rock strived to offer little purchase for any of the cats. The going quickly became extremely slow, for every step had to be carefully measured. If they didn't watch themselves, they could pull a muscle or twist a joint on the unstable surface. Even mighty Therion, whose paws measured nearly three feet across, found himself at a disadvantage due to his immense weight. His paws held the ground adequately enough, but every once in a while he would sink into a dusty crater. Having to immediately resurrect his balance took his concentration away from the valley behind him. He began to experience feelings of doubt and dread, and with the group barely a mile out onto the valley floor, this gave him cause for grave concern.

Surmitang looked about him as they pressed forward toward their objective. The dead trees in the valley were entirely different from the lush, tropical environment he remembered so well. Nothing appeared to grow here – nothing at all. It began to affect his mind; he wanted so badly to see something alive. Anything would do, a sprig of grass, one remaining leaf on the branch of a dead tree, or even a cloud rolling lazily across the sky. The surrounding decay caused him to feel decrepit himself. He would give his right leg to see even a sprinkle of water. Had he kept his attention on the land instead of his worries, he might have noticed the bizarre vines springing up here and there in the valley. He might have even sensed the huge swathe of identical foliage running through the smoky, rock-strewn soil underneath them.

Ajur's muscles tingled all over, from his jaws to his tail. He didn't like any of this and his nervous system reinforced his thoughts. Something about this dead world appeared very much alive to him. He remembered Seefra quite well; he knew the ways of the master of darkness. He would place his enemies in a location designed specifically to lull them into a false sense of unsuspecting calm, and then strike. Although this world appeared benign, Ajur suspected otherwise. He couldn't see, hear, or smell anything yet, but he knew the Champions would be tested early and often. The shadow warriors would be held back, of course, but slayers and keepers were expendable. They might come over the mountains or from a place far across the valley floor. *Maybe*, thought *Ajur, they'll surface from beneath us and take us by surprise.* The giant jaguar flexed his tense muscles, preparing himself for anything.

Maya paced forward confidently. Every so often he would turn his hooded eyes to check on Eha and Therion, and then lift his whiskered face and try and locate Purugama and Conor sailing along in the shadowy sky above him. He said nothing to his brothers, even though he could feel the indecision and tension flowing among them. He could have walked on the apprehension coming from Ajur and Surmitang; it burned so strongly it almost had a voice of its own. He kept his thoughts to himself, though, watching everything as he continued moving forward. He looked back at Therion and saw the huge lion making his way toward them and at the same time taking in everything around him. He saw Eha doing the same at his point, and he saw the remaining Champions watching everything while gliding through the air currents above them. Maya had his own misgivings, but he came to terms with them long ago. The Champions had come here to destroy Seefra and his armies, so it made perfect sense that the very land they walked on was preparing to strike them down. He waited calmly, working on his own strategies for defense and attack. After all, hadn't Gribba told them to be aggressive at every turn?

"Prepare yourselves," he said without emotion. He turned his head and looked at Ajur and Surmitang. "The enemy marshals his forces in preparation for our arrival."

CHAPTER TWENTY-NINE

Janine fought against the two guards dragging her toward Seefra's laboratory. Having been held captive for over two years now, she had finally decided to fight them at every turn, making their jobs as difficult as possible. After almost perishing from a lack of food a few months back, Seefra had ordered her rations increased to one hundred percent of the daily human requirements. With no one else to carry the final key, the master of darkness could not allow any permanent harm to come her way. Janine ate ravenously and exercised three times a day, every day, since coming so close to death. In no time at all her body had returned to premium athletic condition, and her shadow warrior guards were presently paying the price for all that sweat. Neither one of them could move her an inch by themselves, and in her current condition two of them had to work very hard to extract her from her cell and walk her down to their master's laboratory.

Seefra swiveled on his tentacles while watching a corridor in his laboratory blaze in front of him. A picture as clear as a movie screen filled the membrane of the portal. The master of darkness never took his eyes from it. Even while his two servants brought the struggling girl into his presence, Seefra stared into the membrane with a determined expression. With a great deal of effort, the two shadow warriors finally placed Janine next to him. Immediately she attempted to escape but they grabbed her arms and dragged her back. When she pushed one of them down and ran, Seefra silently uttered a few words of dark magic.

"Saszzz. Nivika toxufax."

Janine's body went rigid. Her eyes flared wide open while her arms and legs locked at the joints. Chin jutting out and neck taught, she fell to the floor like a wooden Indian. The two shadow warriors moved to pick her up, but her body stood on it's own before they managed to reach her. Standing at attention in a frozen state, her body floated over to where Seefra stood watching the screen. Even her hair was immobilized, not one strand moved while she levitated over to her captor's side. When she arrived back at her appointed position, she tried to turn her head to look Seefra in the eye. The master of darkness, witnessing her attempts, finally spoke to her, as if just now noticing her.

"I thank you for coming," he said softly.

Janine squirmed, twisting her muscles with all the force she could muster. She tried desperately to turn her face toward the master of darkness, but no amount of effort could overcome Seefra's magic. She wanted to scoff at him, spit at him, at least say something to dim his apparent satisfaction, but she could not move at all. Instead, she stared blankly at the screen in front her, which showed nothing but a barren land with a few beings moving across its surface at a measured pace. It relayed nothing of importance to her. She wasn't remotely interested in exploring it further.

The master of darkness sensed Janine's misgivings. He also perceived her attempts to play down the images placed before her. "Don't be so sure the images you see contain no meaning for you, my dear," he said coldly. "I brought you here for the express purpose of tormenting you a little further before the final battle begins."

Seefra spat out the words to remove the immobility spell on his captive before he continued. Janine dropped to her feet, unstable at first but finally recovering. She barely reached her full height before Seefra continued his gloating. "Behold. Your saviors' final resting place," he said with a twinge of glee, "the valley of infinite deception."

Janine wanted to kick the smirk from Seefra's face, but she knew the punishment for such an affront would be swift and painful. She didn't want to play his games and watch the images on the screen, but she decided to humor him for a few moments. She maintained a relaxed stance while the master of darkness droned on about his plans for the torture and destruction of her companion, Conor of Earth. She allowed Seefra to continue expounding on his strategy for defeating the Champions of the Crossworlds. As her jailer spoke, a radical and dangerous idea sprung into her head. Before she could talk herself out of it, she decided to act on the impulse. Seefra wasn't even paying attention to her, and the guards stood at a safe distance. She decided she had to make the attempt. She tensed the muscles in her legs, prepared to explode from her stance, and looked at Seefra one more time in her peripheral vision. Then she took a deep breath and jumped head first into the membrane of the corridor in front of her.

"Ordaxa!" shouted Seefra. He was so shocked by Janine's compulsive action that he didn't make a move to stop her. "Noralav. Piva!" He ordered her guards to wait by her cell while he fetched her back. The two shadow warriors jumped at the opportunity to leave the laboratory, for they did not want to be the recipients of Seefra's cruel temper. They raced each other around the corner, speeding down the hallway toward the chamber of cells. They heard Seefra cursing and mumbling to himself as he prepared to retrieve his prisoner.

Janine fell through the corridor membrane onto a pile of sharp, dusty shale. She cut herself repeatedly, rolling and grasping at different objects in hopes of steadying herself. After finally coming to a stop, she checked her wounds briefly. She had escaped, that was the important thing. She had gambled on a chance that had paid off. Seefra's chamber and his laboratory could be a million miles away from here for all she knew. The only object connecting the two locations lay just a few feet from her now. The portal she had traveled through sat quietly behind her. It floated silently above the rocks like some bizarre computer monitor or flat screen television.

Hoping to destroy Seefra's only method for recovering her, Janine began hurling rocks at the screen with both hands. She already had deep cuts on her palms and fingers and although the rocks made her wounds worse, she still grabbed anything she could get her hands on and pitched them roughly at the living corridor. Most of the rocks disappeared into the membrane. A couple of them missed the corridor entirely. One of the larger rocks managed to skip off the top of the portal, lightly glazing the perimeter and emitting a small shower of sparks. After seeing this, Janine immediately looked for the largest stone she could lift. She moved it over toward the corridor with her legs, and after pulling the sleeves of her cargo jacket down over her hands; she bent at the legs and hefted the huge piece of shale. She could barely raise it above her waist, but the thought of Seefra sending guards through the portal flooded her body with a surge of adrenaline. She pressed the immense stone up to her chin and then with a mighty exhale, pushed it above her head. The rock equaled more than half of Janine's own weight, and when she brought it down on top of the corridor, the passageway crumpled in an explosion of organic energy. Janine could have sworn she heard a groan in the midst of all the fireworks as she collapsed onto the rocky surface. Seefra could never locate her now.

"Purugama," said Conor, leaning forward in his saddle. "Did you see that?"

"See what, Champion?" queried the great cougar.

"A shower of sparks, far off in the distance," said Conor. "Way up in the mountains, at the other end of the valley. I swear I saw something out of the ordinary – a fire or an explosion."

Purugama looked at the mountain, and then back at Maya and his companions. "It is easiest for us to ascertain its origin, since we can arrive there in a matter of minutes. The others seem to be in no immediate danger. I'm sure they can spare us for a few moments."

Conor braced his feet while Purugama shifted directions and began pumping his giant wings. Already used to his new saddle, Conor rode confidently on his big friend's shoulders, using only his legs and feet for balance. He folded his arms while in the saddle, marveling at how perfectly at ease he felt. It clearly seemed as though he and Purugama had traveled this way together for centuries.

Janine scrambled down off of the steep embankment and found a relatively flat place to stand. She wiped as much of the blood away from her face and hands as she could, and then began surveying the area around her. In front of her lay a vast basin so wide she couldn't even estimate its size. The mountain she stood on, possibly ten thousand feet or so above the valley floor, rose up with its brothers at the extreme edge of the lengthy valley. She looked to her right along the range; it seemed to go on for miles. *The mountains would keep almost anything form entering the valley*, she thought, *although there were a few in the range that had suffered some form of collapse.* An army could breach the damaged areas of the range without too much effort.

Suddenly, out of the corner of her eye, she spied a tiny speck flying through the air. It seemed to glide along the currents of the wind, heading in her direction. She couldn't make out anything yet, but whatever it was, it used wings for flight. The creature would flap its wings vigorously for a minute or two and then glide for roughly the same amount of time. She watched patiently, waiting for it to get closer. Somehow she knew that if it were any of Seefra's minions, there would be a large contingent of them, and not just one solitary creature. She licked some fresh blood from her thumb and index finger as she waited for them to approach. After a while she could make out that someone was riding on a giant beast, a winged beast that took its passenger increasingly closer to her. She watched and waited, suddenly realizing that the creature was a giant cougar, and if that were true then the passenger must be Conor.

Janine jumped high into the air, waving both of her bloody hands and screaming as loudly as she could. With every fiber of her being, she felt relief and happiness that she would finally be reconnected once again with Conor. *She was safe.* But when her feet touched solid ground again, the rocks gave way underneath her.

She panicked momentarily and then felt a smooth and sickeningly familiar surface under her feet. Before she could even think, the floor of the cell of crystals emerged from the rocky mountaintop around her. A small group of very peculiar creatures erected four crystal walls and then a crystal ceiling in a matter of seconds. Once again Seefra's captive, Janine found herself encased in a perfectly transparent cell. She could breathe and move around a bit, but her short brush with freedom had expired.

She banged against the side of the cell with her hands and feet, screaming at the top of her lungs. She saw clearly now that the two travelers were in fact Conor and Purugama. She became hysterical, screaming for Conor to save her and slapping her hands against the sides of the crystal walls. To her horrified dismay, it appeared as though neither Conor nor Purugama could see her while she occupied the cell. "No," she cried as she stared at her savior. "I came so close. Oh, Conor. Why can't you see me?" She mumbled hysterically while the cell of crystals sank into the pile of shale she used to crush the corridor that had brought her to the mountain.

As they cleared the first row of tree-lined cliffs at the top of the mountain, Conor stood in his stirrups surveying the scene before him. The surroundings seemed completely undisturbed, except for a scattering of shale here and there. This meant nothing to him, however, because he searched for the indication of fire or some type of explosion. He knew he had seen something up on this mountain. Something visible from that far away had to leave some kind of sign. He looked down and saw Purugama scanning the area with his great golden eyes. He felt the frustration in his big friend's shoulders. They had come a long way, leaving the other Champions unprotected. If nothing existed here, then the great cougar would want to return to the valley very soon.

"Purugama!" said Conor, excitedly. "Over there, look at that debris." Conor pulled on the thick leathery strap that crossed over Purugama's shoulders, trying to steer the big cat in the direction he wanted. He could no more turn the great cougar than he could control the wind, but the tension on the strap helped Purugama to understand his intent. He banked into a sharp turn and soared over the scattered debris. He turned and glided over the site a second time, making sure that no danger existed there. Finally, he floated over to the debris, elevating just above the broken pieces. Conor jumped off, landing lightly on the loose shale. He examined a few of the pieces, holding one up for Purugama to see. The cougar wasted no time with his explanation.

"A corridor," he said. "Or what used to be a corridor. It may have existed recently, or as long as ten thousand years ago."

Conor felt the pieces in his hand. They gave off an incredible amount of warmth. *This portal was used recently*, he thought, *very recently*. He looked around the immediate area, using a visual grid as his father had always instructed. Something glistened in the brilliant sunlight; it caught his eye as readily as if it had reached out and grabbed his arm. Ignoring Purugama for a moment, he skipped lightly across the rocks until he stood over a huge chunk of shale. The shining object lay just under the left edge of the big rock. As Conor lifted the thin chain, his heart jumped into his throat. Blood-stained and slightly damaged, the bracelet contained a small amulet with the letters "JC" engraved on its surface.

"*JANINE!*" Conor bellowed.

He clutched the amulet in his hand, screaming her name as

loudly as he could. It rolled around the mountain range and through the valley below. He shut his eyes tightly, convincing himself that his girlfriend must be alive, that this served as a message to that effect. No other alternative existed, and he had to return to the Champions and continue the hunt. He opened his eyes and looked over at Purugama. The big cougar floated quietly in the same spot he had occupied earlier. Scanning the valley and the mountains around them, he simply waited for Conor to conclude his investigation. Conor ran back over to him, slipping once and cutting his right elbow. Ignoring the pain and the blood, he jumped into his saddle, clutching the amulet with the small chain.

"I am sorry, Conor," said Purugama as he banked away from the cliff. "Let us both believe she still lives, and dedicate our energies toward successfully rescuing her."

Conor situated himself atop the giant golden shoulders and jammed his feet into the stirrups. He held the amulet tightly, refusing to loosen his grip or place it in any of his pockets. "Yes," he said to Purugama. "Let us do just that."

Janine could feel the floor of her cage dragging through the shale, obviously on its way back to the chamber of cells. While encased within the mountain, she could see nothing but dark stones as they rumbled past her cell. After a while, however, shafts of light began piercing the darkness, and soon she could see the side of an immense wall far out in front of her. The bizarre creatures that had constructed her cell so rapidly now served as her conductors and paced along with the cell on all sides. One of them even rode on top of the crystal ceiling, directing the movements of the others.

The cell emerged from the shale mountain. Janine had quickly overcome the shock of being so close to freedom. She was now used to having things cruelly snatched away from her by Seefra. As she began to examine her surroundings she saw a gigantic cliff face to her right. The creatures appeared to be defying gravity as they walked her cell across the side of a huge mountain. Above her shone a bright sun, and because she decided not to look down at the moment, she had no idea what loomed below her. To her left lay another vast basin; almost a duplicate of the one Conor had overcome to reach her.

This valley seemed quite different in one distinct way. The floor of the valley seemed to be fluid; it swam in a way that could be interpreted as something living. Janine couldn't take her eyes away from the strange sight. She wanted very much to understand the peculiar phenomenon below her. Unfortunately, it was just too far away. She didn't have the eyesight to focus on any particular aspect of the movement. Whatever was surging around the valley floor was gigantic; that she could tell for sure. Janine watched as the entire basin – dozens of square miles, if not more – squirmed and swirled in front of her eyes.

Suddenly the creatures chaperoning her cell began yelling in unison. They barked out a strange chant, over and over again, seemingly to no one in particular. Janine looked over at the creatures on either side of her, and then to the one riding on top of the cell. She watched as they screamed the phrase and saw them looking down at the valley as they did so. Those on either side of her cell raised a small appendage as they yelled out their phrase. Janine wondered what they could be saying, and who might be the recipient of such a strange mantra.

The roar from the valley below took her completely by surprise. The howl was so deafening it hurt her ears until she slammed her palms to the sides of her head. She could see streams of sand and shale fluttering up from the ground in her direction as the sound wave traveled up the mountain. Then it came again, the same bizarre phrase that her escorts had chanted, but this time it had come from the liquid floor of the valley. After several trumpeting roars from below, Janine realized where the movement down below had originated. The floor of the valley swarmed with Seefra's warriors. Slayers, no doubt, and keepers as well. She had heard him babble endlessly about his superior forces, describing them in every possible fashion over her months of captivity. They had to be the first wave of the attack, slayers to overwhelm the enemy, and keepers to build makeshift prisons on the run. She looked down into the valley, trying to gauge the distance between herself and the army below her. She tried desperately to estimate their numbers. She wanted to relay the information to Conor if she were able to escape again.

After swallowing the shock of her calculations, she guessed the number of warriors to be more than one hundred thousand, and possibly as many as five hundred thousand. She couldn't tell for sure. She kept shaking her head and blinking her eyes. For all she knew, there might be over a million slayers and keepers down there. *If Conor tried to defeat Seefra, how could a teenager and a handful of Champions go into battle against a force like this?* It was suicide. By sheer numbers alone they would be overwhelmed and defeated. Janine doubted if even the Lady of the Light could face such a horde and come away victorious. She shook her head a final time, dropping it into her hands. She wanted desperately to find a way to escape again and warn Conor.

The massive host erupted again, bellowing the chant their fellow creatures started only minutes ago. They began moving toward the broken wall of the canyon, very slowly at first, but in a small amount of time their progress increased measurably. They poured through the crack in the mountain, heading into a deserted valley. The warriors squeaked through the small passage, almost single file compared to their previous arrangement. As more and more of the creatures entered the valley, their group widened into the huge horde that had occupied the interior basin. In less than an hour, hundreds of thousands of slayers and over thirty thousand keepers were on their way to meet the Champions of the Crossworlds. They ran and walked and scurried in no particular formal procession, but the creatures made their way as a group nonetheless. As individuals, none of them would pose any problem for the Champions. However, their lack of fighting skills would be supplanted by the size of their host. The giant group marched on, rallied by their repeated battle cries that rolled around the mountains like acoustic boomerangs.

"That's a strange sound," said Conor as he twisted in his saddle to look back at the mountain. "That can't be just the wind. It's repeating itself, and it seems to be something other than a random occurrence."

"Yes," answered Purugama. "It does appear to be organic in nature. It would be worth the trip to determine its origin, although I am somewhat fearful to discover its source."

"We'd better find out what's making that noise," replied Conor, "if not for our own knowledge, then for the safety of the other Champions."

Purugama snarled slightly. Although he felt deeply for Conor, at times his human tenacity grated on his nerves. "We are nearly halfway back to the group. I suggest we let them know of our intentions and then fly back to ascertain the sound's origin."

"But we'll lose valuable time if we travel twice the distance to achieve the same result," protested Conor. "Do you see anything ahead of us besides the other Champions? Is there any commotion occurring anywhere in the valley? Do you think I would object to your counsel if I feared for their safety?"

Purugama could not argue against the young man's last statement. With a quick chuff he reversed course, banked his large, muscular body hard to the left in the direction of the mountain range. Conor had to grab the leather strap above the great cougar's shoulders during this maneuver. The turn had come so abruptly and with so little warning that he nearly lost his seat on Purugama's back. The big cat pumped his wings as hard as he could, hoping to reach the source of the sound and be back among the Champions as quickly as possible. Purugama did not like leaving the others to their own devices for very long. Formidable though they were, he felt that the more time they spent alongside each other as a pack, the better their chance would be when the attack came.

The two travelers reached the edge of the first canyon quickly. They flew over the spot where Conor had found the amulet and sailed over an endless, pale brown valley. The basin was so massive the rocky floor seemed to extend out indefinitely. Purugama flew as fast as he could, pushing his wings to their absolute limit. In no time at all, the two of them formed a tiny speck over a gigantic expanse.

A call traveled up the wall at the far side of the valley, and then repeated itself. Purugama's expression changed when he heard the strange chant from a closer vantage point. He began to think Conor may have been right. His idea to investigate the bizarre sound had been brilliant after all. He listened intently as the cry sailed up over the mountainous wall again. Nearing the far side of the valley now, the great cougar slowed the movement of his wings. Hearing the audible chant again, he could almost pinpoint exactly what it was that made such a sound. He reiterated his earlier feelings to himself. He felt more than a bit fearful about what lay beyond the mountain range in the next valley.

The two travelers appeared over the mountain range on the far side of the second valley, flying high in the sky over the vast horde of slayers and keepers. The chanting from the valley stopped immediately. An ear-splitting roar of vicious hatred replaced the mantra as soon as the two Champions appeared in the sky above the endless host. The multitude below, almost four hundred thousand strong, looked up to the sky as one, releasing their animosity toward a known Champion and his strange passenger. The din continued without pause, as some in the crowd inhaled a fresh breath while others continued screaming at the intruders.

The slayers held their weapons high over their heads, eager to confront their enemy and finish the battle before the shadow warriors were even called forward. The keepers bounced and crawled all over each other in anticipation of erecting another cage of fire for the Champions of the Crossworlds. The roar of the host continued as the warriors jostled each other for the best view of the giant cougar and the young man who directed his flight. Fights broke out all across the valley as the intense desire for battle interfered with any remaining courtesies the shadow combatants held for each other. The lust for war and blood tipped the booming screams rising up from the valley, straining to touch Purugama's wingtips.

"You were right to bring us here," the big cat said, flying the length of the valley. "Those are slayers, Conor, all of them. No, wait, I see keepers as well, no doubt as a rear guard to lock up any prisoners the slayers happen to bring down."

Conor sat in his saddle, speechless, gripping the strap with both hands. He jammed his feet into the stirrups a little further while looking down on the massive army arrayed before him. "There's so many of them," he said absentmindedly. He couldn't believe what he was looking at; it seemed like all of the battle scenes he'd ever seen in any movie theater throughout his lifetime. But this appeared to be even more daunting. He couldn't even see the end of the long line of slayers in the valley. It was so far away from them that the last in the group looked like a blur.

He couldn't see them, but he could certainly hear them. The deafening sound coming from the horde seemed almost surreal. It never ended, nor did it waver in its intensity. Conor looked down at the screaming masses, the endless sea of thousands upon thousands of angry, spirited warriors. They looked like specks at the elevation Purugama was presently flying, but Conor could see the raised weapons waving back and forth in their direction. Even while riding on the shoulders of the most powerful and intimidating beast he had ever known, Conor felt terribly unnerved by what he saw below them.

"How will we ever fight them?" he asked.

"Come, Conor," said the great cougar. "We must tell the others about what awaits them on the other side of the mountains. By the time we return, this horde will have crossed another range." Purugama dipped a wing and turned back toward the familiar mountain range. He began pumping his wings again, flying swiftly toward the safety of the canyon wall. Turning to look back once, he remarked not so much to Conor, but not just to himself either.

"We must inform Maya. He will know the proper course to take."

"The proper course," whispered Conor under his breath, "is to get the heck out of here."

Purugama soared over the valleys and through the sparse trees in the mountain ranges. When he and Conor reached the first expanse, he saw that the Champions had almost crossed the entire span. Maya and his companions were closing in on the first mountain pass at the far side of the valley. The great cougar turned in a wide arc above the group of cats. He looked in every direction for as far as he could see, trying to ascertain whether any other forces might be coming at them from a different direction. Finally secure with his observations, Purugama soared down toward the group below him. In seconds he and Conor hovered lightly above their position. Purugama executed one final turn, dipped his wings forward and hit the ground running. He quickly padded up to Maya and crouched down so Conor could dismount.

Maya halted his advance, and as he sat down casually, the other Champions assumed their protective positions around him. "Your faces show concern," said the leader of the Champions. "Take a breath and then tell us all what you've seen."

"Slayers, my Lord," answered Purugama immediately. "Seefra's serious this time, I'm afraid. There must be close to half a million, including a good number of keepers as well."

Maya sat completely still, showing no emotion or any change in his expression at all. He stared at the lofty mountain range that lay ahead. He closed his eyes as if listening for the mighty roar from the massive host. The other Champions did not disturb his meditation, for they knew Maya very well. He could be conjuring a spell to defeat the slayers at that very moment. He might even be conferring with the creators to determine the best possible mode of attack. He may even be resting for all they knew. One thing they could always depend on, however, was that Maya had never let them down in all the centuries they had served with him. He was supremely intelligent, very courageous, and a brilliant tactician.

"Let us wait for them here," he said finally, still staring at the mountains in front of the group.

"I advise against that," said Therion as he walked up to join the group from behind. "They could bypass this valley completely and come at us from a flanking position. We would be trapped at the foothills of these mountains, with no escape available to us."

No one else questioned the leader of the Champions. Ajur did a most peculiar thing, however. He broke from his guardian position and walked over to Maya. Standing right in front of him, the brawny, black jaguar stared into his Lord's eyes for the longest time. He snarled with great menace, and then looked at every part of Maya's body, sniffing vigorously. He looked for a small flaw in Maya's construction, something that would tell him that another being had taken the place of their leader. After a lengthy inspection, Ajur looked again into Maya's eyes. He bared his huge fangs and roared so ferociously that the black and white whiskers on Maya's face wavered under the force of his breath. Then as quickly as he advanced on his leader, Ajur backed away, glancing at all the other Champions. He was telling them that Maya was indeed Maya, and not some imposter sent here to lead them to their destruction.

Therion took the message to heart. "Tell us then, Maya, what are we to do when an impossible number of slayers pours over the top of those mountains and descends upon us? I will follow your counsel and fight in any way you desire."

Maya licked his right paw and scraped it his over his nose a few times. He did the same with the left, removing the remaining spittle from Ajur's vocal attack. "You will all know what to do when the time comes. Eha, you must be the first wave of our attack."

The gangly but massive cheetah nodded his head as he walked back to the group from his point position.

"Only you have the speed to stay ahead of a horde of slayers," Maya continued. You must lead them away from any protected areas. Take them into the open basin, where the rest of us can deal with them effectively."

"No!" shouted Conor without thinking. "Shouldn't we wait for them to be halfway over the mountain and then strike while their footing is bad and their formation is scrambled?"

Every single Champion looked over at Conor. They didn't know whether to cheer him or shoot him down. To contradict one as wise as Maya made one look extremely foolish.

"My apologies, Maya," said Conor, sheepishly.

"An excellent suggestion," said Maya without even a hint of cynicism. "But you forget, Conor, that Seefra can alter the environment at any time. I expect that when we begin to gain an advantage over the slayers he will do just that. It is best for us to be clear of any large natural structures in case he shifts the surroundings on us. Besides, if we can lure the slayers out into the open we will have the advantage."

Conor bowed his head and backed away from Maya. He walked over to Purugama, grabbed the leather strap and pulled himself into the saddle. As he settled himself, he felt the tip of the great cougar's tail slap him on the back of the head. The small action relaxed Conor, and he pinched one of Purugama's ears as hard as he could. He knew it wouldn't cause any real pain for the big cat, but it made him feel better anyway.

The group of seven gathered close to one another. They began to hear a raucous chant rising over the mountains from the next valley over.

"You will all know what to do," said Maya confidently. He looked at each of the Champions in turn and when he held their attention, he cried out in a low, guttural voice, "For the Champions, the Lady, and the Crossworlds!"

Conor and the big cats roared together as they waited for the enemy to arrive.

CHAPTER THIRTY

The first and fastest of the slayers emerged from the broken section of the mountain range, setting the pace for the others. After a few hundred had passed through, they began wailing and chanting again. The rest of the horde, upon hearing that their enemies resided only a few thousand yards away, joined with the others in the hideous howling. If it had been loud before, now the thunderous roar nearly shook the shale from the mountaintops. The slayers that had crossed, even though they were closest to the Champions, had their voices drowned out by the multitude still passing through the broken range.

When the horde learned that the Champions awaited them on the other side of the mountain, the passage took on a frantic pace. Thousands of slayers climbed over tens of thousands of their fellows trying to be the first in line to attack Seefra's enemies. Keepers found themselves trampled underfoot or kicked aside by the stampeding mass of warriors. Over a hundred thousand occupied the valley with the Champions. An hour after that, another two hundred thousand had crossed through the broken mountain. Soon thereafter, the constant flow of warriors falling through the passes in the mountains slowed to a soft trickle. Three hundred seventy-five thousand slayers and almost twenty-five thousand keepers stood on the valley floor next to the foothills of the mountain, screaming and chanting as they stared at the Champions.

Maya did nothing. He silently instructed the rest of the Champions to do the same. They simply sat there staring at the huge host from a distance of roughly a thousand yards. They didn't show a trace of fear, but they also couched their aggression inside a very calm demeanor. They weren't going to make the first move, but they were showing the slayers they very well might make the last. Therion stood proudly, waving his tail back and forth and letting his dark mane flutter in the shifting breeze. Surmitang and Ajur crouched down on the dusty ground together, eyes locked on the horde in front of them. Conor sat atop Purugama, one hand holding the riding strap and the other resting lightly on his thigh. His fears had all but vanished. Once he saw the other Champions preparing to fight against the giant host he felt a surge of pride and courage rush through his body. He held Janine's amulet and felt his insides steadily rumble into a controlled rage. He wanted to fight the slayers and anything else Seefra could bring to bear against them. He stared straight ahead at the multitude of creatures, lightly flicking his fingers and feeling the magic of the Lady of the Light dancing lightly against his palm.

Eha, as light-spirited as ever, paced in front of the group of Champions making faces at the slayers. Every once in a while he would turn and face his brothers. With a smirk on his face, he leaned down on his forepaws and stretched his body to its limit with his tail high in the air. Eha showed the slayers what he thought of them by proudly displaying a keen view of his rump and anus. Maya merely sat in the same position since they reached their spot in the valley. He waited, listened, and went through a dozen strategies in his head for the remainder of the battles he knew were forthcoming.

The voices of the slayers died down. The cries of the keepers faded away behind them. A single slayer stepped forward, separating himself from the host. He twirled a peculiar weapon in his hands, flipping it from one appendage to the other. He seemed to be engaged in some form of dance, as if he were using the tool to communicate in some way. The other slayers and keepers kept their weapons completely silent during this ritual. None of them made a sound while the strange dance took place. After the slayer finished the bizarre series of movements, he crouched down and bowed to the Champions. Then without returning to the line of warriors, he flung his weapon straight at them. The weapon flew so fluidly that for a moment most of the cats didn't realize it was traveling toward them at lightning speed. A soft whistling noise followed the slayer's weapon as it sped through the air from one troop of warriors to the next. It seemed to gain speed and size as it flew, gobbling up the yards between both forces in a matter of seconds. Something appeared to be controlling it, keeping it on track straight for Maya's nose, for nothing could travel that far and that fast and never waver in the slightest.

The Champions sat watching the weapon approach them. Eha moved to the side, finding a safe place next to Therion. Conor squirmed in his saddle slightly, unsure about what to do. He wanted to jump in front of the weapon and knock it away, but something held him in his seat. The fact that Purugama hadn't moved a muscle obviously played a part in his decision. Still, it pained him to stand by and do nothing.

Maya sat like a stone statue. The huge weapon closed to within a hundred yards as it gained manic speed. Two more blinks of his bi-colored eyelashes and the weapon would split Maya's skull like an eggshell.

343

None of the Champions moved or spoke.

Maya closed his eyes. The weapon whistled feverishly as it closed to within fifty feet.

During the final turn before impaling itself into Maya's forehead, the Lord of the Champions lifted his eyelids. The weapon froze an inch from his face. It hovered for a moment, struggling to find its target. Then it fell to the ground in pieces at Maya's feet.

Conor exhaled.

Maya yowled at the slayers.

Surmitang and Ajur stood and snarled, baring their huge, white fangs.

The entire horde of slayers and keepers charged across the valley. Waving their weapons and screaming, they ran full speed toward their enemies.

The Champions stood their ground, awaiting their destiny.

"Hold on Conor," said Purugama to his passenger. "Hold on to the strap with both hands."

CHAPTER THIRTY-ONE

A dust cloud followed the huge throng of slayers as they crossed the valley and rushed the Champions. Maya waited until the cloud had consumed almost half of the charging host before making his move. Turning his head to the rear, he used his midnight black tail to draw a large corridor above the valley floor behind them. When the membrane solidified, Maya looked at Eha and then Purugama, giving each of them a small nod. As quickly as they could, the rest of the Champions disappeared into the corridor, leaving the two cats and Conor behind. Purugama crouched and wished Eha good fortune, and with one mighty leap, he pushed his huge frame into the sky. The powerful, leathery wings pumped once, then twice, and he turned in the air toward the horde of slayers. They flew over the massive group of warriors but did not attack them. They merely observed and waited for them to find Eha.

The big, gangly cheetah stood his ground, all alone, as he watched the largest army he had ever faced bear down on him. He smiled and chuffed a few times in their direction. He swatted the ground with his long, ringed tail, sending small clouds of rocks in their direction. He couldn't remember the last time he had been able to test himself against a foe this fast. He would be able to run wild, as fast as he could for as long he could.

He knew he could stay ahead of the slayers. They moved terribly fast, but nowhere near as fast as a supercharged, oversized cheetah with magical powers.

Eha waited, watching them come closer. The slayers tried everything they could to outdo each other. Even with the gigantic host, the few hundred at the front of the march climbed over each other in a series of weak attempts to be the first to strike a blow for the Circle of Evil. Eha spit one more snarl in their direction before turning away from them. He swished his hind feet a few times, throwing clumps of sand and a few loose rocks at their front line. With the horde less than ten feet from him, the huge cheetah took off in an explosion of sandy dust.

Eha used every inch of his twenty-foot frame. The long, muscular legs and forepaws churned above the valley floor, putting a good bit of distance between himself and the slayers. He smiled, letting his tongue dangle out of his mouth while he ran.

Every few moments he would look back and check his distance. He didn't want to leave the slayers too far behind. They might get frustrated and design a new strategy, and he wanted them to stay with him until he reached the middle of the main valley. He looked around again to check on their progress, and saw about a dozen small packs of slayers breaking off from the main pack. They sped away to either side of Eha's projected path, possibly with the intent of flanking him. He paid them no mind at all. A few hundred here or there didn't matter; his interest lay with the central force. *Besides*, he thought, *those smaller battle groups wouldn't last long anyway.*

When Purugama saw the small packs of slayers breaking away from the main group, he banked sharply and tucked his wings in pursuit. The main throng presented problems because of its size, but lesser groups could be managed easily. With Conor holding on tightly, the great cougar swooped down onto the first of the smaller flanking groups. He roared at the slayers, a blast of ruby red energy shooting from his throat. The bolt of power increased in size as it sped down toward the group of warriors. The bolt impacted the slayers, causing an explosion of intense red light. When the light dimmed, there was nothing left except a large crater in the valley. No slayers, no weapons, not a thing remained.

Conor had held his breath during the attack. When he saw the energy that came from Purugama and how it decimated the slayers, he exhaled intermittently, trying to control his excitement. He screamed at the big cat, pulling hard on the strap to the left. He wanted to be the one to strike at the slayers the next time, and he urged his mentor to fly him into position.

Purugama complied without hesitation. Elevating away from his first attack, he took a wide turn in the sky so Conor could have a free hand. From six hundred feet above the valley, the big, golden cougar dipped his wings and fell upon the next subgroup of slayers. He didn't say a word to Conor. He didn't want to coach him in any way. He just flew, in attack formation, straight down toward their objective.

Conor held the strap tightly with one arm as he raised his right hand high above his head like a cowboy riding a bucking bronco. He called forth the Lady's energy with a brief incantation. He felt the familiar tingling in his palm as the silver sparkles began their delicate dance. The glistening energy increased until he held a sizzling ball of the creator's power in the palm of his hand. As Purugama banked at the bottom of his attack run, Conor flung the energy ball as hard as he could toward the slayers. He scored a direct hit, but unfortunately had summoned fifty times the amount of energy he needed. The explosion obliterated the pack of a hundred or so slayers. It also took out a few thousand more in the main horde, and nearly sent Conor and Purugama tumbling to the valley floor. Conor grabbed the strap with his right hand while Purugama fought for stability against the blast wave. When he finally returned to a controlled flight, the great cougar addressed his young protégé.

"Mind of the creators, Conor, you'll take the two of us and Eha with you the next time you try and finish the battle with one toss. Temper your excitement when you channel the energy of the creators."

"Sorry," said Conor absentmindedly, forgetting his mistake immediately. "Look, over there to the right. More groups are breaking off from the main thrust. Let's cut them off before they get to Eha!"

Purugama shook his great head as he pulled on his wings, driving the two of them higher and higher into the sky. He looked down in the direction Conor had mentioned and saw additional flanking groups separating from the horde. These groups contained roughly the same number of slayers, and they worked in the logical pattern of containment and capture. They would encircle Eha, pushing him in the direction they wanted, until they finally drove him into an inescapable web. The strategy made perfect sense, but the numbers worried Purugama. After seeing the ease with which they had dispatched the previous groups, even the slayers wouldn't be foolish enough to sacrifice more of their numbers so easily. As he tucked his wings for another attack, the great cougar kept his senses on full alert for any trickery on the part of his enemies.

Now fully engaged in the battle, Conor leaned into the angle of Purugama's descent, enjoying the speed at which they overtook the slayers. For a second they looked like small action figures, and in the next moment they were real warriors, running madly to escape the great Champions of the Crossworlds.

As they swooped by, Conor shot both of his hands out toward the group of slayers, fingers extended. A dozen separate streams of blinding energy consumed every one of the warriors, freezing them for a second before vaporizing the entire group. The young man smiled at the success of his attack and forgot all about the main horde of slayers.

Purugama ducked, trying to take both of them beyond the reach of their counterattack. A string of slayers lashed out at Conor, knocking him clear off his perch aboard the big cat's shoulders. The slayers had formed a giant whip made up of over a thousand warriors. Using the combined magic of the horde, they waited until Conor attacked and then threw the tail of the whip in his direction. They hoped to frighten him into retreating from his attacks on their flanking groups. It was more luck than accuracy that drove the tightly bound string of warriors into the great cougar and his passenger. Conor never saw them coming, and the whiplash from the tail tore him off Purugama's shoulders.

He flew at least seventy yards through the air and landed in a dusty heap on the valley floor. Before he even stopped rolling, a dozen keepers appeared out of thin air. They descended on him like locusts, climbing all over his body as they erected a crude but serviceable cell of shadows. The speed of their craftsmanship shocked Conor. He struggled like a madman against them. Having built cells for millennia, however, the keepers had a perfected technique. The creatures, which resembled a mix between a praying mantis and a lobster, needed no synthetic tools to help them encase an enemy. Their bodies constantly secreted a mysterious substance they used to create whatever type of cell they desired.

Using this frightening skill, the keepers had Conor at a terrible disadvantage.

Terrified of being encased in another of their soulless cells, Conor grabbed the keepers with both hands, flinging them in every direction while he rolled and kicked and bit at the strange creatures. His efforts gained him nothing. The keepers seemed to multiply as the struggle continued. If he threw one away from him, three more would appear, binding his arms and legs in the bizarre, smoky tiles. He yelled at the top of his lungs, screaming for Purugama to save him from the keepers and their horrid prison. He rolled continuously, trying everything to at least slow down as many of the creatures as he could.

While lying on his stomach protecting his face, Conor felt four massive claw-tipped paws grab him from shoulder to calf. The huge talons compressed, lifting him up into the sky and away from the main force of the slayers. The keepers remained attached to Conor's body, fighting to complete the construction of their cell. Every Champion incapacitated in this way would increase the odds for the shadow warriors and the destroyers when they finally came to finish them off. They grappled with the young man in their possession, trying desperately to confine him. His great strength, no doubt supported by the creators, kept them from sealing the last few links in the shadow tiles.

Purugama leaned his huge head down and looked at Conor's predicament. He yelled against the whine of the wind and the shrieking encouragement of the slayers on the ground. "The weapons along the seams of your trousers," he bellowed. "Find one and use it against the keepers!"

Conor fought to comprehend the garbled message from the cougar. One of the keepers scratched at his left eye, momentarily distracting him from deciphering Purugama's words. Conor lifted his one free limb and raked the vile creature off of his face. He flung it toward the ground just as four more keepers clung to his upper body. One of them scrambled down his torso, disregarding the fact that it was flying high above the ground at an incredible speed. Conor felt the tiny hands and feet scrabbling along his skin until it stopped just above his knee. It joined a few of its mates trying to fasten a tile around his legs.

At that moment Conor understood what Purugama had been trying to say. Without looking, he shook his free hand to clear away any of the disgusting creatures. Then he slapped his thigh as hard as he could to drive them away from the small pockets lining his pants. He couldn't have known which of the compartments contained the right increment, so he grabbed at the first one he could feel. He stuck his finger into the small opening and withdrew what seemed like a small piece of rock candy. He brought it up to his face, trying to glimpse the strange material and almost blinded himself. It burned with a silvery brilliance so intense that it nearly blocked out the sun.

The keepers wanted no part of Conor's new device. They forgot all about the cell of shadows as they crawled down to Conor's feet. They hung there like an encrusted beehive, a tightly grouped ball of creatures clamoring for the furthest point away from the young Champion. They shrieked as they watched Conor crush the tiny orb in his palm. They fell silent when he turned his knuckles to the sky and opened his hand.

A minute group of keepers, exact copies of those attached to Conor's feet, danced around in the palm of his hand. With the coloring of the Lady of the Light's hypnotic eyes, the tiny creatures charged toward Seefra's keepers, calling out with high-pitched battle cries. They swarmed over the larger keepers, building perfect cages to house their captives and render them immobile. One by one, the imprisoned keepers fell away from Conor's feet, floating down toward the battleground with a tiny replica riding triumphantly atop their newly constructed container. The cell of silver would encase the keepers for eternity. No magic save that of the creators could ever free any creatures so imprisoned.

Conor twisted his body around, pulling Purugama's gigantic claws away from his skin one by one. With one huge paw still connected to his right leg, Conor grabbed onto the great cougar's wing, using it to lift him back into his saddle. Once there, he jammed his feet back down into the stirrups and used his hands to brush the stray hair away from his face. He continued sweeping his hands all over his head and body, wanting to be sure that none of the hideous creatures were still on him. Once reassured, he leaned down so he could speak right into Purugama's ear.

"Thank you, my friend. You saved my life down there. If not for you I might again be sitting within the darkness of captivity."

"Do not mention it, Conor," replied the big cat. "Use your energy instead to watch my back as well as your own. We have a long battle ahead."

Conor patted Purugama roughly against his giant shoulder. He said nothing further, knowing that his mentor would rather focus on what lay below. The two of them flew just behind the lead line of the main horde. Conor could see Eha out in front of the giant group of slayers, running freely this way and that, trying to tire and confuse them at the same time. Conor knew from Gribba's description that the slayers would never exhaust themselves, but Eha worked tirelessly nonetheless. In fact, he seemed to be having the time of his life down there.

Indeed, had the two Champions been closer they would have seen and heard Eha laughing hilariously as he ran for his life. Although he knew the slayers would cut him to pieces if he fell or if they overtook him, the massive cheetah laughed and laughed every time something happened in his favor. He nearly choked when Conor flattened a good part of the valley with his first energy blast.

After watching the whip nearly finish Conor for good, Eha decided to have some real fun. He began changing directions haphazardly, and every time his huge hind legs shot away toward a different course, he would utter a secret word known only to the Lady and him. Instead of just shooting streams of harmless rocks and dirt toward the horde of slayers, huge streaks of gleaming purple energy shot out from the ground beneath his claws. The bolts expanded as they accelerated toward the slayers, who couldn't avoid the impact because of the giant wave of compatriots behind them. In the time it took for the slayers to comprehend their predicament, the glistening purple essence had reached them. Each small kick from Eha's hind feet propelled enough magical flame to take down at least five hundred enemies – a small number in relation to the total force arrayed against them, but plenty to give Eha reason to rejoice. The big cheetah, running flat out, shook his furry, lined head over and over, laughing his guts out. In the midst of the most serious battle the creators had ever pitched against the Circle of Evil, Eha raced around like a banshee having the time of his life.

Purugama shook his golden head as he watched Eha play his games with the giant host of slayers. He noticed that no additional subgroups emerged from the main horde; evidently they had learned a hard lesson and decided against sacrificing any more of their troops. Purugama held no false hopes about the immediate future. He knew that Seefra would guide the slayers in different and more beneficial directions. What concerned the great cougar now was the juncture in the valley floor approaching Eha and his pursuers. Unless his brother could convince the slayers to follow him into the larger section of the basin, Maya's plans could fall apart before they ever materialized.

It was there that Maya hoped to destroy the bulk of the slayer forces. There was a large enough area to launch a full offensive attack against the horde. But Eha would have to take them there first, and Purugama wondered about the possibility.

Just as he began to dip his wings and take Conor down for a talk with the laughing cheetah, Purugama saw something that altered his course completely. He quickly flicked his wings back and glided along at a good viewing altitude. He almost cautioned Conor to watch the right column of the desert floor, but he thought better of it. The dramatic effect of what was about to occur would best be viewed with an innocent eye.

The huge horde of slayers rumbled along the valley floor, chasing Eha with mindless purpose. Every time they appeared ready to collapse all around him, the big cheetah would flick his hind legs and scamper out of reach. The large, expanding projectiles of purple matter splattered against the slayers at the front of the line, taking them down in large numbers while other groups immediately replaced them. The slayers almost halted their advance out of a lost sense of futility, but something kept them pressing forward toward their goal. If they had possessed even a scrap of wits, they might have noticed the floor of the valley to their right rising ever so slightly. They also might have seen small fissures breaking through the ground as they raced by in pursuit of their goal. Had they used their peripheral vision, they might have noticed the difference between the ground to their left and right, which suddenly looked quite dissimilar. It appeared as though the slayers would have no alternative as to whether they maintained a straight course or turned left to follow Eha. The physical geography of the valley would make the choice for them.

Purugama crooked his neck and looked up at his protégé. He saw the wide-eyed look on Conor's face as the young man stared at the ground with his mouth agape. The great cougar turned his own eyes back toward the valley. "Now watch this, Conor," said the big cat. "Don't look away for a moment. You're about to see some real Champion power."

Conor stared at the scene, not hearing a word Purugama spoke. The whole right side of the valley seemed to be suffering its own private earthquake. A huge underground ridge ran directly parallel to the horde of slayers. It started small, but as it continued, it grew in width and height.

Soon, great blocks of earthen crust were being thrown from the ground, tossed aside like pebbles at the base of a waterfall. The uneven nature of the valley floor increased as the disturbance lengthened, and soon Conor could see movement underneath the displacement to the right of the slayers. The arms and legs of a huge, dark creature appeared every few seconds amidst the confusing jumble of dirt, rock and dead tree branches. The creature would surface for only a fraction of a second before diving deeper into the ground, causing even greater upheaval. Conor thought he recognized it for a moment, but he felt it couldn't possibly be him. He asked himself why not, and with that refreshing outlook he realized that the creature actually was Ajur, the massive black jaguar and Champion of the Crossworlds.

He had disappeared at the onset of the battle along with Maya,

Therion and Surmitang, but now he had reemerged to join Eha in the first phase of their strategy. Conor watched as the muscular cat broke through the crusty shale as if it were sand, tossing pieces aside like confetti at a birthday party. He charged ahead of the horde of slayers, driving through the valley floor, creating a gorge to push the massive host into the huge, flat section of the basin between the mountains.

At the end of his creation, Ajur exploded from the ground, roaring his pleasure upon seeing the distortion he had created in the valley. He bellowed repeatedly as he watched the slayers approach. He challenged any in the giant group of warriors to rush up the embankment and attack him. He would welcome such an exchange, but he knew they would keep their distance. Even with their limited intelligence, the slayers and keepers would recognize the one Champion who had fought and nearly destroyed their master. The name of Ajur the invincible was well-known among the residents of the shadow world. None of them would go anywhere near him, which is precisely why Maya chose him for this particular task.

Ajur stood proudly as Eha raced by him. The jovial cheetah actually looked up at his fellow Champion, chirping a brief greeting as he sped by at over one hundred thirty miles an hour. Ajur saw Eha's face for only a brief second before barely glimpsing the lightning-fast limbs driving through the turn, carrying a large trail of dust and debris behind them.

The bulky jaguar surveyed the horde of slayers and keepers, making certain they followed Eha into the larger basin of the valley. He watched as tens of thousands tried to negotiate the turn together. Hundreds fell while thousands more trampled them underfoot. The dazed but unharmed slayers would merely wait until a break occurred in the rushing horde and then stand quickly on unsteady legs. The lucky ones shook themselves until they cleared their heads and continued the pursuit. The unfortunate ones, mostly the keepers in the group, were never able to get out of the way completely. The horde consumed them again, and after two or three tumbles under the weight of the giant host, they simply disappeared forever. The huge shadow army never slowed for an instant. Even after losing part of its force to the Champions' attacks, or through its own attrition, they always continued forward in a mindless charge.

Ajur calculated that over half of the slayers had moved past him into the larger valley. Satisfied with his work, he ran down the huge mound of earth and jumped toward the ground in front of him. With a mighty roar, he blasted through the cracked surface of the desert floor, disappearing completely save a mild ripple he created as he traveled underneath the shale and dirt.

At first he seemed to be overtaking the horde of slayers, but after a few minutes Ajur switched course and made for the rear of the host. Upon reaching the last few thousand warriors, he abruptly turned right and started to surface. He began digging another trench, similar to the one he fashioned earlier. This time, however, he worked to cut off a section of the pack from its base. In effect, he cleaved the forces of the slayers by a little over one percent. He separated five thousand of their number from their fellows, and by doing so he rendered them vulnerable to attack. As he built the sides of the trench higher, he could sense the confusion in the group he had sectioned off. They knew their safety net had been torn away from them, and the only way to rejoin their group would be to travel around the sides of the shale wall created by Ajur. In a fateful move, the separated slayers split up, sending each team in a different direction. They hoped to divide any forthcoming attack so at least one group might make it back to the horde.

"That's our cue," said Purugama to Conor. "Prepare yourself."

Conor could barely contain his excitement. He held onto the strap as he jammed his feet tightly into the stirrups. From a thousand yards up in the sky above the valley, Conor leaned into the sharp, arcing turn that took the two of them down toward one of the small groups behind Ajur's wall. The two Champions fell out of the sky behind them, literally invisible to slayers and keepers. Purugama flew toward the group on the right, and as he did so, Conor watched Ajur sneaking around the front of the trench on the other side. He understood the strategy now; they would take out their own group while the big jaguar dealt with his. "Let the magic of the creators guide my hands," the young man said under his breath.

At an elevation of no more than a hundred feet, Purugama released a loud and potent chuff in the direction of the slayers. The result came immediately as a sonic boom erupted all around the small group of warriors. It sent them flying in every direction, and as they hovered harmlessly in the air all around them, Conor began to pick them off group by group. With both hands he threw sharp strings of silver energy out into the flailing mass of slayers. With each attack, he destroyed two or three score of the enemy and in no time at all Conor had decimated most of the group on their side of the trench. Those that escaped the airborne attack were trampled underneath three thousand pounds of furious cougar, who smashed the remaining slayers to pulp with his huge paws. Finally ceasing his rampage, Purugama looked around for any strays. Conor stood in his stirrups and watched Ajur deal with those on his side of the trench.

The glistening, black jaguar saw no need for magic at this stage of the attack. He tore through the remaining slayers, his distaste and hatred for Seefra fueling his anger. A few dozen keepers actually tried to encase him in a quickly constructed cage of fire, but Ajur would have none of it. He never even gave them a chance to get a firm grip on his massive frame. As soon as he realized their intent, he began shaking them off and squashing them with his huge body. He smashed their hopes of capturing him while crushing the breath from their lungs.

The other slayers watched this and considered retreating back to the main horde. Yet even with their limited intelligence they realized that the punishment awaiting them back at Seefra's chamber would be a thousand times more excruciating than any they might receive here. So after watching the keepers disappear under the massive bulk of the jaguar, they hurled their weapons at him and charged. The end came quickly as the weapons bounced harmlessly off Ajur's protective shields. He swatted the first wave of slayers away with a slash of a giant paw and the rest of the group saw their fellow warriors disintegrate. In the last moment of their lives, they watched the sky grow darker when the huge cat pounced into their midst.

Ajur descended upon them with a savage snarl, ripping them all to shreds and flinging pieces of their bodies in every direction. The jaguar had reverted to a feral state, and, long after the slayers had been obliterated, he kept searching the area for more potential victims. The look on his face unnerved Conor, and he felt a sense of relief that the big jaguar was on his side.

Purugama had to bellow at Ajur to break into his transformed state of mind. "Ajur, come!" shouted the great cougar. "Eha has found trouble and needs our assistance!"

The untamed wildness would not be put aside so easily. Ajur enjoyed that part of his psyche, especially in times of war. The ferocious rage of a wild cat would serve them well in the battles to come, and he did not wish to extinguish his savage side so soon. If Eha really were in trouble, however, he would need his rational mind to help him think his way through the next challenge. He stopped looking around and held his head still. He let his drool seep through his teeth out onto the ground. He shook his head and focused his eyes, forcing himself to think clearly. As a last tribute to his uncivilized self, he stretched his muscles and threw out a mighty roar. Without a word to Conor or Purugama, the big jaguar ran up the trench and vaulted toward the main pack of slayers.

Just the sight of him is enough to strike fear in any other creature, thought Conor as he watched Ajur sprinting across the valley. Purugama had flown into the sky as soon as he saw his brother head over the trench, and Conor could see Ajur racing ahead to save Eha. His huge muscles flexed and bounced as he raced over the shale floor of the valley toward his brother. His dark ears were pinned back against his skull as he ran with all the speed he could muster. Purugama caught up to him in seconds, soaring down until he paced the jaguar perfectly.

"Eha fell when he encountered a soft section of shale," he said to Ajur. "He tried to rise and run again but the keepers swarmed over him instantly. They encased him in a cell of crystals, but I believe the construction has not been completed. If we arrive in time, we should be able to destroy the cell and rescue him."

Ajur nodded his head once. He detested the keepers and their hideous prisons. The thought of the jovial cheetah locked inside a cell of clear crystals burned in his soul, forcing him to run even faster. He watched as Purugama and Conor flew ahead to find Eha.

Ajur would be able to follow Purugama's signals, so the strategy made sense. Still, he would have liked to be the first one to find the keepers who imprisoned Eha.

Purugama flew past a large stone precipice at the end of Ajur's trench. He immediately caught sight of the main pack of slayers. The horde hadn't stopped moving even after taking Eha prisoner. It merely split when it encountered him, like a parade moving around a stalled float. In the middle of the horde, the crystal cell held Eha completely immobilized. Eha sat still on the valley floor, crumpled in an obviously uncomfortable position. Even his beautiful ringed tail was smashed up against his right haunch, unable to move at all. His handsomely marked face, normally crooked into a smile, was pressed up against the ceiling of the cell in a grotesque image of helplessness. About a dozen keepers danced on top of the cell while a greater number continued working on the crystal tiles. They had nearly completed the cell when Purugama and Conor circled above them.

Purugama roared so forcefully that Conor felt the vibration in his legs. The great cougar took one look at Eha and decided instantly he would give his life to free his friend. The sight of him in that condition, surrounded by a great throng of the enemy, made him lose control. Forgetting all about Ajur or his passenger, he uttered a few words Conor could barely hear and then dove straight down toward Eha's cell. Conor pushed his knees into Purugama's neck and grabbed two handfuls of hair as the great cougar completely inverted his body. They were now heading straight down; the ground raced toward them at a sickening speed, forcing Conor to close his eyes for a second and then open them again. He decided he'd better stay alert to whatever the cat had in mind, so he fought through the tears streaming along his cheeks. Purugama opened his mouth wide, releasing a deafening roar that caused the keepers and a few thousand slayers in the immediate area to look straight up into the sky.

Ajur finally found the back end of the slayer's formation. He witnessed what Purugama had seen through their mental communication, and he held these thoughts in his mind as he penetrated the rear flank of the enemy. Slayers by the hundreds flew in every direction as the huge jaguar plowed through their ranks. Ajur didn't even attempt to fling any of them aside while he ran toward Eha; the speed of his attack combined with the position of his head and shoulders did all the necessary work. He wasn't destroying any of the slayers he came in contact with, but he certainly gave them cause to stop and examine their injuries. A slayer weighing less than a hundred pounds standing in the way of charging jaguar that weighed over a ton would have some explaining to do once his body got over the initial impact. The warriors that sat dazed in disheveled piles could only look up to see the continuing wave of slayers flung to both sides by the powerful Champion. The wake behind the black cat reminded them of the ancient legend of the sea splitter, the one who saved his tribe by walking them between the walls of a great ocean. After regaining their senses, the thousands of slayers cast aside by Ajur rallied themselves and closed the line behind their abuser. To someone high above the scene, it would look like some mystical zipper that opened and then closed behind a creature running for his life.

Conor watched the line of slayers bouncing off one another after being tossed aside like a room full of child's toys. He had little time to confirm what the strange sight was, but he didn't need more than a second or two. He knew it was Ajur coming toward them, advancing roughly through the horde of slayers. Conor returned to his work on the crystal cell, while Purugama laid waste to the endless tide of slayers and keepers.

The great cougar had delivered a ring of fiery crystals of his own while diving straight down onto the keepers. The explosion had atomized an entire section of slayers almost two hundred yards in diameter. The powerful ring of magic had left the crystal cell intact, allowing the keepers to escape the fate of their fellows. Conor, understanding Purugama's strategy perfectly, had leapt from his perch after the detonation, landing squarely amidst the keepers on Eha's cell. Using the Lady's powerful magic, he slew all of them without remorse or hesitation, recalling the cell of shadows they had built for him over two years ago. After dispatching the keepers, Conor immediately went to work on the cell. Placing his hands on individual tiles, he allowed the magic of the creators to disassemble the prison piece by piece. He worked on the ceiling first, aiming to release Eha's head and shoulders. Tile by tile he freed sections of Eha's physique, until at last his head sprung out of the cell right next to Conor. In true Eha demeanor, he leaned his head over and licked Conor's hands roughly. Conor took a brief moment to scratch Eha's ear and then put his hand on the next cell.

"Easy boy," he said to his appreciative friend. "We're not out of this yet."

Purugama defended the circle around the cell with all his might and cunning. He called for Ajur to join him, and soon the big jaguar broke through the circle and stood tail to tail with Purugama. Together they kept the horde at bay, but not without a few scares along the way. There were just too many slayers to deal with, and as they surged forward again and again from different directions, cracks in their defensive shield began to appear.

The magic of the Champions poured forth from the two giant cats, blasting huge throngs of slayers back into the horde from where they came. Many more replaced them, however, and it seemed as though the two Champions fought against an endless enemy.

Purugama and Ajur sensed when the other needed help. Each would send an immense wave of overwhelming power toward the other's side and in the few seconds available to them try and beat back the opposite horde as it closed in on Conor and the cell containing Eha.

"Hurry, Conor!" shouted the great cougar as he raked his paw across the front row of slayers on his side of the circle. Fifty or sixty of the rabid warriors flew back through the air before sinking into the morass of the horde. "We can give you only a few minutes more of unmolested time. Tear away the cells as quickly as you can. You must free Eha, and soon."

Conor worked at a feverish pace, placing his hands on as many tiles as he could without leaving them completely intact. Some tiles he ripped away with bruised fingers and sore palms, others he deftly swatted away as they peeled back from the walls of the cell. Eha did his best to help Conor disassemble the walls. If he saw him struggling with a tile and he had the room to move, Eha would press a paw or his nose against the stubborn surface and do everything he could to dislodge it. He saw the slayers moving Ajur and Purugama back as they closed the circle around them, but said nothing to Conor. The young man worked feverishly to free him and he would not dampen his spirits with any negative reports. He saw another half broken tile and pushed against it with his hind foot.

Regardless of the valiant effort put forth by the two Champions, the circle of slayers crept ever closer to Conor and Eha. The cougar and jaguar were now almost touching the cell of crystals with their tails, and this caused the horde of slayers to grow confident and daring. Keepers began flying from the middle of the pack toward the Champions, hurled by some force called forth by the slayers. Dozens of keepers sailed toward the cell. Most of them disintegrated from the blasts of magic hurled outward by Ajur and Purugama. Some, however, penetrated the Champions' barrier, landing on the cell next to Conor.

The young warrior swatted away as many keepers as he could, but more rained down onto the cell every second. Conor became despondent when he couldn't keep all of them at bay. Some of them fought the young Champion while others avoided him and began rebuilding the cell. Conor screamed with frustration as he lashed out at the keepers closest to him.

A raucous earthquake exploded underneath the cell of crystals. Conor, Eha, and all the slayers swallowed their stomachs as the ground below the clear prison rose into the air like an express elevator. The cell lifted high above the ground – ten, twenty, and then to a height of over fifty feet. Crumpled sheets of shale sprinkled to the ground as Therion's gigantic form appeared between Ajur and Purugama. The huge lion broke through the ground roaring in a fashion only available to the king of beasts. Everything around him froze momentarily, even the other Champions.

In that instant while the slayers paused in their relentless attack, Therion jumped straight up into the air and collapsed onto the ground like a huge golden hammer. Ajur and Purugama dug their claws into the shale and crouched in an effort to escape the blast wave. The circle of slayers expanded by almost a hundred yards as the great lion's magic swept into their ranks like a tsunami. The frontal impact destroyed almost fifty thousand slayers immediately, throwing the rest of the horde back so abruptly that it knocked a good portion of them unconscious. This gave the Champions all the time they needed to complete their task.

Conor quickly went back to work on the tiles. Any remaining keepers had long since retreated after seeing the giant lion appear from beneath the ground. Eha struggled harder than ever to free himself while Conor worked on the tiles, and the other three cats guarded the circle with tempered optimism. Therion, Ajur and Purugama addressed each other briefly before taking their measured stances again. The time for salutation would come later. An urgent task still remained – free Eha and lead the slayers farther into the valley. If Therion had been this close, then Maya certainly wouldn't be far away.

At long last, Eha jumped from the cell of crystals into Conor's arms. The huge cheetah knocked Conor off his feet and the two Champions rolled down the makeshift mound created by Therion's appearance. Eha licked Conor's face and chest a few times before standing and helping the young man to his feet. The other three cats came forward, confident that the slayers would not advance anytime soon. Eha nosed each of his brothers quickly, a cat's way of acknowledging a job well done.

"Thank you, Therion," said Conor as he brushed away a few bits of clinging shale. "You saved us all, and I am grateful."

"No amount of deeds could ever account for my prior actions," answered the big lion, "but I accept your gratitude in the name of our Lady."

"Come, Conor," interrupted Purugama. "The slayers will soon regain their confidence. All of us need to press forward toward our objective."

Conor jumped up into his saddle and inched forward as far as he could, as Purugama instructed. Eha bounced up onto the great cougar's broad back and settled himself in for a short ride. Ajur and Therion waited silently by the mound next to the damaged cell of crystals. Purugama lifted off the ground and floated over to his two brothers. Holding his body directly over them, he reached out with his forepaws and grabbed their outstretched paws. With a mighty chuff, the huge, golden cougar pumped his powerful wings with everything he had. The group of Champions, looking like a sideshow in a roadside carnival, rose up into the air and flew away in the direction of the pack of slayers. Ajur and Therion held on for their life, while Eha sat proudly atop the great cougar, thoroughly enjoying both the ride and the view.

"Maya and Surmitang await us up ahead," said Conor as he pointed out two small figures standing proudly on the floor of the valley. They looked to be a mile or two ahead of the horde, an easy distance for Purugama to cover in the air. They would beat the slayers by fifteen minutes at least. Eha crouched forward, looking over Conor's right shoulder. The young Champion looked back at the cheetah and smiled. Releasing his right hand from the saddle, he reached around and scratched Eha's ears. "Soon we'll be back together again. All of us," he shouted for everyone to hear. "With Maya and Surmitang back in our ranks, the slayers and keepers won't last another hour." He turned and waved at Maya, who looked up at him with a calm but perplexed look.

Suddenly, without warning or sound of any kind, the landscape in front of Purugama and his passengers folded up like a gigantic game board. First the valley developed a rough crease from one horizon to the other. Then the horde of slayers collapsed into each other as the land came together like two hands forming a prayer steeple. The sky followed the valley floor as it was silently sucked into the framework of the disappearing landscape. Conor watched with an unbelieving eye, and then he remembered what they had all said about Seefra. He could not only shift his own appearance, he could also alter his environment. Apparently he didn't care for the current course the battle was taking, and he wasn't prepared to send in the shadow warriors just yet. Instead he would change the battlefield into something more suitable for the slayers. Maybe he would shift the form of the keepers and the slayers as well.

There was nothing to do but wait. Conor waved again at a warped image of Maya and Surmitang as the entire world he occupied closed up around him. Everything became dark for a brief moment. It almost reminded him of corridor travel, but without the drastic changes in temperature. In the pitch black of the changing world, Conor leaned down and patted Purugama's neck a few times. He knew the great cougar must be exhausted after carrying so much weight for such a long time. He gave him whatever encouragement he could and waited for the new world to open up in front of them.

CHAPTER THIRTY-TWO

Slowly a dim light began to emerge. First as a pale impression against an inky background, and then as an outline of thick trees appearing in front of the small group of Champions.

Purugama reared up immediately when he saw the dense forest unfolding before him. He lowered his passengers to the ground slowly so they could take inventory and see if anything threatened their arrival. Satisfied, he set Ajur and Therion down on a moist, leafy trail that sliced a zigzag path through the forest.

Eha jumped lightly down to the ground, but Conor elected to stay aboard his big friend. He had no idea where they had landed; he wanted to be sure of his surroundings before he left the safety of his perch. It did remind him of the rainforest where he found Surmitang while on his journey to collect the Champions. It certainly smelled the same, and the heat and mugginess could not be forgotten. But why had Seefra brought them here, and in what form would the slayers come at them?

"Ajur! Therion!" called a voice not far away in the jungle.

"Here, Maya!" answered the ebony jaguar. "Follow our calls! Surmitang can locate us through this thick foliage."

The four Champions began growling and calling out for their leader. In no time at all, Surmitang crashed through the thick branches of a large tree with Maya right on his tail. They marched up the pathway and rejoined the others. All six of the cats touched noses for a brief moment, acknowledging each other's safety and readiness for battle. Even Conor, still propped up in his saddle, leaned down and grabbed a handful of Maya's and Surmitang's fur as they padded by him.

The group of seven packed themselves together under a large umbrella of fern branches. Conor had dismounted from Purugama's saddle and now sat in between his mentor's forepaws. He felt his big friend's heaving breaths pouring over his shoulders and back. The bizarre sensation gave him comfort and Conor smiled at the thought. He remembered a time only a few years back when he would have been terrified to be this close to animals the size of Purugama. He thought about their first meeting with a smile as he waited for the others to speak. He had his own ideas about what to do, but he deferred to those with greater experience.

"I say we send one of us ahead to scout out the area," said Eha, still licking away the remnants of the crystal tiles. "Or send two of us if it makes sense to separate the group."

"Let us all go forward together," replied Ajur. "I see nothing but trouble coming our way. We can handle our enemies with greater convenience as long as we remain an assembly of Champions."

"I agree with Ajur," added Surmitang as he sniffed around the perimeter of their location. "But let me lead the group through this jungle. It resembles my home, and if it contains the same dangers, I have the best chance of sniffing them out."

Purugama remained silent during this exchange. His greatest asset, the gift of flight, would do no one any good in this thick, leafy environment. If he flew above the rainforest, neither he nor Conor would be able to see anything below them. His huge, heavy wings would be a hindrance to the group on the ground as well. Not only would they make noise as they crept through the trees along the path, but they would slow their progress as a team. Everyone knew this, just as Purugama knew it, but the detriment was not spoken of, and Purugama decided to let the others determine their course.

Maya glanced at the great cougar for a fraction of a second before turning his eyes to Therion. "What is your council, great lion? What course do you recommend?"

Therion bowed his head to Maya, showing respect and appreciation for his Lord. He glanced at the others before responding. "I believe we are in a place of Seefra's making, and this frightens me."

The other Champions looked at each other silently. They were clearly unnerved by Therion's words. None of them disputed him or spoke out of turn; they merely waited for their huge brother to continue.

"Whether we send scouts ahead of us, which I would normally agree to do, or we go forward as a group does not matter. What matters here is that we all keep our senses on high alert. In the dominion of the master of darkness anything we see, hear or smell can destroy us. All of you must open your minds and see every living thing as a threat to our lives. If the decision is left up to me, then I say let us go forward as who we are – the group of seven in service to the Crossworlds. I will travel in the rear, while Surmitang is the most logical choice to lead us through this jungle. I believe that Conor should walk abreast of Purugama until we find a clearing where the two of them can take flight again. Eha and Ajur can flank Maya. If they attack using overwhelming strength, then Ajur will crush their attempt to overtake us. If our enemy uses speed or cunning, then we will let Eha discourage their plans. This is what I suggest, Maya, but I defer to your superior judgment."

"Well spoken, Therion," responded Maya. "Listen well, my Champions, for he speaks truth. We now reside within the hand of the master of darkness. Anything can happen here. The enemy, still a potent force at nearly two hundred fifty thousand, will attack us in forms we may not even recognize. We must all be ready at a moment's notice to heed Gribba's advice, and press the attack against them instead of waiting for their advance. When they come for us, we must be prepared to turn their attack against their forces immediately."

"Let them come," snarled Surmitang as he padded to the front of the group. "I do not fear the slayers and their parasitic companions. I believe we will overcome them with little difficulty. It is the shadow warriors that give me pause. But we will cross that bridge when we come to it." The colorful tiger, now partially hidden by the shades of the forest, took up his station and waited for the rest of the group to form up. One by one the Champions assumed their stations, forming the line that Therion previously described.

The giant lion watched as his brothers set out along the path that led through the rainforest. Finally, with a long look to his rear, he rose up on his huge paws and followed the group at a comfortable distance. He looked everywhere as he walked – up above them, in the trees all around them, and even occasionally behind them. Therion did not like this place one bit, and if this were to be the last stand of the Champions, he would make certain that the master of darkness paid a fit price for the honor of claiming victory over them.

The Champions walked for many miles through the rainforest without incident. The jungle seemed like a thick and steamy blanket, and before long every one of the cats felt their fur becoming heavy with a warm dewy coating. Conor, who did not enjoy humid weather, continued to wipe the irritating sweat from his forehead and hair. His clothing, strangely enough, suffered no ill effects from the immoderate climate. It felt as light as a feather around his midsection and shoulders.

The jungle seemed thicker than anything Surmitang could remember. It could have contained an army of shadow warriors and the Champions wouldn't know it until they attacked. Huge tree trunks sprang forth from the ground in every direction, sprouting into an endless variety of branches and leaves. All around them, every color of the rainbow either grew from the ground or fell from the heights of the crowded rainforest.

None of the strolling Champions could see more than a few feet into the jungle in any direction. The dense foliage grew so close together that the pathway they took seemed to be walled off on both sides. If an attack came anywhere within this jungle, the Champions would be forced into close quarters and combat would prove difficult. This might work to their advantage, but then again, wild cats the size of tanks needed room to fight.

Surmitang halted suddenly and the rest of the group immediately followed suit. No one moved a muscle while the huge tiger turned his head from side to side. Something had caught his attention, and it had to be compelling if Surmitang had stopped their progress. Maya broke ranks and cautiously moved forward. Ajur and Eha did not like their leader taking such chances, but Maya curtly ordered them to stand fast. The Lord of the Champions crept forward so silently even Surmitang was startled by his arrival. He returned his gaze to the object as Maya began to question him.

"Surmitang, what do you think it is?"

"I do not know exactly," answered the big tiger. "An entrance to a cavern or a collection of passageways, perhaps." Surmitang waited a few moments, hoping some of the shadow forces would appear at the entrance. "If we go inside we will be at their mercy."

"Indeed," said Maya. He and Surmitang stared at the strange structure, which looked more like a deep maze than anything else. Lights appeared here and there from within, but neither of the two cats saw movement anywhere inside the cave. It was possible that the occupants of the structure had entered the caves with purposeful intent, perhaps to lay a trap for the Champions. "However," said Maya, "it appears that this entrance is our only option, unless we find another trail leading to a different way into the cavern."

Maya turned and hissed to Ajur, calling him forward to join in their discussion. The dark jaguar listened to their story as he examined the peculiar scene in front of him. "I see no danger in this scenario except for one thing," he said to his brothers. "The rainforest thins for a good mile between here and the structure. Perhaps they wish to use the cavern as an enticement to draw us out into the open."

The leader of the Champions pondered this for a moment. Ajur's instincts were legend, and Maya couldn't grasp the reason for creating a world with a dense jungle if you didn't plan to use it against your enemy. He couldn't fathom any special difference between the rainforest and a grassy plain leading to what could be the entrance to Seefra's chamber of cells. Maya thought deeply about Ajur's comment and about his own feelings regarding their predicament. Then he ordered Surmitang to watch the land ahead of them while he returned to the group with Ajur.

"We'll move ahead in the same formation," he instructed. "Purugama, take Conor aboard as soon as you leave the jungle.

We'll need you in the air in case something happens to us." Maya signaled to Therion and nodded when he received confirmation from the giant lion. Then he shook the residue from his fur and moved forward with the group. His coat remained light for only a moment before soaking up the steamy dew again. Maya kept his eyes on the valley ahead of them.

When Conor cleared the thick leaves of the rainforest with Purugama, he pulled himself up into the saddle across his big friend's shoulders. Before he settled himself, Purugama had taken off and now the two of them soared out over the valley. The great cougar flexed his muscles as he flew around the perimeter a few times. He always felt better when he could use his great wings to their fullest capacity – tucking them into his body while walking through the jungle made him feel uncomfortable and useless.

Conor kept his hands planted on his hips. He looked at the semi-clear sky, trying to find a moon or some stars, and then he remembered that this was merely one of Seefra's creations. He looked down at the group of Champions making their way out of the dense jungle toward the cave opening. Everything seemed normal, even the temperature, which felt cool and refreshing after the oppressive heat of the rainforest. Conor smiled as he felt a raindrop tap his nose lightly.

After a few more minutes of flight, Conor felt another drop of water splash against his forehead. Then he saw a few more sprinkle down onto Purugama's ears. He looked down toward the group as they paced steadily toward the cavern. The valley, lightly adorned with very few bushes and trees, seemed to offer great relief to the group after their trek through the heavy jungle. The raindrops multiplied and Conor soon found himself sheltering his eyes to protect his ability to see.

For some strange reason the droplets caused his face to itch wildly. The bits of rain slapped against his thigh, arm or face causing a strange, ticklish itch. As long as he brushed the water aside quickly the bothersome sensation would go away. The rain grew steadier, though, and soon both Conor and Purugama were having trouble keeping their composure.

Then Conor saw something he refused to believe. The raindrops splashed against Purugama's fur, but the water never disappeared entirely. One would expect it to roll off the side of the great cougar's head, but it didn't do that. In fact, the water remained exactly where it had landed, and even started to congeal into a different form. Limbs sprang forth first, then a head bulged out, and finally a torso formed up between everything else. A minute slayer proudly stood on top of Purugama's head. It looked at Conor defiantly for a moment and then turned away, seeking others of its kind. Apparently, in Seefra's twisted world, the drops of water served as a vehicle for the enemy, and it was raining very hard now.

"Purugama, down, now!" ordered Conor.

The big cat dipped his wings instantly. He had heard this type of urgency in Conor's voice only once before, and it signaled trouble. He followed Conor's instructions and took them straight to the group.

"Maya!" shouted Conor through the rain. "The slayers, they're encased in the raindrops! Once they land they meld together with other tiny slayers until they return to their normal size. You've got to go back to the trees, now!" He looked at the ground around the cats and knew his warning had arrived too late. After sprouting and joining with other warriors, slayers sprang up everywhere. They didn't have to attack from a distance, because Seefra's plan had put them directly in the midst of the Champions. Conor turned his face toward the sky. Even though it still looked mostly clear, thousands of raindrops were heading their way. It looked like some cosmic force had overturned an ocean of water and filtered it through a gigantic strainer. The entire sky was flooded with drops of water. Conor could almost see the slayers riding inside their tiny transports as they descended on the Champions. He looked at he ground again as he heard Maya rapidly issuing orders.

"Take a stance, all of you. Tails together," commanded the leader of the Champions. "Form an impenetrable circle and crush any slayers unfortunate enough to find themselves within our ranks. Let the drops fall outside of our barrier, and wait for the slayers to form an attack before repelling them. Let none of them reach the center of the circle." Maya looked up at Conor and Purugama. "Up in the sky, both of you! Stay aloft until I say otherwise. Find the source of the rain if you can, but more than anything, stay clear of the ground no matter what happens to us."

Purugama pressed his wings against the wind immediately, lifting them away from the circle of Champions. Conor watched as the five of them prepared for battle. He felt troubled by Maya's remark. It seemed as though the Lord of the Champions knew something else was about to happen, and for whatever reason he didn't care to share it with anyone. He absentmindedly brushed away the raindrops as they bounced against his skin. He served as Purugama's groom as well, slapping away any slayers that started to form on the great cougar's body. He glanced behind them, checking once more on the other cats. Conor was very worried – about what he was unsure, but he worried nonetheless.

"Do not concern yourself," said Purugama through the rain. "The Champions are in good hands with Maya there to lead them."

On the ground, the raindrops fell at an astonishing pace. Maya had called forth a conical force field to keep the slayers from falling into their protective circle. Any water falling from the sky would splat against this floating umbrella and fall harmlessly beyond the reach of the cats.

That certainly didn't solve their predicament, however. Tens of thousands of slayers emerged from the ground all around them. As soon as they merged with enough of their fellows and grew to their original form, they attacked the Champions without mercy. No matter how many warriors met their end, the rest of the army weighed in and attacked without reservation. The Champions fought them off with a courageous blend off magical and physical prowess.

Therion, never one to use magic until absolutely necessary, fought the horde of slayers using only his brute strength. Huge waves of warriors came at him again and again, and every time, the giant lion viciously repelled their attack. He swept his tail over Eha's body and slapped it across the ground, taking out a hundred or so at a time. He would rear up on his hind legs and swat ferociously at the enemy, dismembering hundreds at a time when he made a clean connection. The unfortunate few that made it past his tail and claws found their end in Therion's gigantic maw, crushed to pieces by teeth nearly as big as them.

Although Eha had ceased laughing, he still wore an impish grin as he battled the slayers and keepers who chose to assault him. All cats have exceptional speed with their paws, but Eha's flew so fast that few ever saw the movement occur. The lanky cheetah sat back on his haunches firing his paws out like a manic boxer. Supercharged bolts of bluish energy flew from the tips of his claws. The sparkling power deliberately bypassed all of the slayers. It sought out the keepers in the horde, and every few seconds a single keeper or a group of them would explode from the main pack. They flew into the air, spinning like toys before breaking apart and falling back to the ground. Eha dealt with the slayers that managed to break through his energy fields as well, but the destruction of the keepers kept the peculiar smile on his face. They had tried to imprison him during this battle, and they very nearly succeeded. He would not allow them to take him again, even if he had to destroy them one by one during this confrontation.

Maya calmly assessed their situation. He stood by as the others fought furiously. He watched the slayers amass into division strength. The rain had not lessened at all, so they could count on more of them for the time being. The Champions held them at bay, but the golden eyes of their leader saw the tide turning in the not too distant future. Even with the magic of the Crossworlds at their disposal, the sheer number of slayers would eventually overcome them. He needed a plan, a way to divide the forces of the enemy. He watched Ajur and Surmitang as they waded into the packs of slayers trying to break through the perimeter of the circle. They looked so impressive, so formidable, and Maya would not allow either of them to be harmed during this confrontation. The Lord of the Champions raised his masked face and searched through the rain for Conor and Purugama. He spotted them finally and focused his attention on the newest member of their forces.

Conor held the great cougar's fur as well as he could. The leather strap had become useless in the rain so Conor had to grab and hold Purugama's fur to keep himself steady. The drops fell in heavy clusters now, and the young Champion felt nothing but frustration as he watched the endless line of slayers fall to the ground.

Then a thought occurred to him. It came from nowhere he

could recognize, but a voice told him to reach into the next pocket on his pant leg. He obeyed without thinking and poked his finger into the opening, retrieving another of the strange orbs. He held it tightly in the palm of his hand, feeling the warmth of the incredible energy and power encased in the tiny pebble.

The voice returned with a clear instruction about how to administer the magic within the orb. Conor looked up into the sky above him, speaking the incantation while crushing the orb with his thumb and fingers. He bent his arm back at the shoulder, bringing his hand as far back as he could. Then he cast his hand out in front of him, releasing the bizarre silvery dust.

Conor screamed the final chant as loudly as he could, hoping to inject the spell into the sky a bit more forcefully. The silver sparkles from the orb seemed to hang in the air for a few precious seconds. Not a fraction of the silver substance became wet in the driving rain. Suddenly, as if awakened to its purpose, the remnants of the orb shot out in every direction just above Conor's head. It streamed out like a bolt of lightning, solidifying at the same time. The material appeared to have no end, and its infinite nature soon placed a transparent floor between the sun and the group of Champions. Instantly, the raindrops and the slayers within them started gathering on the silvery shield. No matter where they fell, the transparency caught them, because it stretched from horizon to horizon and touched every part of the sky. Using Conor's magic, Maya had effectively achieved his goal of splitting the slayer forces in two.

On the ground, two things happened almost simultaneously. First, the raindrops stopped falling, leaving the slayers with limited forces. Maya acknowledged the change with a nod of his head even as he prepared for what he knew would happen next. The valley where they stood their ground against Seefra's army suddenly sprouted trees and other foliage at a speed that took the Champions completely by surprise. In an instant, the five cats found themselves separated by the same thick, steamy jungle they traveled through to get to their current position.

Ajur had been absolutely right, thought Maya. The structure and the cave entrance had been a ruse to tempt them out into the open. The rainforest would serve as the instrument of their destruction. The slayers and keepers, even the previous world, had been nothing but a distraction. Maya called out to the others, giving them instructions as best he could through the wall of trees between them.

The jungle came alive, brutally attacking the Champions. Huge, heavy branches lifted the cats off their feet, holding them steady while other tree limbs swatted at them. Therion roared again and again, dodging the blows as they waved by his giant mane. He caught a few of them in his huge mouth, crushing the hard wood to pulp before spitting out the remains and ducking other attempts. The other Champions fared no better, but at least no fatal blows had been delivered. Surmitang, confused at first but then understanding the strategy, seemed to be the only one of the group able to navigate through the madness. He did his best to help his brothers, but the jungle reacted like a madman. He had to keep his focus at all times. He silently hoped the others would survive the onslaught.

Maya had seen enough. Flying through the air in the limbs of one of the larger trees, the Lord of the Champions raised his voice and called out for assistance. *"Fingers of the Forest, fight for us!"* None of the others heard him call out, but the composition of the rainforest changed dramatically. Hundreds of new trees, all of an identical species, shot up from the ground and began assaulting the denizens of the original jungle. Huge trunks slammed into each other, exploding in a hail of leaves, splintered branches and pulp.

The jungle dropped the Champions to the ground when forced to fight for its life, and soon the five cats watched the tremendous confrontation between the giants of the forest. Seefra's jungle had no chance because they merely fought under the control of another force. The *Fingers of the Forest* fought as what they were – an individual entity with an important cause. Within minutes, the rainforest had been reduced to nothing. The *Fingers of the Forest* stood their ground, looking for any other threat to the Champions. Maya waved them away, knowing the slayers hid somewhere nearby. The *Fingers of the Forest* were formidable against some foes, but the horde of slayers would eventually cut them to pieces. The Lord of the Champions thanked them for their service and watched as the giant guardians disappeared back into the ground. He turned to the other Champions and spoke.

"Has anyone been hurt?"

No one answered right away, but Surmitang finally broke the silence.

"Ajur has taken a bruise to his right side," said the tiger. "The skin separated. The wound may have come in contact with the pulp of a borrbain tree." Surmitang turned to face Ajur. "I am sorry, my brother, but it must be told."

"It is nothing," replied Ajur. "I hit the ground at an awkward angle, that is all. My ribs scraped against a brace of sharp rocks. I will be fine in an hour, I assure you."

"With all due respect, Ajur," said Therion, "if you are infected with the borrbain virus, there is nothing any of us can do.

Alternatively, there is something you could end up doing to us. Once the pulp reaches your brain, we will have to fight you as well as Seefra, and I do not relish that possibility."

"Speak truth, Ajur," urged Maya. "We have little time."

"It is possible that I encountered the pulp, but I cannot be certain. Everything happened too fast, and I was nearly knocked unconscious during the melee."

"Maya," said Eha softly. "The slayers return."

"Ajur," ordered Maya. "Stay by my side at all times. I will try and communicate with the Lady of the Light and see if she can suggest a cure. The rest of you take your positions behind us. It is time to force Seefra's hand."

The Champions reacted as one, slipping silently behind their leader. Limping slightly, Ajur positioned himself abreast of Maya and awaited orders. Therion lifted his huge head to its full height and scanned the surrounding hills for slayers and keepers. He heard them before he saw them, and then along with the other cats he measured what remained of their forces on the ground. The horde, half a division, nearly fifty thousand strong, swept over a hillside to their left and descended on the five Champions. Waiting for instructions to move, the four cats behind Maya maintained their position, waiting for him to speak. No orders came, however. Maya stood completely still without uttering a word. Trusting their Lord as always, the Champions watched the horde close in on them.

High in the sky above the charging mass of slayers, the transparent silver sheet holding the remaining warriors buckled and lowered approximately one hundred feet. The slayers that were trapped above the transparency slid toward the conical depression in the middle of the silvery mass. Purugama sped away from the descent while cautioning Conor to brace himself. The sheet moved again, this time a distance closer to five hundred feet, forcing Purugama to plunge toward the ground at full speed. Instead of stopping where the transparent floor halted again, the great cougar flew straight to where Maya and the other Champions waited amongst the shredded trees and brush. Both he and Conor almost shouted a warning to Maya, but when they saw his expression they swallowed their words. Purugama landed lightly on the ground behind the small pack of Champions. Without a word they watched the events in the sky unfold as the transparent floor fell toward the ground again.

There were countless slayers and keepers scrambling about on the surface of the transparency. It became difficult to tell where one creature ended and another began. As it continued to fall in sharp vertical increments, the jumble of slayers became even more disorganized. Having mutated back to full size some time ago, the creatures were starved for battle. It drove them mad that they could see the Champions through the transparency but could not break through and attack them.

With the floor continually dropping, the chaos amongst the slayers increased. They fought each other wildly, biting and scraping and hacking away at their own kind with their weapons. Had the transparency not cracked open, the slayers might have destroyed themselves and saved the Champions the trouble.

"Only seconds now, Maya," reported Eha, who watched the horde on the ground race swiftly toward them. The cheetah looked up as the transparent floor fell toward them at an identical rate of speed. At one hundred feet above their position, the shield shattered, cracking apart from every corner of the sky. The rigid material softened immediately after breaking, forming a sparkling, silver pancake of glistening energy directly underneath the falling slayers. The broiling mass of energy and warriors fell directly over the charging army. As Eha heard Maya utter a soft chant, he understood the plan completely. His body visibly relaxed, tensed muscles giving way to the release of anxiety. The big cheetah trained his sight on the approaching horde and waited for the end to come.

The mass of slayers running toward the Champions never saw the immense conglomeration of energy crashing down on them from above. Their single-minded purpose controlled their every step. They wanted to destroy the Champions for their master. They wanted to seek his favor so he might someday elevate them to the rank of shadow warrior and bestow unfathomable powers upon them. They swarmed over the last hill and raised their weapons high in the air, shrieking every curse they ever learned in their short lives. In their righteous fury, they never even noticed the growing shadow within their midst as the other portion of their forces fell from the sky directly above them.

Maya's final chant brought the energy platform to full strength. Blinding streaks of silver radiance exploded in every direction. The light consumed everything – even the Champions on the ground next to the slayers. It did not harm them; however. Instead it fueled them with strength and purpose. Even Ajur, once bent over in pain, now stood tall as his body inhaled the light of the creators.

The slayers did not fare so well. The glistening transparency collapsed onto the forces on the ground. Those falling directly above it crashed into its surface a split second thereafter. The light intensified a thousand fold with the impact, consuming the slayers and keepers in an inescapable cocoon of unrelenting power. The shrieking, once so confident and strong, now peeled forth from the energy blanket in waves of fear and intense pain.

The slayers disintegrated by the thousands in front of the

Champions, who felt the awesome energy bristling from their scorched bodies as they exploded into nonexistence. As wave after wave of warriors fell toward the light and vanished, others inherited their place against the pounding energy. Just as the corridor in Conor's cell of shadows gained strength during its confrontation with the dark tiles, so too did the energy platform rise to the challenge of destroying over a hundred thousand enemy forces. Some of the slayers, understanding the danger from Maya's magic, tried their best to escape the sparkling energy that consumed their fellows. The energy platform would not release its foes so easily, however. Lightning streaked out after the escapees, grabbing them by the limbs or torso and dragging them back to their fate.

The Champions stood strong even while some of the horde advanced on them in their mad rush to escape. They trusted Maya's powerful magic, and, sure enough, every time a group came within arm's reach, the energy field snatched them back into its destructive force. The horrible shrieks died down until only the soft buzz of sizzling bodies remained. The energy platform contorted, changing its shape so it could consume the last remnants of any slayers or keepers that might have rolled free. Finally it lay next to the Champions, a perfect sphere of glistening silver energy. No trace, not even the slightest discoloration from anything it consumed, swirled within the perfect transparency of the orb. The tremendous essence retreated into itself. All that remained was a radiant core of mystical power.

Maya silently instructed the others to stand fast while he approached the energy sphere. He entered the bubble and turned to face the other cats. Blinking his black eyelashes once, he signaled to the others that he felt safe inside the silver orb. He stayed within the sphere for many minutes; he seemed to be communicating with someone. With a serene look on his furry face, the others knew it had to be the Lady of the Light. None of them knew where she presently was, but the fact that Maya could converse with her gave them all a measure of comfort.

The energy sphere eventually began to contract. Appearing as though it might crush Maya, the powerful orb simply disappeared within his fur. A second or two afterwards, Maya smiled as he walked back toward the group. He addressed Ajur directly, but all of the others as well.

"The Lady informs me that there is no available remedy for the borrbain virus. She assures me that Gribba is hard at work on an antidote and will send it through a corridor as soon as he is able. For now, we are to watch you closely. She believes you are in no immediate danger, and should be able to continue the journey. Once we return to the realm of the creators, they should be able to completely rid your body of the sickening disease."

"That is good news," added Conor, grabbing Ajur's tail in a playful gesture.

"Yes," responded Maya, turning to the others gathered close by. "She cautioned me that none of us should touch the infected area on Ajur's flank. It will fester and become rancid before we leave this place. If any of us contact it, we are likely to infect ourselves.

Conor released Ajur's tail abruptly, his face contorting with disgust. Purugama unfolded his wings and stretched them to their limit. He waved a brace of wind against Ajur's side a few times before addressing Maya. "So, we have defeated the slayers," said the great cougar. "What is next for us, my Lord?"

As if in answer to his question, a queer sound reverberated across the small clearing. It seemed to come from the forest behind them, and before any of them could comment, the sound compressed and raced toward them. Something invisible impacted Therion on his right side, knocking him away from the other Champions. Only the huge groan coming from his lungs remained with the other cats as he flew across the clearing. Therion landed in a twisted heap a few dozen yards away and lay there, unmoving. Surmitang immediately started to go to his rescue, but Maya stopped him in his tracks.

"No! Stay here!" he commanded.

The strange sound launched itself from the forest again, whirling toward them at a tremendous speed. They could gauge its proximity by the pitch of its whine, and when it became clear that the sound would strike again, Maya ordered everyone to the ground. Instantly the Champions collapsed while listening to the eerie noise sail over their heads. It corrected its course immediately, however, and turned to advance toward them again. The cats stayed glued to their positions. Purugama placed a protective wing over Conor. The sound bore down on them again, but instead of flying by in a mindless attack, the strange entity stopped directly above them.

The invisible entity plucked Ajur from the ground and pitched him away like a child's doll. Ajur crashed into a knot of trees before dropping to the ground unconscious.

"Ajur, no!" cried Conor. Purugama slammed his wing against the young Champion, knocking him down as he attempted to jump up and save the jaguar.

For the first time since their arrival in the shadow world, a wave of fear rushed through the core of the Champions. They could fight an army of warriors if they could see them, but this they could not overcome. After seeing Ajur meet his fate, Eha whispered something to his Lord.

"This is no shadow warrior, Maya. Something bearing this type of magic must be a destroyer."

Maya nodded his head, letting his chin hit the ground as he did so. The leader of the Champions was clearly unnerved; he had never encountered something so fast and powerful at the same time, and with the gift of invisibility. His head jerked to the left as he heard the ghostly sound pouring out of the trees again. He looked at Therion and Ajur, noticing that both of them still remained motionless. His mind raced as he poured through a series of options – run, stay down, seek out the forest, fling an assortment of spells in every direction, hoping to hit whatever it was with one of them. He spun the alternatives in his mind as the frightening sound approached them again. Just before he was about to rise and face the creature, he saw Purugama's wings take flight and when he looked up he saw the big cougar flying away from the crouching pack.

"Purugama, *no!*" screamed Conor as his mentor soared away, but the big cougar was already out of earshot. The creature changed course instantly, swooping loudly over the remaining Champions. With a crack of thunder, it took off after Purugama, intent on making him its next victim. Neither it nor the great cat could hear Conor's screams. The young Champion yelled encouragement to his mentor, and all the curses of the shadow world to whatever it was that chased him.

Purugama, now free of his human passenger, flew like a madman all around the clearing. He could feel the icy fingers of the destroyer tickling his hind paws as the two of them raced over the trees. He pumped his great, leathery wings madly, dodging here and dipping there, flying like a hyperactive fighter jet with an entire formation of enemy planes behind him. Even while using every maneuver he could design, however, he couldn't shake the bizarre creature that matched his every move. It seemed to know everything he planned to do even before he did, and a few times Purugama even felt a frigid, two-fingered claw closing over his tail. The last time it happened, he remembered Gribba's advice and decided to make use of it. If he couldn't shake the creature, then the next best alternative would be to confront it.

He soared over the brush at the very edge of the rainforest. Flying just over the treetops, Purugama suddenly dove into the thick, leafy walls of the jungle. He listened as his enemy pursued him into the trees, and after only a second or two he heard the familiar sound of something large smacking into one of the trunks.

Purugama reversed course and left the protection of the trees. High up in the air again with a visual advantage, he watched the leafy canopy down below for any movement. Sure enough, he saw the treetops shifting as the creature worked frantically to free itself from its natural prison. The sound coming from the invisible destroyer, once so threatening and controlled, now sounded like a thousand frantic sick animals. With a satisfied grin, Purugama folded up his wings and dove like a falcon straight toward an opening at the edge of the trees. He knew that once the creature freed itself, its only avenue of escape would be through that gap. At over three thousand pounds, Purugama dropped like a stone, soon descending at more than a hundred miles per hour.

A large branch bent back as the invisible creature exited the jungle. The branch had barely snapped back when a golden mountain of fur crashed down squarely on top of it. Purugama grabbed hold of the invisible thing with all four paws, rolling around on the ground as it fought to free itself. No force anywhere in the Crossworlds could have torn Purugama's grip away.

The creature exploded in a fit of surprised shock and anger.

It did everything it could to shake its attacker free. It rolled and bounced, trying unsuccessfully to fly away. It lashed out with unspeakably strong limbs, trying to pry Purugama's claws away from its body. When it realized finally that the big cat wouldn't yield, it began shrieking and bellowing in an unrecognizable language.

The other Champions, less Therion and Ajur, had followed Purugama's progress, and now they stood close by, yelling encouragement to their brother warrior.

"Purugama," said Maya loudly, "a protection packet surrounds the destroyer. See if you can find the seam. If you can peel the shield away we may be able to destroy it."

Purugama went wild upon receiving this new bit of information. He scratched and bit at his opponent, trying to feel anything at all that resembled a seam in the invisible covering. Suddenly he found it, a strip of material slightly different than the rest of the gooey fabric. He hooked a massive claw around the seam, and then managed to get an entire paw inside. He felt the destroyer trying to slice open his paw before he could get a good grip, but Purugama had other plans. Once he popped an opening in the seam he rolled around on his huge back and sunk his teeth into the gap. He released the grip with his hind legs and placed both of them just below his jaw. With one mighty thrust, he ripped the protection shield away from the destroyer. The creature flopped out of the invisible wrapping onto the ground in front of Conor and the group of cats. Dazed only for an instant, it regrouped and faced the small group of Champions, threatening them with a hideous squeal.

The group of seven recoiled at the sight of the destroyer. Without exception, it had to be the most bizarre creature any of them had ever encountered. A huge mouth, surrounded by a set of incredibly muscular arms, screeched at its enemies. The bizarre arrangement of arms, ten in all, had no fur or color to speak of, but they were powerful – strong enough to propel the creature through air, giving the appearance of flight. A single, stout finger with a sharp talon existed at the tip of each arm. It scrambled back and forth like a crab, threatening the Champions with its ear-splitting shrieks.

Before the destroyer could attack again, Maya spit out the energy ball that had previously sank into his body. The sparkling transparent orb bounced once, turned ninety degrees on the ground to look at the destroyer, and then shot forward in a spasm of energy that took the creature completely by surprise. Wrapping itself around the strange body in seconds, the silvery sphere consumed every inch of the Champions' opponent. Then, with the slightest wobble at the bottom of the orb, the energy field lifted itself lightly off the ground. The destroyer couldn't fight, fly or run while encased within the special magic of the creators. It fought madly for only a moment before calmly leaning back against the rear of the silvery orb.

"What do you make of it?" said Eha, nosing up against the gelatinous sphere. "Not very attractive, is it?" The big cheetah stuck his sandpaper tongue out in the direction of the creature, which did not respond in kind.

"I do not know this one. I've never seen it before," answered Maya. "It must be one of Seefra's newest conversions, a shadow warrior who earned the right to be elevated to destroyer."

"If this is the type of magic Seefra can bestow on his servants," added Surmitang, "then what kind of unimaginable power can he command in his own right? Without the wings of Purugama, we might all be unconscious in this field right now."

"Agreed," said Maya. "The invisibility shield is a tool, but the skill to use the wind as a weapon is something else entirely. We will all have to watch out for even the most unlikely occurrences in the future."

"Maya," interrupted Conor. "The creature, it seems to be breaking through the sphere's magic."

"Yes," said the leader of the Champions, a little too calmly for Conor's taste. "Destroyers wield very powerful magic of their own. I assumed it wouldn't take more than a few minutes for this creature to overcome the energy sphere. At least we've had a chance to get a look at it before it departs."

The destroyer had indeed broken free of the transparent field of energy. The creator's invention seemed to have an almost human stubbornness, however. Even though it appeared to have lost the battle with its captive, it would not give up until it was utterly defeated. It clung to the creature with a fierce determination, pestering it with everything it had left. The creature whined and shouted as it tried desperately to free itself from the last of the energy capsule.

"Stand back, Conor," said the Lord of the Champions. "It's broken through the transparency completely. If it confronts us, we will fight it as a team. If it runs, then we will let it escape, see to Ajur and..."

Conor heard Therion's heavy footfalls a split second before his body was swallowed up in the shadow of the giant lion. Therion leapt over everything – the Champions, Conor, and the small mound separating them from the creature. He landed squarely on top of the shocked destroyer, slamming the creature's mouth into the ground. The destroyer shrieked in protest, rolling over and tossing Therion away with minimal effort. Therion landed square on all four paws, growling loudly while setting up his next attack. He ran straight at the creature, the two colliding in mid-air. The destroyer lashed out with its massive arms, trying desperately to find any part of Therion to tear apart.

Although the creature was terrifying, it certainly did not have the coordination of the cats. Therion seemed to know this even before he challenged the destroyer to a one-on-one confrontation. Now it appeared that his knowledge of their differences would serve him well. The giant lion began ripping away parts of the destroyer and flinging them to the ground at the Champions' feet. One-fingered talons, torn away roughly from the grotesque body, lay squirming wildly all over the field. Parts of the creature's arms followed, flying through the air as well. Therion ripped away huge chunks around the screaming mouth with his claws and teeth, tearing them off cleanly and tossing them aside while he looked to strike the fatal blow.

Therion smacked the huge mouth with a vicious swipe of his paw, knocking the creature out. He pounced on top of it, ripping the remainder of its existence to shreds with his hind legs. Finally satisfied that his enemy could no longer put up a fight, he stomped away from the creature while attempting to shake the fury from his mind.

"Well," said Eha, pounding around the group of Champions in a mocking imitation of Therion, "I guess we won't have to decide how to handle this particular enemy." The happy cheetah made a few more circuits before walking up to the disheveled creature. He sniffed at the remains, and then scratched lightly at a few of the scattered arms. To his surprise, the limbs and shredded parts began swirling around as if caught up in a small tornado. Piece by piece, the remains of the destroyer gathered themselves into the dark whirlwind. When every piece of the creature had finally been swept into the billowing funnel, it rose off the ground and floated away toward the cave at the bottom of the meadow. Just before it disappeared into the entrance of the cavern, the creature shrieked one last time. It appeared to be sending a message to the Champions, letting them know they hadn't won. After it vanished into the cave, Eha turned and smiled at his brothers. He gave a bewildered chuckle after seeing such a strange scene unfold before him.

"So much for overcoming them physically," he said. "Although your attack left an impression I must say, Therion."

The giant lion prowled around the outer rim of the gathering. He almost felt civil again, but he needed more time to shake his feral side after such a demanding confrontation. The only gesture he made that showed Maya and the others he was still with them occurred every few seconds when he lifted his huge brown eyes to check on Ajur.

While Therion was battling the destroyer, Purugama quickly flew over to where the black jaguar lay, unconscious and unmoving. The great cougar crouched down to nuzzle the face of his friend, checking for irregular breathing and whispering quiet encouragement. Ajur lay crumpled in a frightening position with his head twisted to the side and his tongue dangling awkwardly over his lips. The helpless look, something he had never seen upon the face of his brother, unnerved Purugama. His eyes seemed glazed over, unfocused. Purugama tried again and again to rouse his friend, but nothing seemed to faze him. Finally, he just sat next to Ajur, guarding him from anything else that might bring him harm. He turned his head to see Maya leading the rest of the Champions over to Ajur.

Maya arrived in front of the rest of the pack and placed his ear against Ajur's chest. The breathing felt shallow but regular. Then he took a long look at Ajur's eyes. After inspecting them for a full minute, Maya placed his right paw against his forehead and uttered a few incantations. He pleaded with the Lady of the Light to bring their Champion back to them, and soon the big, black cat began coughing lightly. He lifted his thick head, slipping it out from under Maya's foot. He craned his neck, looking at each of the big cats in turn. He saved Conor for last, staring at the young Champion with a blank expression.

"Ajur," pleaded Conor, "will you rise now and come with us into the caves? I do not wish to continue without you."

Ajur answered by scrambling to his feet. He was weak and nearly fell over twice, but finally he steadied himself. He looked at Maya with a look of confused anxiety.

"It is the borrbain, my friend," said Maya to his Champion. "Apparently we underestimated its potency. It seems to have infected your nervous system already. That's the reason you feel so unsteady; the virus is affecting your equilibrium." Maya waited for Ajur to speak, but no comment came from the big jaguar. But his eyes said it all. Ajur was scared. He merely stood his ground, shaking his head every few seconds to clear his mind.

"No doubt the impact from the destroyer's attack has affected Ajur as well," added Surmitang in defense of his brother, hoping Ajur's feebleness would soon pass and the borrbain was not to blame after all. "Not one of us would quickly recover from such a devastating blow. Ajur will be ready in a matter of moments. We should stay here and give him all the time he needs."

"No one here doubts his valor," answered Maya. "Indeed, I fear the most formidable attacks will be launched against him in the future. Never forget that it was Ajur who nearly crippled Seefra many centuries ago. If the master of darkness had not received assistance and escaped, he might not have lived to fight in this present conflict. He will expend a great deal of effort trying to destroy him." Maya let this last comment settle for a few moments before continuing.

"Ajur, I respectfully recommend that you travel back to the glade and await our return. I do not wish to be responsible for your untimely demise, and I fear the borrbain might prohibit you from fighting to the best of your ability."

No one said anything after Maya's last statement. The silence lingered among the group like icicles forming on a tree branch. Ajur was a powerful Champion, and an essential addition to their fighting force. He had to be in terrible danger for Maya to put forth such a suggestion.

"You are my Lord and leader, Maya," responded Ajur. "I would lay down my life for you without hesitation. I would give the blood in my veins for any of my brothers and for Conor as well. If this is to be my last battle, then let me spend it honoring you and the creators before I take up permanent residence in the glade. I swear on my love for the Lady that I will not hinder your progress."

Maya stared deeply into Ajur's soul before speaking. "Very well, then. We will proceed into the caverns, but be ready for another shift in the environment. Something tells me Seefra will confound us again very soon. He will not be amused when he learns his destroyer failed to halt our progress."

Worried, Maya sent a quick thought to the Lady of the Light, asking her to watch out for Ajur. He knew he needed all the help he could get.

CHAPTER THIRTY-THREE

The group of seven set out toward the cave entrance. Every one of them, including Conor, kept a close watch on Ajur. The jaguar walked proudly next to Maya, but with a noticeable limp. A few times he seemed to lose his balance, but before anyone could lend a hand or paw, he would steady himself and continue walking. Ajur was a proud cat, and he wouldn't allow anything as insignificant as a scrape against a branch to keep him out of this battle. As the caverns drew near, he took a few deep breaths and peered into the large opening in the mountain. He followed Eha and Surmitang into the cave, walking abreast of Maya.

Conor couldn't understand why, but he felt a deep misgiving about entering these caverns. They reminded him so much of the final corridor he and Janine entered before they were taken captive – dark, soulless, infinite, and the shadows seemed to be alive. He could almost hear the interior of the caverns calling out to him, pleading for him to enter and bring his Champions so they could all be destroyed. The shadow warriors were in these caverns; Conor knew it as clearly as he knew the sun would set later on the far side of the mountain. Just before he passed under the crusted wall of the cave entrance, he turned around one last time to look at the light.

"Purugama, look!" he shouted, pointing his finger back toward the jungle.

The great cougar turned just as Maya crowded in next to him. Both of their fur-lined faces peeked through the opening at the same time. They saw precisely what Maya had predicted would happen. The world of the rainforest was collapsing in on itself, trapping the Champions in the caverns. First the blazing sun turned dark and musty as it fell from the sky. Then the thick stands of trees and the lush landscape doubled over on itself. The flattened horizon rolled up like a bamboo screen, straight toward the cave entrance. Conor and the two cats backed up into the mouth of the cavern, watching the world outside become darker and darker with every passing second. The shifting environment captured the group of seven in its wake. Every bit of light left in the world disappeared. The Champions floated in a sea of milky darkness, calling out to each other to be sure they were not alone.

After a few seconds the light returned, slowly at first, but soon the interior of the caverns opened up for all to see. Instead of one tunnel running through the mountain, now there were thousands of passageways cut into the walls of a vast chamber. They shot away from the immense room from every imaginable location, from every wall, all across the ceiling, and even through the floor in certain areas. It looked to Conor like a gigantic cell of shadows, except with some strategically essential tiles missing. No natural light entered the vast cave containing the Champions, but there appeared to be pockets of minerals everywhere that emitted a dull luminescence. It cast an eerie light in the huge space, letting Maya and the others see well enough to understand their next challenge.

"Who can conjure up physical manifestations such as this?"

asked Therion, thoroughly bewildered by what he saw. "Seefra's powers have truly grown beyond all comprehension."

The chamber appeared to be endless. The monstrous walls shot up more than fifty stories from the sandy floor of the cavern. The Champions couldn't begin to count how many individual caves extended from the massive room. It looked almost like a crude honeycomb, without the precise spacing usually seen in a structure built by a hive of bees. Nevertheless, the caves in the wall, the ceiling and the floor served some specific purpose, and determining that was the first task for the Champions. Finding a way out would be the next order of business, and Maya set about doing both at the same time.

"Conor, Purugama. Take flight and get a closer look at those caves in the walls surrounding us. Do not enter any of them just yet; we are interested only in their composition, and whether or not they serve as a dwelling for a new breed of creature we have yet to meet." Purugama waited to feel Conor's feet in his stirrups before lifting both of them up to the higher regions of the chamber.

The Lord of the Champions turned to the rest of the group. "We need to find a passage that leads away from this chamber. I feel a strange energy here, a kind I cannot understand. It bodes no good will for us, that I can assure you. The small caves that surround us might provide some clues as to where Seefra hides himself, or they might show us the type of magic he uses to bring such a place alive. If you see anything in the smaller caves, sing out and let the group know. Your primary purpose, though, is to find a larger passageway, something we can use for escape."

Ajur was the first cat to turn and leave, showing an eagerness to begin his duties. Maya pressed his jaws together tightly as he watched the black jaguar probing the holes in the ground and along the walls of the chamber. He loved all of his Champions, but Ajur had always been special to him, as he was to the Lady of the Light. It may have been because Maya raised Ajur from a cub, as he had done with Purugama.

The real reason, he believed, was that Ajur always kept to himself, never sharing his emotions or thoughts with anyone. Always ready to help the others, he showed a genuine caring nature with anyone he encountered. He had been the first to defend Conor upon his arrival at the glade all those years ago. The fact that he was so formidable a warrior and yet so tender a personality gave Ajur an attractiveness none of the others enjoyed. Maya silently asked the creators to give strength to the big jaguar until they could return to the realm and find an antidote for his illness.

"Maya, over here!" shouted Surmitang. He straddled one of the smaller cave openings, inserting his head as deeply as he could into the darkness. He raised it only long enough to call out again before reinserting his shoulders into the hole.

Maya signaled to the others to keep looking and then jumped over to where Surmitang crouched into the ground. The huge tiger had his hind feet placed closely together at one end of the cave opening. His forepaws stood inverted on either side of the roughly constructed cylinder, allowing him the opportunity to lower his head and shoulders into the cave.

Maya heard rough snuffling noises coming from within the hole in the ground. Surmitang had obviously found something worth inspecting. The sniffing continued for a few more seconds, and then Surmitang removed his big, furry head from the hole. Smiling, he backed away from the opening and gestured for Maya to take a turn. The leader of the Champions positioned himself as Surmitang had done, lowering his head deep into the cave. He sniffed a few times, waited and then sniffed again. He failed to detect anything out of the ordinary except for one thing. The cave appeared to be bottomless. He felt a steady breeze tickling the light fur around his face. This could only mean one thing, that this cave had an exit somewhere at its end.

"Excellent work, Surmitang," Maya said while backing his body out of the tunnel. "We can send Eha through to ascertain where this leads and..."

A terrified roar poured through the cavern. Every cat except Surmitang, who stood strongly behind Maya next to the bottomless cave, snapped their heads in the direction of the sound. Surmitang, emerging from a cave opening on a jagged ledge roughly a hundred feet from where Maya stood, saw an exact replica of himself standing behind Maya. In a panic, the real Surmitang roared as loudly as he could. In that split second, he couldn't think of anything else to do. He knew Maya was in terrible danger, and he also knew that the Champions would have only seconds to save him, if that was even possible.

Maya looked from Surmitang on the ledge to Surmitang standing immediately to his rear. "Seefra," he said, emotionless. Surmitang's form melted and reshaped itself before the Champions, emerging into his bizarre insect-like appearance. While the cats responded instantly to the real Surmitang's calls, Seefra uttered a simple spell commanding the cave to come to life.

"Pofidiz Haks Yumin!"

Maya braced himself for whatever the master of darkness had in store for him. He felt a brief sensation of bewilderment as his entire body flew into the cave entrance. As he passed the opening, bumping his forehead and paws against the rough edge, he heard Seefra bellow into the cavern.

"Attack! Shadow warriors, attack!"

Maya cursed his stupidity as he watched Seefra jump through the opening in the floor. The master of darkness followed Maya down into the deep recesses of the cave, all the while moving ever closer to him. It appeared at least that Maya had read the cave's dimensions correctly, because it did lead somewhere after all. Seefra had plans for Maya, and they did not include his being a part of the force battling the shadow warriors.

"Silence! All of you!" roared Therion. The Champions had fallen into a controlled chaos after watching Maya disappear. Every one of them jumped forward to offer a plan or a solution to their dilemma. Order returned only when Therion jumped to the middle of the pack and demanded it.

"Maya is gone," continued the giant lion. "We can do nothing to remedy that, but we can honor him and fight the shadow warriors in his name." Therion looked up as Purugama floated down toward the group of cats. "No, my brother," he instructed, "stay aloft with Conor. We will need your aerial fighting skills soon enough."

"Listen," said Eha, bending his head slightly to the left. "The shadow warriors!"

"They come," answered Therion. "Prepare yourselves, and fight for Maya, the Lady, and the five keys!"

They heard the sound of the approach first – an eerie, irritating scraping that seemed to come from everywhere around them. The Champions couldn't discern precisely where it originated from until Surmitang finally guessed correctly. "The caves. They're coming through the caves. Every one of these entrances serves as a passageway. There won't be nearly as many as when we faced the slayers and the keepers, but there will enough. Besides that, one shadow warrior is the equivalent of ten thousand slayers."

"Back away from the cave entrances in the ground," commanded Therion. "Find a solid surface and make your stand there." The Champions followed his instructions, finding a series of ledges where they could fight together as a team.

The scraping sound grew louder. It seemed as though the warriors were nearing the openings leading into the chamber. Eager to please their master, they wanted to descend on the Champions and finish them quickly. Seefra had communicated to all of them that their main threat, Maya, had been removed from the battlefield. This emboldened the shadow warriors, giving them renewed vigor in their quest against the enemy.

Conor and Purugama were the first to see a warrior emerge from the dark mouth of a cavern. Conor gasped as he looked upon it, an almost human form with a small set of spindly wings sprouting from between its shoulder blades. The wings fluttered a few times as the shadow warrior looked out across the chamber at Conor. They operated just like hummingbird wings, allowing the bizarre creature to dart quickly to and fro, just like the small bird Conor imagined. Its body was completely covered in a sickly green skin. Its humanoid arms and legs seemed somewhat restricted by its inflexible composition. The head, human as well except for an extremely large mouth, spun around freely on a flexible neck that looked to be made of latex. The head could turn as many times as it needed to in the same direction, and when it stopped turning, the neck would simply adjust to its new position without any recoil at all.

It wasn't necessarily an ugly creature, but it certainly didn't engender any long looks from Conor. The eyes disturbed the young warrior most of all. Where there should have been eyes, only two tiny concave dark circles existed. Nothing moved in those spaces, and the shadow warriors should have been blind because of it. But when Conor looked at the warrior standing on the ledge in front of the cave opening, he saw that it moved its head just as a sighted person would. It heard a sound and it moved its dark circles in that direction.

It didn't follow any logical pattern at all, and it looked very creepy on top of that. Conor cringed as he watched the creature move its head in the direction of the Champions and back toward him again.

"Don't let their appearance fool you, Conor," instructed Purugama. "Even without the gift of sight, a shadow warrior can see as well as you or me. They have magnificent hearing, and they use it like a sonar beacon, especially in closed areas such as this. If you threw a pebble the size of your fingernail at that one across the chamber, he could pluck it out of the sky as easily as he could a loaf of bread."

A dozen more shadow warriors emerged from different caves along the wall that Conor and Purugama patrolled. They tested their wings hastily while snapping their heads around, checking the room for any danger. They looked at Conor, then at Purugama, and finally at the size of the chamber, as if determining a proper strategy for attacking the Champions. After coming to a decision, they stood rock still and waited for more of their kind to show up. They looked formidable physically and mentally, but they weren't foolish enough to jump into battle prematurely when they could await the bulk of their forces.

Purugama shot a blast of magic from his nostrils toward the main wall of the cavern, where twenty or thirty of the warriors had amassed along a ledge. The energy blast sailed toward them, gaining speed and size with every second. The shadow warriors turned as one, sensing the danger and looking at the energy sphere with their dead eye sockets. It impacted against the wall of the cavern only inches from the pack of warriors. A blast of light and sound occurred in their midst, but when the eruption settled, the great cougar and his passenger watched as the group of warriors fluttered back down to their former position. A few of them darted quickly back and forth, daring the big cat to send another bolt of energy. None of them had been seriously hurt, however, which was exactly what Purugama hoped to find out.

As if called forth by Purugama's brazen attack, over a thousand shadow warriors began moving through the passageways toward the central chamber. They scraped their inflexible wings against the coarse walls of the caverns, crawling on hands and knees until they saw the light of the chamber directly ahead. They emerged from their resting places, hundreds of warriors, all sightless and every one ready to give their life in a battle for the five keys of the creators.

With the throng of creatures finally assembled along the walls and ceiling of the chamber, they began calling out to each other in a bizarre language. They appeared to be discussing strategy, assigning certain platoons of warriors to face individual Champions after the main rush took place. They scrambled all over the chamber walls like flies on human skin, crawling over each other and stopping suddenly to call out a command or to curse the Champions. After all, this was their domain, and the invaders would be fighting them on their turf. In the long history of the Crossworlds, no opposing force had ever defeated the shadow warriors in their own arena.

Conor heard a booming sound echo through the cavern. He looked at the cave entrances along the walls of the chamber. The passageways were disappearing right before his eyes. The chamber appeared to be sealing itself, so that no matter what happened during the battle, no one would be able to escape to regroup and fight another day. Conor watched as the stone doors fell into place at every entrance he could see. Even the floor of the gigantic chamber sealed itself completely, and soon the only sounds he could hear were his own heartbeat and Purugama's massive wings moving against the stale air of the chamber. When the last doors slammed shut along the ceiling, the young Champion looked down to the ground as a sound rose up to meet his ears.

Eha was answering the call of the shadow warriors. He howled like a banshee into the eerie light of the chamber, and before long every other Champion joined in with the others. As a group, the cats growled, snarled and hissed menacingly at their enemies. It may not have frightened them very much, but it did embolden the Champions. Conor began screaming soon after Purugama had joined in the chorus with the other cats. He screamed and pounded his fists against his chest while looking over Purugama's side at the pack. It did make him feel better to cut loose. They may not survive the battle, but he felt certain the shadow warriors would pay a heavy price for their ambitions.

As one powerful force, the shadow warriors shrieked like wild bats and rushed the Champions. They soared down from the fifty story walls like dark hail descending on a village, and as they closed on the Champions, the superior magic of the shadow world poured out from their souls. Beams of power unlike anything the Champions had ever seen streaked down at them from every angle. Some were aimed directly at them, while others impacted against the walls of the chamber close to them. The shadow warriors sent their magic hurling toward the cats and then bounced back up toward the upper reaches of the chamber. Only then would they dive toward the Champions again, flinging everything they had at their formidable enemy.

Surmitang had deciphered their strategy before they ever came near, and with a few spoken words he had thrown up a shield to repel the power of the shadow magic. The force field held all the way through the first attack, but Surmitang could feel the energy buckling under the massive assault. On top of that, a hole existed in their initial defenses because of the strategy of the shadow warriors. By blasting the area around them, they showered the Champions with tons of stone shrapnel from the chamber walls. The big Sumatran tiger took a few sharp rocks to his cheek as he held the shield aloft to protect his brothers.

Eha jumped around like a hyperactive pogo stick dodging and evading everything the enemy threw at them. Ajur centered himself within the protection of the shield. His side had begun to bother him a great deal, and he wanted to conserve his energy until they made their counterattack. Therion, still bruised and angry about the destroyer's attack earlier in the field, stood fighting the shadow warriors at the extreme edge of the shield. He would duck for cover when a particularly harsh barrage headed their way, and then lash out after the bulk of the attack caromed off the force field. He'd lunge forward, extending both of his massive forepaws, and swat at anything that came within reach. Some of the more valiant shadow warriors tried to get under the defenses of the shield to strike at Therion. They met their end quickly, either splattered into nothing by the impact of a giant paw or dragged back under the shield to be ripped to pieces by a gigantic angry lion.

The shadow warriors sensed some of their numbers being destroyed in this way, and after a few passes, the collective group reorganized their strategy. They no longer allowed the bravest of their warriors to attack recklessly, and they also fired their magical bolts from a higher distance, so the Champions would have no chance of striking at them from the ground. Had it not been for Purugama and Conor, the battle might have been very one-sided. In these two, however, the Champions had a volatile flanking force at the top of the chamber.

Purugama noticed Surmitang's shield losing power steadily, and he decided to focus the shadow warriors' attention onto himself and Conor for a while. After warning the young Champion about his plans, the great cougar swooped down toward the main assembly of the enemy. He inhaled deeply, preparing to blow a wall of flame in their direction. Just before releasing his breath, he heard Conor scream triumphantly. Instead of turning to look at his small companion, Purugama kept his eyes forward and watched the reaction of the shadow warriors. Dozens of the strange creatures turned their sightless faces in Conor's direction, trying to determine what type of attack might come from such an insignificant foe. Conor answered them deliberately, extending his arms like rifle barrels and firing intense flashing beams of sparkling energy.

At first the warriors thought little of his efforts, but after the initial impacts they formed an entirely different impression. The first splashes from the creators' arsenal atomized a few score of the unsuspecting warriors. The rest scattered instantly, zipping away in every direction, eagerly dispersing from the one location they knew meant their instant demise. Purugama flew expertly, diving and turning and staying right behind large clusters of the enemy. Conor held his feet in the stirrups as tightly as he could. He held his glowing arms out toward the retreating shadow warriors, sometimes together and sometimes separately. He destroyed at least ten percent of their forces in only a few minutes' time. The explosions and the shrieking of the warriors sounded loudly in his ears, but Conor still heard the cheers and roars of the cats down below at the floor of the cavern.

Out of nowhere, a large bolt of dark energy blasted Purugama from the sky. Conor was hurled from his saddle, nearly knocked unconscious by the impact. He hurtled down the walls of the chamber, and when he landed, he shook his head and renewed the energy source in his forearms. He saw packs of shadow warriors watching him descend as he sailed down toward the floor of the chamber. They wanted him to perish in a painful manner, by crushing his bones as he bounced off the rocky walls on his way to the base of the cavern. The young Champion turned his body in midair, looking at the group of cats rushing up to meet him. He reached out with his hands in an attempt to cushion his impact against one of the Champions.

When he passed the five-story mark in his fall, he felt the familiar grip of Purugama's powerful claws against his back. The great cougar had been seriously injured, but he would never allow harm to come to Conor. He wrenched him out of the air and flapped his tattered wings as hard as he could. He very nearly bounced Conor off the ground; his wings were so damaged they barely even lifted his own weight anymore. He dropped the young Champion into Therion's broad embrace and landed on the ground roughly. His wings, once so perfectly formed, hung like wind-damaged curtains at his sides. Conor looked at his big friend, cried out and ran to him. He didn't touch the wings because he saw they obviously caused Purugama great pain. Instead he pressed his cheek against the golden breast of his benefactor, thanking him for saving his

life yet again. Purugama lowered his head and rubbed his cheek against the crown of Conor's head.

Eha had seen enough. He watched the shadow warriors seize the advantage after Purugama and Conor had been struck down. Now they were closing in on the Champions from all sides. While the cats tended to one of their own, they would strike a fatal blow to the cougar and maybe to the injured jaguar as well. Eha would have none of it. With one mighty push of his lanky hind feet, he exploded onto a nearby wall, hitting the rocky surface in full stride. He began racing around the walls of the chamber, letting his speed defeat the force of gravity. Once he hit his fastest stride, the happy cheetah began spitting huge globs of shimmering energy toward any shadow warrior that happened to be in his way.

The first few packs quickly darted out to the side, thinking Eha's attack was nothing more than an impact strategy. They soon discovered their mistake when the strange bubbles of energy started to enlarge as they got closer to them. The faster Eha ran, the faster the energy balls would chase after his enemy. Finally, after growing to the size of a small outdoor tent, the globs of sparkling spittle would collapse over a dozen or so shadow warriors, pinning them to the nearest wall. The creatures tried everything they could to free themselves from the strange concoction, but no amount of magic would allow them to escape the sticky substance.

Ajur watched his brother trapping different groups of warriors all along the walls of the chamber. Since they were otherwise occupied with Eha, he decided to bring his own magic into the battle. As pained as he felt, he wanted to repay the shadow warriors and their master for his and Purugama's injuries. Following Eha's movements with his huge, copper-colored eyes, the big jaguar started timing the moment that any of the cheetah's globs would slam against a wall, trapping a group of warriors. Blinking his eyes forcefully, Ajur sent a stream of ruby red spikes shooting from his forehead toward the enemy. The spikes split into a multitude of sharp weapons, more than enough to destroy a small group of warriors. The projectiles zoomed toward their targets, and after impacting they dissolved into an acidic potion that sizzled into the bodies of the warriors, melting them into nothing. Ajur held himself steady, turning his head slightly and blinking his eyes every second or so. The red pellets shot forward from his face, accelerating toward the enemy. Group after group of shadow warriors suffered the same hideous demise after coming into contact with Ajur's poisonous serum.

Eha called down to Ajur, encouraging him to continue sending the deadly projectiles toward the enemy. With luck, they might whittle their forces down to half. The cheetah, running at top speed and laughing like a hyena, clenched his teeth only long enough to gather another energy glob inside his mouth. As soon as he released them he continued his raucous laughter while shouting down to Ajur.

Therion had moved Purugama off to the side of the main battle. Ajur and Surmitang held the shadow warriors at bay while the giant lion administered what aid he could to his brother.

"Rest, Purugama," cooed the massive lion. "There is no more you can do in this chamber. Your wings are burnt to a crisp; they will not hold you aloft any longer." Therion used his big paw to move a large stone underneath Purugama's cheek, giving the great cougar a hard but serviceable pillow to rest his head on. "Conor will stay with you until we defeat these vile shadow creatures. I must return to the battle now. Ajur and Surmitang need my assistance."

"Go then, brave Therion," said Purugama. "I will remain here."

The big lion stood, looking one last time at Purugama. Then he hustled off to join the others, readying his own magic as he advanced. He fell in line next to Surmitang, watching the huge tiger lash out at the shadow warriors. He and Ajur had coordinated their attacks and were causing great damage to the ranks of the enemy. Therion looked up, focusing on Eha as he flew around the enclosure. He waved his tail around while preparing to add his arsenal to that of his brothers'. He closed his eyes for a moment while summoning the power of the creators.

A deafening blast rocked the enclosure, and Eha disappeared from the walls of the chamber. In his place was a sizzling crater roughly twenty feet in diameter and nearly six feet deep. The sonic boom that accompanied the weapon almost tore the eardrums away from every remaining Champion. The same weapon had blown Purugama out of the sky only minutes earlier. None of the Champions could figure out from where the energy blasts had originated, the bursts seemed to come out of thin air.

Ajur, Surmitang and Therion circled together on the floor of the chamber, looking at the crater and at each other in remorseful bewilderment. Before they could even blink, Eha fell out of the sky and landed in a heap right next to them. They looked at the mass of crumpled, smoking fur and prepared themselves for the worst. Surmitang broke ranks and walked over to assess Eha's injuries. He nosed the cheetah's feet, then his stomach, and finally his forehead. He sensed light breathing but not much else. As he turned his head to report to the others, he caught sight of Eha's nose twitching slightly. Surmitang leaned down and touched his multicolored face to Eha's nose. He gruffled once, seeing if he could draw a reaction from the cheetah. In return he saw Eha crack his bruised lips into a pained smile. The huge tiger smiled as well and called out to the others.

"He'll be okay. He's not going to function too well for a while, but he'll recover. What's the status of the rest of the enemy forces?"

Surmitang finished his statement and looked up at Ajur and Therion. The two Champions held their heads aloft while watching the main body of the shadow warriors climb the walls of the vast chamber. They appeared to be leaving the Champions to their fate, for not one of them remained behind. Therion looked up at the bizarre scene for two or three seconds and then jumped over to cover Eha's body. "Scatter!" he yelled to the other cats. He didn't have any time to say anything else. He wrapped his limbs around Eha's frail body and held on tightly.

The explosion rocked the floor of the chamber, sending razor-sharp shrapnel slicing through the air in a hundred different directions. Ajur and Surmitang were blown clear of the place they had previously occupied. They slammed into each other once before spinning off in separate directions. Both of the huge Champions crashed into the rocky ledges surrounding the floor of the chamber. Ajur lay on his back with his head and tail drooping over the side of a ledge. After slamming roughly up against a sealed cave entrance, Surmitang fell three stories down to the floor of the chamber. His huge body made a sickening sound each time it thumped against another ledge on its way down. Only Therion, with his superior strength and incredible resolve, managed to maintain his position when the weapon impacted the ground next to him. The fur and most of the skin on his left side had been burned away from his body instantly, but he refused to cry out or leave Eha. Without the giant lion's assistance Eha would surely have perished. As it was, he barely clung to life after the massive detonation took place. His tongue sagged through his teeth, and lay on the dirty ground next to Therion's paw. The beautiful coloring on the cheetah's face appeared to be fading as his breaths came at larger and larger intervals.

"Hold on, Eha," counseled Therion. "We're not finished yet."

Conor couldn't believe his eyes. He stood next to Purugama, who lay at his feet, terribly injured. The other Champions were all but defeated, the only one left with any fighting ability beside himself was Therion, and he was badly burned. Part of his mind told him to crawl behind Purugama and wait for the end, whatever that might entail. But another part of him devoured that timid response. These were his friends, his good friends, and they were his brothers. They had all fought together. Through good and bad they had always maintained their love for each other. Conor loved each and every one of these cats, and seeing them laying about in various stages of suffering filled him with a passionate desire to destroy the shadow warriors utterly. After all, they were responsible for this mayhem, and they might in the end be responsible for the deaths of a few of his friends. He looked down at Purugama's face, at his half-closed eyes and his jaws hanging askew. He glanced over at Surmitang and Ajur, who lay completely immobile at the extreme perimeters of the chamber. Finally, he focused a tearful eye on Therion, who still guarded the sleek cheetah at his feet. The giant lion's majestic mane and fur had been all but seared away, but the proud Champion refused to relinquish his duty to his brother.

Conor reached into the next small pocket on the side of his pants. He walked forcefully out into the center of the circle where the three cats had been standing at the moment they were nearly blown to bits by the shadow warriors' weapon. He withdrew the small orb and rolled it around in his fingers in the same manner he did with a pair of quarters while thinking about something back home. When he reached the heart of the plateau, he looked up at the massive gathering of warriors, all clustered together around the top of the chamber. Summoning the images of his fallen brothers, he shouted out to the hideous monsters.

"Foul creatures, hear me! You have nearly won your battle, but there is one Champion left for you to defeat. I won't be easily overcome, because I wield the power of the Lady of the Light! Do you hear me? The silver queen gave me her abilities long before you even knew who I was and how I became associated with the Crossworlds."

"Conor, no!" advised Therion forcefully. "Even with the Lady's protection, you cannot stand against their weapon. It draws energy from an unknown source. In the end, it may destroy us all."

Conor's eyes blazed with an intense hatred for everything associated with the Circle of Evil. He neither heard Therion's warning nor even realized he was there any more. Whomever the Lady had referred to before leaving the realm had suddenly surfaced from within Conor's soul. He looked bigger, seemed stronger and suddenly shouted with more authority than he had at any other time since he first met Purugama on the mesa over five years ago. It looked to Therion like someone else inhabited Conor's body.

"Shadow warriors! Servants of the Circle of Evil! Flee from this place if you value your lives, for the next exchange will be your last!" Conor raised his line of sight and watched the warriors assess their latest threat. Although they would ultimately fire their weapon again, they did not immediately do so. He watched as they repositioned themselves along the wall, setting up for a different shot and getting a closer look at their target. The young Champion waited quietly, juggling the small sphere in his hand. He did not fear the shadow warriors or their weapon; he only feared the prospect of failing to be brave enough to fight for his friends. Even if it meant his eventual destruction, he would stand against millions of shadow warriors to show them that he valued the Champions' lives and safety above his own.

The enemy started assembling their weapon. They had found their firing position and were planning to use it against Conor. At a measured pace, and with little conversation, they began crawling all over themselves, scrambling to find the proper place for each warrior.

It seemed haphazard and pointless at first as he watched the peculiar dance of the shadow forces. For quite a few minutes Conor couldn't discern anything concrete from their activity, and then, without warning, it hit him. The warriors *were* the weapon! They didn't possess some bizarre atomic cylinder that lowered itself into position before firing and then retracting back into the wall. The weapon was organic, just like everything else in the Crossworlds. With enough shadow warriors clinging together in the appropriate manner, their magic would congeal into a force powerful enough to obliterate the Champions. Conor looked up at them again and saw that they had nearly completed their collective form. He saw the energy surging through their line as it prepared to blast Conor into the forbidden corridors for all eternity. He grasped the magic sphere tightly and began crushing it in his hand. Hoping the creators would answer his strategy, he waited patiently for the attack to come.

Hundreds of warriors bound themselves together in the tight cylinder. They created a crude tunnel by clinging to each other's limbs. Their arms and legs seemed to disappear within the massive structure, leaving a continuous stream of torsos and sightless heads. From the ground, the tunnel looked like a thriving tube with a pulse growing more intense by the second. The shadow warriors, sensing the end of their battle with the Champions, had assembled every remaining combatant to create one final attack. They hoped to finish off their enemies completely before reporting back to their master that he was free to pursue the final key without interruption.

Every warrior focused their sightless eyes toward the young man stationed below. They heard his defiant cries and paid no attention whatsoever. After all, if they could dispatch the true Champions so easily, then what trouble could one human pose for them? Even with the warnings from the master of darkness, the shadow warriors refused to give the small Champion an ounce of respect. They summoned their energies, focusing the entirety of their collective magic in Conor's direction.

Therion watched with astonished eyes as Conor prepared to face the powerful weapon of the enemy. Every other Champion, those that were conscious at least, stared at the small human form standing defiantly in the center of the chamber floor. Purugama blinked his heavy eyes once. His wings caused him so much pain now he could barely spare the energy to lift his head. He did so, however, giving a silent wish to the creators for Conor's safety. Eha had recovered enough to be conscious, and with everything that had happened, he sent a tight smile in Conor's direction. *For luck,* thought the cheetah.

Conor stood strongly in the center of the chamber. The orb was little more than dust in his fingers now, but he could feel an intense buildup in the magical powder. Each of the orbs had been stronger than the last, and this one contained such immeasurable power it felt like it might explode in Conor's hand. The fine grains of sand seemed to push against Conor's palm and fingers, begging to be released into the battle. Completely dormant while in their compacted, spherical shape, the powerful orbs strained to serve their masters when reduced to a handful of dust. Conor squeezed his hand tightly, collapsing his fingers around the orb's contents. *Not now*, he said in his mind. *Almost, but not now.* He looked up at the huge organic pipeline the shadow warriors had constructed.

An inconceivable thrust of dark energy surged from back to front, finally releasing itself from the bowels of the instrument. In seconds the material would crush Conor to pulp, but for that brief amount of time the Champion examined the strange material. The energy itself appeared almost darker than the chamber from where it appeared. It contained imperfections in its shape, giving it a living quality no mechanical device could ever duplicate. As rapidly as it flew toward Conor, the shape drove itself forward just a little faster with the peculiar bubbles on each side of its surface. It almost looked alive, like it felt elated that it was going to destroy one of its master's enemies. Conor stared at it, letting it descend another fifty feet before he released the magic of the third orb. He reached down to the ground with a tightly clenched fist before hurling the dust up into the air as hard he could.

No one – not Conor, the Champions, nor the shadow warriors – immediately understood what happened after Conor released the orb. They all heard something take place, but it was quite a while before anyone realized the true effect of the magic spell. The impact sounded like a gigantic steel hammer hitting an even bigger anvil. It resonated loudly throughout the chamber, and after everyone's ears recovered they began to understand what had happened.

The dust from Conor's fist had immediately solidified upon finding release in the chamber. It also reshaped itself into a wide, flat platter. With this form, it protected the Champions completely from any fallout caused by the redirection of the dark energy. The noise created by that tinny but heavy impact occurred when the shadow warriors' blast interacted with the cylinder. Their weapon had been turned against them. When the energy hit the platter, it reversed course one hundred eighty degrees, heading back up the walls of the chamber at twice the speed at which it had descended.

The shadow warriors never had a chance to break their column and move to safety. The dark energy changed its composition upon impact, becoming a streak of silvery light bearing down on them with a frightening velocity. The sparkles at the forefront of the altered energy shone with a brilliant light, illuminating the shadow warriors for everyone else in the chamber to see. It shifted from completely opaque to partially translucent in seconds. This allowed the Champions to witness the demise of the shadow warriors.

Therion, Eha, and Purugama lifted their heads and watched the scene unfold above them. Even Surmitang, groggy and still physically depleted, stood unsteadily, lifting his great colorful face to the heavens. The huge tiger gave a short chuff of thanks for Conor's presence here in the chamber. Mighty Surmitang, who did everything to discourage the young Champion when they first met, stood proudly, staring at Conor.

The silver energy field raced toward the shadow warriors. Instead of merely impacting on the exterior of the organic cylinder, it altered its form again and raced inside the living tunnel, the weapon made up of hundreds of bodies. A few of the warriors, those farthest from the center of the funnel, managed to disconnect their limbs and scurry away. Their attempts prompted false hopes of escape in the warriors, however, because when the creators' energy finally exploded, it vaporized everything within two hundred feet of its center. The shadow warriors simply vanished, and those that didn't suffer immediate annihilation were bludgeoned against the shuttered cavern entrances. When the blinding light from the blast finally diminished, only the jagged remnants of the walls remained.

Conor had done it; he had obliterated the last of the shadow warriors. Hundreds of minute flaming cinders rained down onto the platter above him. A few of the fiery relics managed to flitter through the cracks between the magical surface and the walls of the chamber. Conor could see them clearly; they were the remains of the shadow warriors. The creators' weapon had overpowered the best that the Circle of Evil could conjure into existence. None of the enemy existed anymore, and all Conor and the Champions had to do now was press forward toward Seefra's chamber of cells. It would be the final stop in the longest journey Conor had made for the creators. The young man took a deep breath and looked around at the other Champions.

"Ajur!" he barked upon seeing the brawny jaguar struggling to gain his feet. Conor sprinted quickly over to his side and wrapped his arms around the cat's huge right shoulder. Pressing against his feet with every ounce of strength he had, Conor helped Ajur lock his elbow and stand straight up. The massive Champion took a few raspy breaths, shaking his head as he did so. He chuffed twice and scraped his right paw over his eyebrows. Only after this bit of grooming did he turn to look at Conor.

"Thank you, young Champion," he said weakly. "I should be able to manage my own weight now. What is the current status of the battle with the shadow warriors?"

"They are destroyed," responded Conor with a smile of relief. "The weapons given to me by the creators overcame their magic and annihilated them. We are safe here in this chamber, for now, but we must gather ourselves and find a way out. Seefra has taken Maya away from us, and our duty is to assure his safety."

"Our duty," instructed Ajur, "is to find and secure the five keys of the creators. Every one of us knows this, and we all knew the dangers inherent in traveling to the world of shadows. Maya understood this more than any of us. We could gain the whole of the Crossworlds, bring Maya back and rescue your companion, but none of it would matter should Seefra crack the code on the fifth key. Maya raised me. I love him as a father and as a leader, but I will not sacrifice our true objective in order to save him, and neither should you."

"I ask forgiveness," replied Conor. "I only hoped to save him from the hellish designs of the Circle of Evil."

"More than anyone in our company," inserted Therion as he limped forward and joined his two brothers, "Maya can take care of himself. If Seefra believes he can control him with any force known to the shadow world, then he is sadly mistaken. I do not fear so much for Maya as I do for us."

"But the shadow warriors have been destroyed," said Conor. "Look about the chamber, and all around your feet. Nothing remains of them at all."

"Nothing of the first wave," said Therion, looking at the walls of the chamber. "If I were in command of such a force, it would not be beyond reason to sacrifice a certain number so that the enemy would be forced to expend all of their reserves. After the initial exchange, it would be an easy matter of ordering the second wave onto the battlefield to finish the task."

Conor shuddered at the thought. If Therion spoke the truth, and more shadow warriors waited in the wings to attack them, then the great Champions of the Crossworlds would indeed perish. In their present state, another large group of shadow warriors would have little difficulty overcoming them. Therion was the last Champion with any kind of mobility, and Conor had used every one of his magical orbs. Escape seemed to be their only option now, and Conor didn't feel like wasting any more time.

"Therion, can you help Ajur make his way over to Purugama?" He turned and yelled across the chamber to the great striped tiger. "Surmitang, meet us over by Purugama!" Conor ran to Eha's side, and as he reached him the injured and weak cheetah leaned his head back and smiled into his friend's eyes. Tears of extraordinary pain marred the beautiful black markings on Eha's face. Conor swallowed when he saw that, and then grabbed Eha around the midsection to help him up. "Come on, happy boy," he said to the immobile cat. "We have to assemble immediately. We must find a way out of here right away."

Eha did his best to stand. At one point he nearly fell right onto Conor's arms. Realizing that he might crush the boy under his great weight, the cheetah caught himself at the last moment. Using Conor's strong shoulder as a crutch, he walked alongside his brother as they moved over to join the others.

Before any of the cats could breathe a word of greeting to each other, a bizarre scraping sound began to emanate from within the tunnels. One by one, cave entrances began to reopen and reveal what crouched inside. As more caves exposed their inhabitants, the scraping grew louder. Every one of the Champions had heard these sounds before. They looked at each other and then looked at the ground around their feet. No one uttered a sound, for there was nothing to say. Only mighty Therion, the tactician in the group, came forth with an assessment of the situation.

"It is as I feared, and as I would also have done. The shadow warriors have sacrificed half of their numbers in order to destroy us. Another force of equal size approaches through the tunnels, and even though I abhor them for attempting to cause our demise, I must say I admire their tactics."

The scraping accelerated as hundreds of metallic wings passed through the cramped passageways. The second wave of the attack was about to commence. The shadow warriors were assembling in the chamber; they would descend upon the helpless Champions with savage cruelty.

CHAPTER THIRTY-FOUR

Maya paced off the length and width of the cell in which he had suddenly appeared. Carefully padding around the perimeter, he realized that the keepers had omitted a certain number of strategically placed tiles in the floor. Even more dangerous than that, the holes in the cell shifted at random intervals. He would never be able to count on a set pattern he might establish for his own safety.

Seefra tormented his subjects quite thoroughly, thought Maya. By the time any of his prisoners entered his laboratory, they most likely were so depleted by the manner of their imprisonment that Seefra had little trouble extracting information from them. The other obvious reason for their cooperation lay a few hundred feet below his cell. Maya had seen many captives falling to their doom since he arrived here only hours before. Whatever lived below the mists in this torturous chamber appeared to be more horrifying than even death itself. The Lord of the Champions lowered his head and sniffed at the perfectly clear floor of his cell.

After failing to discriminate between Surmitang and Seefra's perfect likeness, Maya had fallen quite a distance through the bottomless tunnel. He and Seefra battled wildly as they sailed down into the foggy depths of the shadow world. Seefra had grown very powerful, and it took most of Maya's reserves to hold off the magic the master of darkness hurled toward him.

After inflicting minor injuries on each other, in a flash, Seefra disappeared into the mists. Almost immediately, dozens of keepers fell upon Maya from every direction. The big black and white tabby could do nothing but submit.

So many keepers had attached themselves to him, he felt as though they had become a second coating of fur. One group held his forepaws straight out while another controlled both of his hind legs. At least a dozen keepers crawled all over his stomach and back, and another dozen took control of his head and face. They pried his mouth wide open and jammed heavy sticks between his upper and lower teeth, forcing his jaw to remain open. Other keepers plugged his nostrils with something so foul he nearly passed out after the first whiff. He tried to loosen them, but every time he managed to dislodge one, the keepers would cram several more in its place. This made the stench even worse, and soon afterward Maya ceased struggling. Five or six keepers peeled his eyelids back, and by using some peculiar substance, they locked the Lord of the Champion's eyes into an open position. As the nearest keepers restrained their prisoner, almost a hundred others rapidly assembled a cell of crystals around Maya's body. They accomplished all of this while the whole group continued to fall deeper into the vast reaches of the chamber.

As they descended, strange sounds emanated from the mists all around them. At first Maya couldn't make them out, but after hearing the bizarre calls four or five times he realized they were the millions of souls lost forever in the forbidden corridors. At times Maya heard the voices traveling through the creators' corridors, because all portals, forbidden or otherwise, drew their power from the same organic life force. Naturally they would coexist in close proximity with each other from time to time. Here, however, the cries for mercy and the pleas for self destruction originated solely from the depths of the shadow world.

Maya shuddered at some of the sounds passing through his ears. He couldn't tell for certain, but he thought he heard the gurgling vocalizations of Fumemos, the formless entity that attacked Conor in the surf on that strange world they visited together. It made sense, because anyone who failed the Circle of Evil were either destroyed or locked in the mists of the forbidden corridors for all eternity. Maya paused mentally, wondering which could be worse. He doubted if Fumemos held the power to escape, certainly the Circle of Evil removed all of his magical abilities before marooning him in the mists. How anyone could live there forever was beyond Maya's comprehension. He swallowed hard as he thought of the millions of souls wandering blindly through the mists.

The bindings holding Maya's body in position vanished as the final tiles fell into place. The Lord of the Champions dropped lightly onto the floor of his cell. When he hit the invisible surface, his two hind legs fell right through a large gap in the tiles. While regaining his balance, Maya hadn't even realized that the cell had ceased its descent and docked itself among a huge conglomeration of other crystalline cages. He took his time looking around at the peculiar collection of species trapped in the surrounding cells. Every type of being he had ever encountered existed here in this massive chamber.

The Lord of the Champions examined the inhabitants of the cells closest to him before looking beyond to the remaining population. Far in the distance, maybe eighteen or twenty rows away, one specific cell caught his interest. The prisoner within was the only human he had seen in the entire population. She looked to be exercising inside the crystal walls, first sitting up repeatedly and then running in place. These activities were followed by an additional series of exercises.

Maya moved to the front of his cell, stepping carefully over a gap in the tiles. He pressed his face against the immaculately clear wall, staring at the strangely familiar human across the chasm. He uttered a simple chant that allowed him to move his vision closer to the woman. Soon he gazed upon her as if she jogged only a few feet away.

"Janine," whispered the Lord of the Champions.

The young woman wore extremely tattered clothes. Although she looked terribly unkempt, she radiated an undeniable sense of strength. She paced around her cell like a wild animal, impatient, moody, but at all times calculating. Two shadow warriors stayed close to her cell at all times, standing on a ledge only yards from their captive. A lengthy passageway led away from their station, but where it ended Maya could not see. He assumed it would lead him to Seefra and maybe to the other destroyers as well. He catalogued that information, saving it for a later time. Maya looked back at Janine, whispering another short incantation. Then he settled himself down on the floor of his cell and called out to her.

Janine snapped her head around when she heard the strange voice. Seeing no one there, she immediately assumed it to be another of Seefra's attempts to drive her mad. The master of darkness used everyone she had ever known to torment her, from her father to Conor and then even the Lady of the Light. After months of the same treatment, she learned to ignore the voices. This one, however, seemed altogether different. It was a kind voice, unlike all the other attempts. No matter how familiar the others appeared to be, they all seemed to bristle with a hard edge. Conversely, this one sounded pure and untouched by evil. She couldn't be certain, but nevertheless Janine allowed a flicker of hope to enter her mind. The voice called out again.

"Janine," it said softly. "Companion of Conor, are you there? Can you hear me?"

Janine stayed at the other end of the cell. "Who calls out to me from the depths of the shadow world?" she asked.

"No one from that dreary place, I assure you," answered Maya. "This voice belongs to a friend of Conor's, one he might refer to as his brother."

Janine's heart skipped a beat. Conor had referred to the Champions of the Crossworlds as his brothers more than once. Could it be they had finally made it through Seefra's defenses? Had they destroyed the armies of the Circle of Evil and were they now banging on the door of this very chamber? "Speak quickly, before I lose my nerve," she said. "If you truly are not one of Seefra's servants, tell me your name and something that only Conor would know."

"The name of his mathematics teacher could not have penetrated these wretched halls," replied Maya. "Does the name Hikkins bring back memories of home for you, Janine? As for my name, I am honored to introduce myself. If it pleases the keeper of the keys, I am called Maya, and I am the Lord of the Crossworlds Champions. I have traveled to this place with your companion and five of our brothers. We hope to destroy Seefra, regain the five keys of the creators, and reunite you with the one who loves you above all others."

Janine rushed to the spot where the voice originated, collapsing around it. Her tears soaked the floor of the cell, and some even fell through the open spaces toward the mists below. She cried openly for five minutes, finally releasing all of the fear and pain she had held inside for more than two years. It was a challenge and strain for anyone to remain strong under duress, but for a teenage girl in her bizarre circumstances it demanded nothing less than a heroic effort. Janine had held on with an iron grip for all this time, and now that she sensed an end to her ordeal, she had to allow herself some respite. "Maya," she pleaded through her tears. "Please tell me, is Conor safe? Has he made it all this way without any harm coming to him?"

Maya waited patiently for her to complete her inquiry. He did not understand humans completely, but he did recall that at times his mistress would summon the same cleansing tears. As uncomfortable as it made him, he knew instinctively to let her finish the healing process. He acted the same way with Janine, allowing her to sputter through her questions before addressing any of them.

"Dry your tears, Janine," responded Maya. "I can assure you Conor and the rest of the Champions are quite safe." Although he couldn't make that statement with complete certainty, Maya saw no need to worry the poor girl. She had been through enough already, and one way or another, this journey would be completed soon enough. "Although I was taken captive by Seefra and now exist in this wretched chamber along with you, I know the others will be here soon. After they dispatch the shadow warriors it will be a simple matter of assaulting the last haven of the master of darkness. I assume the passageway close to your cell leads to Seefra?"

"Yes," answered Janine while wiping the excess moisture from her face. "That is, when he is working in his laboratory. At other times I honestly don't know where he travels, but it seems as though he is answering the call of another being."

Maya blinked his eyes and filed this information away. If Seefra obeyed a summons from anyone, it had to be one of the high arcs of the Circle of Evil. The Lord of the Champions wouldn't believe it; he couldn't believe it. The Lady of the Shadows? *Here*?

"Tell me about Conor," asked Janine again. "Is he well and

healthy? Has he been back to earth to check on its condition? Were we able to reverse the altered effects after we gained the fifth key, or has it remained locked in chaos because we failed to return the keys to the creators?"

"I assure you Conor is fine," said Maya. "As is your home world, which returned to its former glory the instant you destroyed Loken and embraced the fifth key. We must be vigilant; however, you know this more than anyone. Seefra has all but one key in his possession, and if he makes the connection to the fifth key then your world as well as thousands of others will fall under his power. No matter what happens to us, we must not allow Seefra to succeed."

Janine listened to an argument she had played over in her own mind for months. She had made and broken so many strategies for defeating Seefra that the hopelessness had finally overtaken her. In the end she decided to do her best to disrupt his work in order to keep a fraction of his mind focused on her at all times. Her small successes and the thought of someday seeing Conor again had kept her going when nothing else would. "You are right, of course, Maya. But what are we to do? You are a prisoner here, just as I am. I assure you, we cannot escape these cells, and you have seen what happens to those who no longer please Seefra."

"A wise girl!" boomed a voice that echoed around the walls of the chamber. "One you might benefit from heeding, Lord of the Champions!"

Maya looked up toward the passageway adjacent to Janine's cell. The two shadow warriors remained still, holding the same military posture. Seefra had not come out of hiding just yet. Maya bellowed into the deep expanse of the chamber. "Show yourself, master of darkness, or are you too afraid of a young woman and depleted Champion, both of whom you hold as your prisoner?"

"In time, Maya, in due time," answered Seefra. "Before I cast you down into the mists I might grant you a short audience. I merely came to inform you that the rest of your group will soon be destroyed. You defeated my army of slayers, and your soldiers fought bravely against my shadow warriors. They have spent themselves, though, and now an entire division of my remaining warriors will descend upon them like locusts on a fresh field of corn. They will pick their bones clean and bring them to me so I can use them as trophies or ingredients in a spell."

Seefra redirected his voice in Janine's direction. "You might be interested in knowing that your companion defeated over half of the initial wave without any assistance. He used a most fascinating device. A pity I won't be able to examine one of the creators' most powerful weapons, one that exists no more." The voice suddenly shifted again, and it spoke to the chamber in general. "In a few moments, you will be all that remains of the Champions of the Crossworlds, Maya. Enjoy your captivity; I might even retain you as my own personal slave."

The echo of the last comment faded while a sickening laughter took its place. Janine knew the sound all too well; she had heard it back on earth, in the final corridor, and in this chamber countless times. She leaned against the clear wall of her cell but did not cry out. From somewhere deep inside, she summoned the belief that Conor would not perish, and that the Champions would somehow destroy the shadow warriors and come for her and Maya. She held on to the thought, saying it over and over in her mind. She ignored the laughter and held unshakably to her belief. She didn't even notice Maya retreating back to the recesses of his cell, taking his comforting voice with him. She stood quietly, holding onto her thoughts with all of her strength.

"Yes," Maya whispered. "You are right, Seefra. A very wise girl."

CHAPTER THIRTY-FIVE

Conor stood with the Champions at the bottom of the chamber, watching cave entrances open all around them. The Champions had arranged their bodies in a circle around Conor, with Therion acting as the spear point in front of the young Champion. Mighty Therion, with his magnificent coat half burned away, stood out in front of the group like a gigantic sentinel. Injured or not, the giant lion would take a good number of the enemy with him before they cut him down. Surmitang and Ajur stood to his rear, guarding the left and right flanks as best they could. Both the jaguar and the tiger, although still impressive in size, had visible massive injuries. The bleeding could be seen coming from deep wounds across their huge bodies. Occasionally they spit blood-filled saliva on the floor of the cavern.

Eha lay on the dusty floor of the chamber next to Purugama. Both of them could barely stand, so they assumed their protective stances and did the best they could while lying in prone positions. Conor stood within the circle, wishing he had one more magical orb. He had the Lady's magic, but he knew how to use only a fraction of it. He knew he would never hold another thousand warriors at bay. He realized this would be the final battle for the Champions, and he, like the others, wanted to make the Crossworlds proud.

After emerging from hundreds of caverns cut into the walls above the Champions, the shadow warriors began assembling at the top of the chamber. Once they freed themselves from their cramped environment, they jumped forth from the caves, fluttering their wings freely for the first time in countless months. They zipped around the chamber, testing their combat flight patterns. Entire groups would sometimes violently crash into other packs, ricocheting off each other. At times struggles ensued, at other times the warriors merely wobbled a bit before racing away to another location. After five or six hundred had gathered along the walls and ceiling, a few of the more courageous flew down to have a sniff of their opponents. They moved so quickly the Champions couldn't put up a legitimate attack, but that didn't prevent Therion from taking a few ill-mannered swipes at them anyway. A few times the giant lion connected, sending a warrior careening against a far wall before slumping to the ground with a broken body. Mostly, however, Therion threw his huge paws at nothing but air. The teasing caused the Champion to roar in frustration. After a few minutes, he finally backed away, saving his strength for the battle yet to come.

"Destroying a few here and there will do nothing to help our cause," said Ajur. "We must all save our strength for what we know will come soon."

"The shadow warriors continue to assemble," remarked Purugama. "Apparently the second wave of their forces will be quite a bit larger than the first."

"We were fools," said Surmitang. "They forced us to exhaust everything we had in the initial attack, and now they will fall on us with a force ten times as large."

Indeed, the shadow warriors' numbers multiplied very quickly.

At least three thousand warriors scrambled around inside the top of the chamber, and the caverns expelled more creatures every second. Soon six or seven thousand warriors crawled around the interior of the chamber, while another two thousand flew around in the open air around the top ten stories of caves. At length, the numbers of warriors emerging from the caves slowed and then ceased altogether.

A peculiar darkness settled over the entire chamber. The Champions couldn't even see the walls anymore. The ceiling of the chamber had also disappeared, having been replaced by a living sea of shadow warriors.

"Come down and fight!" roared Therion, eager to begin the final battle. He squeezed his eyes shut and pointed the tip of his tail straight up at the ceiling. The dark fur at the tip contracted and expanded rapidly while sending blasts of energy into the dense body of warriors. At the point of contact, the energy blasts erupted into a series of smaller, more volatile clusters of power. These smaller bolts scattered randomly into the shadow warriors, taking a few dozen out before dying out themselves. A few of the enemy fell from the heights of the chamber and smacked down on the rocky ground close to the Champions. The remaining warriors didn't even react to their loss. They either refused to acknowledge a defeat of such insignificance or they had other things on their minds.

"Look," said Conor. "They're assembling their weapons. They're not even going to come down and face us. They're going to blast us into the forbidden corridors without even trying to fight us first."

The other Champions shook their heads quietly. They knew Conor spoke the truth. They watched the shadow warriors gather together at different locations around the top of the chamber, assembling their bodies together. Disorganized at first due to their numbers, the warriors soon arranged their forces in such a way that two dozen of the organic energy tubes would soon be ready to fire. They worked efficiently and patiently, forming their torsos into the huge cylinders. Every one of the giant weapons trained its business end down onto the floor of the chamber.

The Champions waited for the first attacks to come. There was simply nothing else for them to do. Purugama could not fly and attack them from aloft. Therion's weapons inflicted a dose of punishment here and there, but it was miniscule compared to the overall force the shadow warriors arrayed against them. Even Conor's efforts with the silver magic of the Lady of the Light proved ineffective. So many shadow warriors could not be conquered by so few and at so distant a staging point. The last of the shadow warriors' weapons were close to being completed when Purugama called out to his protégé, asking him to accompany him.

"Conor," said the great cougar. "Come here for a moment, if you will." After the young Champion complied, Purugama looked at his friend with his huge, golden eyes. "If this is to be our final battle, I want you to know something. I had always dreamed I would meet you someday. For countless centuries, you lived in my soul and mind, always hiding in the background until the day I found you on that mesa beside your small bed. You have lived up to my every expectation, and I am proud to have shared a brief moment of time with you. You truly are a credit to the Champions."

Conor grabbed Purugama's right ear and pressed his face against the golden fur. "I'll always remember you, great cougar, for I too awaited your coming for many years. Some on my world would call it desire, but I prefer to think of it as destiny. We were meant to serve the Crossworlds and to help one another, Purugama, and

I do not believe that our journey is finished. Something inside me tells me that we have more to do together."

With his last comment, Conor looked over at Eha. Bruised and broken, the cheetah managed a pained smile for Conor. The young Champion smiled back and winked, giving Eha as much hope as he could.

The weapons of the shadow warriors glistened with immense power. The interiors of every cylinder radiated a willingness to strike down their enemy. The only thing they waited for was a signal from the collective mind. The cylinders made their final adjustments, aiming directly at the Champions. The energy within the tubes elevated to an incomprehensible level.

A blinding light penetrated the darkness at a high point on the wall of the chamber. Expanding into a manic sheet of vibrant power, the light dropped from its source point and formed the largest corridor Conor had ever seen. The brilliance from the vast screen filled the chamber of caves with a light so intense that night instantly became day. The only disturbance in the purity of the brightness came from a moving wall of some form of organic life. Conor stood, smiled, and raised a closed fist in the air. He knew in his bones who had called forth the gigantic portal. He screamed out to the Lady of the Light, honoring her as a warrior above all others. After yelling her name a dozen times, he stood with his fist raised and waited for the sound of her voice. It came to him soon afterwards, raining down into the chamber like a siren song.

"Ezuvex, assemble behind your leader!" cried the creator of all light. "Avenge your people and your world, and save the Champions of the Crossworlds! Destroy the shadow warriors!"

As one, the Champions raised their heads to the sky. What

they saw in the brilliant light of the corridor caused each one of them to forget their pain and smile broadly. The Lady of the Light, in all her majestic glory, stood at the lip of the portal wall. At her left stood a battle-ready Gribba, showing a fierce expression toward the masses of shadow warriors. They had, after all, destroyed his world, and very nearly extinguished his entire race. The Ezuvex had resurrected their world and their culture while rebuilding their numbers, waiting for the day when they could retaliate against the hideous creatures that swept through their cities, wiping out their loved ones. The day had come, and Gribba called out to his kind, ushering them forward toward their destiny. The Ezuvex armies appeared in the corridor, one step behind their leader.

The Lady of the Light called out a strange chant and dove gracefully off the edge of the portal. As she floated down toward the Champions, Gribba's forces flooded the chamber by the thousands. The Ezuvex had a brand of magic all their own, but it would not be used for this conflict. They had brought their ancient battle instruments with them for this particular confrontation. They planned to pummel the shadow warriors into nothing and leave no trace of their existence. They wanted to remove any possibility of a return to their world some day, so they jumped from the corridor in giant waves and fell onto the huge cylinders of shocked warriors with a burning passion.

The shadow warriors had no time to react, much less do anything about the Ezuvex advance. In the confusion and fright of the appearance of the corridor, they had forgotten all about firing their weapons at the Champions. Their other dilemma lay in the fact that they were packed so tightly together; they couldn't separate and use swift movement against the slower Ezuvex. If they used their individual magic against them, they might have hit each other as easily as the enemy. It would be over very soon. The Ezuvex would have their revenge.

The Lady of the Light descended to the floor of the cavern, herself a beacon of powerful energy. If the shadow warriors had launched an attack against her, they would have witnessed the true power of the Crossworlds. As potent a force as they were the shadow warriors could never hope to withstand the power of a creator. She glided by whole groups of them on her way to address her Champions. Even without the gift of sight, the warriors shielded their faces against her penetrating luminescence.

The Lady looked upon her battered forces after reaching the floor of the cavern. In any other circumstance, she might have paused to shed tears at the heartbreaking sight. This chamber was a battleground, however, and she forbade herself the luxury of emotional freedom. She looked at Therion first, who crouched low in front of her, stretching the singed fur along his body.

"Oh Therion," sighed the Lady. "Rise, brave one, and release the tension in your skin. You owe servitude to no one."

Therion stood without uttering a sound. He walked the few steps toward the center of the circle where Conor awaited the Lady. The young Champion extended his right arm in front of him, keeping his left across his body as he knelt with his head bowed low. The other Champions gave their Lady her due, lowering their eyes until she gave them leave to address her.

"Come to me, my Champions," she said as she lifted Conor to a standing position. "Come and feel the healing power of the creators."

At the top of the chamber, the mêlée between the shadow warriors and the Ezuvex continued. The huge bears with their human features crashed into the organic cylinders with a fury known only to those who have lost everyone they ever loved. They impacted the groups of shadow warriors with such force that the cylinders fell apart at random intervals. Hundreds of Ezuvex clung to the broken sections, hacking away at the warriors with the weapons of their ancestors. Severed pieces of their enemy flew in every direction, bouncing off ledges and flying into the empty caves.

Those warriors who managed to dislodge themselves from the cylinders found unoccupied ledges where they could fire their magic at the enemy. Their moment of freedom soon ended, though, as the Ezuvex quickly located and destroyed them. Many perished in the fighting, however, cut in two by the dark magic of the shadow warriors. All the while, more Ezuvex flooded the chamber through the brilliantly lit corridor. Hundreds more joined their brethren every minute, and soon the strategy of the shadow warriors turned against them. Now *they* were the finite number fighting against an ever-increasing force of enraged Ezuvex. The warriors shrieked as their numbers fell. Even in the midst of mindless battle, they knew what the outcome would be. To their credit, they fought fanatically to the last warrior, serving their master until their final breath.

Remnants of the confrontation rained down onto the floor of the chamber. The Lady of the Light created a glowing, silver umbrella above the Champions so they would not suffer the ugliness of the onslaught. Fighters from both groups fell from the heights of the chamber, careening off the top of the radiant globe. They fell in great heaps around the perimeter of the Lady's protective barrier, mostly shadow warriors, but more than a few Ezuvex as well.

"Remain where you are, brave Champions," said the Lady. The interior of the protective cone will return your vitality to you." As she completed the statement, the wide umbrella began to glow with brilliant silver light. Flakes of silvery dust flickered down from the ceiling of the barrier. In less than five minutes, the Champions found themselves covered with a light coating of the rejuvenating flakes. One by one, the injuries plaguing their bodies vanished. Purugama's wings grew back to their full expanse, stronger and wider than ever. Ajur and Surmitang, healed of their damaging internal injuries, stood and stretched their muscles while instinctively grooming their fur. The black jaguar still reeled from the bite of the boorbain tree, but absent that aspect of his appearance, he looked immeasurably better. Therion's singed skin rolled off of his back like old carpet and was replaced by a glistening coat of thick, golden brown fur. His mane emerged completely renewed, darker and broader than ever, and the giant lion prominently displayed his reinvigorated self for the Lady to appreciate. Conor's scrapes and bruises immediately disappeared, and his mangled limbs adjusted themselves to their former athletic profile. The young Champion bounced up and down in place, testing his body for any pains whatsoever. He felt better than he had at any time since they departed for this strange world.

Only Eha refrained from standing. The sleek cheetah looked completely healed, but something about his bearing spoke otherwise. All of his brothers along with the Lady approached the wary Champion.

"What ails you, Eha?" asked the Lady. "Rise, and greet me with a smile."

The cheetah said nothing. He merely stared into the Lady's eyes. Then he rolled over on his back, displaying the most hideous sight Conor had ever seen. A creature, similar to a shadow warrior, had implanted itself on Eha's body. It appeared to be making its way into Eha's stomach, traveling right through the skin. The pain of such an attack must have been unbearable, so much so that Eha couldn't even find a smile for his Lady as she approached. As he displayed the strange form for the others, the lanky cheetah grimaced again and again.

"Curse them!" spat the Lady of the Light in an unusually rare display of emotion. "May the forbidden corridors consume them for all time! How dare they use such methods so long after the equinox war! This is my sister's doing, no doubt, and she will answer for this transgression!"

The Lady composed herself, saving her anger for a more appropriate time. She held one hand aloft while placing the other directly on the mutant form protruding from Eha's belly. She spoke silently under her breath, a long, complicated chant that would help her Champion regain his strength. As she intoned the magical words, the hand she held against the mutant began to glow. When the brightness gained intensity, the spell caused the light to stream away from the one hand to the other. She was drawing the energy of the mutant form away from Eha's body. Soon her lower hand no longer glowed at all. The energy had been transferred to the creature, which now exuded a silvery metallic sheen. The Lady placed her withdrawn hand against her thigh and waited patiently for the spell to complete its work.

Little by little, the mutant creature peeled away from Eha's skin. One leg after another popped up out of the cheetah's stomach, and each time it happened, Eha moaned and cried with increasing pain. Conor rushed to his side, placing Eha's head in his lap and stroking the spotted neck as lightly as he could. Every time his brother twisted in pain, Conor allowed the event to occur before resuming his nurturing attention.

The mutant creature fought against the spell. It also wished to serve its master, and it would not give up without a struggle. It made every attempt to implant the removed pincers into Eha's skin. This caused the brave cheetah more pain than he could stand, and while gritting his teeth he roared and whined in the same breath. Therion walked over to his brother and placed his huge, weighty body over him, as he had done before when he protected him against the weapon of the shadow warriors. He would hold Eha to the ground while Conor did what he could for him. The mutant creature had to be removed whether it meant Eha's life or not. If it remained on his body very much longer, it would transform him into a shadow warrior with all due haste.

The Lady continued speaking in the strange tongue of the creators. The energy focused itself, concentrating on one tip of the creature's structure. With a huge surge of flashing energy, it ripped half of the mutant's form away from the cheetah's belly. Eha shrieked with unspeakable pain, crying out to his Lady to take the creature from him or take his life. He could not stand the struggle any longer. The Lady crushed her raised hand into a fist and yanked it backwards. The mutant tore away from Eha's skin, sending the cheetah into another convulsive fit of throbbing agony. Then Eha saw the creature stuck to the Lady's elevated hand. He looked at Conor, then at Therion, and finally at the Lady of the Light. He grinned widely, and then passed out cold.

"Stay with him, Conor," the Lady instructed. "He will need your care for a while. She looked at the hideous thing attached to her hand, said a few choice incantations, and watched it disappear into thin air. She shook her hand a few times before cupping it with her other hand in her lap. She looked at each of the cats in turn, and then asked the question she had been dying to ask since she arrived.

"Where is your Lord?" she said quietly. "Why is Maya not with you?"

The Champions neither squirmed nor stalled. Ajur stepped forward to deliver the bad news. "Taken, my Lady," reported the coal black jaguar. "A ruse, put forth by Seefra. The master of darkness assumed Surmitang's form soon after we arrived in this chamber. He coaxed Maya into a cavern and before we could respond to his treachery, both of them plummeted down into a bottomless chasm."

The Lady of the Light offered no reaction whatsoever. She merely accepted the information and nodded her head. She looked up toward the top of her protective bubble and noticed that the battle between the shadow warriors and the Ezuvex had ended. She drew her hand across the width of the chamber above her head and watched the silver umbrella dissolve. Almost immediately, as if he had been waiting for the Lady's permission, Gribba walked forward into the gathering of the Champions. Stopping before he reached the perimeter of the circle, the huge Ezuvex went to one knee and bowed before the Lady and the Champions. Bleeding and covered with the remains of the enemy, the big bear's chest heaved with his labored breathing.

"Come forward, soldier," said the Lady, "and deliver your report. What is the status of the shadow warrior forces?"

"Utterly destroyed," answered a proud Gribba. "My soldiers have asked me to relate their gratitude to the Lady of the Light for allowing them to avenge their families. This is truly a great day for our race."

Surmitang rose and padded over to Gribba's kneeling form. He opened his huge jaws and gently grabbed one the Ezuvex's arms. Pulling him to a standing position, he walked him into the midst of the gathering of Champions. When he had him positioned so that everyone could see him, Surmitang addressed him. "We owe you our lives, Gribba, all of us do. You and your kind fought brave-ly and with great resolve. Let me speak for all of the Champions when I pledge my undying loyalty to you for the rest of my days. All of us will remember this event as a celebration day for the glo-rious race of the Ezuvex."

The rest of the Champions chimed in with their hearty thanks. Conor walked over to Gribba and hugged the huge bear around the chest as best he could before returning to Eha's side. The in-destructible cheetah, now feeling better by the minute, smiled broadly at the large Ezuvex standing in front of him. Seconds later he got to his feet for the first time in almost an hour. A secret spell granted to him by the Lady had accelerated his recovery. He walked over to Gribba and began assaulting his face and cheeks with a barrage of wet kisses. The sandpaper tongue of the wild cat brushing up against Gribba's course fur made such an interesting sound that the entire group broke into fits of laughter. It felt good for all of them, the Lady included, to experience a brief respite from their journey. Just as soon as it began, however, the Lady silenced her Champions and began issuing new orders.

"Gribba," she began. "Take your warriors back through the cor-ridor and await our return to the realm. We must have a superior fighting force on hand in case the Circle of Evil attempts a counter attack."

"At once, my Lady," answered Gribba. "Ajur, we have almost deciphered the boorbain virus. I am certain by the time you return from this journey we will have the antidote prepared for you."

Energized by the sound of the Lady's praise, Gribba bid fare-well to the Champions. He climbed the walls of the chamber and disappeared into its dizzying heights.

The Lady of the Light turned to her warriors. "The rest of us must proceed to Seefra's laboratory in a place located deep within this mountain. I believe that is where the master of darkness took Maya after tricking him into the chasm. Although it looks bottomless, I'll bet that it serves as a conduit straight into the heart of Seefra's chamber of operations. If we're lucky, we might even find a passageway that will deliver us to the inner realm of the Circle of Evil. Maybe today we can finish this struggle once and for all.

"We must travel through the mists that lie beyond the entrance to the bottomless cavern," she continued. "I'll go first, and if you follow each other closely and single-file, we might just make it through together. Conor, mount up on Purugama and wait for everyone to make the jump, then follow us. We'll need his wings and your arms if anything goes wrong. Purugama, you may have to tuck your wings tightly into your body and freefall for some distance, but after you leave the walls of the cavern you should be able to control your descent without too much trouble."

"Ajur, I want you to follow me into the cavern. If anything happens I want you by my side for my protection."

The black jaguar sidled up next to the Lady. She spoke as if she meant what she said, but Ajur knew better. His blood flow had decreased with every passing hour due to the boorbain infection, and now his labored breathing gave his condition away. A noticeable limp didn't help matters either. The Lady was merely protecting him by asking for his proximity. She would never point out a deficiency in any of her Champions, and he loved her all the more for her discretion. He would give his life for her without hesitation.

"The slayers and keepers are defeated," proclaimed the Lady of the Light. "The shadow warriors are no more. Now it is our turn to take charge of the battle. The keeper of the keys awaits her

Champion. After we collect the five keys we will find and rescue her." She looked all the Champions in the eye, especially at Conor, who had already mounted Purugama and sat ready in his saddle. "Everyone into the chasm. We'll reassemble on the other side of the mists."

Conor watched as the Lady fell into the cavern opening. He waited patiently while Ajur and the rest of the cats dove in behind her. When Purugama approached the edge of the chasm, Conor looked around the chamber one last time. "Two down and one to go," he said under his breath. "I bet Seefra will be shocked when he sees me again."

"Did you say something, Conor?" asked Purugama.

"Just preparing myself for the final battle," answered Conor. "How are you feeling now that your wings have been replenished?"

"Strong enough to do this!"

Conor grabbed the strap and held on tightly as the great cougar jumped head first into the chasm. Purugama's massive size caused them to gain speed rapidly, and soon the cavern walls raced by so quickly they became a blur in Conor's watery eyes. He could feel the strength of Purugama's wings as he tucked them tightly against Conor's legs. The big cat dipped his head and curled his legs tightly beneath his underbelly. His huge body zoomed downward like a runaway missile. They fell deeper and deeper into the cavern, at a speed Conor wouldn't even try to guess. He dropped his head down onto Purugama's shoulder, resting it against the strong golden neck. He extended his arms around the huge cat, holding on with everything he had. He shut his eyes, blocking the light out completely. He thought of nothing but Janine, and how close they must be to reaching her. He visualized her face, the features he could remember anyway. He imagined the moment they would jump into each other's arms after being apart for so long.

The two travelers reached maximum descent speed and still the chasm continued. Purugama kept his eyes open despite the irritation from the air rushing by his face. The big cat sensed something changing in their environment. The temperature was dropping drastically, at least twenty degrees in the last minute. He could accept the mists as the cause of the variation, but if that were the case, it would have dropped steadily through their free-fall. This appeared to be something different, but yet something familiar also. It reminded him of the entrance to a corridor, of the extreme temperature shifts of the creator's portals.

This corridor, if authentic, had been created by Seefra, and that concerned him. If the master of darkness could alter any environment he chose, then what could prevent him from changing the path of a corridor at will? He may have traveled to his laboratory through this passageway, but the Champions could end up a thousand worlds away if Seefra desired it.

Purugama shook the thoughts away. Better to believe in the destiny of the group than torture one's self with possibilities. Besides, they had the Lady of the Light as their guide. If any danger arose, who better to face it than her?

Conor held the straps with an iron grip. He had never traveled this fast in his life. He had never seen anything, anywhere move as rapidly as he and Purugama must have been moving at that moment. For a while he didn't even feel the cold. Then it became intense, and he sensed the frigidness of the air against his forehead. He too recognized it as the icy barrier to corridor travel, the equally intense cold and heat one must penetrate while moving between worlds. In all of his other experiences, though, the sensations lasted only a fraction of a second. The icy cold in this chasm didn't seem to be dissipating at all.

In the middle of the most frightening experience Conor had ever gone through, the only thing he could think about was the extreme heat that would follow the freezing cold. If that also lasted for more than the usual time, he and Purugama might be in trouble. Since there was simply nothing he could do, he grabbed the straps a little tighter and held on. He thought of Janine again, and how her ordeal with Seefra must have been a thousand times worse than anything he presently experienced. He focused on the image of rescuing her from Seefra's laboratory, and soon the cold seemed a distant memory.

Both Purugama and Conor would have welcomed the cold back immediately after feeling the fiery heat that replaced it, however. Conor sensed his skin peeling away from his body. He wanted to be strong in front of his mentor, but the heat seemed to double in intensity with every second that passed. Soon his eyes felt like they might burst. His tongue felt like a dried up sponge inside his mouth. His fingernails and every pore of his body penetrated by a hair follicle felt pierced by red-hot needles. He began screaming because he couldn't stand the pain and he didn't know when it would stop.

Seconds later Purugama added his voice to Conor's. He roared in his own suffering with a high-pitched whine. His wings, singed by the heat, felt as though they had burned away from his body again. He wondered if he would able to fly if and when they exited this cursed corridor. He decided that no matter what, he would make certain they landed in a position with his body beneath Conor. If he perished in the fall, maybe his body would cushion the boy's. As he mulled this plan over in his head, the temperature changed again. The piercing heat dissolved almost immediately.

Purugama blinked his eyes and looked around tentatively. When he didn't see the walls of the chasm, he unfolded his huge wings and began slowing their descent.

The great cougar coasted on the heavy blanket of air for close to ten minutes. During the first five minutes he soared back and forth through the sky, letting his wings push against the wind time and again in order to reduce their speed. During the second interval, he maintained a relaxing pattern through the air, taking the time to allow both him and Conor to regain their composure. The freefall had been a frightening experience, but the extensive temperature extremes added a terrifying component to the journey. Purugama felt reassured when Conor patted his flank with a strong hand. He exhaled mightily upon knowing that his young friend had survived their ordeal.

"The adventures just get better and better, don't they?" asked Conor in a relieved tone of voice.

"For a Champion of the Crossworlds," answered the big cat, "the adventure never ends. I am pleased to find you unharmed by Seefra's spells."

"And I you, my friend," replied Conor. "I feared for your wings when the heat reached an unbearable temperature."

Purugama dipped his left wing and dove toward an expansive coastline about three miles away. After straightening his course again, he addressed Conor's last comment. "It would take a great deal more than a portal designed by the master of darkness to thwart my efforts, Champion."

Conor let his friend's statement drift away with the breeze. After patting his flank again, he took great care in examining their new environment. It looked quite different from the chamber of caves. The dominion of the shadow warriors always seemed dark and threatening to him. Compared to that, this environment looked like a paradise. Although the skies teemed with an assortment of different colored clouds, and the ground could have done with a bit more plant life, the area appeared inviting in a strange, mysterious way. The coastline looked similar to those Conor remembered from earth, except that they lacked the wave motion most of those beaches enjoyed.

Conor felt a shiver race down his spine as he recalled his battle with Fumemos, the formless shape that attacked him by the shoreline of the dead ocean of the future. He certainly would not approach any body of water while here in Seefra's domain. He doubted he would submerge himself in any ocean ever again, even those back home on earth. The memory of the pounding surf still frightened him.

The lands beyond the coast drifted away without much variation, although a small hill rose toward the horizon every now and again. The clouds in the sky cast a kaleidoscope of colors onto the terrain below. The ground as far as Conor could see changed colors constantly, giving the entire area an interesting mix of joyful and morose impressions.

Purugama lowered his head and folded his wings. He and his passenger dove toward the coastline where they saw the rest of their group assembled. The Lady of the Light crouched close to Ajur's side, attending to the damaging effects of the boorbain virus. Even at this distance Conor could tell that Ajur's condition had worsened considerably. The proud jaguar stood without emotion as the Lady examined the infected area. Conor saw him wincing in agony as his mistress probed more deeply into the affected layers of skin and muscle. Conor held a silent wish for Ajur's safety, and then prepared for Purugama's descent.

The cougar swooped in over the ocean, flaring his huge wings so they could glide along the entrance to the beach. They landed softly on the glittering sand. Conor heard it crunching beneath the big cat's feet as he ran gently along the shoreline after touching down. Purugama walked up to the other Champions, watching the Lady while she attended to Ajur's wound. The glistening silver creator never stopped working, never turned around, and didn't even address the newcomers after they arrived. She stayed with her task, cleaning and dressing Ajur's wound, trying desperately to remove any of the virus she could find. The big jaguar grunted and grimaced, but otherwise didn't move a muscle. He would never embarrass himself or the other Champions with such behavior. He waited patiently for the Lady to complete her work.

"The boorbain is a powerful virus, Ajur," she remarked. "I am afraid at this juncture all I can do is try and slow its progress."

"My Lady is too humble," replied the jaguar. "Your soft touch strengthens me in ways too numerous to define."

"Your chivalry equals your bravery, Ajur," said the Lady as she passed her hands over the infected area. A silvery membrane followed the path of her hands, ending at the far end of the infection. Ajur bristled lightly when it attached itself to his side, but again he stood fast. "This gauze should draw the virus away from your heart, Ajur. I'm afraid all it can do is halt the progress, because the boorbain elements pursue your organs even as we speak. At least we can hope for a standoff until we can return to the realm for Gribba's antidote."

The Lady of the Light stood and addressed Conor and Purugama with a nod and a diminutive smile. She looked at the rest of Champions while brushing her hands against her clothing. "Come. Now that we are assembled and Ajur has been attended to, it is time to move forward again. Ajur, with me, please." The Lady moved through the group of cats, setting out along the shoreline. She walked for maybe a hundred feet before Therion halted her with a question.

"Move forward to where, my Lady?" he asked. "We are on a strange world, quite possibly of Seefra's making, and none of us has any idea how to find him."

The Lady turned for a moment, and when she did, the group of seven blinked at the sight of her expression. They saw a dozen different emotions in her eyes, lips, and forehead. The most profound of all of them was an extreme sense of sadness. "This is the world of my sister, lion, and I have come here to destroy her. While you battle Seefra for the five keys of the creators, I will seek out the paths I walked as a child. I will follow her scent as I did when we ran together as children on this world she now claims as her own. She knows that we are here, yet she will do nothing to stop any of you. She has waited for centuries for our reunion, and I will not disappoint her."

"Surely a protector must accompany you," Therion protested. "Take me along, my Lady, and let me soften her up for you."

"How long would you last in a battle against one of the creators, Therion?" the Lady queried. "She is not of our caliber, but never think dark magic is any less formidable. She would slap you aside like one of the flies that flew around your rump out on the veldt of your home world, and I will not sacrifice a Champion just to provide a few second's advantage in our confrontation. Stay here, brave lion, and help the other Champions rescue Conor's companion. They will need your strength and cunning to find and free Maya and reclaim the five keys. This task is mine alone. I must return to the place of my father's demise and avenge him."

Conor watched as the conversation between the creator and the Champion unfolded. He couldn't believe what he was hearing; he wanted to jump down from Purugama's shoulders and order the Lady to remain with them. Together, they could destroy Seefra and then seek out her sister for retribution. He held his tongue, however, partly because of her resolute attitude with Therion, and partly because of the look on her face.

The Lady bent at the waist slightly and looked Ajur in the eye. The two of them conversed for a few minutes and then she pressed her cheek against his forehead. After the tender parting, the bulky jaguar returned to the other Champions. As he stepped toward the group, the sand at the base of the small hill fronting the coast began to fall away. As if trickling into a gigantic funnel, great volumes of sand started to disappear into the ground. An opening appeared underneath the small hill, first as a misshapen hole, but after a few tons of sand had fallen away, it began to take the shape of a constructed passageway. As a group, the Champions watched the tunnel expand to a size that would accommodate half their number abreast if they walked through together. At length, the vanishing sands trickled to a stop, and the voice of the Lady of the Light came from within.

"This passageway leads directly to Seefra's chamber of cells. I wish you well, Champions, and hope to join you back at the realm when this journey is complete. The creators will be by your side every step of the way."

Eha was the first in the group to snap his head around after her voice drifted away. The Lady no longer walked on the shoreline, or anywhere else the Champions could see. Their eyes lingered, hoping to see her emerge from behind a rock or a stand of heavy brush. Their silent pleas went unanswered, however, and finally Conor broke the silence.

"Let us be off," he said, straightening himself in Purugama's saddle. "We have one more battle to fight, and the Lady has given us a direct path to our enemy. Surmitang, lead us into the chamber of cells. We must recover the five keys, and I want Janine back with me where she belongs."

The Champions rallied around their younger, smaller brother. Together they walked toward the dark passageway and into the bowels of the shadow world.

CHAPTER THIRTY-SIX

The passageway into the chamber of cells fell away at a dangerously steep angle. As soon as the Champions crossed the threshold of the sandy entrance, the footpath dropped significantly, sloping downward on an extreme decline. The cats extended their massive claws, using them to grasp the unstable ground beneath their feet. Conor, holding the strap of his saddle in both hands, leaned his body back to the point where his shoulders almost touched Purugama's broad back. He tried desperately to see anything ahead of them, but his eyes proved useless. This truly was the abyss of the shadow world, for no light found its way into these depths. Even the entrance, once so permanent, had already closed off their only avenue of retreat. The Champions had expected such an event, so when it happened they hadn't even turned to confirm their suspicions.

The path began to lose some of its width as they moved forward. Surmitang, from his long years in the dense rainforests of Sumatra, knew better than to forge ahead blindly without assessing what lay ahead. Using certain signals that only large wild cats would recognize, he instructed the others to move forward when he felt it was safe, and at other times ordered them to halt their progress if he sensed a particularly dangerous section ahead.

Now that the path appeared to be narrowing, he traversed its width every ten feet or so, determining the precise number of inches available to them. If he felt that walking abreast might pose an unacceptable danger, he would direct the Champions into a new formation. The others, walking helplessly in the inky darkness, trusted their brother implicitly, following his every command.

A dash of light peeked around a corner some distance ahead. A large outcropping of heavy rock tried its best to couch the light in darkness, but the rays kept their relentless vigil, wearing down the stone as the group of seven advanced. The Champions could clearly see small streaks of light pushing through the cracks between the huge boulders. Eha picked up his pace until Surmitang gruffly ordered him back into formation. The immense tiger took his leadership seriously. He would never allow one of his brothers to walk into a trap. He would inspect the intersection of the pathways, and when he felt satisfied of its safety, he would release the others from his guiding hand.

After confirming Eha's obedience and requesting that the others remain behind, he crouched and padded up to the source of the light. Taking his time and assuring himself that no destroyers lurked on the other side of the rock ledge, Surmitang carefully peered around the edge of a small stone. What he saw caused him to forget about Seefra, the destroyers, the Champions, and any protective mission he might have previously taken seriously. He stood there, his golden eyes wide open, staring at the sight before him.

"Mind of the creators!" he said out loud.

Eha, once again avoiding his brother's orders, quietly pressed his head around the corner of the shelf and placed it above the stunned tiger's forehead. Seconds later, he uttered the same sentiment while staring dumbly at the scene before him. The other Champions called out to the cheetah, pleading for a report about what his eyes beheld. After receiving no answer, and seeing that Surmitang would provide nothing either, the remainder of the group trotted down to the junction of the two pathways and craned their necks around the corner. Each one of them stared at the amazing scene, struck dumb by its magnificence. In all their travels for the creators, none of the Champions had ever seen anything so daunting before.

The chamber of cells occupied an interior valley roughly two miles in length and one mile in width. Vast walls of impenetrable rock rose up on all sides of the chamber, making escape unthinkable even if a captive managed to break out of their cell. The walls seemed to have no end; they just continued to climb away from the light and into the shadows until they simply disappeared. The underbelly of the chamber formed its base, but near the bottom the walls sloped inward to the center. It looked like the floor had been carved from the same rock, as if a monstrous volcano had hewed a mammoth hole into the mountain and left its edges as one giant cup.

The Champions guessed about the bottom, mostly because of the thick, swirling mist covering it from edge to edge. A source of light illuminated the chamber just above the crystal cells balancing precariously over the mists. The cells didn't appear very threatening, but Conor and the cats knew otherwise. The young Champion spent almost two years in one of the keepers' contraptions, as had the others around him. If the servants of the master of darkness built those cells, then everyone gathered at the corner of the pathway understood their power. Conor stared at the crystal cells without blinking his eyes even once.

"Janine's in one those things," he muttered to himself.

"Fear not, Conor," answered Purugama. "Before this day is finished, you shall be reunited with your companion. I swear it on our friendship, and on the faith of every Champion here." The other cats scratched at the ground, chuffing their agreement.

As a group, they set out toward the chamber of cells. Conor, amidst a flood of emotions, fielded a passing thought about what he might be doing back home at this moment, had none of this ever happened. Suddenly he grinned from ear to ear, thinking about how drastically his life had changed. Even while heading directly for Seefra's chamber, the young Champion reflected on his life back on earth. He wondered about his friends, about Beau and even Denny back at Mountmoor High School. What would he say to them after he arrived back home? He wondered if he would ever return or see any of them again. He pondered his thoughts as he rolled from side to side with the movement of Purugama's huge shoulders.

The Champions walked along the rocky path for close to three hours. They decided to keep Purugama on the ground for now, in case the wrong pair of eyes might observe him from afar. They had traveled a good distance in a short period of time, but the chamber of cells still looked to be quite distant. They were close enough to discern individual cells now, and everyone in the group stared at the strange creatures occupying Seefra's chamber. Some they recognized, most they didn't, but they knew they were all here because they had threatened Seefra's power one way or another. Most looked bewildered, unsure of their surroundings or why they had been transported to such a bizarre location. Others appeared more seasoned and resigned to their fate. Some of those bore the hideous scars of various forms of torture, a pastime particularly enjoyable to the master of darkness. They sat in their cells, morose and beaten, waiting only for the end to finally come.

Conor strained his tired eyes, looking from cell to cell. He only locked his vision on any cell long enough to determine that none of the occupants were his girlfriend. With every subsequent cell, his hopes sagged slightly. Every time he looked into a new one and didn't see Janine, he entertained the fleeting thought that she might not have survived.

Ajur, now in visible pain, did his best to walk upright and not be a burden to the group. The path had taken its toll, however, and the burly jaguar finally fell against a slanting boulder on the left side of the trail. He coughed harshly, splattering streams of blood-infused spittle all over his forepaws and the surface of the rock. His breathing came at a great cost, and as the other Champions looked upon their sickened brother, they all shared the same thought.

"Ajur," Therion said while walking toward the black jaguar. "You cannot continue. We don't know how much farther we'll have to walk to reach the chamber of cells. But even if it were only a short distance, I fear you would not survive the journey. You must wait here and conserve your strength. We will carry the battle to Seefra and his destroyers. When the day is done, I promise you we will bring the Lady of the Light back to you. She will carry you to the realm herself if she has to, and by then Gribba will have the anti-dote ready."

Ajur looked at his brother through film-covered eyes. He breathed as normally as he could, tried to stand under his own power again, and then nodded his head once. "As much as I wish to deny it, I cannot. If I continue on, I will be nothing but a hindrance for the rest of you. I will do as you say, Therion, and wait here for your return." Ajur coughed loudly before raising his head again, blood and spittle wobbling back and forth on his jaw like a pendulum. "But if the battle goes badly for the creators' forces, you must call for me. If I have one breath left in my body, I will use it to strike a blow for our Lady."

"It will be done," answered Purugama, taking the attention away from Therion. "I will be in mental contact with you, Ajur. Keep the conduit open as you wait for us."

Ajur nodded, half falling against the rock again. He plopped down on the ground, placing his chin on his folded paws. Without a word of encouragement, the huge jaguar closed his eyes and heaved a weighty breath from his poisoned lungs. Within seconds he was asleep, yet even in repose he heard the Champions turn toward the path again. Each one of them silently asked the creators to watch over their brother while they continued their journey. Conor, unable to forget his big friend, turned to look back at him at least a half dozen times before they rounded a corner big enough to eclipse his inert form. Conor made his own plea to the Lady of the Light for Ajur's safety.

Maya languished in the cell of crystals, making every attempt to look like a conquered captive. His mind raced, however, as he examined certain strategies and discarded others. Seefra's penetration into their group while the Champions explored the shadow warriors' chamber had served Maya's intentions perfectly. He could not have planned a better circumstance himself, and now he sat quietly as a prisoner of the master of darkness, alone, helpless and without recourse. That was precisely what he wanted Seefra to think, so he spent his hours acting as though a cunning adversary had dashed his plans.

As he sat quietly in his cell, Maya inspected every inch of the gigantic chamber and the hundreds of crystal compartments. He studied every cell, every occupant, but most importantly, he looked closely at each wall circling the captives. It appeared as though the entrance to Seefra's laboratory was the only way in or out of the chamber, at least at this height. A passageway snaked through the rocks far below, but that was almost a half mile beneath them, and far away from the central chamber. If a line of attack could be created somewhere abreast of the entrance high up on the wall, then Seefra would have no choice but to fight.

The Lord of the Champions lifted his head sullenly and glanced around the chamber. He activated his vision enhancement, carefully moving his head as if looking at nothing at all. He observed a great many of the chamber's residents. After taking their measure, he determined that if given the chance, almost all of them would fight for their freedom. They would turn against Seefra if the opportunity presented itself. Maya plopped his head back down on his paws, looking even more despondent than ever. His gamble might just pay off, but only if he could convince Seefra he had finally accepted his fate. He closed his eyes and began reaching out to Janine's mind. She at least would learn of his plans before they became a reality.

CHAPTER THIRTY-SEVEN

The Lady of the Light walked deftly through the uneven terrain along the shoreline. Twice she felt tempted to stop and gaze upon the beautiful scenery she remembered so well from her youth. She turned her head momentarily, glancing for a moment at the suns hanging low in the sky. Another hour, she thought, and the fiery orbs would touch the horizon. How fitting that their confrontation should occur at almost the identical moment, yet millennia after the fact. Wearing a creased brow, she shook her head as she picked her way through the unstable territory.

She could understand her sister's passion, for it was a trait everyone in her family shared. But she could not comprehend the source of her fury, nor why she had taken to the shadow world so vigorously. Was her hatred of everything she knew as a child that important to her? Could she not value what would be hers in the world of the creators, the world of light? To be denied the training and power of the creators would drive most people to revenge, but she was her father's daughter. That alone should have provided the balance to accept such a fate and find the good behind her destiny.

The Lady stopped momentarily, rubbing her weary eyes with her chapped, lined hands. She did not wish to continue; she felt this journey should have befallen someone else. How could she strike the final blow against her own blood? Then she thought of Eha, and the hideous thing the Lady of the Shadows had used against him in the battle within the chamber of caves. *That must be why,* she thought, *they sent her because she knew her sister better than anyone else.* They also knew that her sister would never be able to persuade her to change her ways. Any of the others, especially the men, might feel pity for a beautiful, heartbroken opponent. The Lady of the Light would entertain no such frailties.

She dropped her hands to her sides and gazed far along the shoreline. She knew what lay ahead, only a mile or two from where she stood. She set out again, toward an invisible beacon only she could sense.

CHAPTER THIRTY-EIGHT

"There, just below the last row of cells," said Conor. *"It looks like an*
opening in the rock wall."

"Yes, I see it," replied Purugama. "We could be up there in seconds. If that's where Seefra hides himself, we could root him out
in a matter of minutes."

"No," said Therion gruffly. "I appreciate your zeal, Purugama,
but we cannot afford to split our forces at this time. We have lost
Maya, and now Ajur. The loss of anyone else might turn the tide in
the favor of the destroyers. If we are to attack Seefra's laboratory,
then I want a strong, united front."

"Do you suppose Maya's up there?" asked Eha.

"I do not doubt anything at this point," answered Therion. "If
he is captive in one of those cells, then his release must be a focal
point of our strategy. We need Maya's magic to defeat Seefra."

"Be silent," whispered Surmitang quickly. "Something tracks
us from behind. Listen! I fear it has found us." The massive tiger
turned one hundred eighty degrees, facing away from the rest of
the pack.

"Prepare yourselves. One of Seefra's destroyers is upon us."

The remaining cats immediately formed an impenetrable ring.
Arranging their bodies so their tails touched at the center of a

tight circle, the Champions created a defensive shield that would warn them of any creature's harmful intentions. Conor, sensing Surmitang's mood and urgency, immediately jumped up into Purugama's saddle. He faced outward along the great cougar's line of sight, watching everything his big friend observed.

The sound came first, long before any physical shape appeared. The hideous noise, it was painful to absorb and difficult to quiet after it penetrated the Champions' ears. It sounded like rough sand being ground into an asphalt road by a heavy boot. The sound appeared and vanished, increasing and decreasing in intensity, as if varying amounts of sand fell under the instep of the hypothetical boot. It made no sense to any of the Champions, but then it wasn't meant to, its only purpose was to drive them mad and remove their strategic advantage. The sound increased in volume as the creature came into view for the first time. It appeared not twenty feet from where they stood, boldly ready to confront the group of Champions.

Whatever it was, it didn't maintain a constant form for very long. It seemed invisible at first, except for the large amounts of sand and rock it gathered from the pathway every few seconds or so. The debris swirled around the creature in its own personal tornado, attaching some or all of itself to the exterior of the body. Almost immediately after making contact, the debris would fly away in a spinning, chaotic pattern before coming back around to connect with the creature again. In combination with the flying debris, the creature's shape changed haphazardly as well. At times it would appear human, at other times, animal-like. Sometimes it wouldn't take on any particular shape at all, and the debris would just congeal against whatever form the creature assumed at the moment.

Conor didn't like what he saw. He couldn't imagine what type of tactics this strange-looking thing might use against them. It reminded him very much of Fumemos, the warrior who commanded the ocean waves. He too changed shape at will, while directing the natural flora and fauna to do his bidding. This creature hadn't tipped its hand yet, but Conor nonetheless stepped strongly into his stirrups. He wrapped his arm through the strap, locking his inner elbow into the strong leather. His other hand gripped a large tuft of Purugama's fur. He could tell by the tightness of the great cougar's muscles that Purugama was ready to fly at a moment's notice. Conor watched the strange creature appear and then disappear with its bizarre cloak of dirt and dust. He never took his eyes away from it.

Eha broke the circle of protection, walking away from the Champions toward the creature. "Pikiwic Lloph," he said, calling the destroyer by name. "Leave us and depart from this place forever. We have no quarrel with you. The master of darkness will soon be destroyed, so you do not have to fear retribution from him. I give you this one chance, adversary of my fathers' fathers. Turn back and we will not harm you."

The gritty sound accelerated for a moment or two, almost as if the creature had broken into a fit of laughter. The debris congealed for almost thirty seconds, allowing it to scrabble out a few words of response. "The massster of darskness will have all of you fooor hisssh evening meal, Ehaaa, prince of the cheetaaahs. You have made a ssseriousss mishtake by coming here. No one, not eveeen someone of my abilitieees can defeeeat Seefra in his own fortresss."

"Look upon the rider of the winged cougar," replied Eha. "He is but a human from earth, and he defeated Seefra in his own castle many years ago, when he was just a boy."

The creature looked shocked for a moment. The debris coating its frame jumped slightly, as if the skin suffered some type of bristling shiver. Pikiwic Lloph gathered his wits quickly, however, dismissing the encounter as an anomaly. "Seefra's powersss are far beeeyond what they were many yearsss ago. If I were you, earthling, I would ruuun back home as quicksly as my little legs could caaary me. This isss no place fooor children."

Eha opened his mouth to reply but instead leapt out of the path of the oncoming destroyer. Lloph shed his debris while rushing madly at the wily cheetah. Eha bounced out of the way, shouting a warning to his brothers at the same time. "Don't let him touch you. If he makes contact with any part of your body, it will instantly become numb and useless. This is how he wears down and destroys his opponents. Soon the entire body becomes ineffective. Only then can he strike the final blow." Eha called down to where Conor and the cougar sat. "Purugama, fly. Now!"

Purugama bolted into the sky. Conor, having prepared for such an abrupt departure, held his place easily while the huge wings pumped vigorously against the air. Surmitang and Therion left the area so quickly that a few leaves floated back to the ground around their former footprints. Lloph smashed into the rock wall with such force it altered the form of his shape completely. Thinking little of his missed chance, the strange creature shifted his shape again and took off after Eha.

A longstanding feud broiled between the cheetah and this creature, and Lloph decided to take this chance to strike a blow for his kind. He quickly caught up with Eha and began keeping pace and pattern with the speedy cheetah. As he pursued him, minute pieces of his form detached themselves from the main body. They held their place for a moment and then sliced through the air at well over a hundred miles an hour. On flat ground with no impediments, Eha could have easily outrun these projectiles. Here in the craggy, rock strewn cavern, however, the big cheetah had trouble keeping up his pace. The slimy bullets chased Eha at an unbelievable speed. It almost looked as though the tiny projectiles had guidance systems linked to the cheetah's thought patterns.

Eha ran like a demon possessed. He had seen the result of contact with his opponent's skin. One of his distant cousins had lost the ability to run because his legs wouldn't function after coming in contact with one of Lloph's kind. Eha wouldn't allow that to happen to him, so he certainly wasn't laughing as he raced around the gritty pathways. Lloph smiled inwardly as he saw some of the random pieces closing in on his adversary. He focused on Eha while waiting for one of the cheetah's legs to fold up underneath him. He couldn't wait to administer a crushing blow to his lifelong enemy.

Lloph never saw the mammoth boulder flying in his direction. It hit him broadside with such velocity that his entire form exploded upon contact. The boulder, twelve feet across and four feet wide, atomized the destroyer as it passed through his body. If that weren't enough, the huge rock smashed against the wall abreast of him, shattering into a thousand pieces of razor-honed shrapnel. To all of the Champions except Eha, it looked as though Lloph had been eliminated.

The scattered pebbles began to stir. They swirled around in a tight circle, almost as if directed by a purposeful thought. The thick mass of debris spun around and around, waiting for something to give it purpose. When Lloph finally gathered himself together, it found its way to him quickly. The creature wore the shattered components of the boulder like a suit of armor. The pieces expanded and contracted as Lloph constructed his next attack. Placing a single sharp piece of stone inside each of his lightning-fast projectiles, the destroyer inhaled deeply. After a massive build-up of internal pressure, he exhaled with an explosion of force. Thousands of poisonous bullets knifed through the air in every direction, flying toward the Champions where they hid.

Hundreds of the tiny projectiles scattered randomly throughout the area, ricocheting harmlessly off nearby rocks or following an endless path toward the top of the chamber. An even more determined set seemed to track their way toward the cats and Conor. Lloph, now completely invisible after shedding his rocky cloak, coughed his grating laughter at his enemies. His work would soon be done, he felt, and after he destroyed the Champions of the Crossworlds his master would give him a place with the inner element of the Circle of Evil. He bent his ever-changing countenance into a hideous smile, grinning inwardly at the thought.

Surmitang flattened himself on the ground behind a massive stone shelf. He planned to wait there until the projectiles shattered harmlessly against the rocky shield. What he saw happening around him caused him to shift his strategy abruptly. He watched Therion assume the same stance as he, hiding behind a shelf of thick stones. At first glance, the cover appeared impenetrable. By all accounts, the projectiles should mindlessly slam into the stone wall while trying to get to Therion.

As Surmitang watched in horror, a far different outcome emerged. The shrapnel, needle sharp and thick enough to pierce the tough hides of the Champions, rode effortlessly within the glassine capsules. The sections of rock contained no organic elements at all, but the tiny bubbles of Lloph's form held every bit of the intelligence their master enjoyed. Instead of wasting their numbers mindlessly, the projectiles actually ceased their momentum upon finding an obstruction in their way. Like a swarm of hyper-intelligent wasps, they moved as a pack to and fro in front of the stone shelf sheltering Therion.

Surmitang gasped as he watched the huge mass of Lloph's servants poking around the rock surface, looking for any opening large enough to stream through and render the giant lion inert. He made his decision quickly, jumping out into the open and calling out to his attackers in a deafening roar that reverberated throughout the underground chamber.

Instantly, thousands of tiny projectiles turned their pointed tips in Surmitang's direction. They hesitated for just a moment, as if surprised by their good fortune, and then raced toward the huge tiger with geometric precision. None of the poisonous projectiles wasted a scintilla of space or energy in their drive to intercept their victim. Their course remained true every inch of the way. Therion, Conor, Purugama and Eha all watched in mute horror as the entire company of liquid bullets streamed toward their brother. Conor called out to the great Champion who had sacrificed his life once already during another journey, but his call fell to the floor unheeded, as lifeless as Surmitang would surely be in a matter of seconds. He looked into the great tiger's eyes as Surmitang watched the armada of projectiles closing in on him at breakneck speed.

When he heard the familiar roar of the Sumatran tiger echoing through the chamber of cells, Maya turned and faced the rear of his crystal prison. *The Champions have arrived*, he surmised, *and not a moment too soon.* He sensed urgency in the tiger's call, however, and he called forth the magic vision he previously used to find Janine. Sighting far away and down into the depths of the chamber, the Lord of the Champions strained his eyes to see what transpired. He spotted Surmitang, standing alone in a clearing while the rest of the Champions either hid themselves among shelves of rock or ran for their lives. Maya's fur flashed when he saw what fell from the sky toward the huge tiger. *Beautiful beast,* Maya thought, *sacrificing himself again for his brothers.* With all of your boasts about who might be worthy to stand with him as guardian of the Crossworlds, there he stood virtuously giving himself up for the safety of those same individuals. Maya shook his black and white head back and forth. *Not this time, brave tiger, we need you for the final assault, and the Lady of the Light would banish me to a forbidden corridor for all eternity if I allowed you to perish in this place.* For an instant, Maya flicked his thoughts to Ajur, whom he didn't sense near the others. Could the boorbain have advanced that fast? He shook the thought from his head and returned to Surmitang.

The Lord of the Champions sent a mental blast of energy straight into Surmitang's mind, ordering him to execute a maneuver immediately. If he obeyed his command, he would live. If he hesitated, he would fade away as nothing more than a furry inanimate object. Maya trusted Surmitang's instincts; tigers were always the quickest to act, especially when their lives depended on it.

The second mental message went to Janine's crystal cell. When she responded to his call, he told her that the time had come to fight for her freedom, for her love for Conor, and for the sake of the Crossworlds. He told her to prepare herself for anything that might happen, and be ready to join him when he called for her. Lastly, he told her that her long odyssey would soon be over, and that she and Conor would reunite soon.

After receiving her assurances, Maya broke concentration with both Janine and Surmitang. He trusted them to fulfill their part of the arrangement, and he had preparations to make. If they were to be successful in their final charge against Seefra, everything would have to come together perfectly. The Lord of the Champions crouched down and closed his eyes. Communing with the council of seven through a special psychic connection given to him recently by the Lord of all Life, Maya explained the nature of his plans to the great council.

Surmitang listened to Maya's command, executing his instructions without hesitation. He stood completely erect, forcing every strand of fur on his body to extend straight outward. In this stance, the quantity of individual black, white and gold filaments far outnumbered the approaching horde of projectiles. Even with seconds left to live, Surmitang relaxed visibly as he understood Maya's strategy. He felt his leader's magic coursing through his body, finding its way into each and every strand of fur. In a deadly and silent explosion, Surmitang's body convulsed in one mighty discharge, sending tens of thousands of tiny needles toward Lloph's weapons. The destroyer's bullets could not escape the rapidly approaching needles shooting out from Surmitang's fur. They intercepted every single projectile in Lloph's arsenal.

Instead of obliterating them, however, they merely inserted themselves through the gelatin sleeve and into the enclosed shrapnel. As this metamorphosis repeated itself, the projectiles merely halted their progress and hovered in mid-air. Frozen by Maya's magic, the deadly bullets waited until all of their members had been penetrated. One second after the last projectile had been brought to a standstill, the entire swarm changed direction and flew back toward their launch point. Mindlessly following their new orders, the horde sought out their new enemy, the destroyer Pikiwic Lloph, who awaited their return with gleeful anticipation.

As the swarm returned to him, Lloph assumed that the Champions had been destroyed. For the first time since he appeared on the scene, he allowed his true palette to show. As his coloring emerged around his misshapen body, the projectiles raced in, increasing their speed. Lloph held a momentary feeling of indecision as he saw the particles of his own form zooming toward him. The sense turned to utter horror as four massive cats and one human found their way into his peripheral vision. He tried to turn his form translucent again, but he might have shouted at them for all the good it would do. Thousands of projectiles slammed into his body simultaneously, injecting his own immobility serum along with a special elixir prepared by the Lord of the Champions. Lloph's eyes sunk into his form as he fell flat against the passageway. Nothing remained except the horizontal blob of a completely motionless destroyer. Some of the projectiles squiggled inside the lifeless form, looking for any part of Lloph in which they could implant their venom. Eventually they ceased moving, and Seefra had one less destroyer to call upon in the battle for the Crossworlds.

CHAPTER THIRTY-NINE

"Well, well," said the Lady of the Shadows, *"punctual as always."*

The twin sister to the Lady of the Light appeared from behind a large stand of thick ferns. Dressed for battle, she made herself visible to her sister, but did not advance toward her. Instead, she walked a wide circle around her, keeping her eyes glued to the Lady of the Light's every move. A twitch of a finger or a flicker of an eyelash would have caused her to attack. "Quite a fitting place for you to perish, don't you think? And I do appreciate your generosity. After destroying you, I can simply carve a hole in the ground next to your beloved father and bury you next to him. That was all you ever wanted, wasn't it, to be eternally close, as you were during our childhood together?"

The Lady of the Light held her position next to her father's gravestone. She had been leaning against the perfectly carved monolith for roughly thirty minutes, communing with her deceased father's memories when her sister interrupted her blessed dream. Now as she lifted her eyes and looked upon the entire scene, her lifelong journey took on a surreal quality. The landscape covering the immediate area glowed with a vibrant aura. Every tree, rock, bush and blade of grass had somehow come alive for her.

Her sister, her twin, exactly the same age as she, looked like a spoiled girl demanding to be allowed to play a little longer. Turned down by a father she felt never loved her, she pouted while pursing her lips and folding her arms petulantly. The Lady of the Light gasped; everything she saw appeared as though it belonged to another dimension.

She still clung to the gravestone with her right hand, the hand whose fingers controlled the magical powers of her ancestors. Her father, wherever he presently resided, was sending her the overwhelming power she would use to destroy her sister. The sensations became too much, ultimately overwhelming her. She began to cry vivid tears of joy and sorrow. She felt overjoyed by the contact with her father, whom she missed terribly, but she couldn't shake the deep pain of her task, to destroy the only sibling she ever had. She didn't even attempt to compose herself. Instead, she let the tears fall freely. She let her body convulse with heartfelt, fervent sobs.

"Crying won't help you, little baby," said the Lady of the Shadows, taunting her sister's passionate display. She watched her tears subside, and the twins locked eyes for the first time in centuries.

"Zelexa," said the Lady of the Light. "Go away from this place if you would live. If you choose to stay, you will be destroyed, I assure you. You cannot overcome the power of the Light. Please, if you ever held a sliver of love for me, leave now and spare us both more unhappiness."

"Come now, Athazia," responded the Lady of the Shadows. "We haven't come here to play, have we? The creators are finished. Seefra has deciphered the spell you placed on the fifth key. I am here to perform a service for the Circle of Evil. Let us be done with it so I can return and plan our ascension to the realm of the creators as the new rulers of the Crossworlds."

The Lady of the Light's vision cleared instantly. Athazia, creator and controller of light, rose and stood next to the grave of her father. She knew Zelexa had lied about Seefra. If the master of darkness had indeed broken her code, there would be no need for this altercation. The world they stood on would have heaved once and disappeared for all time.

Her sister acted foolishly, as always. It never entered her mind that Seefra had intentions of his own. The instant he collected the five keys he would attack the Circle of Evil and take everything for himself. He would destroy Zelexa without a second thought, along with anyone else who stood in his way. Athazia stepped away from her father's gravestone, his memory. She understood her duty to the Crossworlds, and she would fulfill her part of the journey, no matter how painful.

"Step forward then!" ordered Athazia. "I promise you, Zelexa, by my love for you I will shower you with all the might of the creators! Your destruction will be swift and merciful! You will receive everything your masters would never allow an enemy of theirs! Come forward, if you dare!"

Zelexa sprinted forward, and as she did she noticed a change overcoming her sister. Athazia didn't really alter form per se, but a milky cloak began dripping down from the crown of her head, wrapping itself around her. Silver in color, the symmetrical robe covered her from the fine strands of her glowing hair to the bottom of her sandals. At first it glistened, but after completing its metamorphosis the cloak assumed a constant coloration. It looked as though a defensive barrier had simply appeared out of thin air and shrouded her sister in an impenetrable cloak of protection.

Zelexa recognized the strategy and attacked quickly, hoping to destroy her sister before the cone could complete itself. Throwing her arms wildly about and shrieking chants from the depths of dark magic, the Lady of the Shadows summoned the forces of nature to annihilate the Lady of the Light. The land, sea and air responded immediately, lashing out at Athazia and her protective shield. The earth opened underneath her, swallowing the silvery cone completely. Closing again around her, the huge plates of solid ground rubbed together, emitting a sound unlike anything Zelexa had ever heard. It reminded her of bones being crushed by the great beasts of the old equinox armies, breaking and grinding and shattering into dust. The massive sections of the earth fell upon the Lady of the Light repeatedly, sometimes grinding back and forth, and sometimes slamming together like two immense anvils. The noise continued, deafening and sickening, as the ground chewed up what was left of the Athazia. Had it not been for the zeal of the ocean, Zelexa might have ordered the natural elements to cease their activities.

The sea reared up at the shoreline as if possessed. Wave upon huge wave crashed maniacally against the sandy barrier that sealed the dominion of the ocean. The sea wanted to please its mistress, and it wouldn't wait a moment longer for the land to finish its work. In one gigantic surge of tidal power, the sea brought forth most of its existence in a huge wave that had but one purpose.

Over a million tons of water collapsed onto the silver cone encasing the Lady of the Light. The cone exploded from its place underneath the ground, rocketing out of the crevasse in a death roll that might have devastated Athazia right then and there. The ocean chased the relatively small receptacle, landing directly on top of it as it tumbled to the ground again. This time it would not allow it to skip away so easily. The sea poured its contents onto the silver cone with such force it could do nothing but remain in place and accept its fate. Thousands and thousands of tons of seawater crashed down on the small receptacle, drowning it continuously in a torrent of waves. The silver cone must have been submerged for no less than twenty minutes. Finally the water abated, but still it continued its assault on the Lady. Huge waves slapped the silver cone from side to side, knocking it askew and slamming it against the rocky cliffs. Had the wind not entered the fray, the ocean itself might have ended the battle.

The wind around the silver cone kicked up in a ferocious display of speed and power. Before, the land or the sea separately assaulted the Lady's fortification. Now the land *and* the sea, along with punishing gale force winds, pushed the protective nature of the cone to its limit. Whole sections of stone shelves broke off from the mighty cliffs facing the seas. Colliding with the silver cone, the huge clumps of rocks seemed to crush the life from Athazia. Massive walls of water continually rose up to slap against the protective cone, sending the Lady tumbling head over heels again and again. The winds, as mighty as any in the Crossworlds, battered the cone relentlessly, sending it ricocheting off natural structures and careening out off control in every direction.

All through the tumultuous assault, the Lady of the Shadows shrieked with delight. Certainly Athazia must be seriously injured, if not destroyed outright. Every time nature lashed out at her sister, she squealed with pleasure like a two- year-old. Satisfied with their contribution to her demise, she commanded the forces of the natural world to retreat and allow the silver cone to come to rest on dry land. When she saw the cone emerge from the high waves and settle next to one of the fallen cliffs, she quieted herself while waiting for her sister to request terms.

The silver substance surrounding Athazia came alive again.

Sparkling as it had before; it unraveled like a birthday ribbon above the Lady's head. Layer by layer, the protective material sailed away from the Lady's body. In its place stood Athazia, supreme creator, Lady of the Light and commander of the Crossworlds Champions. She graciously bowed, smiling at her sister.

Upon seeing her twin unharmed, Zelexa growled and stomped her right foot on the ground. Removing one of the small batons attached to her thigh, she raised the enchanted staff high into the air. Shouting the horrible curses of the shadow world, she called forth another group of elements to do her bidding. With the final incantation, she summoned the darkness to take her sister from her for all time.

The world went completely dark. Neither sister could see the other. Zelexa continued to call forth all manner of strange combinations of light and darkness. She would leave nothing to chance; this time her sister must perish. As she continued speaking the demonic tongue of the dark magic, she felt an icy presence move through her body. Instead of going around the Lady of the Shadows, the entity merely penetrated her physical being, tasting her juices momentarily before reporting for service. Zelexa shivered uncontrollably, she had heard of the rancid practices of the Sordo Ral, but until this day, she had never called one forth. The sooner she sent it away to destroy her sister, the better. She turned in whatever direction she believed the Ral to be standing.

"My sister is here. Find her and annihilate her," ordered Zelexa.

Without answering, the Ral moved through the Lady of the Shadows once again, although this time quite a bit slower. Apparently it had found something it liked inside of Zelexa, and it wanted to savor it for another second. With an icy exhalation of breath, the Sordo Ral moved away from his mistress.

The Lady of the Light could see nothing. The darkness was so complete she felt afraid to take a step in any direction. Before she could panic, she took a few deep breaths and steadied herself. If she knew her sister, the darkness would serve as a cloak for something else. Zelexa lacked the courage to attack her alone, but if she controlled dark magic, then she could call a host of terrible entities to fight for her.

Athazia felt the skin of her arms ripple. Her delicate nostrils twitched slightly. The tone of her surroundings had changed subtly, she felt sure of it. She closed her eyes, stilling her heart and her breathing. Completely quiet, she listening for the approach of something she knew had entered the battle at her sister's request. The air around her suddenly chilled, growing vastly colder. She sensed an evil so terrible she could not even describe it. It seemed like something her father had described to her many centuries ago, something that existed even before the equinox war. Try as she might, however, Athazia could not identify it.

Her body began shaking with fear. She quieted her muscles and nerves. Just afterward, she felt an icy coldness gliding along the skin of her left forearm. It stopped at her elbow, and she felt the chill spread slightly, cupping her elbow in its hand. She felt another touch, this time on the back of her neck. The tiny hairs lining the skin down her spine stood straight up. The light touch felt so deeply frigid; nothing she had ever encountered gave her the same feeling of dread. She knew without thinking that if she moved a muscle or tried to escape, the thing that caressed her would enter her body and collapse its frosty spirit around her heart.

Sordo Ral! It had to be! The creatures of icy death, how could her sister be so foolish! Did she not know that when the Ral had finished his work he would turn against her and make her his slave? This is why you could never have entered the realm of the creators, Zelexa; you have no respect for the powers you wield. Athazia shook the thoughts from her mind, focusing again on the Ral's touch. If she could distract it for only a moment, it might give her the edge she needed.

"Sordo Ral," she whispered. "My sister acts rashly, as you do for obeying her summons. I am the Lady of the Light – a creator, a protector of the council of seven. If you believe you have the power to destroy me, then have your way and be done with it. If there is any doubt in your mind, however, then reenter the darkness from whence you came and leave the battle between my sister and me to the two of us."

No answer floated up to the Lady's ears from anywhere in the darkness. The icy fingertips fell away from the Lady's neck and elbow. She exhaled visibly, thinking that her adversary had decided against a confrontation. In the next second, however, she understood her miscalculation. The Ral fell against the rear half of her body, penetrating her skin from behind in a rush of frigid motion. The Lady stiffened in a momentary sensation of shock, and then fought back with all the power she could summon. She would not allow one of the Sordo Ral access to her vital organs.

A blast of light illuminated the darkness in every direction but from behind Athazia. The Sordo Ral inhaled every bit of light thrown at it, but at least an outline of the entity appeared. Closing her eyes, Athazia sent impossibly powerful bolts of energy through her back, shoulders, buttocks, and calves. The Ral held on at first, digging its icy claws into the Lady's entrails. Ultimately, however, the magic of the creators proved to be too much for it, and its form fell away from the Lady's being. Once freed from its embrace, Athazia immediately turned and bombarded the Ral with a wide variety of magical spells. In the end, she boxed the Ral inside a shell she found on the beach. With a blink of her eyes, she sent the object thousands of yards out into the ocean. After watching it splash down in deep water, she turned to her sister with a look of amazement in her eyes.

"A Sordo Ral?" she questioned. "First you attach an ancient parasite onto a cat that would harm no one, and now you call forth a Sordo Ral? Have you lost your mind?"

"I would call the Circle of Evil up from the depths of their hellish world if it resulted in your destruction," answered the evil sister. "Don't you see? First my father, and now you, the very bane of my existence! First I am denied access to the light, and then I must spend my entire life watching you receive accolades, increased status, and responsibility from the council of seven. Why you and not I? Who determined a thousand millennia ago that you would enjoy the pleasures of the light while I grovel in darkness?"

"The light was always yours to enjoy, Zelexa," said Athazia. "The creators welcomed you lovingly, as they did all children of the select families. You made the choice to turn away and follow another path."

"To Seefra's dungeons with the creators!" spat the Lady of the Shadows. "Yes, I was welcome in the realm, but only as a servant to my sister! How was it that you received the blessings of the creators' powers and I did not? I have paid a horrible price for that irony my entire life, and now you admonish me for trying to better myself? Tell me, Athazia, what it is like to sit on the throne of power and mock those beneath you?"

"I do not mock you," replied the Lady of the Light. She stood watching her sister break down in tears. Face in hands and shoulders convulsing, Zelexa finally let a lifetime of frustration flood through her fingers. Athazia listened as her sister called out in garbled sentences the pain she had carried with her for centuries. The Lady of the Light walked over to embrace her twin, holding her head softly against her shoulders as the tears continued to fall. She cooed to her, telling her there would always be a place in the light for her. She merely had to ask and it would be so. Athazia felt her sister relaxing in her arms, and she wondered if at long last the light had entered where only shadows existed for so long. Could it be that her sister would finally turn away from the darkness?

Zelexa's body continued to relax. Athazia gathered her up into her arms as best she could, but eventually it seemed there was little left to hold. Before she could do anything to stop it, her sister's form had drooped down into her lap. It finally collapsed all around her, locking her hands, arms and legs in an iron grip so powerful she could barely breathe let alone move. She cursed herself for her stupidity, for trusting her sister again. She wondered out loud whether it would be her final mistake.

"Imprudent creator," laughed Zelexa, "always hopeful that someone might listen to your drivel and change their ways? Your compassion is a wonderful quality, but this time it will be your undoing." Zelexa's voice came from everywhere. The grip around Athazia had been a ploy in the form of Zelexa's body, leaving the Lady of the Shadows to attack from wherever she liked. Before her sister could find a way out of her bonds, she would do precisely that. She appeared before her sister, laughing and mocking her. She raised both hands, directing two wands in front of her. "Goodbye Athazia. Say hello to our father when you meet him."

Darkness took the world prisoner again. The grip around Athazia tightened nearly to suffocation level. The ground reached up, taking Athazia's feet in a bowl of solid granite, and then the power of dark magic rushed forward. Athazia's body fell under an internal and external attack both physical and magical. She endured each blow, each attempt to rip some part of her away from the rest of her body.

An aural assault occurred simultaneously. Hideous noises from the depths of the forbidden corridors assaulted her ears at unspeakable volumes. The Lady screamed intensely, matching the volume of the assault as the pain coursed freely through her body. The darkness overwhelmed her, rushing into her psyche and throwing her into a dungeon without light. She kept her eyes open even though she saw nothing, thinking all the while of Conor in the cell of shadows. For nearly two years, her Champion endured darkness such as this, and she would honor him by doing the same. Then the darkness shifted, and instead of a sensual darkness, it became a mental prison.

The Lady suffered hopelessness the likes of which she didn't even know existed. She wept and wailed and called out for salvation from the light. Nothing happened. No light entered her mind; the darkness endured without interruption. The assault lasted almost an hour, and during every second of agonizing pain, whether crying out or grimacing, the Lady of the Light stared at her sister, unblinking.

When it finally ended, the ground split apart, freeing her feet. The grip loosened and fell to the ground, no longer a threat to her. She stepped forward, staring at her sister the entire time. She said nothing, for no further conversation was necessary. She merely looked at her sister and uttered three simple words.

"Forgive me, father."

The Lady of the Shadows cried out over the injustice she saw before her. They promised that if she followed their plan, her sister would not last the day. They failed her, as surely as her father had failed her those many years ago. Worst of all, she failed herself, and now she would pay with her life.

Athazia stood completely motionless and closed her eyes. She focused on the council chamber, the realm, the Champions, Conor, and most of all, her father. Soon she reached a level of concentration that blotted out all external input. She could taste nothing, smell nothing, hear nothing, nor see or feel anything. She merely existed, and in this reality she did not have to witness the horrible destruction of the only sister she would ever know. She did not hear the shrieking wails of a woman terrified beyond words. She did not see a human form ripped apart and slammed together again so many times it resembled less of a person and more of a mutated abomination. She did not smell the fear her sister radiated as the creators remade her into whatever type of horrible beast they imagined would be a fitting punishment for her misdeeds. The Lady of the Light did not touch what remained of her sister, preferring to remember her as she was when they played as little girls in the realm. She instead chose to fade from view, to leave her sister without tasting her wickedness one last time. As the light took her back to the chamber of cells, she lowered her spiritual eyes; repeating her act of contrition.

"Forgive me, father."

CHAPTER FORTY

"Janine! Get ready. When you see the signal, come to me immediately!" The Lord of the Champions sent out an urgent call for Conor's companion to follow his instructions to the letter. At the same time, he communicated his urgency to Surmitang. After the destruction of Pikiwic Lloph, another message entered the huge tiger's mind, directing him to bring the Champions forward for the final assault. He would know the strategy, Maya assured him, in a very short time.

Maya looked out across the vast expanse of the chamber of cells. Some of the prisoners lay sleeping, but most stood completely alert, aware that some momentous event was about to occur. As a group, they stared straight ahead at the passageway leading to Seefra's laboratory. They looked hungrily at the two remaining shadow warriors, who stood guard without knowing that the rest of their kind had been obliterated by an army of Ezuvex warriors. The prisoners stared hungrily at their freedom, although they couldn't know it was at hand just yet. Even though, something in their minds told them that a life-altering presence stood in a crystal cell close by.

Maya looked at Janine again. Conor's companion appeared ready for whatever lay ahead of her. She looked around constantly, eyes flicking from wall to wall, always seeking a sign. *She had been here long enough*, Maya thought. *She would fight to escape Seefra even if she met her end.* Everything was ready and the preparations had been meticulously attended to. All Maya had to do was set things in motion. The Lord of the Champions blinked once while closing his eyes softly. He communed with the council of seven once again, informing them of their progress. He asked for their wisdom, placing himself at their disposal in the battle against the master of darkness.

Seefra remained calm, understanding precisely what was occurring all around him. His forces had been all but destroyed. His vast army of slayers and keepers had been eliminated. The *Fingers of the Forest* had decimated his own twisted flora, but not before one of the Champions had been poisoned by the boorbain virus. His shadow warriors had fallen to the Ezuvex warriors, and the Champions had beaten every one of his prized destroyers. Now, they stood poised to swarm the chamber of cells. The master of darkness cursed the creators and their servants.

Their achievements held no importance to him, however. Only the fifth key mattered. He felt certain he had solved the creators' spell. He had tested and retested his final formula, forgetting every other concern.

The master of darkness paused to consider his ancient adversary. Seefra had battled Ajur many times, long before Drazian had ever ascended to leadership of the shadow forces. He held a momentary thought, wishing that the boorbain tree had polluted another one of the Champions. He rather liked Ajur, out of respect, if nothing else. The jaguar was a plain and simple being, much like Seefra himself. He knew his task, he didn't complain about it, and he worked to the best of his ability to complete it. He didn't possess the jocularity of Eha, the destructive pride of Surmitang, or the simmering anger of Therion. He was similar to Purugama, the great cougar who destroyed Drazian. *Yes,* Seefra thought, *I will regret Ajur's passing.*

The master of darkness returned to his work. Lifting the potion he felt would penetrate the spell of the fifth key he summoned his last two warriors. When they entered, he commanded them to bring the keeper of the keys to his laboratory. He hissed as they waited for further instructions, prompting the two guards to hurry from the room. They raced into the chamber of cells, eager to complete their master's bidding. As they rounded the final corner that opened to reveal the vast cavern, they chanted the short phrases that would restore Janine's cell and pull it toward the passageway.

They heard nothing coming from the chamber, so they fluttered their wings and hurried along the last stretch of the dark, rocky path. Repeating the magical incantation over and over again, the two shadow warriors panicked when they didn't hear the cell of crystals moving toward the tunnel. They entertained two passing thoughts as they raced to the lip of the opening. If the scenario played out as they feared, and the earthling had escaped, they could either report back to their master or just keep going and hope for the best. Seefra would destroy them if they took the first course. If they followed the second, he would eventually find and torture them for all eternity. Swallowing quickly, the two warriors crested the path.

Maya felt the awesome magic of the creators surging through his body. Even with his eyes closed, he knew precisely what would occur. He stood perfectly still, providing a conduit for the creators' power.

He listened as the chamber of cells altered its form. First, the individual cells sealed every opening in their walls, floors and ceilings. Every gap in the construction of the crystal tiles merged together, creating a seamless cage for the first time since most of the prisoners arrived. Then the cells began to fuse together until they finally collapsed into one singular grid of crystal cubes. Following this, the sides and ceilings of each cell reshaped themselves, creating a flat crystal floor extending all the way to the tunnels leading to Seefra's laboratory. Reaching out to all sides of the chamber, the floor formed a solid base for all of the captives. Within minutes, what once served as a gigantic conglomeration of horribly demoralizing cells transformed into a pathway to freedom. Nearly a thousand prisoners from every race in the Crossworlds suddenly ran headlong toward the passageway and the two shadow warriors who guarded it. Seeing the mass of creatures and hearing their determined cries of freedom, the two guards opted for their second option and ran for their lives.

Surmitang cautioned the others, reassuring them that his communication had been authentic. The other Champions, especially Therion, had argued against waiting for any kind of signal. The giant lion had also pointed out that the mental transmission could easily have originated from Seefra's laboratory, a trick composed by the master of darkness to keep them here and away from the battle raging above them.

"It *was* Maya," said Surmitang. "I know our leader's voice better than I know my own."

"How can you be so certain?" asked Therion again. "The master of darkness fooled all of us in the chamber of caverns, and that was a physical manifestation. Here we are simply talking about voice transference."

"Look!" shouted Conor, pointing toward the chamber of cells.

Surmitang opened his mouth to respond but instead let his jaw fall against the tendons in his face. The entire architecture of the cell area had shifted radically, and now a crystal walkway reached out to them from the main chamber. Like a gigantic, rigid tongue spilling down in their direction, a pathway leading directly to Maya landed softly at their feet. The Champions looked at each other, perplexed for a moment, and then with smiles all around, they trotted onto the path.

Eha led the way, back to his old self and laughing merrily as he stepped onto the crystal walkway. Therion and Surmitang followed the happy cheetah down the path, their eyes constantly darting back and forth, always looking for any sign of trouble. Purugama soared ahead, carrying Conor toward a long-awaited reunion with his companion. Staying slightly ahead of the other three Champions, Conor and Purugama trained their eyes on every inch of the massive chamber of cells. If any more destroyers cared to reveal themselves, then Conor and his mentor would surely detect them before any harm could be done. As they watched their three brothers crest the hill and approach the chamber, Purugama dipped a wing and descended down to their level. Conor and Purugama led the way, and the rest of the Champions followed them into the master of darkness' torture chamber.

CHAPTER FORTY-ONE

Before her cell barely finished its transfiguration, Janine jumped past one of the receding walls and hit the ground running. In a sea of confused and excited faces, she looked frantically for Maya. Bumping into countless creatures and excusing herself along the way, she finally caught a glimpse of the huge black and white cat. He sat serenely amidst a cavern of disharmony, knowing that his plans would come to fruition. Janine dodged a few more creatures and ran headlong toward Maya. The Lord of the Champions turned his furry head slowly at the sound of her advance.

Maya began to stand but found his movements a little tardy. Conor's companion jumped at him, hitting him square in the flank while wrapping her arms around him. She buried her face in his fur, crying tears of joy at the sensation of her finally meeting him face to face. She pulled away finally, and Maya could do nothing but smile lovingly at the girl. *Conor had selected his companion very wisely*, he thought.

"Conor! Where is Conor?" she shouted above the din. "Is he here? Can I see him? Where are the other cats? Oh thank you, Maya, thank you for leading them here!"

Maya continued smiling. Then in answer to her question, he simply turned his head and looked far across the crystal floor.

Janine followed his line of vision until she saw a powerful winged cougar carrying a human male on its shoulders. She instinctively began running to him, but Maya placed a large forepaw in her way.

"Patience, Janine," he said. "Better to keep you safe here and let him come to you. He will be here in seconds, I assure you."

Maya's caution prompted Janine to hesitate, although impatiently. After nearly two years of wondering whether Conor had even survived, now she would finally be reunited with him again. Holding on to Maya's soft fur, she watched attentively as the great cougar soared across the crystal floor toward her. She recognized Conor now, although he did look vastly different. He had grown quite a bit, and filled out as well. His face had changed also; he looked more like a man than a boy. He wore a strange outfit, something matching the leather saddle attached to the big cougar. He looked perfectly at home atop the giant beast, as if he had been doing this his entire life.

She saw him smile when he finally caught sight of her. The huge cougar folded his wings, dipping his huge body toward the crystal floor. Just before they trotted up to join her and Maya, Janine saw an equally massive cheetah, lion and tiger running across the crystal expanse to join them as well. She almost fainted from all the sensations she felt, but the drive to hold Conor in her arms overpowered everything else. She watched him hop down from the cougar's shoulder and land softly on the ground. He ran toward her, mouthing her name and smiling warmly. She watched him extend his arms to her, and in the next second, she felt the one feeling she cherished above all others – Conor's strong arms squeezing her tightly as he said her name over and over again.

The five Champions sat still and quiet, uncomfortably deferring to Conor and Janine's reunion. The human manner of loving com-munication always puzzled the feline race, and this display affect-ed them no differently. They listened as the two humans cooed to each other, whispering their undying love and everlasting commit-ment. After a few moments, Maya stepped forward.

"Conor, the last phase of our journey is at hand. We must lead the prisoners into the tunnel. They will provide the force necessary to assault Seefra's laboratory. They ramble about enjoying their freedom, but we must provide direction for them immediately."

"Stay with me," Conor requested of Janine. "Don't ever leave my side again."

"Always, Conor," she said, her arms locked around his waist. "I won't lose you again." Janine suddenly remembered something of importance. "Maya, the five keys. Seefra has control of the first four. They are in his laboratory."

"And the fifth key?" asked the Lord of the Champions nervously.

"Here, in my jacket pocket," said Janine. "But I fear he may have solved its riddle. We cannot allow him to take control of it. Will you take charge of the key, for safe keeping?"

"I cannot hold it," responded Maya. "None of us can so much as touch it. You will need to serve the Lady of the Light a little longer, I'm afraid."

Janine raised her chin a hitch; looking proudly like the young woman she was – very capable and extremely determined.

"Good girl," said Maya. He turned to the other Champions. "You must assemble yourselves in such a way that the prisoners will recognize and follow you. Each of you post yourselves against a different wall and take positions that will allow you to herd the prisoners toward the passageway leading to Seefra's laboratory. Do not spread so thinly that you cannot maintain eye contact with each other. Purugama, take Conor and Janine to the passageway entrance. I will meet you there and together we will lead the horde against the dark master. Now go! For all we know he may have already deciphered the spell to release the fifth key!"

The Champions flared out across the great crystal expanse. Therion, Surmitang and Eha ran to their positions and began reassuring the panicked prisoners. They explained Maya's plans as best they could, hoping to form up the mass of creatures into some semblance of a fighting force. Conor lifted Janine up onto Purugama's back and then hoisted himself up next to her. As he settled in behind her, he gave the okay to the big cat and put the strap into Janine's hand. He felt his girlfriend's body stiffen as the great cougar flapped his mighty wings, lifting the three of them up off the ground. He looked at her hands as they gripped the strap powerfully and remembered his first few flights aboard the gigantic cougar. He smiled and placed one hand on the strap and the other around Janine's waist.

Maya hustled through the mindless mass of newly freed prisoners. He hoped his three Champions could create at least an organized mob out of the hundreds of creatures mulling about on the crystal floor. That was their task now, however, and he had his own to perform. He had to arrive at the entrance to the passageway before Conor and Janine, so he kept Purugama and his two passengers in sight the whole way. He dodged as many of the roaming creatures as he could, at times leaping over them completely. In a few cases he bowled some of them over. He felt poorly about those interactions, but after seeing the unfortunate recipient rise and walk again, his mind returned to his primary task. Looking ahead, he saw the passageway only a hundred yards ahead. He noticed Purugama and his two passengers gliding down toward the entrance. Dodging a few more frantic creatures, Maya sprinted over to meet them.

The crystal floor suddenly buckled violently, shaking nearly everyone off his or her feet. It settled for a moment and then the chamber of cells rocked on its foundations again. The mammoth walls encircling the chamber began shedding their cloaks, dribbling runaway streams of boulders and soil down toward the entrance to Seefra's laboratory. The ground heaved again, shaking the crystal floor violently. Creatures of all kinds shrieked in panicked terror at the prospect of the floor giving way. Only one thing terrified them more than eternal imprisonment or perhaps death. None of them wanted to find out what kind of hideous monster lurked at the base of the chamber. They had all heard it many times before, and they had also heard the terrible screams of its victims rising up from the mists. As a possible solution to the floor falling away, many of the former prisoners ran to the perimeter, clutching at the rocks on the side of the chamber. If they could find purchase and hold on, perhaps they might delay their end a little longer.

Maya tried desperately to steady himself. He craned his neck as far as it would go, seeking any sign of the other Champions. All hope for a semi-organized advance into the passageway had been lost, he felt certain of that. He caught a glimpse of Therion, standing tall above the horde of creatures. The giant lion was doing his best to calm the creatures around him. His attempts fell on deaf ears as the crowd ran about, hysterically looking for a way to assure their safety.

At least Purugama would remain safe, thought the Lord of the Champions. As soon as he entertained the thought, however, he heard the angry growl of a cougar under attack. Eyes quickly darting into the sky, Maya scanned the chamber for his two Champions and Janine. He saw something only he would believe possible. Purugama fought valiantly against an invisible foe, an opponent that wanted to pull the great cougar out of the sky. *Perhaps it was the destroyer from the magical forest*, thought Maya, *or another of Seefra's minions.* Who it might be was not important, however. The fact that Purugama's wings could no longer save him was. The powerful Champion fought with every muscle in his body, but he could not reverse the course set by whatever wrestled against him. As they approached the passageway, the force pulling Purugama to the ground shifted tactics, turning the great cougar on its back. The maneuver occurred so quickly that Conor and Janine had no time to react. Both of them fell from the cougar's back, down toward the entrance to the laboratory.

As they smacked down onto the ground, a devastating earthquake rumbled through the chamber. It tore the crystal floor from its foundations, sending Maya, Therion, Eha and Surmitang flying like dolls in various directions. The chamber walls erupted in a shower of boulders and debris, and the passageway to Seefra's laboratory was buried under a thousand tons of immovable rock and stone. Janine barely managed to lead Conor into the tunnel before they were sealed inside under the cloak of total darkness.

Maya called out to the other Champions. He watched as close to one hundred of the creatures fell to their deaths in the mists below them. He tried to save as many as he could, but their fear and panic sealed their fate. His main focus now lay in finding and securing the other cats. He would not lose even one of them to Seefra's treachery.

"Maya! Here!" shouted Eha as he bounded up join his Lord. "Therion stands fast against the far wall. He has almost three dozen of the creatures in his grasp, but I fear he will not be able to hold them. I have not seen or heard any sign of Surmitang, but I believe he survived. He would not come this far to consider failure."

"Come then," said Maya. "Lead me to Therion!"

Eha dashed away an instant after Maya completed his request. The cheetah almost left Maya behind with his great speed, but soon he slowed and Maya caught up to him.

Therion stood clamped against the side of the chamber, one giant paw holding his huge body against the wall. With every other appendage, he held as many of the creatures as he could. They hung from his mouth, and from his remaining three paws. A dozen at least hung tenaciously from his huge tail. The giant lion did his best to shout instructions to the panicked crowd, but his efforts fell on deaf ears. Even though the earthquakes had ceased, the creatures simply would not release their benefactor so easily.

Eha and Maya coaxed the creatures from their feline perches. Placing them in various alcoves along the wall of the chamber, they convinced them to stay together for safety. After all of them had been pried away from Therion's huge bulk, the giant lion gingerly placed a paw on the crystal surface.

"It appears to be strong enough to support us, for now," stated Maya. The Lord of the Champions watched as Therion placed all four paws on the clear floor. After testing its strength and stability, he visibly relaxed while letting the tension flow out of his huge frame.

"We must locate Surmitang," said Therion. "I saw him sailing across the expanse in that direction." The big cat pointed with a golden paw, while Eha and Maya followed with their eyes. "We must find him and reunite with Conor and his companion. We might have a chance to save these creatures after all."

"Conor and Janine must follow their own path now," said Maya.

"They are sealed inside of Seefra's laboratory, and none of us will be able to join them. Even with the magic of the creators, it would take far longer than we have to move that much debris. Let us find Surmitang and see what help we can provide for Purugama. I fear he may be injured as well."

"Mind of the creators!" chuffed Therion. "Must we have everything working against us? First Ajur, then this accursed chamber, and now possibly Surmitang and Purugama, not to mention Conor? The creators will have much to answer for when this journey is completed."

"The creators assist us in ways we cannot comprehend," answered Maya. "But that is a discussion for another day."

"Maya! Therion! Over here!" shouted Eha. "I've found Surmitang. He's alive!"

The two Champions hustled over to Eha. Both of them scanned the face of the wall behind the cheetah, searching for their brother. Just as they were about to inquire about his whereabouts, the proud tiger spoke up from his perch below them.

"If you three would be so kind," snarled Surmitang, "I'm not quite sure how much longer I can maintain my hold on this slick crystal slab."

Maya and Therion looked down simultaneously. What they saw almost forced a laugh from their bellies. Surmitang, the three thousand pound Lord of the Indonesian rainforests, hung precariously by one paw from the edge of the crystal floor. His hind legs hung freely, curled up underneath him for balance. He looked like a kitten desperately hanging from a tree branch, all except for his expression, which showed his tremendous embarrassment at being seen in such a predicament. Therion, the only one capable of lifting the great tiger, leaned forward and stepped directly on

Surmitang's paw. Bracing that appendage and making sure the big tiger would not fall, Therion reached over the side with his huge mouth and grabbed the scruff of Surmitang's neck. With a mighty heave, he pulled the tiger up and over the side of the crystal floor. He plopped Surmitang down on the ground next to Maya and Eha, Therion's grip leaving him a pair of sodden shoulders.

Surmitang stretched and shrugged his great bulk. "Well, what are the three of you staring at? Let's go find Purugama and see to his needs."

"You're welcome," chuffed Therion.

Surmitang looked back at the giant lion. Nodding his handsome head once, he looked ahead as he followed Maya. The four Champions ran in unison toward the sealed passageway, looking for any sign of their brother. When they arrived at the endless pile of debris, they found a horde of previously captive creatures removing as much of the rock and stone as they could. They worked frantically, using both magic and brute force. They turned as the Champions approached. Without breaking away from their work, they called on the Champions to help them. They must clear a path, even if only to provide oxygen, they shouted. They could not allow Conor and his companion to perish so close to their goal.

"Save your strength, brave ones," said Maya. "If we were a thousand strong we could not move that much rock and stone in a month's time. Conor and Janine must find their own path. We need to determine the best course for ourselves."

Slowly the creatures ceased their manic scramble. They knew Maya spoke the truth, but they felt terrible giving up so easily. The tales of Conor of Earth were legend, and to see him buried under so much rubble unnerved them greatly. On top of that, they didn't even know whether Conor and Janine were even alive at this moment. They would not give up hope, however, they told Maya as much. They encouraged the Lord of the Champions to press on while they continued their attack on the wall of rubble.

Janine held Conor by his shoulders, letting his head rest in her lap. Terribly frightened by what she saw, she did what she thought might help him until she could think straight.

The two of them had barely made it into the tunnel. The deafening crash of so much debris nearly destroyed their hearing; it certainly limited their ability to communicate. The earthquake that caused the downpour of boulders gave them precious little steady ground on which to run. As they scrambled down the passageway, Conor had been hit square in the head by a dense rock about as big around as a car tire. He collapsed immediately at Janine's feet, and she applauded her earlier decision to eat heartily and exercise while in captivity. Had she not been in superb shape, she might not have been able to drag him through the tunnel the rest of the way.

Raising his hands to his head, Conor groaned weakly. Janine cooed to him while gently pressing his arms back down to his sides. She touched his swollen skull, wincing quietly at the size of the lump on the back of his head.

"Stay still, Conor," she said, lifting a lock of hair away from his eyes. "You've taken a nasty whack on the head. You probably have a concussion. In any case, we'd better wait here for a little while before continuing onward."

"It's dark," murmured Conor. "Why is it so dark in here?"

"We're sealed in," she answered. "The earthquakes out in the chamber grew so violent that the walls caved in all around us.

Something attacked Purugama and tore us right off his shoulders. As soon as we hit the ground, one of the mountains came down on top of us. I don't want to diminish the powers of the creators, but it looks like we're all alone in here. We're separated from the Champions by an entire mountain of rock."

"Then it's up to us," stammered Conor as he rolled up into a sitting position. He grabbed his head tightly, groaning with the intensity of the pain. Then, placing his hand on Janine's shoulder, he stood and steadied himself. "We must find Seefra's laboratory as quickly as we can. Do you think you can locate it in this darkness?"

Janine laughed as she placed a strong arm around Conor's waist. "I know the way better than anyone except the two guards that accompanied me there. I could walk it in my sleep. Before we set out, though, are you sure you feel up to confronting Seefra?"

"For all I know the Champions' lives might depend on what we do next, and how quickly we do it. I'm certain Seefra caused the earthquakes in the chamber, and it was he who sent the destroyer to confront Purugama and separate us from the pack. Unless we stop him he might just send the entire chamber down to the mists and who knows what awaits them there."

Janine held a moment's thought about the creature at the bottom of the chamber. Without explaining anything to Conor about the terrible screaming she'd heard over the last two years, she grabbed his hand and began running down the passageway. Even in the inky blackness of the tunnel, she knew her way perfectly. In a matter of minutes, she and Conor raced around one final corner and saw streaks of light coming from an interior structure. Janine grabbed Conor by his leather vest, pulling him up against the wall. She motioned with her eyes and her expression toward the light.

Conor knew instantly what she meant, so he voluntarily flattened himself up against the wall. The two of them stood silently, backs against the rocky surface, steadying their breathing and staring toward the entrance to Seefra's laboratory.

A familiar voice drifted down from the ceiling of the passageway. "And now, my dear," hissed the master of darkness, "the fifth key, if you please."

Maya and the Champions found Purugama crumpled against what remained of the stone wall surrounding the chamber. The great cougar looked completely lifeless, his powerful legs splayed out beneath his huge bulk, which lay on the rocks like a child's toy tossed away in the midst of a tantrum. His massive wings, the hallmark of Purugama's strength and power, looked weak and useless. One lay folded into itself underneath his heavy flank. The other, flared out as if in flight, covered the exposed side of the cougar's golden face. Purugama's stomach barely moved at all, a signal that the big cat had sustained severe injuries.

About fifty feet away from Purugama lay the remains of the invisible creature from the forest. Arms of every size and shape lay scattered all around the demolished torso of the beast, obviously ripped away by Purugama during the confrontation. Signs of magic existed all around the creature as well, both offensive and defensive in their nature. Huge sections of the stone wall were fused together, most likely the recipients of one of Purugama's attacks. The destroyer had been very tenacious, but in the end the great cougar outwitted the strange creature. The battle had been ferocious, with terrible injuries received by both participants. The Champions would have one less destroyer to deal with now, and that was worth almost any price. But to lose Purugama, however, was a price too great to pay for any reward.

The huge cat groaned weakly. The wing draped across his face fluttered slightly. Purugama's left foot twitched a few times and then stretched noticeably. It was a purposeful act, as if he was testing his limits, and the other four Champions breathed easier because of it.

"Conor," said the cougar with great effort. "What has become of Conor and Janine?" Lifting his great bulk from the rocky surface, he turned his head and faced Maya. "Tell me, my Lord, is Conor alive?"

Maya blinked once but did not hesitate to deliver the news. "After falling from your shoulders, Conor and Janine were buried under an avalanche of rock and stone. We know they were inside the passageway to Seefra's laboratory, but I cannot say for certain that they found protection in the tunnels. They may have escaped the rush of debris, but then again, the mountain might have moved too fast for them."

Purugama lowered his head, grimacing at the thought of his personal failure. Conor trusted him and he had let him down. His blunder may have cost him his life. He squeezed his eyes shut, trying desperately to remove the possibility that Conor may be gone. In his tremendous grief, he forgot all about his own pain, the other Champions, and their quest. His love for Conor overwhelmed him; it took him back to the very first moment he saw him on the mesa, and to every journey they had taken together since. He would not believe that he and Conor had come all this way only to see an end such as this. Maya's voice jarred him away from his reverie.

"Purugama," said the Lord of the Champions. "We do not yet know Conor's fate. It is entirely possible that he and Janine escaped the brunt of the avalanche. We must not assume the worst. The five of us still have work to do here in the chamber. Many lives depend on us. The Lady of the Light might call for our services at any moment. You have served the creators remarkably well, just as Conor has done. Do not allow your grief to overcome you; your young friend would not be honored by such an attitude. Rise and join us in our final act in this wretched place. If you cannot, we will carry you, for without your presence, our group is incomplete."

Purugama scraped his paws against the rough stone on the wall of the chamber. Pressing his huge body away from the rocks, he removed his right wing from underneath him. Now with both wings free, he flexed and stretched his giant appendages, certifying that they still functioned well. Finally, the great cougar struggled to rise and join his companions. Therion, seeing the tremendous effort his brother exerted, moved to help him right himself. Maya stopped him with a glance, however, preferring to let the big cat recover on his own. Purugama stood on all fours, glowing in his golden glory. He looked at his brothers with a mix of sadness and purpose.

"Let us away, then," said the great cougar with great haste. "After all, are we not in service to the creators?"

Conor and Janine froze, their breath catching in their throats. A hundred thoughts pounded into their minds – *run away, respond, go forward into the laboratory, stay where they are* – they couldn't decide what to do, and the voice that echoed around them filled their minds with horrible memories of painful suffering and dreadful fear.

"Conor of Earth!" bellowed Seefra. "Bring me the keeper of the keys, and I will let you live long enough to perish in her arms!

I shall show you no more patience! Bring me the fifth key, or I will destroy you and your precious Champions once and for all."

The cloud of thoughts suddenly cleared in Conor's mind. *Seefra had to be overcome, even if it meant their lives.* That was the meaning of their journey, the reason why he had met Purugama so long ago. Everything hinged on this moment in time, and he and Janine were to be the instruments of Seefra's destruction. He turned to her, whispering in her ear for a moment, and then grabbed her hand and started for the entrance. He called out to Seefra as they approached, taunting the master of darkness with the one sacred object he could not do without.

"Seefra!" yelled Conor. "You do not frighten us, for we have what you desire most. We have that which you will never hold in your slimy little excuse of a hand! The fifth key will forever remain beyond your reach, and your masters will punish you for all eternity for being too weak to acquire it." Conor continued to hurl insults into the lighted area from where he and Janine stood at the entrance of the laboratory. As he took a breath in preparation for more taunting, Janine quieted him with a simple comment.

"He isn't here," she said with a trembling voice.

Conor placed a protective arm in front of her as he crept into the laboratory. It did appear to be empty, but he trusted neither the surroundings nor his enemy. For all he knew, Seefra could be hiding in any of a hundred different forms in this room, just waiting to pounce on them. The young Champion threw out a few blasts of the Lady's mystical energy. These were intended to disrupt the static order of the laboratory, exposing anything existing in a different molecular composition from its original form. Seeing nothing out of the ordinary, Conor lowered his arm and allowed Janine to enter the laboratory with him.

Without any hesitation at all, Conor began ripping draw-
ers away from their housings and throwing aside large cupboard
doors. He didn't even look at Janine, but he knew she followed his
example perfectly. The two of them tore the laboratory to shreds
trying to find the first four keys. Tossing aside anything that didn't
resemble the beautiful coloration of the creators' handiwork,
Conor and Janine grew more frantic as each second passed.

"They have to be here," said Janine, flustered. "Every time he
summoned me here, he showed me the keys he had already mas-
tered. It was his way of taunting me into believing that one day in
the future he would have all five of the keys under his command. I
always saw him place the keys back into one container or another
after one of our sessions together. There isn't any other place for
him to store such valuable items."

"Keep looking then. If they're here in this laboratory, then it's
only a matter of time before we find them."

"You will not find them here, Conor," said a strangely familiar
voice.

Conor whipped his head around and stared at the door of the
laboratory. What he saw there defied all logic, but then again, the
Champions had surprised him before. "*Ajur!*" he said with a note
of shock evident in the timber of his voice. "How did you find your
way here?"

The huge jaguar stepped into the laboratory, nursing a noticeable limp. He shifted his eyes quickly over to Janine before placing
them on Conor again. "I am Seefra's oldest adversary," said Ajur.
"I know everything about him, his ways, his tendencies, and his
habits. Once the crystal bridge extended across the chamber floor
to pick up the rest of you, I knew I'd be able to find the master of
darkness myself."

Ajur took a few more crippled steps into the room. "With a strategy kept within my own counsel, I followed the Champions onto the crystal platform, at a discrete distance of course. When the earth began to shake, I took a side path around the confusion and found a separate passageway to this laboratory."

Ajur swept his big, black tail around the room, measuring its length compared to the area of the laboratory. Checking its progress with a flicker or two of his eyes, he continued addressing Conor. "I do not know where Seefra is at this moment, but I am certain of his absence. I am also certain he took the four keys with him. At this stage of the battle, I doubt he'd be without them for an instant. Perhaps the three of us can find him together. I admit that my present condition precludes me from offering much protection, but I will do my best, as I always have."

Ajur's eyes bounced over to Janine. "I see you have been reunited with your companion, Conor. I am pleased, and if I may be so honored, might I meet the keeper of the keys face to face?"

"Of course," said Conor. "Allow me to…"

"Don't move any closer to him, Conor," called an urgent voice from the other side of the laboratory. "The jaguar you see is only a cloak covering the master of darkness. If you don't believe me, then look behind you."

Conor and Janine stiffened and turned their heads to a sight that took their breath away. On the other side of the laboratory, a duplicate Ajur emerged from behind a large stack of reagents and other shelved materials. This Ajur looked far worse than the one they met at the door. He could barely walk, his eyes were coated with a milky residue, and the wound on his side had mutated into a horrible assemblage of inflamed skin, exposed bone and twisted muscle. Nevertheless, the second Ajur moved across the room and stood next to Conor and Janine, maintaining a guardian position.

"Fools!" shouted the first jaguar. "Do you place your trust so easily? How can you be certain of either of our identities? The imposter standing next to you could strike you down any second!"

"But he won't," replied Conor. "A Champion knows his brother at a glance. That's why I knew you to be the imposter as soon as you entered the laboratory. Now give us the four keys and grant us our leave. You have one chance, Seefra. One more than you ever gave anyone else."

"Listen well, Conor of Earth," hissed the master of darkness through Ajur's lips. "I have four of the five keys of the creators. The fifth key would be a coup, that is true, but I can exist just as well without it. You see, my puny Champion, I have one thing you do not possess, and that is time. I will live another thousand of your lifetimes, and I can always find a way to extract the fifth key during all of those eons. You, however, have only your short lifespan left to you. After you and the keeper of the keys have passed on, I will find where the creators have hidden the fifth key, and I will have it. I assure you.

"So you see, my dear," Seefra said while turning the dark feline gaze to Janine, "I could wait until you perish from natural causes, or just accelerate the process myself."

"Seefra!" snarled an injured but determined Ajur. "Leave these two alone. Your battle has always been with the creators and their servants. Let Conor and his companion return to earth where they belong."

"Never!" replied Ajur's double. "Conor of Earth has served the creators for years, therefore cementing his role as an enemy of the Circle of Evil! He has single-handedly destroyed some of my finest warriors, and despite all my efforts, he stands before me now!"

"Seefra," coaxed Ajur. "You cannot win this battle. The rest of the Champions await you outside in the chamber. The Lady of the Light will return at any moment. You will not leave this laboratory with the fifth key; I swear it on my centuries-long association with the creators. Let these two depart in peace, and I will face you alone; one final combat to decide the outcome of our lengthy history."

"You!" scoffed the master of darkness, dropping the disguise and standing strong on a previously crippled hind leg. "You are but a shadow of your former self, and a beast afflicted by the boorbain virus, no less! I could blast you into oblivion with one swipe of this massive paw!"

Ajur stepped in front of Conor and Janine, placing the length of his muscular body between them and Seefra. "Then do so," he said, baring a pair of enormous fangs.

The laboratory fell into an uncomfortable silence. Janine stepped a little closer to Ajur. Conor opened and closed his right hand while summoning the most powerful spell he could imagine. Ajur tensed, shaking his bulky head a few times to clear his vision. Seefra paced back and forth, but never came any closer to his three opponents across the room. Suddenly, the master of darkness flicked his eyes up above Conor, Janine and Ajur, and recited a small incantation.

"Kyrra vog homonon."

A violent earthquake erupted around the four of them. Instead of a flood of rock and stone tumbling inside the laboratory, however, a vast section of the wall broke away and fell outward toward the main floor of the chamber of cells. It appeared as though Seefra had chosen to give himself another avenue of escape.

The genuine Ajur reacted the only way he could after hearing the wall cracking apart behind him. He pushed Conor and Janine out of harm's way and braced himself in case he needed to jump away at a moments notice. He reacted so quickly and with such instinct that he never saw the long black tail of his counterpart snaking across the room toward Janine. Had he known Seefra's true intent, he might have been prepared for his desperate attack. Instead, in his zeal to protect Conor and his companion, he had opened the door for Seefra's final play.

The master of darkness wrapped his jaguar's tail tightly around Janine's waist and lifted her off the floor. He felt her trying to inhale so she could scream for Conor's help, but he encircled the tail even more forcefully, cutting off the flow of air into her lungs. As the rock wall fell away from the laboratory, he quickly transported her across the room. With his large, golden eyes, he looked up, watching her struggling to free herself. He tensed the tail a little more, watching her grimace with the pain of suffocation. The master of darkness smiled with a deep sense of morbid satisfaction.

From outside the laboratory, the five Champions watched in wonder. "Look at that," bellowed Surmitang as he watched an explosion take out a hefty portion of the chamber wall. A huge section of rock fell away, exposing what looked like a natural window above the area where the landslide buried Conor and Janine.

"Something's moving in there," said Eha. "It looks like a room of some kind, and there are at least two creatures inside."

"Conor and Janine," added Purugama. "It must be." The great cougar stood and spread his wings. "Quickly, we must go to them!"

"Mind of the creators!" said Maya, clearly shaken. "Ajur is with them."

"Impossible," replied Surmitang. "Ajur could barely stand when last we saw him. For him to walk that far in his present condition is inconceivable."

Maya never took his eyes from the laboratory. His jaw dropped open and dangled there for a moment. "It is Conor and Janine, and Ajur is with them. He's trying to protect them against what looks like another black cat. I wouldn't believe it if my eyes hadn't beheld it. There are two identical jaguars in the room with them."

"Seefra!" said Therion, spitting the name from his lips.

CHAPTER FORTY-TWO

"Stay where you are if you desire her life!" commanded the master of darkness. Seefra smiled at Conor with the jaguar's huge fangs. Forcing his enemy into a decision for his companion's life gave him great pleasure, and he delighted in Conor's pained expression.

Seefra watched Ajur pacing around to Conor's right side, preparing for some type of assault. The big cat was right, of course. Even with all the magic he had at his disposal, he could never overcome the Champions, and shadows save him if a creator happened to appear. But Seefra knew he could cause a fair amount of pain before the final outcome of the battle. *Accursed Champions! They had destroyed his armies, broken his hold on his prisoners, and invaded his sanctuary! They would pay dearly for opposing him, maybe not all of them, but some surely would!*

Without another word, Seefra stared at Conor with the huge, golden eyes of his camouflaged form. He peered into Conor's mind and soul, showing the young Champion his intent. He wanted Conor to feel the anguish of exactly what was about to happen.

"No!" shouted Conor. "Seefra don't!"

The master of darkness wound the giant tail into a whip, carrying Janine close behind him. Then with snapping motion, he flung

Conor's girlfriend through the opening above them. Her body danced over the rocks, disappearing into the darkness.

In an instant, Conor summoned his cheetah speed and sprinted up toward the opening. Calling out Janine's name again and again, he assured her that he would find and save her. He crested the hill at top speed and began to lose his footing due to the lack of the crystal floor on that side of the wall. He swayed forward and before he could find his balance, he saw Janine's body disappearing into the mists far below.

Conor roared and dove over the edge of the wall. He had no powers to call upon from any of the Champions, so he imitated Purugama's form when they went into freefall. Closing his legs together and locking his feet against each other, he extended his hands in front of his head and made a steeple out of his fingers. Zooming straight down into the mists, Conor cast a spell that would catch anything falling on a soft bed of invisible cushions as they fell into the chamber below. He knew he'd never catch up to Janine in time to save her, so this would have to be enough until he could find her himself. He uttered a silent request to the creators to let him find her before anything else that lived down there did.

"Foul creature," said Ajur, now flanking Seefra on the floor of the laboratory. "Must you destroy all that is good and worthy?" He charged and pounced on his longtime enemy, taking him by surprise and knocking the master of darkness nearly unconscious. Seefra recovered quickly, however, and by using the much healthier version of the jaguar's physique, he took the advantage from Ajur.

"You will soon join your pitiful friend and brother," said the master of darkness. "You will discover what a horrible death looks and feels like, I assure you."

Ajur looked at his longtime adversary as he attempted to reclaim his breath. He could barely see him, but he knew where to charge when the final attack came. He planned to make certain Seefra never bothered the creators or the Crossworlds again. "Then let us discover it together!"

The big Champion launched himself at Seefra, who sprang from a rock at precisely the same time. The two jaguars collided in mid-air, locking themselves into a ferocious battle. Ajur, using what remaining strength he had, grabbed Seefra by the scruff of the neck and lifted him off the floor. Holding the master of darkness in his mouth, Ajur climbed the rock wall toward the opening above them. Seefra twisted and turned, trying to break free, but Ajur's grip held fast. The massive jaguar used the abilities of his ancestors to haul Seefra up and over the wall. Just as jaguars had been lugging hundreds of pounds of prey into trees for centuries without end, Ajur, with endless adrenaline surging through his body, dragged thousands of pounds of enemy to the edge of the abyss. Holding Seefra in his mouth, he jumped off the edge into the chasm. The mists rose up to greet them as they fell deeper and deeper toward the basin. Seefra squealed and cursed at Ajur, calling him an imbecile for taking them into the mists. What resided there unnerved even Seefra, and that fit precisely into Ajur's plans.

"Mind of the creators, did you see that?" chuffed Therion after he watched Conor freefall into the mists after Janine. The entire scene mystified all of the cats watching from the crystal floor.

Maya immediately sprang into action and yelled, "Purugama, fly, now!" The Lord of the Champions watched as the great cougar soared into the sky toward his objective. Sending him down into the mists was the last thing Maya wanted to do, but time was no longer on their side. Decisions had to be made using nothing more than instinct, and Maya intended to let his inner consciousness flow freely.

"Therion, off you go. Surmitang, stay with him, and offer any assistance you can. I have a feeling we'll need our two strongest Champions at the top of that ridge when Purugama brings Conor and Janine back from the abyss. Eha, come with me. It's time we set a beacon for the Lady of the Light to follow."

Instead of crashing hard on the floor of the basin, Ajur and Seefra landed on some sort of soft cushion. The huge jaguar rolled off the padded surface onto the ground, holding Seefra in an iron grip with his powerful jaws. He looked around the sparse surroundings, trying to get a sense of what lived down in the depths of the basin. What he saw around him didn't provide much comfort at all. Flattened pieces of different creatures' bodies lay everywhere, dismembered haphazardly by a force unknown even to a Champion of the Crossworlds. It looked as though the arms, legs and torsos had been compressed to the point where they simply broke away from the bodies. Even more peculiar, the broken pieces didn't appear to be consumed in any way. The life force had merely been absorbed, Ajur could see that, but it had been done in such a way as to leave the limbs intact. The sight of it sent a chill down his spine.

The rest of the bizarre basin didn't impress him. A stone

passage, constructed from the surrounding rock walls, led to what looked like a channel leading to nowhere. The mists swirled intermittently in a gigantic hallway, some fifty feet tall and twenty-five feet across. After maybe two hundred yards of geometric perfection, the hallway turned to the right and disappeared. A dim, flashing glow illuminated the entire chamber. It looked precisely like what it was – a horrible nightmare where only one outcome seemed possible.

"Fool!" sputtered Seefra, struggling harder than ever to extricate himself from the jaguar's grip. "You have delivered a sentence of death to both of us! Even I cannot control what lives down in these mists. I assure you, Champion, that when you lay eyes on it you will sincerely regret your actions."

Ajur said nothing, contentedly keeping his jaws tightly clamped on the back of his opponent's neck. The master of darkness began altering his form, shifting into every imaginable shape he could summon. Ajur would not yield, however, keeping his teeth securely fastened onto the thick jumble of skin and fur. Seefra began uttering a host of spells, all intended to do his enemy harm and thus free him from his grip. None of them affected the jaguar, and although very sick now, he kept to his vigil, locking his jaws like a vice.

Suddenly, a horrible, terrifying scream cut off Seefra's incantations in midstream. The sound filled the whole basin, but instead of searching the entire area, Ajur instinctively looked toward the corner in the hallway. Following the ear-splitting scream, a thunderous roar filled the basin, shaking the walls and the floor beneath them. This time Ajur saw something appear from around the corner. The two small images looked very familiar to him and as they came closer, he almost dropped Seefra in a tremendous gasp of surprise. He was facing Conor and Janine, clearly terrified and running for their lives.

The sight of the creature rounding the corner behind them caused Ajur to bite down onto Seefra's neck out of utter shock. He had never in his life been truly afraid of anything until now.

The creature's bulk almost filled the entire hallway, stretching easily to cover the twenty-five foot width and almost touching the fifty-foot ceiling. Ajur stared at the strange creature rolling toward him and understood why all the prisoners had met such horrifying deaths. Whatever this thing was, it didn't consume its victims in a manner similar to anything Ajur had ever known. *It must just roll over them*, he thought, *separating what it needed and pressing aside what eventually became waste while continuing to patrol the basin*. It might have seen its victims, but that clearly was the only sense Ajur could discern in the creature's composition.

The Champion blinked his eyes and focused on Conor and Janine for a moment. The basin shook violently again as the creature loosed another terrifying roar. The ground around Conor and Janine trembled so forcefully that the two teenagers had to fight to keep their footing. *Steady*, said Ajur in his mind, giving Conor as much mental assistance as he could summon. If they tripped and fell it would be over quickly, for they would never be able to regain their balance and scamper out of the way fast enough. As near as Ajur could perceive, they appeared to be a couple of hundreds yards away. The creature, steadily slogging down the hall, kept pace and rolled along closely behind them.

Keeping the now terrified Seefra clamped firmly within his jaws, Ajur stared at the extraordinary thing coming toward them. It looked like a gigantic conglomeration of thousands of misshapen pieces of captured creatures. It looked so strange Ajur couldn't even begin to define it. Eyes appeared all over its surface, showing no particular pattern at all. Nor did they all look the same, and their appearance confirmed Ajur's earlier suspicion, that this leviathan had been morphing into its present shape for thousands of years. It might have begun as a single-cell creature, picking up energy and structure from everything it touched during its lifetime. Somehow, at some point, Seefra had discovered it and brought it here. *What could be more fear- inducing than to become a prisoner in the chamber of cells and listen as countless others fell into the mists to meet this unspeakable death?* Ajur bit down harder on Seefra's neck, snarling as he did so.

The creature roared again, clearly frustrated by Conor and Janine's quick feet. Most of the other prisoners stood completely still, their fear immobilizing them until the creature could pulverize and absorb their essence. Forgetting the Champion and his companion, Ajur watched the creature howl its frustration all over the basin. He stared at the thing with eyes wide open, watching the mouth roll over and eventually under the huge sack of a body. That explained the intermittent roar; the mouth had to follow the rest of the body as it rolled aimlessly down the hallway. *Does it even possess a brain,* wondered Ajur? *Did it register what it saw, or taste anything that it consumed? Or was it still just a mindless one-celled creature, marching along on its endless route around the basin, looking for beings to exterminate?*

Conor lost his footing and fell and Ajur almost dropped Seefra again, this time to assist his brother. The big cat leaned forward, urging the young Champion to regain his feet and run for his life. Janine crouched at Conor's side, lifting his shoulder to help him to his feet. Conor shouted orders, pleading with her to keep running and save herself. She would do no such thing, and soon the two of them were up and running again. Conor suffered a severely sprained ankle, however, and their progress down the hallway slowed significantly. Sensing victory, and with its mouth reappearing from beneath it again, the creature loosed a shriek that shook blocks of stone from the rim of the hallway.

Purugama broke through the mists at the moment he heard the third roar echo through the basin. Closing his wings, he swooped down into the hallways. Upon rounding one of the corners in the basin, his wings flew into overdrive. What he saw caused him to plead to the Champions for any spare energy they might release to him. "Mind of the creators!" he growled, horrified beyond belief.

Conor jerked his head around, judging the distance between the creature and himself. He knew they wouldn't be able to outrun such a relentless foe forever, so he began hurling magic with reckless abandon. He flung every spell he knew at the beast, firing off incantations as rapidly as he could. The magical spells were formidable, but as a deterrent they only served to infuriate the creature even more. Some of the energy blasts took away a dozen or so eyes from its bulk. Others severed whole sections of its form, leaving them writhing on the ground behind it. The mammoth dimensions of the creature invalidated any attack Conor could conjure up, however, and it continued rolling close behind them, bellowing incessantly. Conor ran as best he could on his injured ankle, but he knew that soon he would have to stop. The body only served for so long while wounded. Sooner or later it would just give out, and unless he could convince Janine to go on without him, they would soon be rolling along with the creature as part of its hideous form. He despaired, and at that moment he became aware of a large shadow flashing across the floor of the basin. In his depleted state, he couldn't discern the source of the irregularity. He only thought of Janine, and how he wished he had never exposed her to any of this. He dropped his eyelids, and at that moment he felt a massive paw clamp onto his arm with great urgency. He looked to his right and saw two things, golden fur and another identical paw lifting Janine from the ground as well.

Purugama seized the two teenagers, lurching away from the ground with adrenaline pumping through his wings. Whatever pursued them had very nearly overcome Conor and Janine. If he had been a second or two slower, he might not have been able to save them at all.

The creature howled its displeasure rudely, as Purugama pulled them away from the floor. It roared so hideously that Purugama felt that all the demons of the shadow world had joined in the chorus. The creature actually stopped howling for a brief moment, turning some of its eyes upward to look at him and his two passengers. Grunting with enough force to clear the air of any floating debris, the massive creature turned its attention toward Ajur and Seefra. With another surging roar, it started forward again. With a new pair of victims locked in its vision, it forgot all about Conor and Janine.

"F-Fool!" stammered Seefra. "Release me and I'll reverse the effect of the boorbain tree. I swear it on our long and divisive association. Ajur, if you have any sense of justice in your heart, let me go so we might both survive!"

"I'll release you," said Ajur after opening his huge jaws. "But only because our end is near and absolute." Seefra immediately tried to shape shift again, but Ajur fell upon his form in an instant. "Not today," said the jaguar. "Not this time, my friend, for I am here to assure your demise." Covering Seefra with his giant, muscular body, Ajur continued speaking. "I will stay with you, Seefra, and give you all the justice you deserve. I will not allow you to perish alone, for that would truly be spiteful, and the Champions are a far better sort than that. We will wait for your creature together. Your only hope is that the Lady of the Light finds us in the next few seconds. Maybe her magic could overcome this thing that serves you."

"The magic of the creators?" scoffed Seefra. He broke into a fit of nervous laughter that echoed all around the basin. "The creators do not care for any of their former servants, or for their current Champions!" He spat the words into Ajur's face. "Look at yourself, great jaguar, and tell me, *where is your Lady now*? Is she here? Has she come to save you? You are as meaningless to her as I ever was while I served in her protection forces. She will leave you here to die today, and tomorrow not give you a moment's thought."

Ajur freed one of his forepaws and smacked Seefra in the face as hard as he could. "Blasphemer! Serving in the protection forces was never enough for you! You tried to break into the council of seven by force instead of merit. The creators abandoned not a loyal servant, but instead a greedy, power-crazed opportunist! I do what I do today to honor the Lady and all of the creators! They have given me what all creatures desire, a lifetime in which to serve others! Never speak her name again, or I will destroy you myself before that beast has the pleasure."

"Ajur!" shouted Purugama, breaking into their conversation.

The jaguar turned his head and saw the great cougar floating in the air about twenty yards from him. Conor and Janine sat confidently in the saddle, beckoning to the big Champion. All the while the huge, hideous creature rolled toward them, gathering up everything in its path.

"Come with us, Ajur," shouted Conor. "We can ride on Purugama's shoulders, and he can carry you with his paws. Come, now, before the creature overtakes you!"

"Yes," added Purugama. "Let me carry you to safety, my brother. Come with us back to the realm where Gribba can remove the boorbain poison." The great cougar urged his friend vigorously, even though he felt in his bones what Ajur's reply would be. He heard it seconds later, confirming what he had always believed about the friend he had known since they romped around the glade together as cubs.

"Take Conor and his companion to safety," replied Ajur. "I have almost reached the end of my time, and you know as well as I there will be no remedy awaiting me in the realm. Gribba is a skilled medic, but even his capable elixirs cannot touch the boorbain virus."

"No!" shouted Purugama. "You cannot be certain of that! Come with us, Ajur. Give yourself a chance at least!"

"That is precisely what I intend to do," responded Ajur, heaving a pained breath through his infected lungs. "I will give my Lady one last service by assuring her that Seefra will never torment her again. The Crossworlds will be rid of its most powerful and vindictive adversary for all time. My life will be my final gift to the creators and the Crossworlds."

"Ajur, no!" shouted Purugama. "Do you realize what you are doing?"

"I understand perfectly," answered the huge jaguar. "You will not turn me away from this course, Purugama. Give my love to the rest of the cats, and especially to the Lady of the Light. It has been my deepest honor to serve with the Champions of the Crossworlds. Now go, before the creature makes martyrs of us all."

Purugama looked up at the thing approaching all of them. Ajur spoke the truth; it would be on top of them in seconds. The great cougar flapped his mighty wings, pulling away from the floor of the basin. With tears streaking his cheeks and a sense of hysteria in his voice, Conor shouted down to Ajur, telling the jaguar how much he loved him. Janine clung to Conor, burying her face and trying unsuccessfully to hold her tears back. The creature roared mercilessly as it rolled over Ajur and Seefra, crushing the life from their bodies. The only sound louder than the reverberating echo of the creature's victory call was Purugama's howl of agony and loss. As he disappeared into the mists, carrying Conor and Janine on his shoulders, he kept yelling Ajur's name as loudly as he could.

CHAPTER FORTY-THREE

Purugama and his two passengers burst over the edge of the crystal floor, flying over Therion, Surmitang and a host of former prisoners. All present in the area cheered wildly upon seeing the return of the young Champion and his companion. Although they did not understand the solemn looks and behavior of the returning heroes, they applauded nonetheless. Therion and Surmitang roared their approval momentarily, until they noticed the pain in Purugama's eyes. They watched as Janine convulsed into Conor's shoulder blades. They immediately understood the meaning behind her dreadful sorrow.

Politely ignoring the crowds of newly-freed creatures rushing to meet the trio of heroes on the crystal floor, they hustled around the bulk of the throng toward the perimeter of the chamber. They sought Maya and Eha, hoping to break the devastating news to them. Running quickly but not full out, the two massive cats checked every inch of the crystal floor. They finally caught sight of their Lord constructing a huge beacon of light at the juncture of the pathway toward the laboratory of the master of darkness. Eha assisted Maya, helping in his efforts to locate and summon the Lady of the Light. Surmitang and his companion reeled themselves up upon reaching the location of the beacon.

"Good news, my Lord," began Therion. "Conor and his companion are safe. Purugama broke through the mists only seconds ago with both of them securely on his back."

"They should be here momentarily, Maya," added Surmitang. "Those who used to be prisoners in this place have surrounded them. They wish to thank them for all they've done."

Maya checked the beacon one last time before activating it. His comment came at such a low volume, Therion and Surmitang almost missed it completely.

"And Ajur?"

Both lion and tiger glanced at each other, neither wishing to relay the sad news. It was Surmitang who finally spoke. "If you ask, then you must already know. Ajur must have followed us on the crystal bridge. We can only assume that when he arrived at the chamber of cells, he went directly to Seefra's laboratory. He battled Seefra to the end, Maya, and held him to the ground to assure his destruction. He gave his life for the Crossworlds, my Lord."

Maya nodded his head once uncomfortably. "Say nothing to the Lady of the Light. I will break the news to her after we leave this foul place." The Lord of the Champions uttered a spell that caused the beacon to flare with a silver intensity so bright it bathed the chamber in daylight. He turned to see hundreds of creatures coming toward them, surrounding Purugama and his two passengers. The chaos had ended, their journey was complete, and the creators would reign supreme in the Crossworlds for another thousand millennia. Despite their painful loss, the journey into the shadow world had been a resounding victory.

Behind Maya, a brilliant doorway appeared. Immersed in a magnificent aura of silvery precision, the corridor solidified and the Lady of the Light strolled through with a gentle, regal gait.

The portal flashed before vanishing, leaving the creator standing amidst her Champions. She looked around at the gathering of giant cats, greeting each one silently. When she had seen all but one, she softly inquired as to his whereabouts.

"Where is Ajur, off scouting about again, I presume?"

Purugama turned his huge head, looking up at Conor and Janine. The two teenagers met his eyes and immediately looked down in sadness. They said nothing about the events beneath the mists.

"We had to leave Ajur along the path some time ago, my Lady," said Maya, calmly. "I will collect him personally before we leave for the realm."

The Lady blinked once while staring at Maya. "I understand," she said softly before turning to the crowd of creatures who had been held captive by Seefra. "You are all free to return to your respective worlds. We will provide transport for you through the corridors of the Crossworlds. Follow the instructions of these giant Champions, and shortly you will all be home with your families."

A rousing cheer echoed throughout the chamber. The creatures began milling about, half positioning themselves for portal travel, and half bumping into a Champion here and there. They wanted to touch them, to say thank you and physically sense the majesty of their rescue. They wanted to remember their saviors, so they could relate the encounter to their grandchildren with great enthusiasm when the time came. Many of the creatures passed by the Lady of the Light as well. None so much as even grazed her robes, however. She was a creator, after all, and she deserved a certain measure of restraint from those she watched over. Still, they exchanged smiles with her, even though in each instance hers dissolved rather quickly. Although inspired by the victory over the Circle of Evil's forces, the Lady's expression carried a vague silhouette of loss. The brightness, usually apparent in the silvery glow of her aura, had departed for some reason. The creatures could not understand it, and they didn't bother trying. They simply presented her with a smile as thanks for their release.

The Lady of the Light called forth a vast group of corridors to carry the creatures back to their respective worlds. After all of them had finally left, she grabbed the beacon Maya had used to direct her to the chamber of cells, wrenching it from the ground. Holding it like a spear, she hurled it across the chamber and over the far edge of the crystal floor. It disappeared after passing under the makeshift window in Seefra's laboratory. No one remaining in the chamber heard it penetrate the mists and clatter on the floor of the basin.

Without discussing her peculiar actions, the Lady turned and drew the boundaries of a huge corridor into the stone wall of the chamber. Looking over her shoulder and counting the Champions one last time, she glanced at Maya before entering the membrane. "Go, my Lord. Collect Ajur. Bring him to me and together we will take him to see Gribba." Looking forward again, she walked briskly into the corridor and disappeared.

CHAPTER FORTY-FOUR

The realm of the creators bathed its returning heroes in a warm serenity unlike any sensation Janine had ever experienced. After traveling through the intense cold and heat of the portal, they walked into what she perceived to be paradise. Every aspect of the environment, down to the smallest detail, gave forth a strong, positive quality that made her feel perfectly at ease. Every moment she spent in the realm seemed to fuel her body with increasing amounts of energy. The injuries she had sustained while under Seefra's control disappeared within seconds. Her teeth, chipped and loosened by the impact against the floor of Seefra's laboratory, regenerated themselves completely. Her skin, bruised and torn over her two year imprisonment, glowed with the pristine appearance of any young woman from her home world.

After arriving at the realm, Purugama had excused himself, leaving the two teenagers alone to explore the grounds. Conor had taken her on a long, rambling walk, showing her the tumbling waterfalls, shimmering pools, and the endless forests interspersed with emerald green meadows. It was during this time that their bodies, regenerated and became strong again. At the end of their stroll, Conor had showed her Gribba's healing water walls. Before he could explain their function, two of the walls sensed the visitors and glistened with knowledge of fresh assignments. Soft beds, coated with flowers from the realm, rose up to greet Conor and Janine. At Conor's urging, Janine sat down on the relaxing bed of flowers. Lying down on her back, she watched as the water wall moved closer and began dripping with a multicolored intensity. She blinked her eyes once and fell into a deep, restful sleep. The wall had gone to work immediately, completing the improvements the realm had already initiated. In no time at all, Janine and Conor once again enjoyed the peak of health.

When she awoke from her lengthy nap, Janine looked over and noticed an empty bed next to a dull water wall. Conor had left without waking her. She rolled on her side and swung her legs over the bed, placing them on the ground. A huge, furry hand grabbed her shoulder as she stood, gently helping her to her feet. Janine looked up into the face of an extremely tall and muscular bear, with a human face. He smiled at her, releasing his grip when he felt assured of her steadiness.

"I am Gribba," said the furry giant. "Conor asked me to wait here with you. You must be Janine, the keeper of the keys."

Janine remembered mention of this gentle, intelligent creature. "I am, and I am pleased to meet you, sir. I understand you saved Conor and the Champions in the chamber of caverns. I will always be in your debt. Please give my thanks to those who accompanied you."

"It is an honor to serve the brave companion of our seventh Champion," replied Gribba. "However, I must ask after your well-being. How are you feeling? May I bring you food or drink? Is there anything you desire to make your stay here more comfortable?"

"Nothing that I can think of," responded Janine, although she felt rather lonely. "Do you know where Conor is?"

"Purugama has taken him to see the Lady of the Light," said Gribba. "They shouldn't be away for more than another thirty minutes. They left over an hour ago, so I expect them back shortly."

"Over an hour ago?" queried Janine, "How long have I been here on this bed of flowers?"

"Only a short while," answered Gribba. "You arrived yesterday with Conor, so I expect you've been rejuvenating for slightly less than thirty hours."

Janine stared at the Ezuvex with her mouth agape. "*Thirty hours?*"

Walking through the forest at Purugama's side, Conor heard a soft whimper around a brightly lit corner. At first he thought the sound originated from one of the many natural phenomena in the realm. As they drew closer to its source, however, Conor knew it came from a living being.

The Lady of the Light sat against a stone outcropping holding her face in her hands, crying openly. Maya, the Lord of the Champions, sat calmly facing her as he delivered a tale about a truly courageous act. As he told her more about Ajur's heroics, the Lady seemed to slip further into a sadness Conor had never witnessed before.

"With his final breath he swore his allegiance to the creators. He begged us to thank you for his life of service, and he spoke of the pride he always enjoyed while serving you. He loved you deeply, my Lady."

Upon hearing this last sentiment, the Lady of the Light broke down anew, convulsing with a fresh flood of tears. One of her Champions was gone, and this time there would be no rejuvenation. No power in the Crossworlds would ever bring Ajur back. She loved all of her cats without limit, but Ajur had always held a special place deep within her soul. He seemed solemn to most, indeed, even to her most of the time, but she knew that inside his thick, muscular exterior, Ajur stoked a happy heart and a playful personality.

As she sat there allowing her grief to run its course, she recalled the images of Ajur's youth. Purugama had been a handful, but Ajur never strayed from acting like an imp each and every day. He would lie in wait for anyone, creature or creator, playfully falling on their shoulders from a hiding place in the trees. Nipping at the neck of his victim, Ajur would sprint back into the forest as soon as he felt he had overstayed his welcome. The rebuke wouldn't keep him from his playful habits, however, and as soon as another target walked by, the fun would begin again. The Lady pressed the image of his coal black face in her mind, remembering the dark golden eyes that consumed anyone they observed. She had watched him grow from a tiny cub into one of the most feared Champions in her assembly. He had given his life for the Crossworlds, for her, and for the rest of the Champions. It made perfect sense to her that his last conscious act would be in the service of others. The Lady wiped away a face full of tears with delicate hands, and looked up at Maya with a pleading gaze.

"I knew," she said. "I felt it my bones. I sensed that something dreadful had occurred, something so painful that you dared not relate it to me before we returned. I could feel the absence of one of the Champions, and yet I couldn't bring myself to question you about it. I understand now, Maya, why you waited to tell me."

"It was the creature at the bottom of the chamber," answered Maya. "We lost Ajur, and I wasn't about to risk losing you as well."

"He speaks truth, my Lady," added Purugama. "Nowhere in the

vast reaches of the Crossworlds have I ever seen such a hideous and powerful enemy. If all the Champions had stood against it, we would have been obliterated in seconds."

Conor stayed silent up to this point, deferring to the Lady and the other Champions as they discussed Ajur's passing. He couldn't hold his question any longer, however, especially in light of past events. "My Lady," he asked respectfully. "Why can't you resurrect Ajur in the same manner you returned Purugama and Surmitang to the glade? If they were reborn, cannot Ajur be revived as well?"

The Lady of the Light held a hand out to Maya, who stood ready to answer Conor's question. "I only wish it were so simple, my Champion. Purugama and Surmitang perished in locations where the creators held dominion. The shadow world has never been such a place. The Circle of Evil reigns supreme in that sector of the Crossworlds, and as potent as our magic is, we cannot penetrate their barriers. Believe me, could we retrieve our Champion, we most certainly would, but we have no recourse in their world. We can travel beyond their walls, even do battle there, but finding and resurrecting a soul is beyond out capabilities so long as they retain their authority."

"I am sorry," replied Conor. "If there is anything I can do, anything at all, my Lady."

The Lady of the Light smiled broadly, as did Maya and Purugama. "Oh Conor, what you have for us already can never be repaid. Come. Let us find the keeper of the keys. The two of you have an appointment to keep." The Lady wiped her face one last time, took a deep breath and brushed off her robes. She stood, and when she walked to the middle of the pathway, Maya and Purugama stepped to either side of her soft gait. They escorted her to their next destination, attending to her every need. She presented a polished exterior, but the two cats knew her very well. She was hurting deeply. She missed Ajur quite terribly. They would stay close to her, making sure she passed through her grief with as little disturbance as possible.

"Conor Jameson, COME FORWARD!" boomed the robust voice of the Lord of all Life. "Be well, and enter the chamber of the Council of Seven."

Conor glanced at the Lady of the Light. She smiled demurely and nodded her head once. Swallowing the encouragement, he returned his gaze to the entrance of the council chamber. No less a personage than the Lord of all Life had prepared his personal corridor so that Conor could enter the presence of the creators emeritus. Passing through a tunnel of jasmine, the young Champion carefully ascended the seven steps leading to the creator's portal. He entered the membrane, purposely keeping his eyes open. He saw nothing of any consequence, and the familiar sensations of cold and heat did not accompany his passage. He walked right through the membrane as if emerging from a pool of warm, scented water.

The other council members sat quietly upon seeing Conor enter the chamber. Directed to a seat in the center gap of a seamless round table, Conor smiled inwardly as he watched the table create an opening for him to pass through. He bowed to each creator in turn, as the Lady had instructed, waiting for their acknowledgement before taking his seat. After removing his golden headband, Conor noticed a second chair rising out of the ground next to him. He knew without hesitation who would be sitting by his side through this hallowed reception.

The voice boomed again, calling out for another attendee. "We also request the Keeper of the Keys!"

Janine followed Conor's pattern to the letter, even bowing slightly to the assemblage before taking her seat. Although she still wore the tattered clothing from Mountmoor High School, she looked refreshed and strong. After sitting down, she took Conor's hand in hers, squeezing it tightly.

"May we see the fifth key?" asked the Lady of the Light.

"Yes, please," added the Lord of the Stars. "Produce the fifth key."

Janine glanced over at Conor, who gave her a quick wink. She saw him smile, and the sparkle in his eye filled her with a joy she hadn't felt in over two years. They were free, together again, and that's all she needed right now. She worked the damaged zipper on her cargo jacket until it released itself and removed the dark box that encased the powerful key. She unfolded the flap carefully, pulling the lid open slightly. A brilliant light, whiter and more potent than any light in the realm of the creators, blasted through the small crack in the case. Janine looked at the Lord of all Life, who gave his silent consent, and she opened the box completely. Before the key was even in view, all the creators on the council leaned forward, trying to bathe their bodies in the beautiful, pure light.

Janine reached into the box and removed the fifth key. With a smile, she held it high above her head, like a trophy she recently won in a competition. The creators rocked back into their floating chairs, eyes glued to the brilliance of the key. It was all colors and colorless at the same time. The breathtaking beauty of the metallurgy defied all description, and for a full minute, all were silent in the chamber of the Council of Seven. Finally, the Lord of all Life addressed Janine.

"We cannot show you the depth of our appreciation, young lady. Throughout this journey you showed immense courage and an admirable devotion to your companion, as well as to the Crossworlds. We appreciate everything you have done for our cause, and deeply apologize for any suffering you endured."

Janine couldn't speak a word. She merely smiled and nodded her head a few times.

"Conor Jameson!" roared the Lord of all Life.

Conor nearly fell out of his seat. He stood quickly, banging his knee against Janine's chair. Trying his best not to show the result of his bumbling attempt to rise, he stood with his hands behind his back and his feet slightly apart.

"Roughly two of your years ago you revealed information to your companion that very nearly destroyed the Crossworlds. Even the Council of Seven was forced to abandon the realm until you could find and regroup the five keys of the creators. The Champions of the Crossworlds found themselves stranded on the other side of limitless galaxies. Your own world came close to annihilation. The council members have convened more times in the last two years than in a hundred centuries prior. You have single-handedly caused more mayhem than all residents of the Circle of Evil during an equal amount of time." The creator leaned forward toward Conor, his aura flaring as the volume of his voice rose. "What have you to say for yourself, young Champion?"

Conor stammered for a moment, not quite sure what to say.

"You act much the same way as you always did," said the Lord of all Life, continuing to berate Conor. "And it has always been thus with human males of your age. The immediate is the only consideration for you, and any consequences of your actions be damned. This is precisely why we nearly denied Purugama's request to mentor you during your initial journey together. Had it not been for the Lady of the Light and her steadfast belief in you, his request would have received a very short hearing indeed!"

Conor's hands tightened against each other, twisting back and forth behind his back. Lord of all Life or not, he wouldn't take this much longer. Ajur had given his life for the creators, and for all of the Crossworlds. *Wasn't that more important than a royal tongue-lashing from an overbearing mystical presence?*

"We understand what it is to be human, Conor Jameson. We have studied your race for as long as you have existed. We celebrate your curiosity, although at times it leads to your undoing. We also honor your commitment to one another, even though you exist in a large vacuum of strangers. You may never notice each other from one day to next, and yet when tragedy strikes, you swarm together in a wave of caring that defies all expectations. This trait is unique among all the planetary populations within the Crossworlds system, and we find it most intriguing. Even so, we find some of your actions most disturbing."

The Lord of all Life straightened and cleared his throat. He seemed uncomfortable preparing for what he had to say next, almost as if he had been outvoted and still had to deliver a speech he found distasteful. His aura flared inconsistently, showing his discomfort to the entire council.

"However," pressed the Lord, clearing his throat again, "your transgressions pale next to the extensive list of your accomplishments, and we are not so impolite as to brush them aside without comment. You fought quite bravely against a host of destroyers early on in your association with the Crossworlds. Along with your companion, you followed the clues left by our seeker and recovered the five keys of the creators, the symbols of all power in the Crossworlds. You endured capture and imprisonment, as did the Keeper of the Keys, and ultimately reassembled the Champions for a successful assault against the forces of the dark master."

The Lord of all Life paused for a moment, glancing over at the Lady of the Light. "We understand one of the Champions gave his life during your last journey. We mourn your loss, my Lady, and wish to make a declaration regarding Ajur's station."

The Lady of the Light bowed deeply, giving her Lord her consent. As she straightened, she looked at Conor, smiling beautifully.

"Conor Jameson," announced the Lord of all Life, "it is our wish to certify your association with the Champions of the Crossworlds. Moreover, we hope you will accept with our blessing the position of chief protector of the Lady of the Light, a title Ajur proudly held for over three centuries."

Conor's hands relaxed noticeably. He exhaled, hoping to recite his next utterance with some form of decorum. "The honor is to serve, my Lord."

"So be it," said the creator, turning to address Athazia. "My Lady, your wish has been granted. Whenever the Champions respond to a summons for a journey in the service of the Crossworlds, let it be known that Conor Jameson will serve as your shield. Let it be known throughout the Crossworlds."

"Thank you, my Lord," responded the Lady. "Your wisdom is unmatched."

"Step forward," said the Lord of all Life to Conor and Janine. "We realize that both of you have given of yourselves to a great extent. We wish to repay you, in whatever way you wish. Tell us, Conor, Janine, is there anything we can give you in return?"

Janine looked at Conor and smiled. She turned back to the

Lord of all Life and gave their request. "If you please, we wish to return home, back to our families and our community. We appreciate all the wonderful friends we've made here, but home is where we belong."

"Let it be done!" declared the Lord of all Life. "My Lady, will you see to their transport?"

"I will be pleased to accompany them, my Lord," replied the Lady.

She directed Conor and Janine to the portal and had them turn and bow one last time to the Council of Seven before leaving. The three of them passed through her Lord's corridor, entering the realm of the creators once again. At the bottom of a small hill waited Therion, Eha, Surmitang, Purugama and Maya. Conor halted his steps as soon as he saw them, knowing that within minutes he would be a hundred galaxies away from a pack of friends he would cherish forever. He accepted Janine's hand, following her down the hill toward the big cats.

Eha smiled and licked Conor's face. "We'll see each other again, I'm sure of it."

Therion allowed Conor to grab a handful of his large, dark mane and pull his huge head down to eye level. "Take care of the keeper, Conor," chuffed the giant lion, "and of yourself. We will need you if crisis ever rears its ugly head again."

"Chief protector," spat Surmitang. "Too regal a job for anyone other than a tiger, but you'll do in a pinch, I suppose." The beautiful tiger licked his flank a few times. "You have proven your valor an untold number of times. Watch over yourself, Champion."

Maya kept his words in his soul. He merely glanced at Conor and Janine with a knowing smile, brushing his huge, black and white cheek and ear against their faces. As all domestic cats do from time to time, he winked subtly at Conor before moving away.

Conor walked up to Purugama while holding onto his emotions with an iron grip. The great cougar, wings flared to their full fifty-foot span, looked so majestic and powerful that Conor felt he was seeing him for the first time. It wasn't until Purugama lowered his left shoulder, inviting Conor to climb aboard again that the young Champion ran toward him and jumped into his saddle. He leaned down and pressed his mouth to one of Purugama's golden ears. Kissing it in a place where no one else could see, he whispered to the great cougar.

"We will see each other again, my mentor."

Purugama began to purr. "Yes, Trolond Tar, you speak truth, for our paths will cross again."

"Trolond Tar?" Conor whispered back into the giant, furry ear. "What is this strange name? If there is another mystery I have yet to learn, don't keep me in suspense, Purugama. Tell me, who is this Trolond Tar?"

"He is you," answered the great cougar. "Or rather, you are he, reborn after countless millennia. You will learn more as your life progresses. Now off with you, and not a word to the Lady, she would skin me alive if she knew I breathed a word of this to you."

Perplexed but not deterred from his farewells, Conor slipped off Purugama's shoulders. Grabbing one of the big, furry ears in one hand and a scruff of neck in the other, he hugged the great cougar with all his might.

"Be well, friend," he said, and turned back toward the Lady and Janine.

He saw a blazing corridor standing independently just to Janine's right. He walked over to his girlfriend, grabbed her hand, squeezed hard and stepped toward the portal. The Lady of the Light addressed them both before they left.

"Thank you, Janine, for holding the keys in safekeeping for all of us. Conor, I suspect the threat from the Circle of Evil has vanished, but should we ever need to assemble again, I will feel safe knowing my protector will be at my side. Safe journey, and remember, the creators will always watch over you."

Conor smiled and winked at the Lady. Janine bowed demurely, also smiling. The two travelers looked at each other, walked into the corridor, and vanished.

Conor and Janine stepped out of the invisible membrane into the small, rural community of Wimmits, California. Almost together, they took a deep breath, inhaling the scent of redwood burl and fern forest. They stood about thirty feet from the main road, Highway 101, dubbed the Redwood Highway for the obvious reason. As far as they could see, immense trees, some rising three hundred feet into the air, lined the road, the town and most of the residential and commercial structures. After what Conor had seen and experienced over the last two years, the sight of home nearly brought tears to his eyes.

"Well," said Conor. "May I walk you home?"

Janine threw her arms around him, kissing him hard on the cheek. She broke off, suddenly shocked by a realization. "What are we supposed to say to our families?"

"Just tell them the truth," answered Conor. "That you and I went on a long journey together, unless of course you want to tell them about the Crossworlds, the Champions and the creators."

"Not a word," replied Janine, shuddering and smiling at the same time. "Not one single word about any of it."

CHAPTER FORTY-FIVE

The chamber of cells lay still, smothered in a dark, murky silence. After the departure of the Champions and the Lady of the Light, all remaining illumination had vanished from the crystal floor. Seefra's laboratory, and the deep basin located far below the main chamber lay quietly in a vacant slumber. The mists separating the cell of crystals from the basin had dissipated somewhat as well. Instead of a fluid, constant drift of milky air, they flowed haphazardly above the floor of the basin. It seemed as though the wandering waves of cool air were looking for something to give them direction. Without guidance or an entity to possess them, the mists sought out any form at all to assist in their search for a new journey.

Seefra's laboratory and the surrounding environment had essentially passed into another dimension, leaving no life at all within the vast chamber. Only one creature remained. It leaned sloppily against one of the huge walls in the basin. Seefra's ultimate destroyer, left with nothing to do and no one to consume, had fallen into a deep hibernation. It had the resources to stay alive for years before it needed to feed again, so it saw no immediate need to try and escape its lonely passageway. The beacon lying by its side provided the only source of light and energy anywhere in the chamber.

Quietly at first, and then with a more pronounced beat, the beacon began pulsing rapidly. The tip of the beacon glowed with a brilliance known only to those frequenting the realm of the creators. After a minute or two of constant rhythm, it illuminated with a silvery blast of pure energy. The owner of that aura could not be mistaken, and within seconds of the beacon's activation, a corridor appeared at the other end of the passageway. It was a small portal, slightly larger than necessary for one passenger to use. The membrane flashed with a bright silver luminescence, solidifying all at once and preparing itself for transport. Through the portal stepped Athazia, Crossworlds creator and Lady of the Light. All alone and weaponless, save her magic, she strode forth from the passageway. Once clear of the membrane, she turned, giving a soft command. The corridor closed in on itself, disappearing completely and removing her one avenue of escape.

The creature snorted roughly, stirring from its intense sleep. Something tickled its sense of smell, something delicious. Steadily emerging from its hibernation, it raised its hideous form and moved away from the wall. One by one, the hundreds of eyes unfolded from its body, searching in every direction for the source of the enticing aroma. It rolled back farther away from the wall, allowing its gigantic maw to release a volume of stench that infected the basin with its foul insides. It coughed a few times, spitting the remains of countless victims from its gullet against the wall. In one giant heave, it righted itself, pressing evenly against the walls of the basin. Mouth open and eyes wide, it began its search for whatever it was that disturbed its sleep.

On the back of its huge bulk, one of the eyes caught sight of an anomaly in the passageway. A source of intense light caught its attention, flashing in its retina a little too brightly. Knowing by instinct that something out of the ordinary had entered the chamber of cells, it rolled backward slowly to allow more of its eyes to witness the disturbance. When it finally determined what lay behind it, a thunderous roar came forth from its bowels. Shifting its focus without turning, the creature advanced on the Lady of the Light with great purpose.

Athazia looked upon the gigantic creature with a sense of dread and awe. That Ajur had sacrificed himself to assure Seefra's destruction was bad enough, but to think he suffered a horrible death in this dank pit at the hands of such a creature was beyond conception. The Lady shivered as she stared at the thing rolling toward her. Then she collected herself, remembering why she had traveled here after Maya's warning.

"By the force of the Crossworlds, and in memory of the great Champion Ajur, I come here to summon the magical keys of the creators!" She stepped forward, extending her delicate hand toward the creature. "Tyu okum sadax!"

The creature's form convulsed harshly, causing it to lurch to the left, splattering a few eyes against the wall. It had no idea what lay deep inside the tons of blubber surrounding its former victims. Had it any semblance of intelligence, it might have grasped the irony that its former master was about to become the instrument of its destruction. Its huge body convulsed again, rocketing forward toward the Lady of the Light, refusing to give up any part of its perceived nourishment. Then the thick, obese skin exploded outward in four distinct locations, yielding to the awesome power of the creators. Four keys, each a unique shape and brilliant color; flew from the form of the creature toward the Lady at the other end of the passageway. The creature bellowed with the knowledge that something terrible was occurring. Leaning forward, and in extreme pain, it drained its insides all over the chamber basin. Apparently, Seefra's body had traveled deep within the creature's intestines, and the keys, traveling from a secret pocket in his coat, had burst almost every organ on their way to freedom. The giant destroyer sagged against the wall, screaming loudly toward the Lady of the Light. With whatever life it had left, it would make her pay for the pain she had brought to it.

Athazia spread her fingers as the keys approached her. They slowed their progress as they encountered her essence, falling lightly into the palm of her hand. One by one, the beautiful keys flashed once and disappeared into the fabric of her robes.

She turned her attention to the creature writhing in the passageway. Her aura flared brightly many times as she remembered her Champion and his horrible encounter with this monster. She opened her eyes wide and shouted the command given to her by the Lord of all Life.

"Destorum Llif, Destoro Ddef!"

The beacon beside her flashed once and vanished. The chamber basin was instantly cloaked in an inky blackness. The creature howled like an army of shadow warriors while the creators' spell destroyed it from the inside out. Athazia felt an energy she never dreamed existed rising up within her, and the force of all the galaxies in the Crossworlds shot forth from her eyes like a laser cannon. Two identical beams, powered by the fifth key of the creators, streamed forth into the creature, cutting it to ribbons and laying waste to the surrounding rock and stone walls behind it. Everywhere the Lady looked, the titanic energy blasted the form of the creature to ribbons. She rose up from the ground, elevating her assault and hitting the grotesque form on all sides. Rock walls exploded into hot, molten cinder as the creature screamed in agonizing pain.

Athazia rose above the mists, directing the pulverizing energy onto the surrounding chamber walls. Armageddon replaced the former silence in the chamber as the entire mountain crashed down on top of the creature. The Lady of the Light elevated through the open ceiling of the chamber, leaving the hideous beast in its own grave for all time. She blinked her eyes once. The beams flashed and were gone. She looked down one last time and whispered softly to herself.

"Rest easy, Ajur, Champion of the Crossworlds. I shall never forget you."

Look for the next installment in the series:

Conor and the Crossworlds:
The Author of All Worlds

Coming October 2010

CHAPTER ONE

"*Preposterous!*" *boomed the Lord of all Life.* "*No one commands that* much power. If this council meditated for a thousand centuries, it could never approach the type of cataclysmic force you describe." The red aura flared as the supreme councilor threw out his hands in disgust. "I refuse to believe it. Your findings must be flawed."

"The precision of the mathematics cannot be disputed," answered a calm and reserved Mr. Hikkins. "The sequence I am illustrating for the council is occurring even now. I cannot speak as to the source of this phenomenal power, but I assure you my figures are correct. Not only is the entire system in jeopardy, but I also believe Conor's world may be in the most immediate danger. If my calculations prove reliable, earth will be wiped away from the Crossworlds system in approximately twenty-two days."

"This is madness!" shouted the first councilor as he rose from his floating seat, slamming an open palm against the table. "Entire worlds disappearing without a trace, do you realize what you are suggesting?"

"I am *not* suggesting," replied Mr. Hikkins while clenching his teeth.

Arriving two days prior to his session, the soft-spoken but determined seeker had demanded an immediate audience with the Council of Seven. Merely stating a request in so bold a fashion would keep most visitors in the gardens for weeks, but Mr. Hikkins had always been something of an enigma to the creators. His intellectual capabilities had never been questioned, but his decisions left some on the council suspicious of his motives. Indeed, the crafty seeker had solved many of the most perplexing dilemmas during his service, including the final calculations for the protection packet used by Conor in his first battle with Seefra. But his judgment often troubled some of the council members. His decision to travel constantly instead of dedicating himself to the realm had not sat well with the Lord of all Life. The council debated whether to restrict his movements many times, but in the end they understood the overall value of his contribution. Mr. Hikkins, on the other hand, had never allowed his relations with the council to hamper his precious responsibilities for a moment. He preferred close contact with the beings under his guidance. He enjoyed traveling through the corridors acting as mentor to the Crossworlds' most valuable inhabitants.

He discovered the anomaly in the system almost by accident.

Staring up at the stars one evening, he noticed a tiny discoloration appear and then disappear in deep space. He thought nothing of it, until a few days later he spied an identical shift in the pattern of the night sky. His disciplined mind would not accept a random occurrence repeating itself in such a short period of time. He began investigating the phenomenon immediately. He contacted most of the preeminent mathematicians and astronomers in the Crossworlds system. He ran simulations in his mind constantly while jotting down bizarre sets of equations. Most he threw away, but the few that remained began to form a most interesting model indeed. The result, when he had finally dismissed all other possibilities, astounded him. He didn't feel fear or dread, instead he appreciated the purity of the strategy. The Circle of Evil couldn't possibly annihilate every planet in the Crossworlds system. That would take too long and they wanted immediate revenge. Instead, they had devised a formula that depended on random selection based on calculated odds, slating worlds for destruction while shaving the probability of error to less than five percent. It was brilliant and deadly, and unless the creators could decipher the source of their power, Conor would have to be notified at once.

"There is no mistake, first councilor," repeated Mr. Hikkins. "I haven't determined the physics of the weapon, but I have deciphered the pattern of their attack." The seeker waited a few moments to allow the reality of what he reported to settle in with the council. When he felt he had their collective attention, he dropped the one statement he knew would ignite controversy. "The situation leaves us no choice. We must notify Conor immediately and inform him of the circumstances."

"No," said a delicate, soft voice. It came from the rear of the chamber. The Lady of the Light stepped forward, announcing her presence to the members of the council. Up to this point she had listened quietly while Mr. Hikkins delivered his account, preferring not to become directly involved unless absolutely necessary. This, however, must not be allowed.

"We cannot turn to him again so quickly," she continued. "He has established a life for himself back on earth. He and his companion have worked tirelessly to pick up the pieces of their shattered lives and move forward again. They have selected a path for their futures, and we must not intervene and disrupt their progress."

"We appreciate the zeal with which you defend your Champion," interjected the first councilor. "Let me remind you, however, that your presence here is only tolerated so long as you observe and remain silent. You may not interrupt the proceedings no matter how strongly you feel about the subject matter."

The Lady of the Light gently lowered her chin in submission, but did not retreat to her former position. Her silver aura flared briefly, highlighting her apprehension with the contents of the discussion.

"My Lady, if I may," began Mr. Hikkins. "You must know how deeply I care for Conor, as well as for Janine, his companion. After all, I spent a good deal of time with both of them during Conor's first year of high school. I do not wish to disturb their happiness, nor do I find the prospect of throwing the young man into another journey appealing. However, you must understand the complexity of the situation and grasp the mortal danger we all face."

Mr. Hikkins turned to face the Council of Seven directly. "The ability to wipe away the existence of an entire planet has never confronted us before. Due to your design and the collective power of the system, the Crossworlds have successfully existed for untold millennia. What I tell you now I say with the support of empirical evidence. Earth will not be the final target for the Circle of

Evil. I believe they will continue their offensive after destroying the birthplace of our latest Champion. After obliterating that target, they will turn the focus of their mighty weapon against the glade of champions and the realm of the creators. I do believe, first councilor, they intend to destroy every world that holds positive dominion over the system itself."

The council chamber exploded with comments and argument. Mr. Hikkins accepted a barrage of challenges to his suppositions. He stood silently while accepting the flood of criticism. He knew better than to try and debate the council, especially after delivering a message as shocking as this. Even under intense scrutiny, however, he felt comfortable with his conclusions. After all, he held the conviction of his science and a consummate belief in what he put before them. In his opinion, they could only come to one conclusion. To be certain of the outcome, though, he allowed the council to exhaust themselves before delivering the final blow.

"May I remind the council," he stated quietly, waiting for the last points to be aired before continuing, "that we haven't touched upon the most important aspect of their strategy."

"And that is...?" demanded a clearly exasperated supreme councilor.

"The corridors, my Lord," answered Mr. Hikkins without hesitation. "Imagine if you will the network of portals connected to the combined energies of just one world."

The chamber went completely still. The council members froze in place, none of them uttering another sound. They stared at Mr. Hikkins for what seemed like the first time. Their expressions softened towards him, as if their opinion of his intelligence climbed a notch or two. As one group, they changed their posture, looking directly at him with open minds.

"Yes," continued the brilliant mathematician. "Not only are the complex organic connections throughout the system in jeopardy, but consider this, esteemed council members. If we do not act, and act promptly, we may not be able to recruit Conor and his companion at all. We may be cut off from them permanently. What's more, if the portals that bond the glade of Champions to the realm of the creators are severed by the elimination of a symbiotic world, then you will be without the services of your most powerful protectors."

The Council of Seven sat in stunned silence. The Lady of the Light placed her head in her hands, sighing deeply. All present in the chamber now began to grasp what Mr. Hikkins already knew as fact. The Circle of Evil, whatever remained of them after the great battle with the champions, had devised one last deadly strategy to destroy the Crossworlds forever. The desperation of the tactic confirmed their depleted state, Mr. Hikkins had said as much when he referred to the random aspect of their attack. They were gambling that the worlds they wanted to eliminate would fall within their projected line without touching their own provinces. The first councilor had spoken the truth, for the plan *was* madness. The Circle of Evil had decided to gamble with a weapon strong enough to erase an entire galaxy from existence. There appeared to be only one logical course of action, as distasteful as some in the chamber found it.

"How soon can Conor be contacted?" asked the Lady of the Light.

"Preliminary calculations have already been arranged," replied Mr. Hikkins.

"Proceed then," commanded the supreme councilor. "My Lady, I assume you wish to travel to the glade?"

"I will leave immediately," she answered with a slight bow of her head.

"Then let it be so," stated the Lord of all Life. "Let this be the final battle between the Creators and the Circle of Evil. I will hear no more about them after this journey."

"I assure you, my Lord," said Mr. Hikkins. "One way or another, this will be our final confrontation."

Lightning Source UK Ltd.
Milton Keynes UK
19 September 2010

160085UK00002B/11/P